Running by Night

by
G. Russell Overton

This is a work of fiction.

Names, characters, places and incidents are the product of the author's imagination. Any resemblance to actual persons, living or dead, business establishments, institutions, events, or locales, is coincidental.

First Edition

Copyright © 2011 by G. Russell Overton

Cover artwork by artist William Wisehart II

ISBN: 978-0615438061

This book is published by arrangement with the author by *Aarquives Publishing Group*, a division of *Aarquives Unlimited, LLC*, 2517 East Mount Hope Avenue, Suite 10, Lansing, Michigan 48910.

Genres

Action, adventure, Gay/Lesbian/Bisexual/Transgender rights, politics, Great Lakes, drama, sailing, coming of age, international politics, civil rights, civil liberties, suspense, intrigue, danger, friendships, love and relationships, human rights

Visit us on the Web at: www.aarquives.com

Acknowledgements

Running by Night could not have become a reality without the help of a few others. The greatest help came from my life partner, Bill, who encouraged me during the entire drafting process. He was also the first person to read it, offer editorial comments, and insist that the story was worth publishing. C. Corbin Talley, a long-time friend, performed the first detailed editorial work and provided the kind of critical comments that brought the work close to being ready for publication. My comfort with the Russian language has never been what it should be, and friend Nadya Sporova assisted me in drafting current, colloquial Russian dialogue. I wish to thank author Neil Plakcy, who encouraged and provided valuable pointers to a new author. Finally, all that I am I owe to my late parents, George and Nita, who showered me with the best loving guidance parents can give.

I dedicate this work to the memory of John Robert McGraham [2008], Matthew Shepard [1998], James Earl Chaney [1964], Andrew Goodman [1964], Michael Schwerner [1964], Allison Krause [1970], Jeffrey Glenn Miller [1970], Emmett Till [1955], Tsar Nicholas II [1918], Vokivecumsemosta (White Antelope) [1864], and all of those who died too young at the hands of intolerance and hate. May their memory serve to motivate people of good character to create a world where ideological and religious fanaticism can find no home.

Table of Contents

Chapter 1   Tobermory

The early morning sky offered no glimpse of the
Canadian shoreline. I stood on the bow of the *Polar Star II*
hoping in vein to catch site of land. It was late May, and we
had a steady spring breeze out of the southwest pushing us
along. If the wind held, we would make Tobermory by late
afternoon.

Harry was asleep in the forward cabin. He was my
life partner of seventeen years. Harry and I had left the east
coast of Michigan from Tawas the night before. I tried to
be quiet on the bow so as not to wake him.

We had sailed the *Polar Star II* into Tobermory
many times on pleasure trips. Tobermory, at the tip of the
Bruce Peninsula dividing the waters of Lake Huron and
Georgian Bay, had always been a refuge for us away from
the hectic lives we led in Michigan. We often went scuba
diving among the shipwrecks around the Bruce Peninsula.

This trip, however, was not for pleasure. The
Federal Bureau of Protection had started arresting gay rights
activists the night before on charges of terrorism. My only
crimes had been to declare my sexuality openly and oppose
the policies of an illegal regime. That was enough to
consider me, Joe Kelly, a threat to national security.

For more than twenty years I had known that
certain elements in American society sought to eliminate the
gay rights movement. I considered us fortunate to have
lived in Michigan and to have a sailboat. We were close
enough to the border that we could make our way to Canada

whenever circumstances required. Gay men in the interior states would have little chance of escape.

I paced from side to side on the bow, trying carefully not to trip on the tether of my safety line. It was a few minutes after four o'clock, and according to GPS we had been in Canadian waters for only half an hour. I scanned the horizon, hoping to spot visible evidence that we were in Canada. I knew that even in bright sunshine land would have been beyond visual range, but I hoped to see a ship with a Canadian flag or a glow on the horizon that might indicate something substantial.

The sky was clear and with a full moon, and I could see for a long distance in the early morning darkness. Occasionally a puff of cloud on the eastern horizon made me think I saw land, but it was nothing more than the Ojibwe trickster, Manibozo. I was tired and vulnerable to illusion, but I managed to keep my wits. Though we were in Canadian waters, we were still close enough to the boundary that a U. S. Coast Guard patrol could snare us without causing an international incident.

I walked quietly back to the stern and scanned the sky and horizon for any signs of a ship or aircraft that might be searching for us. I caught sight of some running lights on the water from the northwest. It was a fast moving ship of some sort, and I started to grow nervous. It appeared to be coming from the Michigan side of the Lake, probably from around the Straits of Mackinac. I thought about firing up the engine to push us a little farther inside the Canadian boundary, but I knew the engine would wake Harry.

I grabbed my binoculars and looked at the approaching ship. It was too large for a Coast Guard patrol. A few more minutes passed, and I was able to discern the outline of a cargo ship. It was a freighter of some sort, probably coming either from Chicago, Green Bay, or Northern Michigan. I went back to the bow to scan the horizon for site of land then back to the stern to check my heading. I made a slight course adjustment to ensure we were on a direct course for Tobermory and trimmed the sheets accordingly.

Except for the lapping sound of waves against the *Polar Star II* and the wind fluttering the sails it was dead quiet on the water. The air temperature was a chilly forty degrees. I zipped up my windbreaker and pulled the hood up over my head.

I peered across the stern again, back towards Michigan. I was no longer concerned about U. S. authorities. We were far enough into Canadian waters that I knew we were safe. I thought instead about Michigan. I could imagine the Lake Huron coast of Michigan. I pictured Alpena, Oscoda, Tawas, and Port Huron. I thought about Bay City and Saginaw. I thought about the highways that had taken me back to my native Oklahoma many times over the years. I imagined driving from Bay City through Flint, to Lansing, Fort Wayne, Indianapolis, St. Louis, and Tulsa, my home town. I thought about my friends in Bay City, my family in Tulsa, and friends and adversaries in Oklahoma City where I had attended college and started my career as a gay rights activist.

I thought about the life I left behind and wondered what I could have done differently. How was it possible that I could have accomplished all I had and still ended up as a refugee? The answer was depressing. Like many other gay rights activists I had deluded myself into thinking we had accomplished something of significance by an occasional court battle win or preventing a piece of legislation from passing Congress. While fleeing for my life I had to realize that I had failed to render my enemy *hors de combat*. I had known my enemy well, and I knew his agenda for my annihilation.

I had only been gone from home eight hours, and I was already homesick. I wanted more than anything to be able to turn the boat around and head home. As I looked across the water towards Michigan the refrain from a Woody Guthrie song played over and over in my head:

> So long, it's been good to know yuh;
> So long, it's been good to know yuh;
> So long, it's been good to know yuh;
> This dusty old dust is a gettin' my home,
> And I got to be driftin' along.[1]

---

[1] Woody Guthrie, *So Long It's Been Good to Know Yuh* (1940).

Chapter 2   First Loves Lost

Mark Wisner was my first love. They say, "You never recover from your first love," and I've thought that to be true. As much as I loved Harry, Mark was always a part of me. We were best friends in high school in Tulsa, Oklahoma, and became lovers at an early age.

Tulsa was a pretentious town with no reason for such airs. It was Oklahoma's second largest city, and when oil pumped from Oklahoma wells, money flowed into Tulsa bank accounts. It is a well-founded perception that Oklahoma oilmen in the 1920s were ignorant rubes with too much money. They built gaudy, extravagant homes, but had no idea how to function in polite society.

Their coarseness stemmed from the fact that many of them were nothing but a pack of common criminals. Much of their oil income came from leases on Indian land. These criminals bribed and cajoled a pliant court system to have them appointed as "guardians" over "incompetent" Indians and their children. These guardians had the power to negotiate lucrative oil leases on their wards' lands. These guardians grew instantly rich, while their Indian wards suffered in poverty. Though morally bankrupt, it was all done with the sanction of the legal system. These oilmen, with their ill-gotten fortunes, became Tulsa's aristocracy.

The Tulsa they built was a visually appealing town at first presentation. Its downtown had a handsome skyline. Just south of downtown were the graceful estates of the wealthiest Tulsans. These homes were tucked into the gently rolling hills of the city built on the Arkansas River, and at the sight of a Muscogee Nation Tribal Town.

Tulsa was a segregated city, even into the twenty-first century. South Tulsa was reserved for white people with means. North Tulsa was what they used to call "Colored Town" (or worse). West Tulsa was for oil refineries and "poor white trash." Even in the 1970s when I was in high school, the only time people from the north or west sides of town dared venture into south Tulsa was to work as housekeepers, gardeners, or gas station attendants. People from south Tulsa simply had no reason to venture out of their exclusive paradise.

My Father was a bank executive, and we lived in a comfortable home in south Tulsa. He interrupted our idyllic existence while I was in Junior High to divorce my Mother and marry his buxom secretary. In the divorce agreement my Mother kept our family home. She received alimony and child support for my sister and me. Mother had enough money for us to be comfortable, but she had to let the housekeeper from north Tulsa and the gardener from west Tulsa go, and she could no longer afford her seasonal Dallas shopping trips to *Neiman*'s.

Our home put us in Memorial High School's district. It was known then as the rich kid's school, a problem for me because my family no longer had the means for me to be a spoiled brat; buxom secretaries tend to drain family finances. I no longer had an allowance, which meant that I had to take a part time job after school, and when I was old enough to drive, I had saved just enough money to buy a used *Pontiac* sedan. Most of the other kids at school drove flashy new sports cars that their parents had given them.

I never complained about my circumstances though. Sure, I was angry with my Father, and it was hard to have to socialize with a school full of *Little Lord Faultnoroys*, but I

quickly grew through the experience. I knew right away
that I was a fighter and could survive almost anything. I
made my own niche and found a circle of friends who, for
reasons not unlike my own, had little use for up and coming
Oklahoma oil executives.

I met Mark Wisner at a party through Allen, a
mutual friend. Allen's parents were strict Southern
Baptists. They had no idea what a wild kid he was. They
had gone away for a weekend church retreat, and Allen
invited everyone he knew in school for the party. He had a
full bar set-up and marijuana for everyone. Allen
introduced me personally to Mark. I will never forget
looking into his grey-blue eyes for the first time.

That first conversation cinched our friendship. I
revealed my passion for history, and Mark expressed how
concerned he was that we were about to lose some
important historical buildings. The railroad industry was in
the midst of a restructuring. They had stopped passenger
service across the country eight years earlier, and in so
doing had abandoned many of the passenger stations along
their rights-of-way. By 1975 these stations were rotten and
crumbling.

The next Saturday, Mark and I took off for some
small towns in eastern Oklahoma. We followed the route of
the *St. Louis and San Francisco Railway*. Most of its
stations were long gone, but we found a few gems that were
intact. Mark reasoned that we should scavenge whatever
we could in order to preserve a bit of history; we took log
books, signs, and a doorstop.

That weekend set the tone for how our friendship
developed. Mark was a year older than me and had his
driver's license. He drove a 1962 *Sunbeam Alpine*. The
Alpine was a tiny car and, for the next year at least, we had
to confine our treasure hunts to collecting small items.
Sometimes we took longer excursions and made a weekend

of it. We took a tent and sleeping bags and camped wherever we could. It was on a cool spring night in a tent that our friendship turned into romance.

Before retiring, we reasoned that we could keep warmer if we zipped our bags together and slept naked (we had been taught that in Boy Scouts as a survival technique). The low that night was fifty-seven degrees. We stripped and crawled into the uni-bag and pretended to go to sleep. I felt my heart race every time I breathed, inhaling the smell of his body next to mine. Before too long, our hands began to wander and when the occasional brush of a hand turned into a caress, we passionately embraced.

I knew then that I was gay. I had fantasized about Mark from the moment I had met him. The night we first had sex I was madly in love with him. Yet, I was unable to accept the reality of that love. The next morning we drove back to Tulsa in dead silence, neither of us commenting on the previous night's event. We both were masters at denial and acted for the next few weeks like nothing had happened.

Mark had a girlfriend at the time; her name was Sonya. They went out on dates, but I think to Mark she was just for show. Mark made it a point to introduce me to Sonya's best friend, Stacy. That worked out perfectly. As two sets of best friends, we went out on double dates together all the time, and I mean *all the time*. It was known at school that if Joe and Stacy were going to be somewhere that Mark and Sonya would be there too. By then I was driving. Our dates settled into a weekly routine where I picked up Mark first (my *Pontiac* had ample room for four), then the girls. We went to dinners, movies, school dances, and many of the combinations of things that high school kids do. After each date, we dropped the girls off early (I'm sure their parents loved having us date their daughters) then

Mark and I headed off to the sand bars on the Arkansas River for a more intimate date.

Had things been able to continue like that, I might have ended up with Mark as my life partner. In my senior year he went off to college. We kept in touch and stayed close, but the distance made it too difficult to see each other frequently enough. Neither of us had dealt with our sexuality, and we had never discussed our sexual relationship. I knew, by everything I had been taught, that I was committing a mortal sin and was destined for Hell. Then in the fall of my senior year, a friend of my Mother's invited my mother, sister, and me to visit her Pentecostal church. My Mother would have nothing to do with it, but I went. In the sermon that Sunday, the pastor said in such a sweet and convincing tone, that prayer and faith could cure all kinds of sins, even things like drug addiction and homosexuality.

I decided to be 100% straight. I gave my life to Jesus and became the best member of a congregation. I prayed and studied the Bible. I volunteered for everything the church asked, but every time I saw Mark, I made love with him. Each time I wept, prayed, and begged God to take away my burden. Finally, I decided Mark was the problem. I told him I could never see him again, that I could not get the sin out my life as long as he were there to tempt me. He was crushed and never spoke to me again. There was my real sin, turning away a trusted friend and blaming him for my failure to accept the beautiful relationship we shared. I never forgave myself for hurting him so badly.

I went off to college and continued my religious struggle. I was a freshman at a small private university in Oklahoma City. It was in the heart of town in a 1920s middle class neighborhood. I had no idea what my major would be, though I leaned towards pre-law. I had good study habits and did well in my classes, but emotionally I was as unsettled as ever.

My first semester was spent trying to find a new "church home" and screwing a young man by the name of Caleb. Caleb had wavy red hair and a red-haired chest. He was a little guy, about five feet four inches and handsome as all get-out. I treated him just like I had Mark. I screwed him at night then blamed him the next day for making me do it. I finally broke it off. I reasoned that I would stop being gay if he were not around to tempt me. I never once considered that it was a fucked-up religious mentality that caused my discomfort.

In my quest for a new "church home" I began to grow skeptical of the shenanigans in the Pentecostal churches. I never did understand all the "miracles" that happened in church every Sunday. One would think that wheel chair and hearing aid companies wouldn't do much of a business in areas with a large Pentecostal population. And talking in tongues was just bizarre. In the middle of each church service, someone invariably began babbling, even in the middle of sermons. Often it was kind of like when a dog barks at night; when one starts several others join-in. Those were the services that made me increasingly impatient. Just because someone interrupted the sermon did not mean that the sermon was to be cut short. No, God had a message to deliver through the pastor, so sometimes church went well into the afternoon.

What opened my eyes to the farce of it all was the phenomenon of "slaying in the spirit." That was an event where the pastor called people to the front to receive a special blessing from the Holy Spirit. Because the Holy Spirit was so powerful, the simple human body could not handle all that energy flowing through it and temporarily shut-down, making it appear that the person so blessed had fainted, then the slayee writhed and moaned on the floor as though he or she had been clubbed. During the time of this special blessing all the other congregants were either supposed to have their heads bowed and eyes closed or be gazing at the ceiling with their hands upward stretched and singing "Alleluia" or speaking in tongues. I rarely sat at the front of the church, but on one Sunday I did, and during that part of the service, instead of keeping my head bowed, I mistakenly looked over to where people were being "slain in the Spirit." Elders were positioned behind the slayees, and, at the right moment, the elders pushed their knees into the back of the knees of the slayees and pulled quickly on a shoulder, thus forcing the Holy Spirit's victims to buckle and fall to the ground. The elders, of course, were ostensibly placed there to catch the slayees so as to prevent injury.

I never went back to a Pentecostal church again. I searched six months for a church that could promise me a cure from my homosexuality. Finally, I found a small Presbyterian congregation near campus. I was raised Presbyterian, so I thought I would give it a try. This was not a mainstream Presbyterian church, but one that still taught the fundamentals of John Calvin. I liked it. It brought together the familiarity of a church service I had known as a child and the austere fundamentalism that I needed in order to keep from coping with my sexuality. It also introduced me to a religious-political symbiosis that would evolve into a dangerous social movement bent on the destruction of open democracy.

Though I later grew cynical about organized religion in general and hostile towards right wing extremists, my faith in God was never insincere. I honestly believed that if I prayed hard enough and had enough faith, God would turn me heterosexual. Every time I stumbled, I blamed myself for not having enough faith and for failing God.

I looked for other ways to contain my sexual urges, and I became a physical fitness nut in the process. I ran and worked-out, thinking physical exhaustion would curb my longing for male intimacy. I enjoyed running the most. It was a great way to stay in shape, and I became quite buff in the process. It never dawned on me that a physically fit homosexual was more likely to have homosexual encounters than one who was out of shape.

I ran forty-two miles a week, averaging six and one half minutes per mile. During the week, I arose at 5:00 AM and went for a six mile run. It was the perfect time for street running because there was no traffic, and I could get lost in deep thought. Saturdays I allowed myself to sleep a little later and then took off for a ten to twelve mile run. On most Sundays I rested.

One Saturday I took off across campus and noticed another runner headed towards me from a perpendicular road. He was tall, handsome and had a full chest of hair. Instinctively I did several double takes. I think he noticed my attention. We met at the intersection and he asked if I minded if he ran alongside for a while. I said, "Sure." I was thinking more lustful responses.

He introduced himself as Tom David. He was a junior and was in a pre-law program. He asked me where I was headed and was impressed when I told him my route. He asked if he could tag along.

We became great friends. He tried to get me to join his fraternity, but I resisted. I was afraid of how I might handle the all-male environment, but I told him, always using religion as a cover, that my religious beliefs were opposed to fraternities. We started spending a lot of time together. What started as lust, turned into the worst crush. I never let my feelings show. I was determined not to screw up another friendship. Besides, for all I knew he had no interest in a sexual relationship.

Tom was a strange, off the wall kind of guy, fond of offbeat films. He took me to my first John Waters movie, *Polyester*. It was showing at an alternative theatre, the one that showed *Rocky Horror Picture Show* on Friday nights at midnight. The people in my church thought that particular theater was a den of iniquity. When I saw where we were going, I was mortified. When I realized that the star of the show was Divine, a drag queen, I told Tom I wanted to leave. He insisted I give it a try. He promised that if I was too insulted after the first ten minutes we could go. I roared with laughter, and after about twenty minutes, he leaned over and asked me if I was too insulted. I whispered, "Yes, I am terribly insulted, and this is too funny. We have to stay."

I spent much of my weekend time away from church with Tom. Saturdays we went for long drives, much like I had been used to with Mark Wisner. On one of these Saturdays he took me to Okemah in east-central Oklahoma. It was a small depressed town. He wanted me to see the birth place of Woody Guthrie. I have always been a fan of American Folk music, and Woody Guthrie is an icon of that genre. I was like a child going to *Disneyland*.

I expected it to be a museum or some kind of tourist attraction. To get to it, we had to park next to a wooded hillside. There were no signs, no markers of any kind. There was a dirt trail worn through the woods that led to it. Once we got to a clearing, we saw a wood frame structure that was a shell of a house. The wood was grey and rotting, not a speck of paint to be seen. The window openings were missing their sashes and no doors were left in the doorways. The roof was open to the sky and what was left of wall plaster had fallen through the rotten floor. Birds and snakes slept where Woody Guthrie once had a bed.

I was shocked, "How can this be?" Tom explained to me that the people of Okemah had turned their backs on

Guthrie when he started associating with Socialists and
Communists in the 1930s. All those songs about the plight
of migrant workers and "This land is your land, this land is
my land," sounded too much to them like intentions of a
Bolshevik takeover in America. They wanted no part in
honoring or even acknowledging their native son. They
even went so far as to prevent outsiders from preserving the
Guthrie home. In fact, the only reason the home stood at all
was that it was a protected historic site.

Like other well intentioned visitors to the home, we
left a note pinned to a doorway with a message. It read,
"We will never forget you, Woody, rest in peace."
Afterwards, we drove back and forth through town with the
windows rolled down singing *This Land* at the top of our
lungs. After our third pass, Tom noticed a sheriff patrol
following us. Tom drove right on out of town. The sheriff
continued to follow until we crossed out of Okfuskee
County.

Tom graduated the following December. He
wanted a break from school before submersing himself in
the drudgery of law school. He went on a cross-country
sight seeing trip. He told me he would be back by early
summer.

I decided not to enroll for a fourth semester in
January. Some friends at church worked in the oil industry,
which was then in one of its boom cycles. Brian Meeker
owned a land leasing firm, which signed up drilling
contracts. He needed people who were willing to drive all
over the region researching land titles and signing up land
owners. It sounded like an exciting job to me and the
prospect of making so much money at a young age was too
much to resist.

Brian was only a few years older than me and was
already a confirmed millionaire. He was in the process of
building his trophy wife and new baby a 4,000 square foot

home on a forty acre estate. The house would include a three lane garage. Each lane was deep enough to handle three cars. He "needed" that space to accommodate his *Mercedes 560sl, BMW 633 CSi, Jaguar XJ12*, and a gaggle of other rare and high end automobiles.

It was great work and I enjoyed it. In those days we thought that the oil pools underneath Oklahoma's red earth were a continual fount of wealth. We never imagined that we would pump them dry.

Tom came home in May and was surprised to see me out of school and with a full time job. We resumed our friendship as though nothing had been lost. He was getting ready for law school in the fall, but wanted to enjoy what was left of his "freedom." He traveled with me on many of my business trips. Whenever we traveled together I was always careful to get rooms with two beds. I never knew for sure whether Tom was gay. I still had a crush on him, but I was no closer to coping with my sexuality than I was in high school.

I continued to stumble. I had no idea that a gay community existed and no clue where to find it. God's Providence being what it is, I unwittingly rented an apartment two blocks from the strip where the gay bars were in Oklahoma City. Soon after I had moved in I was on my way home from a church function on a Saturday night and realized I had forgotten to buy milk. I turned right onto Northwest 39th Street, hoping to find a quick turn around. I saw the strangest spectacle of men wearing bizarre clothing and making out in the parking lot. I wanted to jump out of my car and join in, but I was horrified. I turned onto an alley. My headlights hit two guys, both naked, one on his knees giving the other a blow-job. I really wanted to join in, and I was even more horrified – what if Pastor Stan or someone from the church saw me there?

I bought my milk and went home that night. Every night, however, knowing where I lived gnawed at me. A few months went by, and I ventured out on a Saturday. I went to the *Park*, a pick-up bar on 39th, and hooked-up with a trick. The next morning I could barely drag myself to church. I was convinced that I was apostate, but that event established the cycle. I prayed, volunteered for work at the church, and waited for God's cure, all the while growing more sexually frustrated. I gave in to my urges went to a pick-up bar like the *Park* or the *Nail*, tricked with an unknown character, and then went through self condemning remorse for the next few days afterwards. It was almost like a manic depressive cycle.

I was ever more committed to the church, hoping that my faith and exposure to "Godly things" would bring that elusive cure. I prayed and took on more and more responsibilities. I was the model member of the congregation, and my efforts were noticed by Pastor Stan. He appointed me to teach Sunday School classes and eventually nominated me to the Board of Deacons.

Reverend Stan Chalmers was the catalyst for the tiny Presbyterian Church I joined. Pastor Stan was one of those dynamic, eloquent preachers of the 1980s, who could motivate large numbers of people to follow his personal direction. He was tall, reasonably good-looking, and had a voice that sounded like the Archangel Michael. People came to church just to hear him speak.

The church was a part of the Reformed Presbyterian denomination, a fundamentalist splinter group, claiming to be the true followers of John Calvin. When I first visited, the congregation was made up of thirty aging remnants of a neighborhood church. Within a year of Stan's parsonage the congregation had trebled with a contingent that was in my age group.

I felt a sense of belonging and made friendships that seemed to be meaningful. It was an environment where I could have friends without any sexual tension – I didn't dare. We had picnics, volleyball games, and pot luck dinners. It was like a huge extended family.

After Tom left for law school, I needed a new best friend. All my church friends were great to hang out with, but one developed into that closeness that I had always enjoyed. His name was Bob Fenton, but his closest friends called him "Stormy." It had nothing to do with his disposition, as he was a soft spoken character that was too easy-going for his own good. His father called him Stormy because it stormed violently the night he was born. He pretended to hate the nickname, but he never protested too much.

Stormy was a few years older than me. He lived across the street from the church in a tenement and was kind of down on his luck. He visited the church when he saw all the renewed activity. We immediately hit it off and spent time together away from church and all the church related activities.

He enjoyed running, so he often joined me for my Saturday long runs. Oftentimes we spent an entire Saturday together, going for hikes, biking, or some other outdoor activity. He was terribly handsome and "just my type," a hairy chest, muscular, but not a body builder, light brown wavy hair with natural blondish highlights, a bushy mustache, and thunderously muscular legs. I always tried to watch myself around him. Still, the friendship progressed and a sort of affection developed between us.

On a late May Saturday we went for a drive to Lake Keystone, one of the many manmade lakes in Oklahoma. There we could go for a long run, then in the heat of the afternoon, jump in the water for a swim. It was a hotter than normal day and we went running wearing only our

shorts. The sweat glistened and highlighted every feature
on his body. On days like that I had to keep myself under
strict control. On a stretch of flat surface on a deserted
gravel road near the end of our run, he challenged me to
race to the next intersection. That day he was a bit faster
than me and pulled slightly ahead. I focused on his broad
back, narrow waist, hairy legs, and tight buttocks. The air
was stifling, but I could smell the sweaty scent off his body.
It was more than I could handle. The only way I could get
away from it was to pull ahead. I mustered every ounce of
energy I could and beat him to the intersection.

Huffing and puffing at the finish line, he said,
"Wow, where'd you get that burst of energy?"

"It was either win or get in big trouble," I replied.

He looked perplexed, "Really, how so?"

I tried to diffuse the issue, "Don't worry about it,
you don't need to know." I thought that would be the end
of it and darted over to a nearby field of lush green grass
and collapsed.

He followed me over and lay down next to me, "So
what's all this trouble I don't need to know about?"

I said, "Drop it. It's nothing"

He stared at the sky for a few moments, "What if I
told you I already knew?"

I was getting scared. "What is it you think you
know?"

"For now, let's just say we both could have gotten
in trouble."

I was intrigued. "How so?"

"Well, I think we both wanted something back
there, but we're not supposed to have it."

My heart beat faster. "Like what? Show me."

Stormy sat up and looked around. We sat in a field
of tall grasses, there was no one around and couldn't have
seen us if there were. He leaned over and planted a wet kiss

on my lips. I knew what to do. My arms wrapped around him, and we fucked.

The difference between this encounter and all the others so far, was that we talked about it. Perhaps not so honestly, but we talked. Stormy initiated it while we swam. He said, "You know I am really straight. I am saving myself for the right woman. It just seemed like you are a nice looking man and I sensed you were thinking the same thing. We needed a little release. That's all it is, a couple of friends who help each other out now and then."

I was baffled and asked, "So you don't think there was anything wrong with what we did?"

"Well, I have to admit, it's not exactly orthodox, and Stan certainly wouldn't approve, but he doesn't have to know either. It doesn't make us gay or anything like that. We're just being good friends to each other."

"When you say, "help each other out now and then," do you mean that we might do it again?"

He shrugged "Why not?"

I smiled and thought, "What a great solution."

We drove back to Oklahoma City, stopping in Davenport to have some barbeque at Dan's Restaurant. It was the best place in the state for smoked ribs. Stormy was driving. As we got closer to town, I asked if he wanted to stay at my place for the night. He said, "Sure, I just need to get up early enough to run home and change for church."

Chapter 3   A Faithful Servant, But With Issues

July was miserably hot, and the last place I wanted to be on a sultry Sunday in Oklahoma City was in an un-air-conditioned red brick building. I was, however, deacon, and I taught Sunday school. Saturday evening I had gone down to the church to put the lesson on the chalk board when the air conditioner quit again. I called Pastor Stan and told him what had happened. The weatherman had predicted a high of 104 for Sunday, and I suggested that a shortened service might be in order.

Stan did not see how that could be possible. The sermon alone would take up at least thirty-five minutes, and he needed every minute. Besides, this might be God's Providence in action. People should be a little uncomfortable during this particular sermon. Why, he might have even entertained the thought of deliberately turning it off just for the sermon anyway. After I hung up the phone, I finished my lesson and went home. As soon as I stepped through the door I turned my own air down to sixty hoping the heat would feel good the next day.

In the morning I fixed a large thermos of iced tea to take for my Sunday school class. At nine in the morning it was already eighty-seven degrees inside the building. I taught the adult class on the *Westminster Confession of Faith*, our rule of faith, theology, and polity. My lesson for the week was Article XXI, "of Religious Worship and the Sabbath-Day." The main thrust was that even in "today's

20

work-a-day world," Christians should keep the Sabbath holy by worshipping God with other believers.

Before I was half way through I had loosened my tie and removed my blazer. I knew what Stan would say, "As a deacon you have to set an example. God did not put you in that position to be comfortable." I didn't care. It was too damned hot. Stormy was in my class and had also taken off his jacket. He was sweating profusely under his white pinpoint oxford, and I could see the thick mass of chest hair outlining his firm pectoral muscles. He had been out of town for a few weeks. We had not been able to "help each other out" for a while, so it seemed to get even hotter in the church.

We only had ten minutes between the end of Sunday School and the start of the church service. I always sat on the aisle in the third pew from the back on the north side. The sanctuary was laid out in a semi-circle with the pews broken into three sections facing the pulpit. The choir loft was behind the pulpit, and an ancient pipe organ was fitted out behind the choir. In all, with the overflow rooms opened up in back, the church could seat about two hundred.

Stormy sat next to me as usual. It was stifling. Congregants were anxious to get a bulletin just so they could fan themselves. The sermon was always the last part of the service. I could tell by the way Stan wound-up during the first half that the service was going to be a long one. After Dee, the church's favorite soloist, sang *O Sacred Head Now Wounded*, Stan stood up for the Scripture reading. Dee stepped down to sit with her husband. By then her blond curls had fallen completely straight.

Stan began to speak. He was a tall, haunting figure. His voice was booming and charismatic. "Turn with me in your Bibles to the Book of Romans, Chapter Nine." He read the entire chapter and then prayed for the hearing of

God's Word. I knew by the scripture reading that the sermon would be a classic predestination message and would go at least forty-five minutes.

In fact, Stan used the opportunity of a predestination sermon to promote his political agenda. Some Calvinists have always misused the doctrine of Predestination as a measure of social control; if a person does not follow the pastor's lead, he or she must, therefore, not be one of God's chosen. The mid-term congressional elections were approaching and Stan preached that it would be ungodly and reprobate to vote for political candidates who did not support prayer in school and oppose abortion and gay rights.

By quarter after twelve, people looked as though they were going to pass out. Stan was still going strong. Stormy leaned over and whispered, "Why don't we walk out; I can't stand it any longer." Horrified, I shushed him, and a couple in front of us turned around to see what the commotion was. Finally Stan said, "Let us pray."

After the service, Elder Barrett asked me to call an emergency meeting of the deacons to discuss a new air conditioning system. I set the meeting for Tuesday night after I was due to return from a short business trip. Rob Montgomery said he would try to get some estimates by then.

I went to *Furr's Cafeteria* for lunch with a few friends from church, including Stormy and Pastor Stan. While eating, Sam Haugan, who had been in my class that morning, asked me if he thought that by eating-out on Sunday, we were violating the Sabbath. I replied that since we were preventing the women from working in the kitchen, in fact, we were keeping the Sabbath better than those who ate at home. Sam asked about the people who worked in the cafeteria. "Aren't they breaking the Sabbath, and aren't Christians who eat here contributing to the violation?"

Stan interjected that because people who worked at these jobs on Sunday probably were not saved, they could not keep the Sabbath holy anyway. So what difference did it make where believers ate? He further stated that those Christians, who have to work on Sunday, such as himself, have to use one of their days off during the week as a Sabbath. They have to keep that day holy just as other Christians keep Sunday Holy. He went on to quote several Scriptures and preach for another fifteen minutes.

When Stan was done, I brought up the subject of the mission drive in the church's neighborhood. I suggested that the next Sunday after church, instead of going out to lunch, everyone bring a sack lunch. We could eat quickly and go door to door, inviting the residents around the church to attend the Wednesday night dinner and fellowship.

Stan did not like the idea. He thought the only reason the local people would come would be for the free food. I failed to see why that would be a problem. Most of the neighborhood people had no idea where their next meal was coming from anyway. I thought, after all, ministering to the poor was a function of the church. Stan argued that the main function of the church was to preach to unbelievers and to minister to the spiritual and physical needs of believers. He asserted that the church did not save people simply by filling their bellies.

I went on home around two thirty in the afternoon. Normally I went to a park or something to enjoy the afternoon, but it was too hot to do anything outside. I took off my church clothes and put on a pair of running shorts. Stormy called and said he wanted to drop by. He thought maybe we could go for a run later that evening after it cooled a bit.

I greeted him at the door, and he said it looked like I was ready to go for a run right then. I told him I saw no reason to dress for the occasion. He asked if I had any beer in the refrigerator. I told him to grab us both one. We talked about Stan and how wound up he was that morning. Stormy remarked that Stan had the tendency to get out of control. Stormy took off his shirt and shoes and stretched out on my sofa.

After about fifteen minutes, Stormy asked me if I wanted to "limber up a bit before our run."

I said, "Yeah, let's do it here on the carpet." I went to the bedroom and grabbed a bottle of lube and some towels. We were good friends and fuck-buddies, but that was it. We were still delusional enough to think that someday we would get married and forget we ever had sex. When I walked back in the room, I said, "You know, there are some people who would think it a sin to have sex on Sunday."

He was putting *Isle of View* on my turntable; it was our favorite sex record. He replied, "Yeah, well, those are the same sorts of people who do not think it necessary to feed those who are starving."

The deacon's meeting convened Tuesday at the Montgomery's house. Rob Montgomery was one of the five deacons and was my closest friend of the bunch. I had made the unusual request of asking their wives to attend. The women had no vote, but I wanted them there to discuss the mission drive. Rob had gotten some estimates for the air conditioning. We decided on the more expensive one, which could be partially operational by the next Sunday.

After we had decided on that, I turned attention next to the mission drive. I explained, "Stan and the Elders are totally uninterested in it. I think it is utterly deplorable that all these rich white people drive into town from their suburban homes twice a week wearing blinders to a poor black neighborhood. These past few years most of this congregation has done well during the oil boom. Money has been flowing like water in this town, but not to everyone. We have been talking about doing something for the neighborhood for months. It is time for us to take action. I have $2,500 I can use to start the fund; I am challenging each of you to contribute a similar amount. We'll call it the "Deacons' Fund." With $10,000 to start, we can make a serious impact on the neighborhood. We'll use it for food, clothing, and shelter. Stan is opposed to us inviting them for the church's Wednesday night gatherings. Instead, I think we ought to use some of the money to host a Sunday afternoon dinner. Once the congregation sees our success, they will want to be a part of it, and Stan and the Elders will have no choice but to go along."

Brad Mitchell said, "Although I am in favor of the idea, remember the elders are currently considering a proposal to sell the church building and move the congregation out to the suburbs."

Rob suggested, "If this plan works, people in the neighborhood might join the church. Then it would be difficult for the elders to pass a vote to move."

Dean Albertson was skeptical, "Somehow I can't see our congregation being all that welcoming. I don't think many of the locals will feel like joining."

Walt Hammond, who was much older than the rest of us and was often the voice of wisdom, said, "If anyone in the church has a problem welcoming local poor blacks, he can just as well go out to the suburbs and establish a white's only church. That's not the Lord's work and I want no part of those kinds of goings on. God placed us in that building on Shartel Avenue for a reason, and I believe it was so that we could make a difference. If we can't minister to the needs of the neighborhood, I can't imagine that the Almighty would have much use for us anywhere else."

That pretty well ended discussion on the matter and my plan was adopted. The next Sunday we planned to canvass the area and invite people for the following Sunday services and lunch afterwards. I suggested that everyone bring a change of clothes. I thought it inappropriate to canvass the neighborhood with men wearing *Hickey Freeman* suits and the women in *Christian Dior*'s highest fashion.

Thursday night about 10:30, Rob called. "I've got a serious problem. Charlotte and I went out to dinner tonight. Afterwards, we went to a club to listen to music, have a few drinks, and dance. Just as we got out of our car at the club, Stan drove by. He slowed down and gave us a nasty look, but didn't stop. I think he might try to cause some trouble."

I thought, with horror, about my own forays into the gay bars. I was thankful that God provided me with Stormy's "companionship." I hadn't felt the need to visit the bars for a while. Stan could be following me just as well.

I said, "You may be right, but I am about fed up with his attempts to control every aspect of our lives. If Stan tries anything I will stand behind you. I'm sure all the other deacons will too. Why don't you and Charlotte sit with Stormy and me on Sunday? If Stan confronts you, we will at least be there for moral support. Don't worry about it in the mean time. If something happens before Sunday, let me know."

I waited until Sunday morning to put my lesson on the board. Rob and Charlotte came in while I finished. Charlotte looked pale as a ghost and had a nervous quiver in her voice. Stan walked in behind them. He walked directly up to Rob and said, "I will not tolerate my deacons behaving like the unregenerate. I have already discussed the issue with the elders and they are all in agreement. You must resign as deacon. If you refuse, you will be suspended

from office until a new election can be held. I will
announce from the pulpit this morning either your
resignation or your suspension. Which will it be?"

Rob replied, "Could I have a hearing before the
elders, it seems like I should be able to offer some kind of
defense or apology or something."

Stan insisted, "The matter is settled. I need an
answer right now."

Rob retorted, "Fine. I'll make it easy for you, Stan,
I'll resign my position as deacon, and I will also resign my
membership in this church." Charlotte began to sob.

Stan reminded him, "You can't do that. You know
very well church doctrine clearly states that the only way
you can leave the church is to transfer to another. In which
case, you must be a member in good standing. I suggest,
therefore, that you calm down, repent, and remain, in fact, a
member in good standing."

Rob retorted, "I really don't give a flying fuck
whether you take my name off the rolls or not." Charlotte
gasped; my eyes popped out. "You will never see me in
this church again. C'mon Charlotte, let's go."

Stan coolly replied, "Very well, Rob. I will place
you under interdict, and you will be unable to attend any of
our denomination's churches or receive the Lord's Supper
until you repent." Stan turned to me, "I trust that you will
discuss this situation with the other deacons. Let them
know that their behavior is under my scrutiny, and I will
tolerate no deviant behavior in any of my church officers."
I nodded, and Stan left the room.

Rob and Charlotte were still there. Rob said that
they would be going. I assured him he was still my friend.
Rob told me to keep the $2,500 he had donated to the
Deacons' Fund, so long as I made sure Stan knew whose
money it was.

After church, I met with the other three remaining deacons as planned in the basement. I told them what had happened with Rob, and I went on, "I don't know how the rest of you feel, but I have had it with that megalomaniac. Rob is my friend and is a good man. He did not deserve that kind of treatment. If it weren't for the fact that I am committed to the people around here, I would have walked out this morning too."

Brad Mitchell spoke, "Like you Joe, I am first committed to the people around here. I find Stan's behavior deplorable, but we are powerless to do anything about it right now. As long as we are a part of this church, we are subject to his tyranny."

Walt Hammond said, "I agree, Stan should have at least given Rob a chance to explain himself, and Stan has been acting a little dictatorial lately, but if God has placed us here as deacons, we have an obligation to fulfill His will."

Dean Albertson interjected, "I am not sure if Rob was wrong or not, but Stan was definitely wrong. The signal I get; maybe I am a bit paranoid; but it seems that Stan is looking for an excuse to replace us all. Ever since we first started talking about reaching out to the people around us, he has developed a more belligerent attitude toward us. If this is the case, either we are going to have to stick close together and watch every step we take and every word we say, or we might as well give it up right now. I say let's do what Rob wanted us to do and go help some people."

We ate our lunch, changed clothes, and set out for the neighborhood. Several local families came to church the next Sunday and stayed for lunch. In the months ahead we helped local residents with medical bills, housing, and food. A few members of the congregation began to appreciate the work we were doing. Money poured into the

Deacons' Fund, and for awhile we had a sense of euphoria. We had worked hard and invested a lot of our own money, and we could see results. The neighborhood started to look good again, and five families regularly attended church.

The only concern we had was that a majority of the congregation was still lukewarm about the whole thing. Many were rather cool to the neighbors who came. We hoped that in time their prejudiced attitudes would change. Stan kept quiet; he seemed to have other things on his agenda that were more important. For the next few months the Deacon's Fund program progressed smoothly and without incident.

Stan's biggest agenda item in the autumn and early winter was in preparing for a seminar our church was to host. Reverend J. Paul Peterson of the New Life Evangelical Church in Colorado Springs led the seminar. I was surprised that Stan would want someone like Peterson to speak authoritatively in our church. He was not affiliated with any denomination and his theology was somewhat nuts, blending differing elements of non-traditional theology. Stan insisted that, even if he did not agree with Peterson's theology, he was a man of God and had a message all Christians should hear.

Peterson's seminar was entitled, "What Have Our Founding Fathers Done?" His message was one of, using his own lingo, "super-constitutionality." His premise was that in writing and adopting the Constitution of the United States, our founding fathers never meant for it to become supreme law over the law of God. He claimed that it was part of a liberal conspiracy to promote atheism and communism that had perverted the church/state separation clauses in modern society.

Peterson argued that the Constitution was only a framework for government and that Christians had a duty to subvert it when it came in conflict with the fundamentals of

Christianity. He argued that evangelical Christians could set aside their theological differences to work together to "save" the country from the evils of liberalism. He also argued that we should try to work within the framework of the Constitution by electing fellow evangelical Christians to high offices, but that if such a tactic proved futile, we should be prepared to abandon the Constitution altogether and establish a Massachusetts Bay style theocracy.

I was horrified by Peterson's message. I attended all of the sessions, primarily to learn what his agenda and tactics might be. In the end I concluded that he was too wacky to gain much of a national following. Still, I was unnerved by the way his common-sense language and dynamic presence excited a positive response even among my fellow congregants, a normally emotionless crowd.

Stormy and I were virtually married by the time of Peterson's seminar. Ours was a monogamous relationship, not so much out of love, but out of necessity. Everyone knew we were friends and hung out together. As long as we kept the blinds drawn and were careful in public, nobody suspected a thing. Stormy stopped coming to church shortly after Stan's blow-up with Rob. I was concerned that our shenanigans were responsible, but he insisted that he was just tired of Stan. I understood. Stan, for all his charisma, could, at the same time be equally irritating.

In April, Presbytery held its semi-annual meeting. It was in Stilwell, Oklahoma, about two hundred miles due east. Stan and three of the elders went together. I could imagine what a fun car ride that would be for three hours.

Stormy called me Friday afternoon and said, "Hey, with Stan out of town we can have some fun. Let's go somewhere." He convinced me to take a three day weekend. I cleared my schedule at work for Monday and called Walt. I told him I had a family emergency and wondered if he could cover Sunday school for me.

I made reservations at the *Sheraton-Dallas* and picked up Stormy at his place around ten at night. On the way out of town we stopped at *Beverly's* for some coffee and a piece of pie. I had my favorite, butterscotch cream. Stormy had lemon chess. As we approached Norman, I remarked that I hoped nobody saw us heading south together. Stormy assured me that he had kept an eye out. He said, "Wouldn't Stan shit if he knew what we were doing."

When we approached Ardmore, heavy rain drops splattered the windshield. I flicked on the radio to see if there was a tornado watch. The wind picked up and the rain turned into a downpour. When a weather report finally came on, we learned that a tornado watch had been issued for south central Oklahoma. We drove on through Ardmore and on to the Texas side of the Red River. The storm lifted just south of the border. We checked into the posh downtown hotel around two o'clock in the morning.

Stormy and I had a late breakfast and spent the afternoon in the hotel's indoor pool and spa. We swam for hours, taking periodic breaks for the whirlpool, sauna, and bar. Around four in the afternoon we went back to our room on the eighteenth floor. I asked Stormy if he wanted to shower and go out to dinner. He said, "Sure, but why get in a hurry? Let's go out in a few hours." I smiled as the bulge in my swimming trunks began to swell.

We were showered and dressed for dinner by eight. I called for a table at the *Port o' Call*, a Polynesian restaurant on top of the adjacent office tower. I ordered a *Dewar's* "Rob Roy," and Stormy had a "Jack and Coke." The restaurant had always been one of my favorites. It was decorated with grasses and bamboo; it kind of looked like a set from *Gilligan's Island*. The food was always striking.

After dinner we decided to go to a few night spots. I hated driving in Dallas traffic, and we wanted to keep drinking so we took a taxi. Dallas's hottest night spot in the gay district was "*JR's*," named after the television show's J. R. Ewing. The lesbians had there own version, "*Sue Ellen's*." We could go out and dance all we wanted without having to worry about who might be watching us.

Sunday was spent much the same way. We shopped and went back to the pool. That afternoon when we were done at the pool I lay down on the bed. Stormy crawled on top of me and we locked lips. After about fifteen minutes, I pulled back and said, "You know Stormy, I could fall in love with you very easily. It frightens me. We have the best sex I could ever imagine, but I keep telling myself that I will be totally straight when I get married. I'm starting to think that isn't going to happen. Do you ever think about what we're doing?"

He said, "Yeah, I do. I guess I kind of love you already, but I still want to get married and have a family too. I'd be really jealous though if you took up with another guy or a girl. I like what we have. I try not to think about it too much."

Monday morning we woke up early, ate a quick breakfast and checked out of the hotel. It was clear, sunny, and about eighty degrees. I suggested we stop at *Chickasaw National Recreation Area*, a wooded park along the way with a clear stream flowing through it, and go for a walk.

We hiked for over an hour. On a Monday the place was deserted. We came to a clearing in the canopy near the stream. The sun warmed our faces, and we enjoyed a deep wet kiss. During the embrace, Stormy unbuttoned my shirt and jeans. I unfastened his as well and ran my fingers through the mat of hair on his chest and back. He slowly moved his lips over my chin and down the skin of my throat. He worked his way over my chest muscles and began nibbling at the hairs forming a line above my naval.

After we made love I rolled onto my back in the grass and stared at the sky through the clearing. I fantasized about taking Stormy back to Dallas and abandoning our lives in Oklahoma City. For two days I had lived what seemed like an ideal existence. The thought of going home and resuming the double life I had created made me ill. Still, I was not prepared to accept the fact that I would never be straight.

We were back in town around eight that evening. I called Dean to find out if anything had happened while we were gone. He said it was a quiet weekend, but was kind of hurt that I had not called him. I apologized and asked if he had spoken with Rob. He said that they had played racquetball Saturday afternoon. Rob seemed fine.

Stan was back for the Wednesday night fellowship services. He asked the deacons to meet with him and the elders after the service that night to discuss the Presbytery meeting. When we met, Stan began to read from his notes, "The Tulsa church has elected a new elder, Paul Wagner. The Pastor of the Coffeeville church has been formally removed. He admitted to violating the Second Commandment." Apparently he had permitted a picture of Christ to be hung in the church building. Stan continued, "Presbytery reached an agreement on the Sunday school question. Women can only be permitted to teach Sunday school to pre-school and kindergarten children. Presbytery instructed us to hold immediate elections to replace Rob Montgomery, and, finally, they urged us to place your Deacons' Fund under direct control of the Elders."

Dean interrupted, "What was that last item?"

Stan continued, "Since Church members contribute to the fund, it needs to be under control of the elders."

I said, "Stan, do you remember that we created it to address a problem that the elders refused to address?"

Stan replied, "As far as I am concerned, the problem that existed was none of the church's business. With the funds under elder control, at least it can be used properly."

Brad said, "Does that mean that the poor in the neighborhood will once again be neglected?"

Stan replied, "Of course not. Those who are members will be helped as they should be."

I interjected, "What are you talking about; you know darn good and well that none of the people around here have joined the church yet."

Stan continued, "The money will not be used for non-members."

Walt asked, "What about Betty Olson?" She was another pregnant woman due any day. "Will our commitment to her still be honored?"

Stan shrugged and replied, "She hasn't joined any membership classes and seems only interested in having the birth of her child paid for by someone else. I think our discussion is pointless. You have no authority to maintain this account. Who has control of the checkbook by the way?"

I said, "Dean and I are the signatories on the account."

Stan asked, "Where is the checkbook? Is it here with you?"

Dean lied, "It is at work in my office."

Stan said, "Fine. Tomorrow, at three in the afternoon, the two of you need to meet me and the two elders who will assume control of the account at the bank." Dean and I left abruptly.

As soon as I got home I called the other Deacons and asked them to meet me at the Village Inn the next morning for breakfast. That morning we were all more furious than we had been the night before. Dean told us we

had $13,379 in the account. He said he was not turning it
over to the elders until we agreed it was the right thing to
do. Brad suggested that we had six hours to spend the
money on the neediest people we knew. Walt wondered if
there would be any legal problems. I said that the money
had been given to us to use at our discretion, and that as
long as we had control of the money, there could not be any
legal ramifications. Besides, technically the money had
been given to Dean and me for the express purpose of
helping the poor. There could be nothing illegal about
doing that. Dean reminded us that we would likely be
removed as deacons. Walt said, "Stan and the elders are
preventing us from performing God's command to minister
to the poor, so I have no further function as deacon anyway.
I'll resign before they remove me." We agreed to withdraw
all but one dollar from the account and distribute the money
to the neediest people in the Community. Brad wrote out a
formal resignation, effective at three o'clock that afternoon,
and we all signed it.

I called my secretary and cleared my schedule;
then, Dean and I went to the bank and made the withdrawal
in cash. We stopped first at Betty's and gave her enough to
cover the birth. We made sure she understood that there
would be no more money. Next we went to Charlie's, a
recovering heroin addict. We paid his rent ahead for a few
months and set up a grocery account at the local
supermarket. We made a few other stops to take care of
those we thought needed the most assistance.

It hurt having to tell people we could not help
anymore. We knew that if we could have continued, the
neighborhood could have made a real turn around. Now,
many of them, like Charlie, would probably end up back on
the street, in jail, or dead.

We exhausted the cash and finished our last stop in
time to meet Stan at the bank. We signed the account over

and handed Elder Barrett the checkbook. Stan inquired about the account balance. When the bank officer told him, "one dollar," he flew into a rage. Dean handed him the ledger which detailed all the expenses up to the last moment (he had finished the last entries in the car on the way to the bank). Stan threatened to have us removed as deacons, but I handed him the joint resignation.

Dean and I left the bank and stopped at Beverly's for some coffee. Dean said he had no further interest in the church. He said he would come for the Sunday service that week to say good-bye to his friends.

I told him I was committed to the Sunday school program and unless Stan tried to cause problems there, I would at least fulfill that spiritual obligation. I asked what Sandy, his wife, thought about leaving the church. He said she had lost interest some time ago and did not care one way or the other. I had not seen Sandy in a few weeks and asked Dean why. He said she had gone to help her sister in Tulsa settle into a new house and was going to stay for a few weeks. I thought that was odd, but did not pursue it. Dean was anxious to go. It was his racquetball night with Rob.

Stormy and I went for a run that night. I told him what had happened and that Dean and Sandy were leaving the church. Stormy wondered if anyone else would leave. He said it was about time people woke-up to what a nut case Stan was. I told him I was just as fed-up, but wanted to stick it out for awhile.

Our running circuit took us over to Harry Rogers Park and then back, altogether about six and a half miles. I kept thinking about Sandy out of town to help her sister move for several weeks. It did not seem right. Dean had been acting funny anyway. I wondered if they were having marital problems. I thought about calling Rob to see if Dean had said anything at their racquetball sessions.

Stormy advised against it, thinking that would come across as gossip. He was right. If Dean wanted to talk, he knew how to find me.

Saturday evening I went down to the church to put my lesson on the board as usual. Stan came in, and I thought, "What now?" He was cheerful and greeted me as a long lost friend. I responded as warmly as possible. Stan asked, "What are you teaching this week?"

I responded, "Right now we are going through Harris's *Inspiration and Canonicity of the Bible*. This week we are studying chapter seven which deals with the Old Testament Canon."

Stan replied, "You know, there are not too many teachers who would attempt to cover such in-depth material. I feel blessed to have someone like you as a teacher. Several class members have spoken highly of your abilities and have told me how much they have learned from you."

After he left the room, I thought, "What brought that on? Was he gloating or is he trying to cut his losses?"

At worship service the next day Stan announced a congregational meeting that would be held in two weeks to nominate new deacons. He said nothing about what had happened or why we needed to elect new deacons. Everyone knew anyway. The pews sat empty where the neighborhood people had sat. My former colleagues and I were saddened by the conspicuous absence. Most of the others in the building were oblivious to the empty pews. After service, Dean said his goodbyes and walked out for the last time.

Stormy and I decided to go for a long bike ride in the afternoon. He told me he was concerned that he was about to be laid off at work. In fact, all of us were quite concerned. *Penn Bank*, the largest bank in Oklahoma City had just closed and left hundreds of businesses with no operating capital. The oil boom had busted. He said he was not sure if he could stay in Oklahoma City. Apart from me, he really had nothing to keep him there.

The following Saturday I was about to run over to the church when Rob called. He asked if we could talk that evening. I told him I needed to put my lesson on the board and wondered if he could meet me there. He said it was extremely personal, but thought that would be a quiet, safe place. He walked in and we greeted warmly.

I said, "What's up? You sound worried."

"You'd better sit down; are you sure no one's here?"

"The doors were locked and the lights were out when I came in. Unless you saw someone, we are quite alone. Now, what's going on?"

"Dean and Sandy are getting a divorce."

"I sort of suspected something like that, but why, and why are you so upset about it?"

Rob replied, "There are lots of small reasons, but the big one is why I'm so upset. Last week after you guys were done with the Deacons' Fund meeting with Stan, Dean and I played our weekly racquetball game. We met at the "Y" and played vigorously for an hour. While we were in the showers, he asked me if I would like to come over for a few beers. I figured Dean needed to talk about his divorce, so I ran home and left a note for Charlotte. I told her not to wait dinner. I thought I would take him out for pizza or something.

"He greeted me at the door and asked me what I wanted to drink. I told him a *Pearl* would be great if he had it. He ran to the kitchen. I sat down on the sofa in the middle of the living room facing the fireplace. When Dean walked back from the kitchen with the beer, I was rubbing my shoulder and said, "I think I might have pulled a muscle during that last set." Dean set the beers down on an end table and put his hand on my shoulder. He started massaging and said, "Let me take care of it." Well, one thing led to another and Dean started rubbing other things."

I interrupted, "I don't understand."

"Well, he rubbed something one doesn't normally rub casually. He got kind of personal."

"What are you trying to say Rob? Spit it out."

Rob hesitated, took a deep breath, and said, "Well, Dean said, "Where does it hurt?" and I said, "Right where you are rubbing, that feels good." And it did feel good. Then, God help me, I said, "My other shoulder doesn't feel so hot either. So he massaged it. The skin under my shirt started to get raw, so I took it off. Then I said, "I'm kind of sore all over." Dean leaned forward and his hands caressed my chest. He seemed to enjoy it. So did I. Next thing I knew, we were both naked and our bodies were intertwined. He asked me to make love, and we did. It was like nothing I have ever experienced. I never knew two people could feel like that."

Rob and I talked for over an hour. He told me that he had known for more than a year that he was in love with Dean, but never knew how to act on his feelings. Rob talked graphically about what it felt like to be intimate with Dean. About the time he started to describe their intercourse, we heard scuffling and footsteps. The front door slammed, and we both jumped up in time to look out the window. Brad Mitchell was running to his car.

Rob said, "I was afraid of something like this. What do we do now?"

I said, "Look, I have to tell you some things too. You are not the only one in this boat. I have been having the same kind of affair with Stormy for more than a year."

Rob was stunned.

I went on, "We'll have plenty of time to talk all this through later. We have some damage control to deal with

now. What about Charlotte? She's not the type to handle
any of this very well."

Rob replied, "I can't tell Charlotte. That would kill
her. I do love her, just not like I should. I don't want to
hurt her."

I said, "Rob, you may not have a choice now. We
don't know what Brad heard, but that scuffling was right
outside this room. The walls are paper thin. If Brad heard
half of what you just told me, he will tell Stan. Charlotte
will find out. Here's what we do. I'll run home and call
Brad. I'll try to find out if, and what he heard. You go
home and stay by the phone. Don't let Charlotte answer.
Who knows who might try to tell her something? Wait for
my call. I'll phone right after I talk with Brad." Rob agreed.

I hurried in the door as soon as I got home. Stormy
was already there waiting for me. He asked, What's
wrong?"

I replied, "I'll tell you in a minute. In the
meantime, fix us both a stiff drink." I called Brad. There
was no answer. I told Stormy the whole story; all he could
say was, "poor Charlotte."

I kept calling Brad's number. Finally on the third
try he picked up. He was cold and had nothing to say. I
asked as, nonchalantly as I could, "What have you been up
to?"

He replied coolly, "I stopped over and visited with
Pastor Stan for awhile before coming home."

I asked, "What did you talk about"

His reply was, "Nothing much, church stuff. You
know, the kind of thing one can pick up late on a Saturday
night?" I knew that the worst had happened.

I called Rob to tell him the bad news. I told him he
had no choice now. Either Charlotte heard it from him now
or from someone else at the wrong moment. He told her
immediately. She screamed and pounded him with her fists,

ran to the bedroom, and shut the door. He ran in after her to catch her with a razorblade aimed at her wrists.

He called me back and said he needed some help. I called Walt Hammond. He and his wife were already in bed. I told Walt a quick summation of the situation, minus my own details, and asked if Mrs. Hammond could go over and stay with Charlotte for the night. He said she would. Rob was packed, and as soon as Mrs. Hammond arrived, he left.

Rob came over to my place first. I called Dean, and he came over as well. The four of us sat up and talked for hours. They asked me what I thought Stan would do. I feared he would make a public spectacle. Rob and Dean said they really did not care anymore anyway. They wanted to get their divorces over with and then move on as a couple. They speculated that they might move to Denver. Seeing, two of my closest friends officially come-out ahead of me, made me realize that I was fighting a lost cause as well.

Brad did not come to church until time for the worship services, and when he did, he ignored me completely. Stan opened the service as usual with announcements. He asked the congregation to support overseas missionaries and the denominational scholarship fund. Then he said, "We have a grave crisis in the church that needs the prayers of the entire congregation." Everyone listened with full attention. I knew what was coming. He continued, "Rob Montgomery and Dean Albertson have fallen together into the abominable sin of homosexuality." The congregation gasped in shock. "Until such a time as these two men repent and return to our flock, no one, absolutely no one is to offer them comfort or friendship. Anyone who does, will himself be considered apostate."

I could stand it no longer. I stood up and interrupted Stan, "Where did you hear this; was it from Dean or Rob personally?"

"It wasn't necessary. A faithful member of the congregation reported Rob's confession, which I believe you yourself heard. Is that true?"

"If I had a private conversation, and a person thought he overheard something and carried that to you, then by making this announcement, you are both guilty of the sin of gossip and slander. That is equally abominable in the eyes of God, and you, Reverend Chalmers, should resign your position as pastor."

Stan chuckled a bit, "I think you know the truth, and I wonder, will you maintain a friendship with either or both of them, or will you abide by my direction?"

I picked up my Bible and walked out. I could hear Stan ask the congregation to turn in their hymnals to number 73, *A Mighty Fortress Is Our God.*

I called Stormy as soon as I was home. I told him I needed to go for a long run. He came right over. We hit the pavement, and I told him about the service. He was in disbelief. He said, "Just wait until they find out about us. They'll think it a satanic homosexual conspiracy."

We kept running. After a bit I said, "So what about us? Are we gay now? I really don't have any interest in women. In fact, the idea of having sex with one repulses me. I really do enjoy the hot sex we have. What do you think?"

Stormy replied, "Yeah, I think I made up my mind a few months ago. That weekend in Dallas was kind of a point of no return. I've had sex with women, but it really is no great thing. They smell funny, and tits feel all squooshy and icky. When we get back from our runs and are all sweaty and smell like a locker room, that's what gets my blood pumping. I can't imagine going back to women now. It just seems gross.

"Besides, I've been reading the scriptures and doing some serious study on the subject. I've come to the conclusion that homosexuality is not a sin, certainly not in the Christian era. Stan and John Calvin would have been proud of my methodology. I decided to set all of the man-made rules and laws of the church and society aside and, with prayer, devote my study solely to the scriptures.

"It worked, just like Stan and Calvin said it would. I had read through all of the passages that modern Christians use to condemn homosexuals, and I could find nothing in the Scriptures to support their views. Then, while scanning through the Book of Romans, my eyes were drawn to that passage of Chapter Eight, verse 38, "Neither height, nor depth, nor things past, nor things present, nor things to come, nor powers, nor principalities, nor any created thing can separate you from the love of God." I read that and a light bulb went off. It was as if God himself spoke to me, and I believe with all my heart this was the unction of the Holy Spirit. The church, laws, social rules, the teachings of John Calvin, all are created things. It doesn't matter if the church insists that homosexuality is a sin, what matters, is that those created things cannot separate me from the love of God. Then I remembered all those Calvinistic beliefs of predestination and the Scriptures that support those notions, "Before the Foundation of the world I knew you," etc. If we believe that God is sovereign and that he knew who we would be before he created us, then he knew we would be gay. And being gay is a created thing. Even that cannot separate us from the love of God. God doesn't make mistakes; everything is a part of His big plan for us. It is not that God loves us despite the fact that we are gay, it is that God loves us and created us gay."

That was it for me. I finally said the words, "So that's it. We're gay. I'm gay. I am gay. I AM GAY!" We came up to an intersection and had to wait for a light. I danced around waving my arms, yelling, "I am gay; I am gay!"

Stormy motioned to get my attention, "Geez Joe, settle down. People will think you're crazy."

Rob and Dean got their divorces. Sandy did not care and gave Dean an equitable settlement. Charlotte, under the advice from Rick Horton, an attorney at the church, took Rob to the cleaners. As soon as Rob and Dean were free they packed up and moved to Denver as they had suggested. Some years later I heard they were doing well and active in a local gay rights organization.

I stayed in Oklahoma City. Stormy and I continued our relationship for another six months. We talked at one point about moving in together. Stormy was a bit of a slob, though, and I knew it would destroy what we had. I loved him in a way, but it was not a romantic, life long commitment sort of love. We characterized our relationship as best friends who liked to fuck each other.

Once we were both out and away from the church, we considered dating and meeting other guys. Stormy wanted to get out of Oklahoma City. He eventually found a job in Phoenix. I was sad to lose his companionship, but we both realized it was time to move-on. He left on a Sunday morning. He drove by for a good-bye kiss. I gave him a blow-job for the road. He pulled out of my driveway and turned onto westbound I-44. I slipped on my running shorts and hit the pavement. I ran twelve miles that day.

Chapter 4   Mirror Balls, Dance Floors, and Harry

The oil business was shut down, and I was unemployed so I went back to school. This time I went to a large state university nearby. It was almost like recovering from a period of insanity. Suddenly I was back in classes, reading books at a feverish pace, and leading a gay rights organization. The year was 1984.

Having seen an ad in the college paper for the Gay and Lesbian Student Organization I attended their first meeting of the semester. I made comment in the meeting that I hoped the organization would focus on educating society and winning political battles. Next thing I knew, the name of "Joe Kelly" was on the ballot, and I won the presidency of the group, an unexpected honor.

I did my best to live up to my rhetoric, becoming the public image for the group right away. When we protested at the state capital or on campus I was the one in front of the cameras. My name and photograph were headlined in the newspapers and local television stations. There were times in grocery stores when mothers steered their children away from me, and many nights I came home from class to find hateful and threatening messages on my answering machine. Nevertheless we achieved some of our goals during my administration. We gained university funding for our organization, established a helpline, and pushed a sexual orientation protection policy through student government and the faculty organization.

I had not been personally afraid of or intimidated by the rednecks and religious fanatics that made such a fuss against us. They shouted Biblical quotes and condemnations, but rarely initiated violence. Though I was not personally afraid of our detractors, I knew that the real threat they posed was not in beating up a few fags, but in politics. If they ever gained enough political power, the gay rights movement, along with democracy in the United States, would be dead. It was J. Paul Peterson's agenda I feared the most. The way I hoped to defeat them was through education and in demonstrating that we were a productive part of mainstream society. I embraced the concepts of peaceful resistance and opposed violent rhetoric. I thought we could marginalize our opponents by maintaining civility in our political struggles. I was wrong.

No matter how much we tried to present ourselves as normal everyday people, conservatives pushed the political mood of the country further and further to the Right. Incompetent and corrupt politicians could easily win elections as long as they allied themselves with religious extremists. The J. Paul Petersons and Stan Chalmers of the country did not care if their politicians were inept or even corrupt. In fact, to them it was an ideal setup. A decaying political system was exactly what they wanted.

Campus life at a state university in Oklahoma was quite different from quiet collegial life elsewhere. The university was well respected nationally for its liberal arts, engineering, and law schools, but it was famous for football. The state university football team was the *Booming Pioneers*, a name eulogizing those earliest of Oklahomans who had illegally crossed into Oklahoma Territory before it was supposed to have been open to settlement. The *Booming Pioneers* had won numerous national championships and always finished in the top ten in the country. They had no choice. Any coach failing to have a winning season or letting the team fall out of the top ten was fired on the spot.

University football was arguably the most important issue in the state. It was as though the state fathers decided long ago that Oklahoma had to be good at something, and football was it. It was common for news channels to pre-empt regular television programming when breaking news revealed a scandal with a *Booming Pioneers* football coach or the team. The state legislature was known to have spent more than a day's business debating whether or not a coach should be fired, though they had no official say in the matter. Above all, it was considered a statewide disgrace for the team to lose to Texas, our bitterest rival.

As a child I had thought the statewide preoccupation with football was silly. As a college student, however, I saw how football drained resources from every other university program. It was a constant source of outrage. While all the other departments struggled for adequate funding the football program's budget just grew fatter and fatter.

The History Department, though still staffed with some of the greatest minds in the country, was as under funded as any in the liberal arts. For that reason I made it a point to rely on my own resources and not seek assistantships. I supported myself as an electrician. I apprenticed for the mandatory three years, before earning my journeyman's license. I knew that it would be difficult to find gainful employment as an historian, and I thought I should have a fallback trade just in case. I was in the last year of my Master's degree when I passed the state exam and obtained my journeyman's electrical license. By that time, all my classes were at night, so I could work full time during the day.

I worked for a large electrical service company in Oklahoma City. It was difficult to be the only gay apprentice in an electrical shop. This was "good-ole-boy" hell. I had not formally come out at work, but most everyone at work saw the news coverage of my first public appearance on television as the Chair-person of the Gay and Lesbian Student Organization.

Doug was my work partner the next day. He did not say a word to me until lunch time. Then he said, "I'm going to *Wendy's*, where do you want me to drop you off?"

I feared that my thumb would have to provide my next ride, so I said "*Wendy's*."

Doug was the nicest and the least of the rednecks in the shop. Still, he was ice-cold. I sat down with him at a table. He plowed into his food and said nothing. I could stand it no more, so I said in a perky tone, "Did ya watch the news last night?" Doug nearly spewed French fries and Coke at me. After he swallowed, he started laughing. I said, "I didn't think you could keep up that macho-tough-guy thing too long."

He composed himself and got kind of serious. He said, "Why didn't you give us some warning or something?"

I said, "What was I supposed to do, call a shop meeting to tell everyone I'm gay? There is no easy way to do this, and I figured if a few people saw it on the news, they might not even pay attention. I guess I didn't count on the entire shop being glued to the TV last night."

Doug ended the conversation by telling me, "I'm OK with you being gay and all, but I don't want the other guys to know I'm OK with it because they might start thinking I might be gay or something."

The next four months were hell. The dispatcher made sure I was the apprentice on every job that required crawling under a house or in an attic. I was given the messiest, nastiest, dirtiest, and most physically challenging tasks in the shop. The other apprentices were sent on jobs

to help with changing light bulbs and fixing switches. I
never complained though. I knew that was what the "good-
ole-boys" wanted me to do. Then they could tell the shop
owner that "the nelly faggot couldn't cut it." I did my job,
kept to myself, and never let on like anything was different.

Some of the guys started to come around after a
while. They finally realized that "the faggot" really could
cut it and, in fact, was not all that nelly. Gradually they
started to treat me more normally and things were fine.

Once I had my Journeyman's license I was lead
man on my jobs, and no longer had to put up with anyone's
crap. The work we did was interesting. The connection
between my historical life and my electrical life was in
solving mysteries. The best jobs were when someone had a
switch or a plug that was dead and I had to trace the circuit.
I also enjoyed the variety of work that my shop did. We
were a service shop only. We did not do new construction.
In a typical day, I could make up to ten service calls, each
one with a unique problem or need.

One morning Richard, the dispatcher, told me that
someone had called and specifically requested me to make
the service call. I looked at the name on the ticket; it was
Brian Meeker, my former boss from my church-going days.
It was at his estate in the country. I wondered if Pastor Stan
had arranged for a witch burning or something. It was July
and already ninety degrees by the time I got there.

Brian greeted me at the door. We shook hands
warmly. I said, "How did you know I was an electrician?"

He said, "I've heard a few things about you here
and there."

I said, "If you know that I am an electrician now,
you must know about my other activities."

"You mean that you are gay and a gay rights
activist?"

"Well, yeah."

"I kind of always knew anyway, especially the way you and Stormy spent so much time together."

"Well, what about Stan and all his pronouncements about Rob and Dean?"

Brian rolled his eyes, "Oh yeah Stan. What a piece of work. I don't know how we all put up with him so many years."

I said, "So you're OK with me and everything?"

"Heck yeah. I wanted someone out here I could trust. You are the only electrician I know."

I asked him what he needed. He said he wanted some ceiling fans installed. His house was miserably hot, and all the windows were open. I asked if he was having air conditioner trouble. He said, "Joe, I can't afford to run the air conditioner. That's why I want ceiling fans installed." He had most of his millions with *Penn Bank*. I had never known that. He had paid our last paychecks out of what he had left.

After I gave him the estimate, we chatted for bit longer. I had heard that Stan had taken a larger church in a Dallas suburb. He had become a regional leader in the burgeoning conservative movement and an adviser to several up and coming conservative politicians. Brian told about how our church had sold the building and moved out to the suburbs. Attendance was down to the core "faithful." He thought they were mostly a bunch of hypocrites. After he lost all his money and could no longer tithe the hefty 10% he used to, Stan and the elders had gotten rather cool to him. He asked if I knew anything about Stormy, Rob, and Dean. I told them that we had pretty much lost touch, but exchanged cards now and then.

It was on another service call where I met Harry. It was the late 1980s and I was out and gay. On any given Saturday night, I was at the hottest disco in town, *Angles*, on the dance floor twirling to *Dead or Alive*, Martha Wash,

and *Duran Duran*. The high point of any Saturday night
was when the hush fell upon the floor then the quiet
thumping sound that led into "Relax, don't do it, when you
want to go to it . . ." Then the bottles of poppers surfaced.
After a while the entire dance floor smelled like amyl-
nitrate; each person took a hit, and then passed the bottle on
to the next fellow. Dr. Paul was the most popular person on
the dance floor; he was an obstetrician and brought pockets
full of medicinal poppers to hand-out. I always made sure
to get a couple of vials, they were much better than the
over-the-counter ones we had to buy at the sleaze stores.

One Friday afternoon I had finished my last work
order and hoped to cut out early. My dispatcher called and
told me to go to a nearby drug store. The store had been
robbed several times and was installing a security system. I
was needed to run a dedicated circuit for the cameras. The
security company's installer was Harry. The moment I laid
eyes upon him I was mesmerized. Harry was a little guy,
about five feet, two inches. He had stunning features, nice
arms gorgeous legs, and a tight butt. A nice tuft of thick
chest hair was poking out of the collar of his uniform, and
Dickies trousers encased his bulging basket nicely. What
more could a gay man want? I was at work of course, and
did not dare make a move. I did get enough out of him to
know that he worked for a company in Georgia and traveled
all over the country installing security systems. He was
only going to be in Oklahoma City for a few days. I tried to
put him out of my mind.

Saturday night I was on the dance floor, and about
half way through *You Spin Me Like a Record* I twirled
around to see Harry step onto the dance floor. I nearly lost
my balance. I recovered and made a beeline for him. I
asked him if he remembered me from Friday afternoon. He
said he had hoped to run into me there at *Angles*. We
danced for a while longer before going back to my place.

We made love all night with a little assistance from several vials of Dr. Paul's poppers.

We slept until noon on Sunday. This was Harry's first trip to Oklahoma City, so I decided to show him around. I took him to the *Patio Grill* for breakfast. The *Patio* was an Oklahoma City institution. During my time with the church I had been part of a men's prayer group that met there on Saturday mornings. In the late 1980s I was a regular there again on Sundays with all the other gay boys who had been out dancing until 2:00 AM.

The *Patio Grill* had been in continuous operation since 1950. When it opened, it was at the outskirts of development in Oklahoma City and was at the intersection of U. S. Highway 66 and Classen Boulevard. Classen was a main drag leading directly to downtown, so the location was ideal for a successful diner. I could always imagine many a weary traveler coming into town hungry. A place like the *Patio Grill* would have seemed like an oasis. The quality of the food and service was the reason the *Patio* remained a viable business long after Route 66 ceased to exist in Oklahoma City.

It was a small restaurant. In fact, the *Patio*'s neon sign out front was probably as big in surface area as the seating area inside. The décor was stereotypically 1950s pink and green. The booths and stools at the counter looked as if they had been made the day before, and the pink and green terrazzo floor sparkled as if *Mr. Clean* had polished it himself. On the wall at the side of the eating counter was a small marquis with each waitress's name and her years of service. The youngest in 1989 was Earline with only eighteen years. Fay Lynn was next with twenty-two years. Ruby was the oldest with thirty-one years.

The cuisine was the best artery-clogging, waist-widening southern food a person could ever hope to find. For supper, my favorite item on the menu was "chicken-fried steak," pounded round steak that was breaded and battered, then pan-fried until golden brown. It was served with a heaping portion of mashed potatoes, and everything was smothered with cream gravy.

I took Harry there to have one of their famous omelets. A three-egg Denver Omelet included the juiciest Virginia ham, sliced thin, sweet white onions, and red peppers. They whipped the eggs with heavy cream until frothy then slow cooked the omelet, usually about twenty minutes. It came out almost like a soufflé, light and fluffy, and melt-in-your-mouth delicious. Harry was impressed.

We spent the rest of the day running around town. From the Patio we went downtown to the *Myriad Gardens*, Oklahoma City's glass-domed arboretum. Then we went to the zoo. We exchanged numbers and he went back to his hotel. I wondered if I would ever see him again.

The next morning I was getting supplies together for my first work orders. Richard, the dispatcher, stopped me and told me to go first to *Balliet*'s, a fine clothing store for women in the *50 Penn Tower*, which was only a few blocks from the *Patio Grill*. He said they needed some receptacles installed. The store manager had requested me personally. *Balliet's* was the kind of upscale clothing store where trophy-wives shopped. The manager and all the women who worked there looked like models right off the cover of *Vogue*. Richard said, "How'd you get in with a fine piece like that? You turnin' straight on us or something?" I shook my head. I had no idea why a store like that would request me specifically. All the other guys in the shop were furious. They all wanted to go as my "helper." It was a one-man job though, and the manager had made it clear they wanted me and no one else. Just before I left, Bobby Don said, "What a waste, the only fairy in the shop among all those sweet looking ladies." I smiled and walked off to my truck. While driving there I thought perhaps the reason the store manager had requested me was, indeed, because I was the only "fairy" in the shop.

I walked into the store and asked for the manager. She told me they were having a security system installed and that I needed to add some receptacles in the mechanical room. I smiled. I walked to the back and there he was, Harry grinning ear to ear. As soon as we entered the mechanical room, he closed the door. We embraced and kissed as though we had been apart for years. He said, "I thought about you all last night; I couldn't sleep."

He started to go for my belt and I jumped back and said, "Harry, no, we'll both get fired!"

He said, "Don't worry, I've fixed everything. I told the manager that we need about three hours back here to do our work and that if she or her staff disturbed us, it would take longer and cost more. She said we would be left completely alone."

I rolled my eyes. I said, "I've never done anything like this, I don't think I . . ."

He pulled out some lube, condoms, and poppers and said, "C'mon, show me how you lay pipe."

By then the swell in my trousers gave lie to my protestations.

That was Harry's last job in Oklahoma City. From there he went on to Amarillo and then to the west coast via Albuquerque and Los Angeles. His company had sent him on a six month journey that would take him from San Diego to Seattle, then back to Chicago before turning south again.

We talked frequently while he was on the road, but I spent most of the next six months finishing my dissertation. He told me about everything he was seeing as he stopped in each city. At the end of his trip, he had a month off before starting all over again. He decided to spend his time off with me in Oklahoma City. I turned my dissertation into my committee the week before he came back. I would not have my defense until after he left again.

We spent that month in wedded bliss. At that point we both knew it was a life partnership and admitted as much to each other. It was a difficult time to start a relationship. I was already interviewing with universities all over the country. Harry could not simply quit his job and move to Oklahoma City knowing that I would likely have to move in the next few months. He decided to go back to Georgia and start another circuit until I was in a more settled situation.

Four months later I accepted the position with *Bay City State University*. Harry and I had tried to coordinate our job-hunting efforts as much as possible. Once it looked like I was going to have an offer from a school, he sent out resumes in the same area. He found a growing security company in Saginaw that made him a handsome offer in management. We were both delighted with Bay City, and there we started our lives together.

Chapter 5   Bay City, Michigan

    Life with Harry in Bay City had been one of the happiest times of my life. Bay City itself is a great place to live. When I first traveled there to interview at the university I fell in love with the town right away. I had not felt that way about the other two prospects, a small university in southern Ohio, and a major university in Nebraska. Southern Ohio was interesting, and I might have accepted a position there if Bay City had not come through. There was no way in Hell that I would have moved to Nebraska though. I had grown up in a Great Plains state and I wanted as far away from the oppressive culture and climate as I could get.

    Bay City turned out to be everything I had hoped it would be. I had moved from the "Great American Desert," as Stephen Long had so aptly described Oklahoma in the 1820s, to a land surrounded by the greatest fresh water supply in the world. In Oklahoma, months of summer sun and temperatures daily in the 100 to 104 degree range baked the cracking earth until not a drop of moisture was left. In Michigan, summer rains and rich moist earth grew tall green trees, luxurious grass, and the best musk melons. If, on occasion, the temperature crept up into the mid-nineties, all we had to do was drive ten minutes to the beach where we could cool off in Saginaw Bay.

    The first snows often fell around the first of November. Our base snow was usually in place by Christmas. Winter hung on solid until early March, but it

was preferable to the miserably icy, blistery winters of
Oklahoma. Snow is much easier to deal with than ice
storms, and with snow one can partake in all kinds of winter
sports. Harry and I took to cross-country skiing.

My first impression of Bay City was of a charming
Victorian town that had grown grudgingly through the
twentieth century, but at one point, say around 1942, had
put its hand up and said, "Stop! We don't want to
modernize any more." It had a lively business district in its
city center, with privately owned clothing, drug, jewelry,
and hardware stores. On any given afternoon downtown
was bustling with people carrying their shopping bags and
darting in and out of stores.

When I first visited downtown Bay City, I thought I
had passed through some kind of time warp. I did not know
cities like it still existed. I knew I had passed into another
dimension when I went shopping in *Krepp's*. I had
forgotten to pack clean socks, so I stopped in to buy some.
I also needed to use the men's room, so I asked a clerk. He
told me to go up the stairs to the mezzanine and turn left.
When I topped the stairs I looked to my right. There was
their accounting department. It was staffed with middle
aged women, sitting at desks with adding machines (not
calculators) and manual typewriters; this was in 1990. The
clerks downstairs wrote up the purchase slip, then sent it
upstairs through pneumatic tubes, where the women at the
desks punched numbers into their adding machines, pulled
the handles several times, and sent the finalized sale back
downstairs to the clerk. I was shocked, enamored, and
horrified all at the same time.

The buildings in the town revealed a rich history.
Bay City had been a wealthy town at one time and its
fathers had obviously wanted to leave a legacy of grandeur
for future generations to admire. All of the major structures
had impressive archways with ornately carved stone or

marble, elaborate chandeliers in their entryways, or some
other feature or collection of features intended to inform the
visitor that they were entering a place of substance and
wealth.

East of downtown was the grand Victorian
neighborhood. Center Avenue ran east from downtown,
and its way was lined with palatial homes of carved stone
from the 1870s, 1880s, and 1890s. Scott and Allen, our best
friends, owned one of them. Many of these homes in the
1990s had only had three owners, often from succeeding
generations. Most had never fallen into states of disrepair
and were in great condition.

South and west of downtown were the more modest
working class neighborhoods. The South End was a Polish
émigré community. That was where Harry and I first lived
in Bay City. The people that live in the South End are the
finest people in the world. They are not rich or necessarily
well-connected, but they always treated Harry and me with
the greatest respect. We never felt uncomfortable or afraid
to be out and gay in that community. The "Sout' End" is
easy to spot in Bay City. The appearance of Blessed Virgin
Shrines in almost every front yard is the dead give away.
These shrines have been ridiculed by outsiders as a visual
blight and "a bathtub turned on end with Mary inside."
Actually most of them are not made of bathtubs, and even if
they were, it is an expression of spirituality and community.
I would never ridicule that, especially toward the people
who welcomed a couple of queers into their community. I
have to admit though, that when I learned that Madonna had
been raised in Bay City, her bathtub spread in *Playboy*
made me laugh; my neighbors failed to take it with much
levity, though.

The northwest part of town was the French-
Canadian community and the southwest part of town was
German. The Germans were the descendants of the wave of

German immigration that had swept over many parts of the United States during the European upheavals in the 1840s. The French-Canadians had come down to work in the lumber camps in the 1860s and beyond. It always amazed me how these communities had stayed intact for so long.

The lumber camps were what made Bay City a wealthy town in the late nineteenth century. In fact, in the 1870s Bay City continuously vied with Muskegon for the position of wealthiest town in Michigan. Many of the lumber barons, as they were called, settled in Bay City, but the richest of them all, Henry Williams Sage of Cornell University fame, never lived in Bay City. Sage had the largest lumber mill in Bay City and was one of the greatest land owners in Michigan; that is until his lumberjacks stripped his land of all its native white pine.

The U. S. Civil War, its subsequent reconstruction in the south, and mass migrations to the Great Plains, where there were no forests, had created an unprecedented demand for building lumber. Michigan's vast wealth of virgin white pine was mostly to disappear by the end of the 1880s. Much of it exited Michigan through Bay City. Sawmills lined the Saginaw River, which was the means of transport in the region for fallen timber.

During the lumber era of the 1870s and 1880s, Bay City's waterfront was as rough as any frontier town. At the end of the cutting season in the spring, hordes of cutters descended upon the town for two reasons, to pick up their pay for the season and to spend it in the brothels and bars. Water Street in the spring was not the place for polite folk, and it really was not until the end of that era that the city began to look more civilized.

By the 1890s the lumber era was finished in Bay City, but the city fathers who had grown wealthy off of it, were well set for many years to come. As a result of the lumber industry, Bay City, along with Saginaw, Flint, and other towns nearby, had attracted a wealth of highly skilled machinists, boilermakers, and others necessary for building and maintaining state-of-the-art lumber mills. Southeastern Michigan had built the greatest industrial infrastructure in the country. That is why, when men like Will Durant, David Buick, and Louis Chevrolet had visions for industrial empires, they needed to look no further than their own neighborhoods.

Bay City was, however, on the edge of that industrial infrastructure. It remained on the edge of the resulting wealth from the auto industry. Bay City had its plants and machine works, the greatest were the shipyards, but Bay City would never be so dependant on *General Motors* as to be devastated by plant closings like Saginaw and Flint. Bay City never was the wealthiest city in Michigan again, but it never was the poorest either.

In the middle and later twentieth century, Bay City became more of a sleeper town. *GM* plants in Saginaw and *Doxxen Chemical* plants in Midland often drew on the population of Bay City for their workforce. Bay City remained largely unnoticed by the outside world, and at the end of the twentieth century it looked much like it had at the beginning.

Our first home on the South End was a modest two-bedroom frame structure. It was our honeymoon cottage. Harry took the job with the security company for a while, but after a few months found an opportunity with a large national non-profit organization. It was a great career move for him. I went to work at the university. It was a small history department, so I had to teach everything from freshman U. S. history to European history, but I was able to get one course in the catalog in my field, Russian history.

Russian history had been my passion since childhood. Why I am not sure, but I remember that my high school history teacher could never explain satisfactorily

enough to me why such a great country could have
imploded the way it did in 1917. Before returning to
college I had read enough to know that traditional
explanations were wrong. They typically theorized that a
corrupt and inefficient regime had left the country with no
alternative but revolution and that revolution grew out of
the yearnings of oppressed peasants for freedom.

After much scholarly consideration of the topic, I
concluded that the Russian Revolution of 1917 was a
terrible mistake that should never have happened. Camps of
treasonous criminals had instigated both the overthrow of
the monarchy and the Bolshevik seizure of power. Despite
the criticism of opposition parties in the Duma, Russia's
elected legislative body, the Tsar's government was
winning its war with Germany, and though economic
hardships existed, the Russian economy was healthy and
growing. That was something no other belligerent in World
War I could claim. The Provisional Government, which
first replaced the Tsar, demoralized the army and lost
territory that had not been occupied by a foreign army since
Napoleon's. The Bolsheviks, an obscure party of fanatics,
ousted the Provisional Government in October and quickly
made peace with the Germans, ceding even more territory.

I found myself, a liberal Democrat, siding with
Russian monarchists. All criticism understood, Nicholas
II's dynasty, the Romanovs, had brought Russia three
centuries of growth and stability. They had taken a nearly
defunct nation in 1613 and turned it into the greatest empire
in the world. Their biggest mistake in the early nineteenth
century was a complacent failure to lead Russia into the
industrial age quickly enough. Nicholas II's father,
Alexander III, had realized the dangers of failing to
industrialize and pursued it with vigor in the 1880s.
Nicholas continued and expanded his father's industrial
policies. He succeeded, and by 1914, just before World

War I started, Russia was an industrial and economic super-power. In fact, Russia's pre-war levels of industrial output would not be matched again by the Communist regime until the late 1930s. I had thought that if the criminal regime of the Communists ever faltered, the Romanovs would return.

The Romanovs have, however, always been their own worst enemies. Even before the war and revolution, the Tsar's family constantly caused him embarrassment. In the post revolutionary period, some Romanovs sided with the Nazis in Germany, and many fought petty battles amongst themselves with only a handful demonstrating a true sense of loyalty to their motherland. By 1990, they were so scattered and fragmented that it did not seem likely that a Romanov could make a successful bid for the throne.

In my studies, I had always found Nicholas II to be a good tempered man. He rarely lashed out at his relatives no matter what trouble they caused. He tended to be tolerant of their eccentricities. Homosexuality was common among the Romanovs. Two of his favorite uncles were homosexual as were several near relatives. His only published comment on the subject was in reference to a gay relative who had just married. Nicholas said, "I didn't think he was the marrying type." Perhaps his accepting attitude towards homosexuality was also what endeared me a bit to him.

My career in academia was controversial as a result of my interpretations of Russian history. I gave a talk at a conference just after finishing my Ph. D., and a colleague interrupted me by calling me a "revisionist." I replied, "If the historiography on Russian history is so flawed, then, perhaps, some revision is necessary." Nevertheless, I did my required publishing and gained a bit of a following – quite unexpectedly. By the time I left teaching, I was a well respected historian.

My first year teaching at *Bay City State University* was the year that the Soviet Union was in its final collapse. I quickly became the most sought after professor at the university for interviews with the media, and for general opinion on what was happening. My classes were always full, and students seemed to like my teaching style.

I enjoyed teaching, but political issues at the university made me rethink my career. The income was modest, but that was not the problem. Though it was a state university, it was heavily endowed with money from the Douglas family, who still owned controlling interest *Doxxen Chemical*. They were a conservative bunch and used the influence they had purchased to direct university policy. The idea of an openly gay professor, especially one who had been an activist seemed to bother them somewhat, but my "liberal" political ideas were what caused problems. In my first *U. S. History 1002, Post Reconstruction to the Present* course, I had severely criticized the Reagan administration's acceleration of the concentration of wealth into the hands of an elite few. Some of my students in that class were part of the Douglas clan. Before my next semester started, my department head "suggested" I refrain from criticizing recent administrations so briskly.

I blew that off. My department head was not an historian, and I was not going to compromise my teaching ethic to appease a few rich bastards. That incident, however, prompted me to conduct some local research, historical of course, on the Douglas family and *Doxxen Chemical*. I had no issues with *Doxxen Chemical* as a corporation. They had seemed to clean up their image in recent years. Their pollution of the Saginaw River watershed had been reigned-in, the fish were safe to eat again, at least in small doses, and trees actually started to grow around the *Doxxen Chemical* complex. I am enough of an environmentalist that I don't think industry should

willfully pollute the air and water; I think we should
develop fuels that are renewable and non-polluting; and I
think people should recycle everything they can. Beyond
that, I am not one to chain myself to pipelines or support
wanton destruction of property in the name of
environmentalism.

My curiosity was piqued and I had to know more
about *Doxxen Chemical* and its role in local society. The
world headquarters for *Doxxen Chemical* was in a small city
a few miles away. It was a strange town. The only industry
there was *Doxxen Chemical*. Should *Doxxen* have ever
moved its world headquarters elsewhere, the town would
have dried up and blown away. The city was beautiful. It
had no slum, the streets were clean, and everything was, oh-
so-tasteful.

Charles H. Douglas, the company's founder, started
drilling brine wells there in the 1890s. In the beginning of
the twentieth century *Doxxen Chemical* was well
established and growing into the global corporate power it
became in the twentieth century. Douglas was determined
not ever to move his world headquarters and his heirs so far
have respected that wish. The rapidly growing company
had to have a pleasant living environment to attract world-
class executives. By the 1920s the town had been
transformed from a dying lumber town to a *Doxxen*
company town.

In my research I uncovered a brochure that *Doxxen
Chemical* had used in the 1950s to recruit new executives.
It played right into the "Leave-it-to-Beaver" mentality of
the time. The brochure presented the town as a clean, well
kept city with everything one would need and want to find
in a city without the crime or the slums. It was perfect for
the white middle class family with two children and a car.
It is where the Cleavers and the Nelsons must have lived,

and Ward and Ozzie must have really been *Doxxen* executives.

That brochure stated emphatically that the town was not a company town, but simply the place where *Doxxen Chemical* headquarters was located. Company spokespeople, even into the late twentieth century, dismissed the notion of it as a company town. I begged to differ. The way the town kept slums out was to keep property values throughout the town inflated beyond what low income families could support. Maids, gardeners, gas station attendants, and others of the "servant class" did not need to live there. They could and did live on the outskirts of town or commute from Saginaw, Bay City, or Freeland. When a *Doxxen* executive was recruited, he was strongly encouraged to live within the city limits with promises of property buy-outs should he be transferred and better-than-market mortgage terms at the local banks. It all made perfect economic sense for *Doxxen*. There was no danger in the company losing out on the property buy-outs, because executives transferring-out were quickly replaced with executives transferring-in to buy the houses. With *Doxxen* guarantees on the mortgages, the houses where *Doxxen* executives lived were, arguably, company homes.

Doxxen's town certainly had more than its fair share of the arts, and the city encouraged theatre, opera, visual arts, and music. However, every foundation, society, or other philanthropic organization had at least a few Douglas family members on its board. The Douglas family influenced and controlled, at least to a certain degree, how the town was governed and how people lived. When a company controls real estate, consumer services, and social life in a town, and determines who can and cannot live there, it is a company town, regardless what the company may claim.

In my next semester of teaching History 1002, I made it a point in my discussions on industrialization to talk about the development of *Doxxen Chemical*. I pointed out how, in the mid-twentieth century, the air and water pollution that spewed out of its bowels made the fish in the Saginaw River unsafe to eat. Trees would not grow within a ten mile perimeter of *Doxxen* facilities. I also pointed out that this situation persisted until the *Clean Air and Water Acts* forced *Doxxen* to clean up its emissions. I was nearly fired mid-semester.

I managed to keep my job, and I toned it down for awhile. I knew that *Bay City State University* and I would have a short term relationship. I began thinking about alternatives.

I was not the only professor to get in trouble for exercising academic freedom. Betty Stanton was an English professor and one of my best friends. She was straight and a perfect fag-hag. Betty was a poet from Berkeley and was very well published. She was a diehard socialist, and we had many heated discussions about the failures of Communism. One spring the university's arts council thought it would be a good idea to have a poetry reading in the rose garden. Betty was asked to lead the presentation with selections from some of her own published works. She chose her favorite, *The Death of Lenin' Dream*. This particular poem was a recent publication lamenting the demise of the Soviet Union. It contained the word "fuck." She was brought before a disciplinary board for teaching profanity to students.

Feeling my political voice stifled in the university environment, I reacted as I always had – I rebelled. I first tried to organize a gay faculty group on campus. My attempts raised attention, but not much of a following. Because it was a small university, there really were not that many gay or lesbian professors, and certainly not enough who were willing to be acknowledged publicly.

While involved in that attempt, a pastor from a local Presbyterian church contacted me. The Reverend Charles Gibson was affiliated with the mainstream branch of the Presbyterians. He said he wanted to help.

My most recent conversation with a Presbyterian minister had ended with me calling him a gossip and him declaring me apostate. It did not matter that Gibson was from a mainstream denomination; I was skeptical. He was persistent, and I agreed to meet him for coffee.

We met at McDonald's. I did not expect the meeting to last long. Gibson was an older man, distinguished in his appearance, and articulate in his language. His first question was, "Why are gay people not interested in religion? I have tried for years to reach out to your community, but have so far been unable to interest more than a few. What am I doing wrong?"

I was startled by such a question. "It's not so much what you are doing wrong, but what your church and most churches do that drive gay people away. Many of us are deeply spiritual and would like to be a part of a greater spiritual community, but don't feel safe in most churches."

I proceeded to tell him about my experiences with the Presbyterians in Oklahoma City. When told him the part where Pastor Stan announced Rob and Dean's sexuality from the pulpit, Gibson hung his head in his hands. With an apologetic tone, he said, "I am surprised you agreed to meet with me at all."

In the next two hours Gibson convinced me he was an honorable man and had the best of intentions. He wanted to find a way to reach out to the gay community in some kind of meaningful way. He thought the university environment might be the best venue, but was unsure how to proceed.

I told him my clout with university administrators was rather thin. Because I was faculty I could reserve certain rooms for special lectures and seminars, so I suggested hosting a special seminar designed to open dialogue between organized religion and the gay community. Gibson said that he knew several members of the local clergy that were likewise interested in reaching out to gay people.

Although I had faculty privileges to reserve rooms, it still had to be on behalf of a community organization. I made up the name "Bridges Foundation" and registered a room for a Tuesday night early in the next semester. Over several bottles of red wine, Harry, Betty Stanton, and I designed a provocative advertising campaign for the event. The posters featured an archetypical preacher holding a Bible in one hand and gesturing with the other from a pulpit. Gathered around him were drag queens, bull dykes, and a host of other queer themed congregants. The caption read, "Religion and Sexuality, an Open Forum." We stuck posters on every bulletin board on campus and had public service announcements on the local public radio station. We sent flyers to every campus organization and all the participating ministers made announcements about the event from their pulpits.

The structure of the event was to have a panel discussion led by three ministers and three leaders of regional Queer organizations. We had no idea what kind of turnout we would have. The room I reserved could seat no more than 100 people. The room was packed, with people standing around the perimeter of the room. Most of the people who came were genuinely interested in the event.

There were, however, a few hecklers. After the panelists made their opening statements, we opened the floor to questions and comments. The first respondent was a young man who, when recognized, stood up and with an arm and index finger outstretched toward Heaven declared, "Homosexuality is an abomination in the eyes of God. Jesus saved me from all sorts of sin. I robbed convenience stores, did drugs, and stole cars, but I never went so far as homosexuality." Reverend Gibson coolly and effectively shut him down. After that outburst, the dialogue was generally positive and constructive.

The end result was that the Bridges Foundation became an overnight legitimate organization. Its mission was to continue to promote ways for religious institutions to reconcile with Queer people. Like most other activist organizations we succeeded for a number of years to achieve definable goals.

Though I was once again a gay rights activist, it was my academic career that gained a national following. Media attention about my unique interpretations of the Russian Revolution attracted business leaders, who intended to expand into the burgeoning markets of the former Soviet Union. They sought out my advice and consultation services. The next several years brought more clients and I found myself making more money at consulting than in teaching at the University. It seemed pointless to keep the position at the university when I could do even better consulting full time. After my fourth year, I submitted my resignation and left the university. It was a great move. Consulting work had its challenges, but they were all related to my ability to perform to client expectations; political machinations were irrelevant.

Soon, Harry and I decided we had outgrown our cottage on the South End. We wanted to move into the Victorian neighborhood east of downtown. With my job, we had the financial resources to buy just about anything we wanted. At first we thought about the Center Avenue mansions. Our best friends, Scott and Allen, had a lovely Victorian house on Center, and we thought how wonderful it would be to have one like theirs. There was not another one like theirs, and we were disappointed with the ones that were available.

We decided that the Victorian ideal was not necessarily for us anyway. Victorian homes in original condition were not well suited to a post-modern lifestyle. They had rooms that no longer served any earthly function. They were hard to heat and cool, and they had no closet space.

South of Center Avenue was a neighborhood of homes built in the 1950s. They were *chic* structures with an obvious Frank Lloyd Wright-Bauhaus influence. In fact, the architect had studied under Wright and was none other than Allen Douglas, the errant son of Charles H. Douglas. Allen had grown up with no interest in the chemical business and a burning passion for architecture. His sense of design was unique and embodied the spirit of the post World War II era that rebelled against all things traditional. He designed ultra-modern buildings that featured clean functional lines and little or no decoration.

One had been on the market for almost a year. Victorian homes in Bay City rarely stayed on the market for more than a month, but a 1950s home, no matter how elegant, had to wait for the right buyer to come along. Harry drove by the house one day and suggested at dinner we call our realtor, Bob Horgath, to set an appointment for us to walk through it.

The moment I stepped through the front door I knew it was our home. It was built in 1959. I could picture Jack and Jackie Kennedy, Cary Grant, Audrey Hepburn, Elizabeth Taylor, Rock Hudson, James Dean, and Doris Day dancing a Bossa Nova on the gleaming terrazzo floors. I could imagine serving dry martinis and perfect Manhattans. The garage was large enough for the biggest tail-finned *Cadillac*. This house was meant for furnishings

with understated lines and clean crisp design. Knick-knacks
had no place there, and a table in this house should have no
more than one piece of fine *Steuben* sitting atop.

The following year we paid off the house. We were
living well. Harry traveled with me whenever he could.
Trips to San Francisco, Berlin, St. Petersburg, Moscow,
Paris, and Washington all became normal vacation spots for
us. We had an ideal life that seemed secure and perfect.

The gay community was open and welcoming to
newcomers, something that many other communities,
Oklahoma City for example, tended not to be. Sure, Bay
City's gay community had its cliques, but they were not so
exclusive as to scare people off. Hardly a weekend passed
without someone having some kind of social function. In
the summer it was cook-outs, boat outings, and trips to the
beach. In the winter, holiday parties, dinner parties, and
cocktail parties were the norm.

The operative word in all of those events was
"cocktail." Ours was a drinking crowd. Gin, Scotch,
Vodka, and olives were considered the four basic food
groups. One had to plan for these gatherings of fifty to a
hundred people on average. At a typical party we could go
through several cases of liquor. I don't think most of the
crowd had a problem; it was simply our way of socializing.

As a new couple in town, our first order of business
was to throw a party and invite everyone we could. That
was a great way to put us on the "A" list. It also neutralized
our position in the crowd; everybody liked us right away.
Though we had our closest friends, we avoided, quite
skillfully, getting drawn into "family" squabbles. We were
the peacemakers, not the pot-stirrers.

And there were pot-stirrers. Chief among them was
Matt DuPont. "He's a high maintenance girl," I used to say.
He constantly looked for drama; when he found none, he
invented it. He loved to prey on new people, though he left

Harry and me alone. I remember one new couple that had
moved to town about two years after us. There names were
Rodney and Herb. They were a bit nerdy and their attire
was a bit dated. Matt referred to them as "Peaches and
Herb." Matt, using an unidentifiable alias on the Internet,
stumbled onto them in a chat room. He acted like he was
interested in a three-way with them and asked all kinds of
probing questions. Rodney revealed that he had a foot
fetish. At the next social gathering Matt then goaded people
into walking up to them and saying things like, "You know,
I found a really interesting set of feet the other day." We
never saw Rodney and Herb again.

Halloween was always the most important social
event of the year. That was where most of the crowd
"hustled out their finest drag." They gave the Castro
District stiff competition. At first Scott and Allen hosted
the festivities at their home, which was big enough for
about one to two hundred people, but the event grew larger
and larger each year, and eventually we had to put a
committee together and arrange for a public location that
could handle at least four hundred. There was no place
suitable and willing in Bay City, but the owners of the old
Shuck Hotel in Old Town Saginaw were open to the idea.

Each year had a theme. Contests during the
festivities were for best costume, best theme representation,
best drag, and best group. Drag was not required, but
costume was. Matt DuPont, one of Bay City's premier
female impersonators, and his two best friends, Darryl and
John, always did a group theme. They were known as "The
Diors." They always did a perfectly choreographed stage
show. They did all the standards, *We Are Family, Lady
Marmalade, Stop! In the Name of Love.* They even did
some newer numbers like, *Absolutely Not!*

Harry and I never did drag. That wasn't us, but we
had a great time putting together costumes to fit the theme

anyway. The steering committee always tried to set a theme that would force people into drag. The one where they nearly succeeded was when they made the theme "beauty pageant" and everyone was supposed to come as "Miss" something. I came as close as ever to real drag by fashioning a nun's habit and came as "Miss Belief." Harry would not cave, so he did butch *Village People* drag and came as "Miss Chief." The best costume that night was "Miss Conception" (Miss Della Shus or Greg McDonald). Her outfit was that of a pregnant woman of loose morals. In her mile-high hairdo were strewn condoms (which obviously hadn't worked). Matt DuPont asked Greg, "Now tell me Della, did you have to use any padding to achieve that with-child look?" Greg went on a diet the following week.

Greg was a piece of work. He had a tendency to want to be the life of every party. His favorite pick up line was, "Highhhhhh, my name is Della Shus; are you hungry?" It rarely worked. He was obsessed with penises; I guess most of us gay boys are, but most of us do not verbalize it publicly. Greg did. I have seen him, after a few too many cocktails, walk up to total strangers and say things like, "You have nice arms; how big is your dick?"

What fueled his liveliness in most social situations was typically a combination of vodka and *Vicodin*. Greg had apparently been using these substances for some years and had developed a tolerance to the combination that would have killed most people. Though his "V & V" cocktail, as we often called it, bordered on serious abuse, it never seemed to impair his ability to function as a professional. By all observations he only consumed his "V & V" during social gatherings.

In fact, the only problem he encountered from it was a supply problem. He could only complain so much to his doctor about feigned aches and pains, so he had to resort to obtaining his supply of *Vicodin* from friends. Some willingly shared the remnants of an unused prescription, but even that was not enough. It was well known in our community that he raided friends' medicine cabinets whenever he came to visit.

Harry and I had our own experience with his clandestine acquisitions. I was recovering from a back injury and had a bottle with about twenty pills in our medicine cabinet. Greg was part of a dinner party one night. The next Monday Harry noticed that only ten were left in the container, asking if I were in severe pain. I told him I had been doing fine and had not taken any for several weeks. We wondered if it could have been the housekeepers or Greg. The following weekend Greg was at a party, obviously well livened on his "V & V" cocktail. We knew for sure then.

To confirm it, however, we set up a test. I had the prescription refilled; then counted the exact number of pills in the container right before another social event where Greg would be in attendance. At one point in the evening, Greg excused himself for the bathroom. Harry discreetly went to the bathroom right after Greg and checked the bottle. Another ten pills were missing. The next time, we left only one pill in the bottle, but included a note that said, "We hope you enjoy this, Greg, it is the last one." He came out of the bathroom red-faced and never raided our medicine cabinet again.

Scott and Allen went through a brief period where, although they loved each other dearly, they were not entirely monogamous. The "Jacks," as we called them (Jack Mitchell and Jack Upshaw), always threw a fabulous Christmas party and invited upwards of three hundred people. They had the means and the house to support such an event. At one of these functions, Greg McDonald walked into a closed bedroom to find Allen servicing a

twenty-something cock. Greg burst back into the party and
started telling everyone, in his Della Shus voice, "I just saw
Allen sucking off that gorgeous tall blond that I've been
lusting after, and Allen was going all the way down to the
base on him." As quickly as he could, Scott grabbed a hold
of Greg and took him upstairs to shut him up. Greg was
close to passing out anyway and decided to "rest" for a
while. Scott then went to the bedroom where Allen and the
blond were still at it. He told Allen to pull himself together
and rejoin the party as if nothing had happened, but to make
sure that he and the blond did not reenter together. They
stayed for the rest of the party, but with Allen getting a lot
of smiles and winks. A few weeks later Scott had a new
Mercedes 560 SL. I always assumed Allen was making the
payments.

Greg was an older member of the crowd, and in the
midst of his forty-ninth year, Matt DuPont initiated Greg's
mid-life crisis. He was sitting across from Greg at a dinner
party and said, "Greg, I never noticed that you have hooded
eyelids. You don't usually see that sort of thing on people
until they start to show signs of aging." Within a year, Greg
had his eyelids tucked. Then he bought a new convertible,
and continued with more plastic surgery, including a
tummy-tuck and skin resurfacing. He finished the year out
with a new hair piece.

The wildest night of all for Greg McDonald was
while he was dating Toby, a cute young airhead. If Greg, or
Della, could put away mass quantities of liquor, Toby made
Della look like a Prohibitionist. I was finishing my last
semester teaching during the holidays and had rounds of
university parties to attend. Greg was a Geology professor
and attended many of the same parties. The finale was the
President's Ball at *Bay Valley Inn.*

The President's Ball was one of the social events of
the holiday season to receive a written review in the *Bay*

City Times. High society was always well represented at
the Ball. It was Saturday night and Greg was there with
Toby. Greg, as usual, had too much to drink too fast, and
when he realized this was the wrong place to turn into Della
Shus, excused himself, left Toby behind, and drove home to
nap it off. Toby was in too much of a stupor to realize at
the time he had been left behind with no transportation.

About twenty minutes later someone burst into the
grand ballroom shouting something about a stolen limo.
Harry and I ran out into the parking lot to see what had
happened. A stretch limo was crumpled into a telephone
pole at the end of the parking lot, and a man in tails and a
woman in her disheveled bridal gown were standing next to
the vehicle.

The police and an ambulance arrived and pulled
Toby out of the driver's seat. He appeared to be dazed and
had blood streaming down his face. The police asked if
anyone knew him. With Harry tugging at my coat to be
quiet, I spoke-up. On the way to the hospital, I called Greg.
Greg had just awakened from his slumber and was ready for
the disco.

Greg burst into the hospital and demanded to see
Toby. He looked at the cuts above Toby's eyebrow and
thought about that beautiful boyish face being ruined for
life. Greg demanded that no doctor touch him until a plastic
surgeon could be found (the two cuts were about an inch
each). When the resident physician came in, the nurse
informed him that, "The kid's father wants a plastic
surgeon."

Greg hired the best attorney in town to help lighten
Toby's fines and jail time. They worked out a plea bargain
that dropped the kidnapping and hijacking charges, leaving
only the grand-theft and DUI in place. Their relationship
ended a few months later.

Our idyllic life in Bay City also included sailing together. Harry enjoyed it, but the boat had been my hobby. I enjoyed sailing alone, as it gave me time to meditate. I remembered the first time I saw the Great Lakes. It was on my move from Oklahoma to Michigan. My frames of reference for large bodies of water were the muddy reservoirs we had back in Oklahoma, where a "big lake" was anything deeper than twelve feet and wider than fifty yards. Soon after crossing the Michigan state line, I pulled off the freeway at South Haven. I was awestruck to see an inland sea of clean, fresh water. It looked like an ocean, except the air smelled fresh, not salty or fishy. The beach was nothing but pure fine-grain sand. You could walk barefoot for hours. I saw sailboats out in the water and determined I was to have one.

It took me several years before I was ready to purchase a boat. In the meantime I learned how to sail from a good friend, Alfred Vickers. Alfred's boat was, in those days, the handsomest boat on the water. Alfred was an accomplished sailor, and he loved to teach people about sailing. To him it was serious business; he would have no time for anyone approaching it with half a heart.

I wanted to learn sailing more than anything, and I spent almost every weekend for an entire summer on Alfred's boat. He was delighted to have an apprentice. I learned everything I could about sailing. By the end of summer he was letting me pilot in and out of the channel and even dock the boat.

I found the *Polar Star II*, then christened the *Fighting Chance*. It had been a racer some years back, but had fallen into disrepair. It had won the Chicago to Mackinac race in the seventies and finished second in the Governor's Cup in the early eighties. I was not interested in racing so much, but I did want a fast boat. I did most of the restoration work myself, taking a summer just to make her seaworthy. I finished it out as a pleasure craft, with all the amenities necessary for taking long trips. I knew Harry would only enjoy it if he could be comfortable.

In the summers I made it a point to let people know that they were welcome to join us for sailing on Saturdays. The *Polar Star II* pushed off from the marina promptly at 10:30 AM every Saturday. Anyone who wanted to come had to be on board by that time. Greg McDonald was one of the regulars. On one occasion I was about to push off and walked around the entire boat to ensure that all was in order. Greg, or Della in this case, was stretched out topside on the bow on her beach towel. He struck a 1940s cheesecake pose, throwing one hand behind his head and said, "Hhhhi Joe, do you find me wanton and alluring?" I replied, "No, it's more like wanting and leering."

Those Saturday sails were the most entertaining. As the captain it was necessary for me to refrain from consuming alcohol. I quietly picked up on more gossip and news than in any other venue. I heard the story about Martin Upshaw and his breakup with Timmy Lewis. Martin, or "Marty" as he was best known, was a successful construction engineer. He was a nice looking man in his upper thirties, but, I think, had a bit of a self image problem. No one had ever been able to figure out his relationship with Timmy. Timmy was a dashing twenty-something gold digger, gorgeous face, blond hair, and blue eyes. He had a "past" and was known to have taken advantage of older wealthy men. Marty knew all about Timmy's sordid past, but was smitten anyway. Marty insisted, "That's the old Timmy. The new Timmy is a changed person; besides, I'm not old."

The only thing Timmy had changed was his sugar daddy. They stayed together for about four years. When they met, Timmy's sole means of support was running a fry-wagon at fairs and special events. Marty shed his

pinstriped suit for a white cook's uniform on the weekends
to help Timmy in the fry-wagon. Marty claimed it was fun
to do something different. It was Matt DuPont that coined
the phrase, "Fry Daddy and Fry Baby."

Into the fourth year of their relationship Timmy had
been spotted at the *State Bar* in Flint, a popular cruising bar,
picking up all kinds of trash. I had just come back from a
trip to London the Friday night they broke up. The next
morning I went down to the dock as usual. Matt DuPont
showed up about 9:30 grinning like a Cheshire Cat. Matt
rarely went sailing with us, so I was a little surprised to see
him.

After everyone was on board, and we were
motoring down the Saginaw River, Matt said in a tone loud
enough for everyone on the boat to hear, as well as most
people on shore, "You'll never guess what I witnessed last
night." Everyone gathered round while he told the story.
"Last night I went down to the *State*. Timmy Martin was
there as usual, hitting on everyone he could find. I guess
Martin Upshaw had heard (can't imagine how) about
Timmy's philandering at the *State* and showed up
unannounced. When he walked in, Timmy was hitting on a
man in a wheelchair, a wheelchair no doubt! Marty walked
up to them and asked Timmy what was going on. Timmy
said it was a surprise to see Marty and introduced him to his
"old friend Bob." Bob certainly was old, but I'm not sure
how long they'd been friends. Timmy winked at Bob, and
Bob wheeled his way out of the bar. Timmy put his hand
on Marty's shoulder and said, "Honey, why don't you get
us a drink." Marty went up to the bar, ordered drinks and
when he got back Timmy had disappeared out the front
door. When Marty realized what had happened he threw
the drinks on the floor and stormed out of the building.
Some of us quietly followed, just so we could make sure
nothing bad happened. Martin walked around every vehicle

in the parking lot until he found Bob's chairlift van. He
opened the door, which was unlocked, and there was
Timmy, doing his part for charity. Bob's and Timmy's
pants were on the floor and Timmy was sitting in Bob's lap
with Bob's dick in Timmy's ass. We all saw everything."

Everyone on my boat was aghast. I was aghast that
this tale had been told on my boat! I knew it would be
labeled the "gossip ship." I asked, "C'mon Matt that is too
fantastic. How much of that story is embellishment?" He
assured us that it was the real story. The way events and the
break-up went, I was finally convinced.

Much more than the "gossip ship," the *Polar Star II*
was my refuge. While friends were generally welcome on
Saturdays, I always made it clear that Sundays were for
Harry and me alone. Those were the quiet days we set out
for a day sail refusing to think about work, friends, or any
other responsibilities. Often we sailed out into the expanse
of Lake Huron to see nothing but water. Some of our most
remarkable love making was in the sun on the bow of the
Polar Star II. All that could be heard was the lapping of the
waves, the fluttering of the sail, and the moaning of two
passionate men.

Chapter 6   . . . And the Wall Came Tumbling Down

All the while we ran with the cream of gay society
and lived a fabulous life, American society grew more and
more conservative. My sense of history caused me to be
increasingly alarmed with the social trend in the country.
My experience with fundamentalists gave me a cold sense
of reality knowing well the people who opposed us. For
more than the ten years before the time we made our escape
to Canada, the conservative propaganda machine had
vilified gays so much that we were as hated as Jews in
1930s Germany. I knew what to expect.

Conservatives operating mostly within the
Republican Party splintered into several special interest
factions. The most dangerous of them were a group who
self-identified as "Proto-Conservatives." They pretended to
embrace the "true philosophy" of the American Revolution.
They were not, however, moralistic ideologues, but
pragmatic political actors. They used the Religious Right
when convenient, but could deploy the most irreligious
tactics to achieve an end result. They were never able to
articulate a particular philosophical agenda. In fact, the
only thing that was clear about their agenda was the goal to
gain power by whatever means possible.

The media labeled them the "Proto-Cons." Liberal
commentators further abbreviated it to "Pro-Cons." The
Proto-Con propaganda machine invented an idealized vision
of America before it had been ruined supposedly by liberals.
This pre-liberal America was unsurprisingly pastoral, white,

Protestant, and, of course, exclusively heterosexual. The image of an isolated frontier family sitting around the fireplace in their log cabin, reading from the family Bible was their most prominent theme. Never mind that the entire Proto-Con leadership in Congress came from or had powerful ties to the largest investment banks on Wall Street and the military-industrial complex. The Proto-Cons were articulate, and their simplistic message resonated with many Americans.

Even still, the last election took me by surprise. We had seemed to have a momentary pause in the conservative trend two years earlier. We had elected a liberal President, who seemed to be extremely popular.

Our new President, Brandon O'Hara, stepped into a financial mess that the Proto-Cons had created through *laissez-fair* economics. Though he implemented aggressive programs targeted at righting the economy, his measures took too long. Unemployment averaged ten percent throughout the country, but in Detroit, Cleveland, New York, and Los Angeles it was sixteen to twenty percent at the mid-point of his administration. Proto-Cons had the gall to blame him for the state of the economy.

The Proto-Cons kept quiet during the election, preferring to let a loose grass roots movement, known as the "Liberty Snakes," fight the political battles. The Liberty Snakes movement brandished the Revolutionary era "Don't Tread On Me" flag. Those of us in the gay community often referred to them as "trouser snakes," an epithet they found highly offensive. They really did not have a coherent agenda, except for accusing liberals of making the federal government too intrusive. They had no idea just how intrusive the federal government was about to become as a result of their actions.

Republican success in the mid-term elections was mixed. They took a majority in the House of

Representatives, but were just shy of taking the Senate.
They were widely successful in many state races. What the
Liberty Snakes and most other Americans failed to realize,
however, was that when they handed control of the House
to Republican leadership, they in fact gave a great deal of
power to the Proto-Conservative leadership within the
Republican Party.

Leading the pack, and destined to become Speaker
of the House, was the always dapper, Mike Crooks, a Texas
Republican. Crooks was one of those Machiavellian
politicians, who had risen to the top by the most ruthless
and conniving methods. It had been common knowledge,
and even, at times a point of public scandal, that Crooks had
for many years endeared himself to the military-industrial
complex by supporting lavish defense appropriations.

He had no morals and no conception of the meaning
of hypocrisy. On his way to his party's leadership, he had
ousted his predecessor by exposing an extramarital affair –
all the while married, but sleeping with a powerful
Washington lobbyist himself. When the media exposed his
affair, Crooks then tried to divert attention by submitting a
new proposal for a new constitutional amendment banning
gay marriage. It was entitled, "The Sanctity of Marriage
Amendment Act."

Rather than running for President outright, an
election he knew he would lose, Crooks devised another
scheme by which he could seize power. In the first weeks
of the Congressional session accompanying O'Hara's
accession to the presidency, Crooks dropped a hardly
noticed provision into an omnibus spending bill. This
provision created a special bureau within the Department of
Homeland Security. The title of this new agency, "Federal
Bureau of Protection" or FBP, was nebulous enough to
sound like something everyone could support.

The language creating the FBP was vague and authorized funding through covert appropriations. Most pundits saw the fact that Crooks created this new agency under the administration of an opposition President as an act of bipartisanship. Crooks played the bipartisan role long enough to ensure that he was able to handpick most of the new agency's operating staff. Using covert funds Crooks built a private army that was concealed from the President and the Joint Chiefs of Staff. It was a hodge-podge of retired special operations personnel, reservists, and other active and inactive duty soldiers, all sharing one thing in common, their zeal for the agenda promoted by Crooks, and their love for the money he funneled into their hands. After two years of preparation, the FBP was fully operational and ready for any emergency.

Harry thought I was a bit nuts when I insisted on opening Swiss and Canadian bank accounts right after the election handing control of the House to Crooks. Over the ensuing six months, we shifted the majority of our financial resources out of the country. As refugees we would not want.

Crooks was too powerful and apparently had too much dirt on most of his colleagues, so when the Republican Party took control of the House in January, he took the gavel as Speaker of the House. Crooks dropped all pretense of bipartisanship, and on his first day as Speaker he made it clear he was at war with President O'Hara. Most news commentators interpreted that to mean that Crooks would aggressively try to block the President's legislative agenda. They underestimated the Speaker.

His first target, however, was not the President, but the Vice President. Eliminating the President first would only have handed power to an old-school liberal. Our Vice President was Jimmy Waite. Waite had entered politics from Pennsylvania in the 1970s and had come in to national office, first in the House of Representatives in 1974. As a teenager he had campaigned for Bobby Kennedy in 1968, and Eugene McCarthy after Bobby's assassination. Waite had been on the fringe of every left-wing initiative since. He even supported the concept of gay marriage. Crooks had to eliminate Waite before he could go after the President.

Though proof at the time was lacking, few had little doubt that somehow Crooks was behind the assassination of Vice President Waite. Waite had been scheduled to attend the re-opening of a grade school in Rock Island, Tennessee. The school, which had been destroyed in a tornado, had been rebuilt with federal funds that were part of the President's plan for reinventing education. The Vice President traveled by motorcade from Nashville for the ribbon cutting. On his way there, while driving through the winding roads of the Appalachian country, a pipe bomb exploded underneath his car on a hairpin curve. The car flipped and tumbled down a two hundred foot hillside. No one survived.

Crooks had to move fast. Though the President ordered a full state funeral, he also quickly submitted a nomination for a new Vice President. As Speaker of the House Crooks was next in line to the Presidency, but only for awhile. Immediately after the funeral, the President had been scheduled to take part in an economic summit in Brussels. Wishing to demonstrate that the United States was not shaken by the death of its Vice President, O'Hara had decided to attend as scheduled.

In the meantime, Crooks had fabricated executive memoranda indicating that the President had planned deep cuts in the defense budget. Crooks had, with the help of lobbying efforts from his private FBP army, convinced top Pentagon brass that the President was their enemy and Crooks was their ally. Crooks successfully made the argument that the President's policies put national security in danger.

Crooks made his move while the President was *en route* in Air Force One. The U. S. Ambassador to Belgium was a Republican. President O'Hara had made the appointment in an effort to promote bipartisanship. The Ambassador, Frederick Arnold, was a moderate Republican from Nebraska. He had been narrowly defeated by an equally moderate Democrat in a close election. Arnold was considered a moderate, not so much because of a political ideology, but because he tended to support whatever political trend in vogue at the moment. He had no political spine and was easily bought. Crooks re-purchased Arnold before the President's plane landed.

The President was scheduled to go directly to the U. S. Embassy in Brussels upon his arrival. Once in the embassy compound, Arnold, with FBP special forces on his flank, informed the President that security concerns would require him to remain in the compound for at least another day. At that point the President was effectively cut off from the entire U. S. government. Crooks quickly moved to seize power. With the President out of the country and out of communication, the Speaker of the House was the only legal source of administrative power.

Speaker Crooks called a press conference, from the East Room of the White House, no less. He said that the President was incapacitated, though not how. Crooks went on to say that he was exercising his Constitutional responsibility to ensure that the government of the United States was not interrupted. He was flanked at the press conference by the Joint Chiefs of Staff. The *coup* was working as planned.

Six hours later, Crooks declared a state of emergency and suspended the Constitution. President O'Hara and his family quietly disappeared. Administration

directives barred the White House Press Corps from asking
questions about the President. On rare occasion Crooks or
his press secretary would only say that the President was in
a safe place where he and his family would remain until the
crisis was over.

Crooks's first order of business was to replace the
entire Cabinet. His replacements were all Proto-Cons.
With the Constitution suspended his replacements required
no Senate confirmation. In fact, he had asked a now
powerless Congress to refrain from enacting any legislation
for the next month. Both houses dutifully complied. He
also appointed a new Secretary of Homeland Security, who
was none other than the Reverend J. Paul Peterson.

I was on my way home to Bay City from a business
trip and hurrying to a connecting flight in Detroit when I
saw the announcement about the *coup de tat* on an
oversized monitor in the terminal. I stood still for a moment
and listened to the news. I sat down on a bench in a
deserted waiting area and thought back to a class I had
taught a few years earlier. It was "Holocaust as a Concept
in History." Though the class contained a component on
the German Holocaust of World War II, it was a thematic
course that examined genocidal movements worldwide. I
included discussions on the Bolshevik genocide of the upper
and middle classes in post-revolutionary Russia, the Turkish
genocide of Armenians in World War I, and the Frontier
genocide of Native Americans in the United States in the
nineteenth century.

The course was all about answering the two
questions usually associated with the German Holocaust:
how could it have happened in a country with such a rich
cultural tradition, and why was there so little resistance? I
told my students on the first day of class that these would be
the only questions on their final exam. They had all
semester to learn the answer. A passing grade would state

that genocide can happen anywhere, anytime. The elements of it exist in all cultures; they include populations that perceive themselves as victims of an ill-defined nature, social groups that mistrust and vilify other social groups, and people who are easily given to a mob-rule mentality. The trigger that can cause these elements to coalesce into a dangerous mix of genocidal behavior is usually some kind of event or dynamic enabling the elements of hate to gain political power.

For the few moments that I listened to the news in the Detroit airport, I shuddered in horror. When the news cut away to a commercial for anti-diarrhea medication I snapped out of my shock. I realized that hundreds of other people in the airport had stopped to listen to the news. It was dead silence. Then before the commercial break was over, all of the people quietly picked up their laptop bags and continued on to their connecting gates. I did the same thing.

The airport and the flight home were quiet and uneventful. No one wanted to talk about the news. It was as though people wanted to hang on to a last moment of normality before the storm hit.

I closed my eyes for the forty-five minutes we were in the air. I continued thinking about the concept of holocaust and how we had all of those elements coming together. I knew when I heard the news about Peterson's appointment that the United States was in trouble. Why would Crooks put a preacher in that position? What qualifications did Peterson have to direct the security of our borders and cities? This was the man, after all, who had declared that terrorist attacks were God's wrath poured out upon a sinful society.

When I arrived home, I told Harry we needed to think about the fact that the United States might not be safe for us much longer. He thought I was overreacting. I told him nothing might happen, but we simply needed to be better prepared. At my insistence, we contacted our attorney, John Elliott, and had him place all of our tangible and real assets inside the country into a trust. He would become trustee upon our absence from the country. Our standing instructions were to liquidate everything and transfer the proceeds to an account in Switzerland. It was an arrangement that would protect our financial interests as long as we set everything in motion upon first warning.

The next three months proved to realize my worst fears. At Peterson's first press conference, he talked about "dangerous elements" in American society, and that the FBP under his direction would go far beyond rooting out Islamic extremists. He did not spell out those "dangerous elements," in his initial statements, but I inferred from that to mean a new definition of terrorism that could include political opponents.

Peterson's first target was the Senate. It was still controlled, at least marginally, by the Democrats. Speaker Crooks had an aggressive legislative agenda and needed both houses of Congress functional. Peterson discovered that seven Senators were also members of a "subversive" organization, the Council for International Strategies, a liberal think tank. There were many more than seven senators who supported the Council, but it just so happened that the seven identified were also from states with Republican governors. Once those Senators had been forced to resign, they would be replaced with Republican appointees and Crooks would have his majority in the Senate. Congress could be allowed to go back to work.

Crooks's legislative agenda included "An Act to Identify and Eliminate Subversive Organizations." This act could never have passed judicial review, but without a functional constitution, that did not matter. It called for the Federal Bureau of Protection to compile a list of subversive

organizations and publish the list in the *Federal Register*.
Any organization so listed had fifteen days to disband and
report its membership lists to the FBP. The act gave the
FBP a five year mandate to continue compiling and
updating the list on a monthly basis.

   The first list published in March included mostly
pacifist organizations and women's rights groups. Most
notable was the *Coalition for Nonviolent Intervention*
(CNI), a radical left group that had a habit of disrupting
international events and protesting against even some of the
most liberal politicians. Though they were outspoken and
their philosophy radical, they never posed a serious threat to
anyone. Their core agenda was promoting peace through
civil disobedience.

   Some of the organizations listed in the *Federal
Register* cooperated, handing over their membership lists,
only to see their members arrested and harassed by the FBP,
the IRS, and other federal agencies. The CNI refused to
cooperate. On the fifteenth day, Peterson moved to arrest
CNI's leadership and raided their headquarters in
Washington, confiscating all of their computers and files.
The next day he issued a statement about the CNI. He said,
"We suspect this organization of colluding with terrorists,
and we are diligently inspecting the records of this
subversive organization for all of their contacts with those
who would do harm to America. This evil organization is in
every community across the country, and we encourage
loyal Americans to purge their communities of this ungodly
evil." This was Peterson's style, to make outlandish claims
that sounded real, but without a shred of evidence.

   Later that day, Crooks gave a press conference.
The first question was whether he knew about and agreed
with the statements of the Secretary of Homeland Security
regarding CNI. The Speaker said he had the fullest
confidence in the Secretary, and that he hoped "good

American citizens" would root out of their communities any un-American activities. That night vigilante squads formed in about thirty cities. They raided and burned their local CNI offices. With membership lists in hand, vigilantes detained local members of the organization and held them until the FBP could take the detainees into custody.

The next day, Crooks issued emergency curfews and stay at home orders, ostensibly to quell the violence. Instead of trying to suppress the vigilante squads, however, he mobilized the National Guard, and sent them to finish the job of "peacefully" closing down all CNI operations within the United States and arresting community leaders. Within a week he declared the operations to be a success and lifted the emergency measures. One more element of political opposition was now quiet.

I knew who was next. The country settled back into a state of guarded normalcy for about a month. Then, with a calculated plan mirroring the CNI operations, Secretary Peterson put gay rights organizations on the April list and issued a similar statement about the *Human Rights Campaign* and the *National Gay and Lesbian Task Force*, two of the leading gay rights organizations in the country. This time, however, the Federal Bureau of Protection operated more deliberately. I think they were trying to close down both without the violence. Peterson's public statements, however, only served to inflame public attitudes.

Peterson singled out homosexual men. Either he did not perceive the lesbian community as a threat, or entertained a perverse heterosexual male fantasy about them. He talked repeatedly about why homosexual men were subversive. According to Peterson, it was incompatible with American ideals of family and patriotism for men to live a homosexual lifestyle. He said that we were a danger and menace to society. Crooks did nothing to quiet the Secretary of Homeland Security. Soon enough angry mobs began to form again. As yet there was no call to action from Washington, so for most of April, it was mostly rhetoric and protests by vigilante groups.

Gay rights activists, like myself, tried to form a reasonable response. We staged counter demonstrations. Some of our allies in the religious community came to our defense. In Saginaw, the Reverend Charles Gibson of the First Presbyterian Church called me to see what he could do. I suggested contacting the other supportive ministers in town, and asking them to preach acceptance and understanding from their pulpits the next Sunday. Reverend Gibson agreed and thought we should also try to reach out to the less supportive clergy in town. After what had happened with the *Coalition for Nonviolent Intervention* riots, he thought even the most conservative ministers would want to avoid further violence and bloodshed.

Reverend Gibson put together an impromptu meeting with most of the religious leaders in the area for Thursday night. He asked me, as the president of the *Bridges Foundation* to speak publicly about our concerns. Then one by one each clergyperson would respond in a way to appeal to their constituents not to escalate the violence. He had contacted all of the local media, which would be present, and the program was to be aired on local television stations and radio.

These religious leaders had agreed to come solely because of Reverend Gibson. He was the kind of man respected by leaders of all faiths, both conservative and liberal. The conservatives there, primarily Pastor Joe Don Hartge of the Calvary Assembly of God Congregation, had no intention of saying anything supportive of gay rights. They simply were there to help stop the attitudes escalating towards violence.

Joe Don Hartge was a colorful character. He had moved to Michigan from Mississippi a few years back. Word had it that he had been run out of the state for embezzling money from his church in Biloxi. When I was teaching, one of my students, Ray Welsh, attended Hartge's church. Ray frequently stopped by my office after class. I think he was trying to convert me. I once asked him about those rumors of embezzlement, but he always replied that, "The Pastor is a man of God, and he would never steal from the Lord's work." Ray thought it was a liberal rumor concocted by the devil to confound people and keep them away from the Holy Spirit. I remembered my experiences with fundamentalist religion in Oklahoma and understood.

Hartge's church was located in Saginaw Township, just about twelve miles from Bay City. I think he had moved to Michigan in 1991 not long after I had. When I first moved to Bay City, the religious community was split mostly between Roman Catholics and Lutherans. It had been refreshing to see a society dominated by these old world churches and not by Southern Baptists and Pentecostals. When I saw Hartge attracting a large congregation, I was dumbfounded that people in Michigan could so easily be duped by a man who was obviously a charlatan.

The congregation grew so much that by the early 1990s the church needed a new building. The structure they built in the township was like many of the flamboyant fundamentalist churches then popular. The building was five stories tall with a front entry of glass rising to the peak. Pastor Hartge arrived every Sunday morning for services in a white *Rolls Royce Silver Shadow* convertible. A news reporter once asked him if it was appropriate for a minister to drive such an ostentatious car. Hartge replied that it was a sign to the world that God had blessed his ministry. The approach to the church from Tittabawasee Road was a three block long drive lined with flagpoles waving banners of the world. Some people called it "Six Flags over Jesus."

I have to say, though, that for all the flamboyance of the church, Hartge himself impressed me at that Thursday meeting with the religious leaders in town. His statement was aimed at his congregation. He appealed to them not to wage violence in the name of God. After the meeting he pulled me aside and put his hand on my shoulder. In his Mississippi drawl he said, "Boey, Ah've done all Ah kin to he'p you out. Ah hope this does the trick, but ya'll see what's going on in this country. If'n Ah was you, Ah'd be makin plaens to do somthin' differ'nt. You know Ah cain't say nothin' to support you bein' a homasekshal an' all, but Ah understand the fix yur in, an' Ah just don't wanna see yah get hurt. You seem like a nice boey. Ah'll be prayin' for ya."

I thanked him for his words and kind thoughts. I told him I fully understood the dangers we faced. We shook hands, and I left for home.

The Thursday forum and the appeals from the local ministers bought us a few weeks. When I came home after the forum I told Harry, "We needed to start putting our escape plan in action and notify our attorney to accelerate transferring our assets out of the country." I had launched the *Polar Star II* two weeks earlier. We had a slip at the marina in Bay City. I told Harry, "We need to take as many of our belongings that we can carry in two cars to the boat tomorrow. I'll sail it to Tawas, while you drive to the other end of the bay to pick me up. We'll leave the boat there for the time being. I'll make arrangements with the marina in Tawas to rent a slip for a few weeks."

We packed as many clothes as we could that night before bed. Harry and I lay down and kissed before going to sleep. He asked me, "Do you think all this will really be necessary?"

I said, "I don't know. I have a bad feeling about
what is going to happen. I think we need to be prepared.
I'm not going to let us end up like the Jews in 1930s
Europe, blindly going about our business as though nothing
is wrong." Harry had heard me give this speech a few times
before. He knew I was right though.

The story that kept haunting me was Elie Wiesel's.
In the opening of his book *Night* he described his home
village of Sighet in Hungary just before the Germans took
control in 1944. He told about Moshe the Beadle who had
warned the village to evacuate while they still had time.
The Jews in Sighet thought all the horrors they had heard to
be mostly fiction. They thought the Germans would have
no reason to do them harm. Besides, the war was almost
over, and, surely, the Germans were more concerned about
fighting the Russians than rounding up a few harmless
Jews. But the Jews from Sighet did become victims of the
German Holocaust. Elie Wiesel was one of the few who
survived to tell the story. If only they had listened to Moshe
the Beadle.[2]

I knew what had happened in Germany. A defeated
and bankrupt nation had to look somewhere for the cause of
its misery. They could not blame the military. The German
army had fought so bravely during the Great War and had
brought Germany much glory. They could not blame the
Kaiser; life had been good when he was in power.
Somebody had to be the cause of Germany's misery; why
not the Jews? They were a relatively small part of the
population, they were different, had strange customs,
nobody really understood them, and they were rich. So
Germany blamed the Jews.

Now, in twenty-first century America, things were
falling apart. Our legitimate government had not

---

[2] Elie Wiesel, *Night* (New York: Bantam Books, 1982).

accomplished enough, quickly enough to suit the impatient
demands of our media and voters. Our new dictator had to
make a show of success somehow. If he could not eliminate
the economic source of America's misery right away,
maybe he could eliminate another source. With Secretary
Peterson sounding out the justification, homosexual men
were to become the next cause of all of America's trouble.

I was determined not to be a "Sighet Jew." I would
do everything in my power to protect my family and my
loved ones. I had talked with all of our friends and begged
them to prepare to evacuate the country. I was starting to
sound like Moshe the Beadle. Most of my friends thought I
was crazy. Scott and Allen, our closest friends, seemed to
be among the few to understand the gravity of the moment.
They had, at my urging, recently met with our attorney John
Elliott and had their trusts in place.

Saturday morning, Harry and I went to the marina
about eight o'clock. It was a brisk morning, the sun was up,
and I had a good breeze out of the west. I could set a steady
course to the north-northeast and sail on a beam reach. I
hoped it would make for a faster trip to Tawas. We loaded
everything into the boat, and I pushed off from the dock. I
motored the *Polar Star II* down the Saginaw River. I
waited for the Lafayette Street Bridge to open and thought
about the names of so many streets and buildings in the
United States like Lafayette, Washington, Patrick Henry,
Paul Revere, and other national heroes. Those names had
been honored as a symbol of our Constitution and freedom.
Soon our freedoms would be gone, and all those
revolutionary names rendered meaningless.

The bridge opened and I sailed on through to the
next three bridges, then to Saginaw Bay. The wind was
pretty strong by the time I got out into open water. The
Polar Star II was easy enough to sail alone. The only
challenge was in hoisting the mainsail after I entered the

Bay. The wind was a bit gusty, and while raising the main halyard, I had to keep an eye on the channel. Saginaw Bay is shallow for several miles out, and veering out of the channel can find a boat run aground easily.

With a few gusts of wind, I got the mainsail up and unfurled the headsail. I resumed my journey and was slicing through the water at five knots in a matter of minutes. I trimmed my sheets and she was up to six knots. On the way out, I passed the *Paul Theyer*, one of the freighters that delivered crushed stone up the Saginaw River. It was a handsome ship, and one I always enjoyed watching go by. I made good time and hoped to be in Tawas by late afternoon.

I wanted to move the *Polar Star II* to Tawas to make our escape as quiet and quick as possible. Tawas was a bit more than an hour's drive from Bay City, but then, once out of the harbor, we could be in the open water of Lake Huron in minutes. Depending on the circumstances, it could take hours to get to open water from Saginaw Bay.

I caught sight of Tawas about three o'clock in the afternoon and called Harry to come and pick me up. On the drive back home, he said that Scott and Allen had called and wanted us to go to dinner. I was tired, but knew we might not see them again otherwise. We went to their house for cocktails and hors d'oeuvres.

We decided to have dinner at *Alfredo's* Italian restaurant. The food there was always fabulous and sometimes they had entertainment. In the old days, Alfredo got up on the stage and sang. Now, his oldest daughter, June, ran the place, but she did not sing. I think she had always been embarrassed when her father did.

The four of us arrived at the restaurant and noticed Matt DuPont was there with some of our other friends. He frequently took the stage at *Alfredo's*. He had a beautiful voice and always made an evening memorable.

The four of us were having a great dinner and looking forward to some of Matt's entertainment. He didn't just sing, he did a stage show, but out of drag. In one show he sang a couple of numbers and then looked across the patrons in the restaurant. He picked out a couple near the stage. It was a young straight couple – he loved to prey on people like that. Matt did a once up and down look with the woman and said, "Honey, what were you thinking with that hairdo? Women haven't done that sort of thing since the sixties!" He then looked at the man and said, "Do you think she's pretty . . . no don't answer that." The room was in an uproar, and Matt broke into *Hello Dolly*. He had the entire room singing, swaying, and laughing, including the couple he had just trashed. We fully expected another evening like that.

In the moment of fun and great food, we had forgotten the times in which we lived. We finished our meal and ordered another round of martinis, hoping that Matt would get up on stage soon. From my back approached two mid-twenties leather-necked idiots. Leather-neck #1 said, "Where are youse girlfriends?"

I didn't know the two men were standing there, and turned around and said, "What?"

He said, "Don't youse guys have any girlfriends?"

Growing wary of the situation, I said calmly, "Why is that your concern?"

Leather-neck #2 said, "'Cause we didn't think this was a faggot joint. Maybe youse oughtta go to your own kind of place."

Scott spoke up, having had a too much to drink, "Oh, I thought you were asking because you wanted to go home with us to have a hot and steamy, six-way orgy." Allen kicked Scott under the table and tried to shut him up, while the two leather-necks' faces glowed redder.

I thought they were about to turn the table over when Matt and two waiters came over. Apparently they had been monitoring the situation. Matt asked the leathernecks in a Bette Davis staccato "What seems to be the problem?" Leather-neck # 2 said, loud enough for the entire restaurant to hear, "I think you have a table of filthy, stinking, AIDs infested, faggots in here! What are you going to do about it?"

By that time June, the proprietor, was in the middle of it and said to the leather-necks, "These patrons have been valued customers of this establishment for years. I don't want any trouble in here, so please leave. Now!" She and her staff then escorted the leather-necks out the door, followed by their very embarrassed dates. June came back to our table and apologized profusely. She offered us a round of drinks on the house.

Matt, with his, "save what's left of the evening" and "the show must go on" mentality jumped up on stage. He nodded over to the piano player, who began thumping the keys, and Matt broke in, "What use is sitting alone in your room, come hear the music play. Come to the cabaret old chum, come to the cabaret . . ." Matt knew what he was doing. So did I; I felt like we were a table of Jews in Berlin, circa 1932.

We stayed for another hour, hoping the leather-necks were long gone. It was a lovely spring night, the stars were shining brightly, and the air was crisp, but not too cool. The four of us walked up Water Street and stood at the old bridge abutment at Third Street. A bit tipsy, I looked over at Scott and Allen and said that I hoped they would be able to get out of the country in time. We walked towards home, down Center Avenue. At each intersection, we warily looked over to see that no one was lurking in the shadows. I had never before felt the need to wonder about my safety at night in Bay City.

Harry woke me up with a steaming cup of coffee at my bedside Sunday morning. I went downstairs after I had sipped some coffee to the living room where Harry was reading the Sunday paper. He handed me the front page section without saying a word. The headline read, "GAY BAR IN ATLANTA FIREBOMBED, RIOT ENSUES." The night before, about 200 gay bashers descended upon a popular gay district in Atlanta. Their first target was the *Heretic*, one of the hottest bars in town. The bashers had a military rocket, which they launched into the bar around 11:30 PM, a time when the bar would have been at its busiest. About 300 people were killed and many more critically injured.

The bashers stayed out front and chanted biblical quotes. Their goal was to slow emergency access to the scene. Fire and rescue workers were held at bay until police backup could arrive to deal with the bashers. In the meantime, news spread down the strip and the other bars emptied out. Their patrons descended on the Heretic. At first, they simply wanted to move the bashers out of the way. However, the bashers were armed and began shooting. That sparked a riot and about 2,000 gay people converged on the bashers. Before police could gain control, another 1,200 people had been shot or severely beaten.

Harry said, "I was going to question whether or not we really needed to move out of the country, but there's my answer on the front page."

I said, "Yeah, I'll give us two or three weeks at the most. The mood of the country is such that I don't think anyone can stop the violence from spreading." We turned on the television to see the news updates. The media circus had begun. Every channel had full, round-the-clock, coverage of the *Tragedy in Atlanta*.

I was stunned. Harry and I had been in Atlanta in February and we had spent a few hours at the Heretic.

What alarmed me even more, was the reaction from the religious community in Georgia. I knew that outside Atlanta, the rest of Georgia was a wasteland of bigotry, but I thought there would at least be some reaction from sensible people to an event like this. The reactions from most prominent persons in Georgia could be summed up by the statement of the Reverend Jimmy Lee Swarthout, pastor of the First Southern Baptist Church in Atlanta, "It's unfartunate this kind of vyelence had to 'ccur, but this is nothing more than Gawwd's wrath being poured out upon unrepentant sinners. Ah hope this terrible event sends a message to all homasekshals to repent and come to Je-esus. Should they fail, Gawwd will send more of his ahmies to their lairs until they have no place to hide."

By mid-afternoon, Atlanta was again in turmoil. Riots broke out after the church hour when religious zealots marched up and down Cheshire Bridge Road, Piedmont Avenue, and across downtown. They carried anti-gay posters, chanted Bible verses, and sang hymns. These were not peaceful demonstrators. When gay people and their allies tried to block the zealots' routes, the zealots responded by beating anyone in their way with their posters. A few had guns and began shooting into the crowds. That sparked more rioting. By evening, the governor of Georgia had called in the National Guard to restore order.

Atlanta settled down by Monday morning. Most businesses downtown stayed closed for the day. Otherwise the city was generally quiet. There were only a few minor incidents.

Monday morning, I got a call from a client in California. He needed me to come to San Francisco for a few days to review some project plans for the upcoming year. I knew I wouldn't be around for the next year, but I had to oblige. I was still under contract, and I couldn't afford to wreck my reputation just yet. I called Harry to tell him I had to fly out the next morning. I asked him to be sure to be home for dinner, so we could have the evening before I left.

We talked about what had happened in Atlanta. I told him I hated being gone so far from home while all this was happening. Harry assured me everything would be fine until I came home. I told him I would try to make adjustments in the contract so I could work outside the country.

He dropped me off at the airport around nine in the morning. From Midland-Bay City-Saginaw Airport my flight went to Detroit. There I had about a two-hour layover before catching a direct flight to San Francisco. I knew this route well. On this final trip to San Francisco, having been booked at the last minute, I found myself in steerage, what the airlines called "coach." No upgrades were available. The trip was less painful than most. There were only two screaming children, and they were several rows away from me. I had a book, but found myself unable to concentrate. I put the book away an hour into the flight and stared out the window, worrying about how my life seemed to be falling apart.

I thought mostly about what was happening to the United States while in flight. Most of the other liberal activists, who hadn't been arrested, had already left the country. That left the gay community even more isolated than normal and the country with an even stronger conservative majority. The situation was hopeless. If conservative extremists would so willingly go after an organization like the *Coalition for Nonviolent Intervention*, I knew gay rights activists had no chance to survive. The only thing that spared us so far was our financial strength. As a social group gay men and lesbians tended to be wealthier than average heterosexuals; I felt increasingly like a Jew in 1930s Europe.

The weather in San Francisco was clear as we
landed. The weather there was usually delightful. I could
understand why it had been such a desirable place to live. I
had no doubt that our opponents in the Bay area looked with
lustful eyes towards the Castro District. A message
indicator appeared on my cell phone when I turned it on
after landing. It was Harry. I called him back as I was
walking down the terminal to pick up my luggage.

He asked, "Have you seen the news?"

"No, I just got off the plane."

"Crooks called a press conference today."

I grumbled, "Great; what delightful things did he
have to say?"

"He talked about Atlanta." My heart sank. "He said
he hoped the violence in Atlanta could be brought to an end,
and it was too bad that so many homosexuals in Atlanta had
chosen an immoral path. He warned them to stay in their
homes and not to try to interfere with federal attempts to
pacify the city. He then said that he had nationalized the
Georgia National Guard. They and an Army battalion, on
its way from South Carolina, would demolish the remainder
of the known homosexual hangouts in town. Joe, they just
showed pictures on the news of tanks demolishing the *Eagle*
and the downtown bars."

I felt moisture on my cheeks. "Is there any news of
this spreading beyond Atlanta?"

"No. For now, Atlanta seems to be the focus."

"Well, at least that may buy us a few more days.
Let me see if I can catch a plane out of here tonight. I don't
want to be this far from home right now."

Harry sounded worried, "Joe, I want you here. I am
scared to death."

"I'll see what kind of a flight I can get as soon as I
hang-up. I'll call you back as soon as I know what I can
do." All flights were booked for all airlines for the next

thirty-six hours. I called Harry back and told him I was
stuck. I would be home on Thursday. I said, "Even in a
worst case scenario, we have about five days before our
situation grows critical. What is your schedule supposed to
be on Thursday?

"I am not leaving the house until you get home."

"Harry, you can't do that. You have to maintain an
air of normalcy. In a worst case scenario, they may be
looking for me and for any signs of escape. Look, I'll call
you when I get to my room." I took the hotel shuttle and
checked into my room at the *Drake*. I started thinking about
the worst that could happen. I was holding my cell phone in
my hand, about to dial Harry, and I thought, "They could
have my phone tapped by now." I picked up the hotel
phone and called his cell. I didn't think his phone would be
on a first priority tap list. Harry was a known homosexual,
but not an activist like me. They didn't really consider our
relationship valid, so just because we lived together did not
immediately put him in harm's way. "Harry, listen . . ."

Harry interrupted, "What phone are you calling
on?"

I replied, "The hotel line. Listen, I want you to . . ."

He interrupted again, "That's the most expensive
way to call; why are you doing that?"

I sighed, "I am worried my phone might be
bugged."

Harry exclaimed, "Good Lord, this is getting
ridiculous. What are we going to do?"

"You are going to work tomorrow, just like nothing
is wrong. I am going to meet with my client, and tell him
that we need to make some changes to the way our contract
is completed. I need to know where you are going to be on
Thursday."

"I am supposed to be in Petoskey. I have a conference with the staff at the office there. My meetings should be done about 4:30 in the afternoon."

"Good, that should work out. Listen, I am going to go to dinner, I'm starving. While I'm out, I'm going to stop at a kiosk and buy a pre-paid cell phone. I'll call you with the number. I want you to do the same right now. Use cash, do not use a credit card."

"Joe, it is after nine. I'm ready for bed, and I don't want to have to get dressed again."

"Well then, go first thing in the morning. I'll call you on my regular phone later tonight. We can't talk about anything but superficial stuff. I love you. I'll talk to you later. Hey wait. I'll give you the phone number in cryptic terms, just listen for the numbers as I talk. I love you."

"I love you too, be careful Joe."

I walked down Columbus Street to one of the Italian bistros lining the street. I had a delightful linguini with duck and an Alfredo sauce. I walked back towards town. My meeting didn't start until ten o'clock the next morning, so I decided to have one last night in the Castro District. I hopped on a Metro train at the Montgomery Street station and exited at the Castro Street Station by the *Diesel* store. The mood in the Castro was somber. Normally, even on a Tuesday, it was a festive place. The Castro District had always been a place where people could be themselves without fear of attack or abuse. I ran into some old friends, John and Fred, in front of *Badlands*. We went on in to have a few drinks. I had met John and Fred at a regional conference for gay rights activists. I usually tried to look them up when I came to San Francisco.

John and Fred were worried about what was happening in Atlanta. They asked me if I thought the same thing would happen in other parts of the country. I told them that it would be happening there in the Castro within a few days. I suggested they get out of town as soon as possible. I told them that Harry and I were headed to Toronto as soon as I got home. They seemed bewildered at the concept of San Francisco turning into another Atlanta. After a few drinks I was ready for bed, so I gave them a big hug and said, somewhat tearfully, "Take care of yourselves; please don't stay here too long. You could hop on a plane and be in Vancouver tomorrow.

I stopped in at a phone store and picked up a prepaid cell phone. I felt like a drug dealer. Those things are expensive too; it cost me $79 just to get a basic phone and a hundred minutes. Even though it was late, I called Harry when I got back to the room. I told him that I had run into John and Fred and how depressing the Castro was. I gave him my phone number as we had discussed, hoping he would get it. I told him to call me in the morning when he had done his "errands."

Harry called about 6:30 AM, it was 9:30 in Michigan. He called to give me his phone number. I was still asleep, so I hadn't seen any news. He told me the FBP was making arrests in Atlanta – all gay activists, of course. I got ready and went on to my meeting. I told my client that I couldn't stay the remainder of the week. He said, "Atlanta?" I nodded yes. He asked what time my flight was, and I told him it was an early flight the next morning. I suggested we continue with our work session and try to develop a plan for working long distance. He agreed. After our session, he insisted on taking me out to dinner.

I didn't sleep well Wednesday night. I was up and ready to go to the airport two hours early. My plane arrived in Detroit at four in the afternoon. I had a two and a half-hour layover so I went to a kiosk to buy another pre-paid phone. I didn't want to take any chances. I walked on to my connecting gate at the other end of the terminal. Stepping off of the moving sidewalk, I noticed two men in black suits showing their badges to the agent at the gate. I assumed they were FBP. Without missing a step, I wheeled around onto the opposite moving treads and headed straight for the exit. I didn't look back to see if they had spotted me. I figured if they had, they would have already been on top of me.

On one of the oversized news monitors, I saw Speaker Crooks making a statement in the oval office. He said that he had ordered the detention of all known gay rights activists to prevent the violence in Atlanta from spreading to other communities. I went straight to a car rental agent, and rented a car. I called Harry once I was safely out onto I-275. I told him, "I'm driving from Detroit to Tawas in a rented car. Two FBP men were waiting at the connecting gate for me. They must not have spotted me because I made it out of the airport and the car rentals without incident. We have to hurry. How long will it take you to get to Tawas?"

Harry replied, "About three hours, but I have to go home first. I forgot my passport."

I replied, "You go straight to Tawas. I can swing by the house on the way. Even with that extra stop I'll still be there in two and a half hours."

Fortunately traffic in Detroit moves well. Even though it was rush hour, I was cruising at eighty-five. From Detroit, I whizzed through Pontiac, Flint, Birch Run, Saginaw, and I was in Bay City at 6:12 PM. I ran in the house, without turning on any lights, grabbed his passport, and headed up Pinconning Road towards Standish. My flight from Detroit to Saginaw was just then pulling out from the gate, so those FBP agents knew that I had missed my flight.

About 6:45 my regular cell phone rang. It was Jimmy from the Bay City Marina. He asked me where I was, that two men with badges had just been in looking for

me. Assuming my phone was tapped, I told him I was in
Detroit at the airport waiting to catch a plane. I said that I
had missed my first flight, and I was in one of the bars. I
said I had too many drinks watching a game. He acted
bewildered. I told him I would call him back later.

Jimmy was a twenty something gay boy, cute, buff,
and a little flighty. I called him back on my first pre-paid
phone. I told him what was happening and asked, "Did they
ask about my boat?"

He said, "Yes. I told them that it was down at the
repair shop for some work. They asked if they could see it
anyway. I said, "Sure, but it's in the paint booth. It's all
taped up right now. The paint is wet; you'll likely ruin your
pretty black suits. Of course, if you do," licking my lips,
"I'll be more than happy to take your suits off and clean
everything up." They grimaced and walked out."

I laughed, "Jimmy, you are too good. You know, I
think I have a spot on my suit, perhaps I should come back
there and you could clean me up."

Jimmy giggled. He knew I was joking, but he said,
"Joe, you just keep on going wherever you are headed. I
don't want to know what those nasty FBP men had in mind
for you." I told him not to worry, but that he should get out
of there right away.

I called Harry and asked him where he was. He
said he was at West Branch. I said, "The FBP is already
looking for me. By now they must know that I have a rental
car. I can't take it into Tawas. Meet me at the parking lot
at the *Corsair Trails* where we go cross-country skiing."

I only had to wait about twenty minutes. I had sat
there with the lights out. I quietly sat in the car. Harry
showed up at 7:30. We took his car, abandoning the rental.
We were at the marina in fifteen minutes. I told Harry to
get rid of the car. He drove the car over to the boat launch,
let out the parking brake, and it rolled into the water.

Nobody would be using the launch until morning. By then we would be safely in Canadian waters.

We pushed off from the dock and motored at low RPMs so as not to raise any alarms. As soon as we were far enough out, I had Harry raise the mainsail and unfurl the jib. We had a good tailwind and headed easterly towards Canada. Harry had the idea of rigging some fenders over the sides and stern to cover the letters of the *Polar Star II's* name. Normally, I would cringe at the idea of sailing out of port with fenders dangling around the hull. I raised the Stars and Stripes, but not the Russian Imperial flag as I normally did. Later, Harry suggested sleeping in two hour shifts like we normally did on overnight trips. I told him I couldn't sleep. I told him to go on down and get some rest and that I would wake him later to give me a break. I knew he would fall fast asleep and not awaken until daylight.

I steered the boat at an irregular diagonal toward the Canadian border. I knew the Coast Guard beacons would trigger an alert for any vessel heading straight towards the border. I hoped to make it look like a boat unaware of its heading. We crossed the border at 3:42 AM. I promptly lowered the American flag, raised the Russian Imperial banner, and hauled in the fenders in open defiance. Harry was sound asleep, and I set the *Polar Star II* on a direct course for Tobermory.

Chapter 7 Michigan Maple Syrup

With our heading at due northwest in early May, I could see the first glow of red on the Canadian horizon around five o'clock. I eagerly scanned hoping to see land, but we were still in the middle of Lake Huron. The black sky began to give way to blue. It looked like we would have a day of perfectly clear skies. I called down to Harry.

Harry came stumbling up the ladder. "What time is it? Why didn't you come and get me sooner?"

I told him, "You needed your sleep, and I was fine, but I could use some coffee.

He went into the galley and put a pot on the stove. He yawned, "Where are we?"

I replied, "Safely inside Canada, but we still have about thirty miles to go." I let him take the helm while I sat down and sipped some coffee.

While Harry steered, I called John, our attorney and told him we were in Canada. He called back a few hours later and said he had most of our tangible and real assets secured before the Justice Department could try to seize them. I told him we needed to get to Toronto as soon as possible, and asked him to have someone drive my *M*6 over to Tobermory. He said it was already retagged and ready to travel. John asked if I had any suggestions for a driver. I said, "Get Jimmy from the marina in Bay City to drive it. He needs to get out of the country, now. When they figure out how he lied to them about my boat, they will be after him. Be sure to have him call me as soon as he clears the

border. What about Scott and Allen, have they made plans
to leave yet?" He said that they, along with many of our
friends were either on their way out of the country or had
already left. Scott and Allen were driving to Toronto that
day.

I went down below and drifted off for a long nap.
Jimmy called about three. He had no trouble crossing the
border. I told him we were near Tobermory and would be
safely docked by the time he arrived.

Scott and Allen called a few hours later to say they
were near Toronto. I asked them where in Toronto they
were headed. Scott said that John had worked out a
package deal for all of the Saginaw area refugees at the
Perseus Suites, a spa and hotel complex. It was in the heart
of Toronto's shopping district and catered to upscale
urbanites. John had booked us there as well. I told Allen
that Jimmy was bringing my car and we would stay the
night in Tobermory. We would drive to Toronto the next
day.

We entered the harbor about 4:15 in the afternoon.
After docking I went up to the harbor master's storefront
and reserved a temporary slip for a week. They knew us
well in town. The Harbor Master told me that the U. S.
Coast Guard had warnings out all over Lake Huron looking
for my boat. He had wondered if we were in trouble or
something. I told him what had happened, and then,
because he was the harbor master, I gave him our official
plea for asylum. He looked down, and said that it was
unbelievable that this sort of thing could ever happen. He
assured me that he would contact the Ministry of Foreign
Affairs immediately.

Tobermory was a little fishing and tourist town.
The harbor was long, narrow, and quite deep. It sat at the
tip of the Bruce Peninsula, which separated Lake Huron
from Georgian Bay. The Bruce Peninsula was part of the

Niagara Escarpment, which ran from Niagara Falls through lower Ontario, up the Bruce Peninsula, across Upper Michigan, and back around Lake Michigan on the Wisconsin side. The land formations of the escarpment around Tobermory were particularly dramatic. The escarpment was what made for the long narrow harbor. Though the water was sparkling clear, on foggy nights and in stormy weather boats could easily succumb to the underwater craggy rock formations of the escarpment. That coupled with the cold waters of Lake Huron made for a wealth of interesting shipwrecks to explore.

Flowerpot Island guarded the entrance to the harbor at Tobermory. It was so named because of bizarre remnants of the Niagara Escarpment that dotted the shoreline of the island. Natural erosion had worn around these remnants to form tall rounded towers of rock that someone thought looked like flowerpots. I often wondered how those tall cylindrical structures of rock continued to stand. They looked top heavy like they could tumble at any minute, but they stood for centuries.

Tobermory catered to people like Harry and me. Not so much because we were gay, but because we enjoyed the water. It was a place where people could relax and be themselves, leaving pretentious airs behind. Several restaurants dotted the harbor. Whitefish was the delicacy on every menu, and a couple of entertainment establishments offered music and drinks. The rest of the storefronts around the harbor were antique and souvenir shops. Tour boats, private yachts like mine, commercial fishing boats, and an occasional Russian peasant boat, where the proprietors flew the double eagle and peddled a variety of wares, lined the harbor. It was always delightful to sail into the harbor at Tobermory, even after the sleepless night of a frantic escape.

Harry checked us into a hotel at the other end of the harbor, while I closed up the *Polar Star II*. As soon as I walked into the room I collapsed on the bed. Jimmy arrived around six in the evening. Harry had reserved a room for him next to ours. We went downstairs for a nice supper and then back to our room for a cocktail on the porch. Jimmy said that he had listened to the radio on the way over. Speaker Crooks openly accused gay rights activists of terrorism, and several hundred leading activists had been detained. He also said the news channels reported a number of these suspected terrorists still at large and presumed them to have left the country.

We turned on a cable news station. They said that Crooks would address the country at eight. Canadian news stations would air the broadcast as well. Crooks announced that intelligence reports had established a direct link between several leading gay rights organizations and two foreign terrorist networks. For this reason, he had ordered the detention of known gay rights activists and the confiscation of all of these organizations' records. Because he was concerned about the escape of these suspected terrorists, he was closing the borders with Canada and Mexico, and all ports of entry in the United States for the next seventy-two hours, after which FBP Special Forces units would be stationed at all border crossings to check traffic leaving the country. He apologized for the economic difficulties this would cause, but insisted that it was necessary for the safety of the country. We were thankful we had gotten out when we did.

The reaction of Canadian Prime Minister McConihe was one of indignation. Following the address of the President, McConihe addressed Canadian television. He said that he had reviewed the so-called intelligence linking gay rights organizations with terrorism and that it was nothing more than the same kind of tom-foolery used to trick the world to go to war in the Middle East. He said that both he and Mexican President Virgil Mateo had refused to stop the flow of gay refugees fleeing the United States, and that was the reason Speaker Crooks closed the borders. He went on to assure the refugees in Canada that they would be protected and permitted to remain in Canada as long as they chose. He closed with an appeal to the people of the United States to restore constitutional government.

Things seemed to quiet down for awhile. McConihe's comments reassured us, and we began to settle into our new lives in Toronto. The *Perseus Suites Hotel* was home to about four hundred gay people from the Saginaw area. Other hotels housed gay escapees from Cleveland, Detroit, Chicago, Fort Wayne, and other communities around the Great Lakes.

The revival of gay life on Church Street was amazing. In all, Toronto had ten thousand new gay people. On Saturday night Church Street was closed to traffic from Dundas to Bloor Streets. *Woody's* and *Sailor's* had to open their third floors. *Sailor's* had always been my favorite bar in Toronto. I never really understood the connection between the two. From the street, they looked like two different bars with very different themes. On the inside, it was one big complex, and it was not clear where one started and the other ended. On the *Sailor's* side, however, there was a nautical theme. They had numerous pictures of historic boats, including the original *Polar Star*, with hunky Russian Sailors manning the decks.

On our first Saturday in Toronto, Harry and I decided to take Jimmy to *Sailor's*. I told him to wear his marina uniform. He did, and besides the fact that he was a twenty-two year old stud, the uniform made him a hit at the bar. After his third proposition within fifteen minutes, Jimmy realized he was on to something, and grew quite particular about whose affection he returned. He ended up

walking back to the Perseus with us, and there were some
broken hearts at *Sailor's*. He did get a young man's
number, who had moved to Toronto from Quebec City. His
name was Jean Luc; he was French-Canadian. Jean Luc
was 5'6" to Jimmy's 6'1." They made a handsome couple
and seemed to spend a lot of time together right away.

As refugees, we knew that we had to have some
kind of political voice. We organized and called ourselves
the Saginaw Valley Queer Association. We drew up a set
of by-laws and a constitutional structure for operations. At
our first election for officers, the organization elected me as
chairperson. I had the most experience in gay rights issues
in the group, and, as in college, I had the right vision. In
that position, my first duties were to coordinate with leaders
of the other refugee organizations that were forming in the
other "camps." I also was responsible for representing my
organization to the Canadian government and the public. I
handled all of the issues with visas and work permits for
members of our organization. As chairperson I cultivated
relationships with well connected people in the Foreign
Ministry, who eventually introduced me to Foreign Minister
Beckwith.

This, once again, put me in a prominent position
and elevated my public notoriety. I became the go-to
person for many media organizations. Each time Crooks
made a new attack on gay men in the United States, I was
the one on the evening news to express the alarm of the
refugees and to express our gratitude to Canada for
welcoming us into their society. I always ended my
comments, though, with an expression of our desire to go
home.

Going home was impossible. Decent people, like
our attorney John Elliott, started smuggling gays into
Canada once the borders had been closed. Secretary of
Homeland Security Peterson ordered the arrest of anyone

associated with gay rights organizations or known to be homosexual. Then he began acquiring title to abandoned and closed factory complexes around the country. Michigan had more than its fair share that became FBP compounds. Most old factories had a security perimeter around their complexes to keep vandals out, which could also be easily adapted to keeping prisoners inside. Detroit, Saginaw, and Flint housed more gay prisoners than any other cities.

When I found out about how old factories in Michigan were used as detention camps, I discreetly contacted John Elliott. He came to Toronto to meet with me. I suggested setting up an antebellum style underground railroad. He agreed something needed to be done, but was not sure how to get the prisoners out of the camps. I asked, "What are they doing with these guys anyway? Are they used as slave labor, or are they just waiting to die?"

John said, "I think they are using them as slave labor. I've seen a lot of construction vehicles going in and out of the old *Saquaquom Iron* foundry on River Road. It had been closed for about ten years. Most of the vehicles carry *Ballithorun Corporation* logos. There must be some military connection."

I said, "Why in the heck would there be a major military contractor involved?

John said, "I don't know, but that is a terrible place to house people."

I replied, "Yeah, we gotta get them out of there."
John asked, "How?"

I answered, "Here's the deal. Unless the FBP completely re-did the perimeter, those fences are not so secure. The river is just across the road, and if we had low-profile water transport nearby, we could easily get a few people out each night. We could hold them in safe houses until we could arrange for transport out of the country."

John said, "Possibly, but you can't empty the compound by just getting a few people out each night. The Federal Bureau of Protection will catch on to how those guys are getting out."

I said, "I know, but if we get enough of them out, maybe The Federal Bureau of Protection will move them off the compound to a safer place."

John said, "Yeah, or just shoot them."

I said, "That's possible, but we can't just leave them."

John asked, "You keep saying we. You don't intend on crossing the border yourself, do you?"

I answered, "Just to lead operations."

John chided me, "You know, I risked my neck and my license to get your property out of the country. Now you want to come back?"

I said, "Look John, I don't intend to risk my life. I want to help these guys get to a safe haven. Can you help me?"

John gave-in, "I don't suppose I have a choice do I?"

The Canadian Ministry of Industry arranged for *Canadian Royal Shipping Company* to assist us with our mission. They had a ship that made a regular run to Saginaw. The *Mississaugee* brought nickel ore mined from Sudbury to the *Grey Iron* foundry up river from the *Saquaquom Iron* site. The shipping company agreed to provide us free transport both ways. At first we thought it would be ideally convenient to use the ship as our transport from *Saquaquom Iron* back to Canada, but the Federal Bureau of Protection supposedly conducted a thorough search of every vessel entering and leaving Saginaw Bay. It was too dangerous.

We decided to carry powered dinghies. The *Mississaugee* would drop us about twelve miles away from the river mouth. At night, we would be undetectable. From there we would run to the State Park beach near Tobico Marsh, portage, and hide the dinghies in the rushes.

I called John to find out what he had arranged in Michigan. He had gotten a list of workers for *Ballithorun* in the area and did some background checks. John found a couple of guys who had hidden their criminal record from Human Resources at *Ballithorun*. He persuaded them to give him a layout of the barracks and the security system at *Saquaquom Iron*. John also found some former plant workers.

Bob, Fred, Tom, and Joe were the former *Saquaquom Iron* employees. They had worked in physical plant when the foundry was operational and knew the buildings in and out. They were die-hard union members. They opposed everything the Crooks was doing and thought it an abomination to have "their" factory turned into a defense plant, manned with slave-labor while there were so many unemployed people in the area. Bob, Fred, Tom, and Joe would do anything to help us.

They picked us up where we portaged the boats. Then they drove us down Bay Road. Fred's house was near the Saginaw River in Carrolton, just across the river from *Saquaquom Iron*. The "Guys," as we called them, brought whatever canoes and fishing boats they had to Fred's place. We could row across the river, do our business, and row back. It seemed easy enough.

We put our team together in Toronto. Harry was furious about me going back into the United States. He was even less pleased with my insistence that he stay in Canada. Jimmy went with me; we needed his youthful agility. Scott came. So did a character about whom I knew little, Marc Cranmer. Marc was shadowy. We had seen him occasionally at *Bambi's*, a gay bar in Saginaw. He was what we had publicly called in a condescending tone "rough trade" (privately, I think many of us had entertained a fantasy or two). Marc did not seem bright, but was built like a shipyard. He was about 5'8" and 200 pounds of solid muscle. I remember him from *Bambi's* wearing skin-tight, ripped Levis. The package he carried between his legs made the most monogamous of us squirm. Harry was livid when he found out Marc was joining us on this trip; so was Allen. Scott and I assured our spouses of our fidelity as best we could.

We drove to Tobermory and spent the night. I checked the others into a hotel, while I stayed on the *Polar Star II*. She was scheduled to come out of the water in the next few weeks, and I wanted one last night. Besides, sleeping in the v-berth, gently rolling back and forth with the motion of the water, beats sleeping on a landed bed any day. I called Harry to make sure he understood that I planned to sleep on the boat alone. He still seemed unconvinced. I could always tell by that tone in his voice.

I took Scott, Jimmy, and Marc over to see the *Polar Star II* on our way to supper. Marc seemed enthralled with it, like he had never seen a sailboat before. Jimmy stopped him from walking up to the bow, Marc wore black soled shoes, and they were marking up the deck. I told Jimmy not to worry; I doubted if I would ever sail her again. After that we went up to the *Crows Nest* for dinner and some drinks.

The *Crows Nest* in the summertime is a hopping place. They always have live entertainment, even if the entertainment they bring in is the dregs of the musical barrel. A few years back Harry and I were there in July and a singer/pianist/drummer/harmonica player was doing his rendition of Jimmy Buffet's *Margaritaville*. This singer entitled the number, *Tobermoryville*. The lyrics sung out of key and off beat went like this,

Wastin' away in Tobermoryville,
Lookin' for my salt shaker of salt,

Some people claim that there's a Mormon to blame,
But I know, it's the phone jam vault.

I wanted so badly to ask him what Mormon and to
explain to him that "Salt shaker of salt" made no sense, but
Harry told me it was not important and to leave it. The
singer's next song was, *Sweet Dreams are Made of Cheese*.
Sitting up there with Marc, Jimmy, and Scott in September,
there was, thankfully, no entertainment.

The next morning we took the first run of the *Chi-
Cheemaun*, the car ferry that connected Tobermory with
Manitoulin Island. From there we could drive to Sault Ste.
Marie, Ontario, to meet up with the *Mississaugee*. It was
about an eight-hour drive altogether. We stopped at the
Carolyn Beach Motel in Thessalon for a delightful lunch
and a slice of coconut cream pie that tasted as though the
coconuts had just been plucked from a tree and cracked
open.

Harry and I had stayed at the *Carolyn Beach Motel*
many times driving through Ontario on our way to a
backpacking trip. The motel was unpretentious, but sat atop
Lake Huron at a point that juts into the water with a smooth
rocky slab. A short trail through tall grass led to the point
where guests could sit and watch a spectacular sunset. The
food was all homemade with the freshest ingredients. It
was the kind of place that gave weary travelers a sense of
comfort.

The *Mississaugee* took us aboard as soon as we
arrived. It was early September, and the weather was
starting to cool off. It was a wet September. That made it
good for remaining undetectable. Patrols would not be
looking for people on the open water or on the river.

Everything went like clockwork up to the point of
getting into *Saquaquom Iron*. The *Mississaugee* dropped us
out in Saginaw Bay as planned. The "Guys" picked us up
and drove us to Fred's place, where we spent the night.

There was a bit of a catch there; Fred had a three-bedroom house. His kids were grown so his wife, Martha, had made up the double bed in each room for us. I stammered something about sleeping on the sofa, but Martha said, "Nonsense. You wouldn't get a good night's rest on that thing. Our two sons shared a bed all through high school, and they never had one complaint. You boys will be just fine." Scott and I quickly volunteered to share a room. Jimmy glared at me with daggers. I figured he could take care of himself, and, besides, Jean Luc and Jimmy were not a declared couple yet. Jimmy could afford to stray. Scott and I were like sisters, so, no danger there.

When we woke up the next morning, Martha had washed and pressed our clothes that had been drenched with rain and water from Saginaw Bay. She also had a large breakfast ready for us with bacon, eggs, pancakes, and Michigan maple syrup. Michigan maple trees give syrup a distinctive flavor, quite unlike that from Vermont, which tends to be smoky, and that from Ontario, which tends to be bland. Michigan syrup is sweet and has a pungently rich taste. For a moment I felt I was home.

Martha and Fred were part of the German community in Michigan. Their ancestors had immigrated to America in the aftermath of the 1848 revolution in the German states. Excellent farmland in Michigan had just been surveyed and was open for settlement. Entire German villages immigrated and reestablished their communities, virtually intact. They retained much of their native identity and culture, some to the point of capitalizing on it as with the little town of Frankenmuth. Frankenmuth promoted an idealized version of a Bavarian town, complete with a Glockenspiel playing each hour. In their Lutheran churches, most recited the Lord's Prayer as, "*Vater unser, der Du bist im Himmel . . .*" In fact, many of these Lutheran churches, on special occasions, especially Christmas Eve,

conducted the entire service in German, and a good
Christmas Eve service would have ended with *Stille Nacht*
having been sung by all.

These German Lutherans in Michigan, and Martha
and Fred were no different, took their religion seriously.
They were conservative folk, who clung to as much of their
ancient German past as possible. They resisted a fast paced
life of rapid and constant change, testing and trying new
ideas and gadgets slowly and reluctantly. Conservative
though they were, the persecution their ancestors had
experienced as new immigrants to America, and distrust and
suspicion they experienced during the world wars of the
twentieth century taught them a unique brand of tolerance
and acceptance for others different from themselves. They
no more wanted to preach to others about their beliefs and
attitudes than they wanted someone to tell them to recite the
Lord's Prayer in English.

Martha started to walk towards my plate with a
fresh spatula of pancakes hot off the griddle. I put up my
hand and said, "Thanks but I couldn't eat another bite."

She pointed at me with that loaded spatula and said,
"Look here buster, you are not going out to dance under the
mirror ball at the disco tonight, and you don't have to worry
about someone imagining a fat roll on your waist. You are
going to be doing hard demanding work, and you need your
energy. My boy, Randy, is safe in Canada now, but he
could just as easily be in that prison camp. If he were there
and you couldn't rescue him because you ran out of energy,
I would never forgive you." I ate the next stack without
another word.

We stayed inside most of the day; we didn't want to
take a chance on being noticed. We watched TV and read
the last week's worth of the *Saginaw News*. In the
afternoon, when Martha had finished cleaning the kitchen,
stripping the beds, washing and ironing the sheets, and

starting to prepare supper, she came in to check on us. She sat down next to me on the sofa, "Do you really think you can save those boys? I know some of their mothers. They are desperate to see their sons set free."

"Tell me about Randy." I asked. "Do you know for certain that he is safe? Are you in touch with him?"

Martha replied, "Yes, we helped him get across the border before it was closed. He is in Toronto."

I asked, "Really. Where is he staying? Most of the refugees from this area are in the hotel I'm in."

She said, "He had a cousin living there. He is staying with her. We write twice a week."

I nodded, "I see. I'll make it a point to look him up when I get back. Is there anything I can take for him?"

Martha shook her head, "No, you have your hands full. I send packages about once a month."

Martha told me that Randy had a boyfriend before he left. The boyfriend wasn't able to get out of the country in time, and she didn't know where he was or what happened to him. She hoped he would be in *Saquaquom Iron*, and that we could rescue him. His name was Kyle Reddick. I told her we would do what we could.

The sun began to set and we gathered our things. Fred and the other guys were ready to take us down to the river around ten o'clock. That was when things quieted down at *Saquaquom Iron*. We crossed the river and hid our boats in the reeds along the riverbank. We were dressed in blackout suits. Surprisingly, there were no guard towers or patrols along the outer security fences. We could see guards stationed at the entrance gates on River Road, but nothing on the backside. It seemed too good to be true and frightened us somewhat.

We cut through the rusted chain link fence with no trouble. There was only a barbed wire barrier at the top of the fence. We made our way to the barracks at the north end of the compound, which was closest to where we cut through. All the windows had been painted over. We tapped on one, hoping to find a friendly face.

A curious face greeted us and, after ascertaining our intentions, let us in. It was pitch black inside. I asked if we could turn on a light. Our greeter said no, the light would shine through the glass; even though it was painted out, filtered light came through. I suggested putting blankets over the windows facing the compound. We used our flashlights instead, so we could aim them away from the windows. Once we had some light, I saw about 250 men in orange prison suits staring at us.

I scanned the crowd for familiar faces, but saw none. They were gaunt, ill-fed, unshaven, and dirty. When I started talking, however, a man near the door walked towards me. He extended his hands and said, "Joe, don't you recognize me?"

"Matt!" I exclaimed, "My God. I thought you and Bob would have escaped. At least you are all right. Where is Bob?"

"Bob is dead." Matt looked to the ground. He had no more tears left. Matt Crossly and Bob Dunsmore were a jet-setting gay couple that set the standard for how to be successful, wealthy, classy, and well-liked. Harry and I were successful and had enough means to live comfortably, but we weren't wealthy, not like Matt and Bob. Their home in Midland was a 5,000 square foot mansion, complete with servants and groundskeepers. They also had a home on Sanibel Island in Florida, a villa in the south of France, and a condo in Palm Springs. It was nothing for them to fly to Paris for a long weekend. In fact, I had just assumed that they had gone on to Europe before the border closed.

Matt told me about the day after the borders were closed. He said he and Bob had reservations to depart for Paris the next day. That night, while they were in bed at home in Midland, a knock on their door awakened them about midnight. It was The Federal Bureau of Protection. Matt answered the door. Bob waited at the top of the stairs. The captain of the arrest squad told them to pack whatever they could in twenty minutes. They were being detained for a "few days." Bob tried to argue, he said he wanted to call their lawyer. The captain said that they could not call their lawyer at that moment, and that the more he argued, the less time he had to pack and dress. The captain went on to say that Bob could go in his robe if he so desired, but that their twenty minutes was ticking. Matt told Bob to get packing and get dressed and ran upstairs himself to help Bob get ready.

They came downstairs, each with a bag and Bob carrying their pet dachshund, Milly. The captain told Bob he could not take the dog. Bob said, if Milly doesn't go, neither do I. The captain motioned and a guard snatched the dog out of Bob's arms, threw her on the ground, and shot her. Bob lurched at the guard, and the captain shot Bob through the head. Matt said that a few days later his attorney was permitted to visit him in jail, primarily to tell him that all of their property in the United States had been confiscated under racketeering laws. Matt was labeled a suspected terrorist, like the other men in the barracks.

We heard other horror stories about the past few months. The commandant of the compound was fond of getting his rocks off frequently. Each night he rounded up a few of the "nancy boys" from the barracks to service his needs. At gunpoint they would be forced to give him a blow job or to get fucked – all without condoms. I was mortified. "You mean to tell me you have eight hundred gay men bare-backing with the commandant? That might as well be a death sentence to all of you!" They understood the danger, but what could they do? And all the while, the

commandant considered himself straight because he was the
top man in all the action.

We told them we intended to take a few out each
trip. Matt said, "Joe, how many do you think you will get
out all together before the guards figure what is going on,
ten, twenty, fifty tops? After that, they'll crank down
security. You will never get anyone else out. Right now,
security is pretty lax at night. You could empty this entire
compound in one night if you had a means of escape."

"How lax is security?"

"We've thought about escaping several times, but
with no means out of the country it would be moot. We've
been hoping to find outside help. You're it. They lock us
in our barracks at 10:00 PM each night and bolt the door
from the outside, so we can't go out the front. The idiots
think that by painting the windows so we can't see out, we
would be too afraid to open them at night. We've been
using the back windows you tapped on to go between
barracks the whole time. We could have a pool party
behind the barracks and they would never know. Guards
are stationed by the front gates at night and that's it. We
just assumed they must have some kind of patrol outside the
perimeter."

"Nope. There are no patrols. Not on the river, not
around the back of the property. Nothing."

"So we could all get out of here tonight if we had
transport. Bummer, all you've got are a few canoes and a
couple of bass boats?"

I hesitated and thought a moment, "I think we might
have something more substantial. Hang on." I turned to
Scott, Jimmy, and Marc and told them I wanted to empty
the entire compound.

Scott rubbed his forehead. "I knew you would do
something like this. Are we going to have time to get to the
Mississaugee and back before dawn?"

"Yeah, we can do it. Marc, you are with me. Scott, Jimmy, I want you to go with Matt and get the other barracks ready to go. Matt, do you know if anyone is not physically able travel on his own or to swim?"

"There are a couple of guys in barrack #2 that were beaten pretty badly a few days ago. They might be the only ones who would need assistance."

"Alright. Check on them and get them ready one way or the other. We'll keep a couple of the boats here in case we need it for anyone in bad shape. We should be back by midnight. Be ready to go."

The two of us went back to the boats and rowed one back to the other side where Fred and the guys were waiting. They were surprised to see just the two of us and wondered if something had gone wrong. I told them, no, but we needed to get up river and find the *Mississaugee* right away. We loaded the canoe in Tom's truck and drove up river. The *Mississaugee* had already dumped its cargo and a tug was turning it in the river.

We waited for it to be running under its own steam again, down river. Marc and I took the canoe and rowed out to meet the *Mississaugee*. The captain was none to happy to see us. At first he refused to take any passengers on board in the river. Marc I and described conditions at *Saquaquom Iron*. We told the captain about the beatings and Matt's story. He called all stop to the engine room. The captain told us that his father had served in World War II and had been a part of the Canadian regiments that entered some of the Jewish camps. He asked if we could get them to swim out to the boat about a quarter mile down river from the camp. I said we could.

I asked about how we would hide eight hundred men on board. He told me that they had only dumped half their load at *Grey Iron*. The rest was destined for *River Rouge* in Detroit. He could hide them in the cargo hold behind a mound of ore. It would be unpleasant, but they would be safe. The captain gave us a rendezvous time of 2:30 AM sharp. If we weren't there, he would go on without us. I assured him we would be there.

Tom got us back to the down river launch site around12:30. My team stationed around the outside of the compound to observe any movements of the guards. Matt and the other barracks' leaders focused on getting their men out. There were four barracks altogether with about two hundred men each. We saw the *Mississaugee* steaming very slowly down river around 2:15. The men hiked down River Road about a quarter mile. In a line of about eighty men each, they swam out into the water towards the ship. The captain had ordered a net running the length of the ship to be dropped over the starboard side to the water line. The captain had set his speed at a slow pace so that the ship would not have to stop, which could have raised suspicion. It was also imperative that the operation be over with in less than an hour. By then the starboard side of the ship would be within direct sight of the Zilwaukee Bridge, which was heavily guarded by The Federal Bureau of Protection.

The whole operation went off without issue. By 3:30 everyone was on board except for Jimmy and Scott. They had taken the boats back to the other side of the river so Fred and Tom could retrieve them. The two men who had been beaten had to be ferried in one of the bass boats. They both had broken legs and cracked ribs. Apparently they had refused to give the commandant a blow-job. Jimmy and Scott met up with us about ten minutes later.

The captain had sent some of his crew down into the hold to adjust the ore piles. In the bow of the ship, they shoveled a depression in the ore and built a bit of a higher mound towards the middle of the ship. The men hid in the bow section of the cargo hold. This would do.

As soon as the men were on board and down in the hold, the captain gradually began increasing speed. Getting through the lift bridges at Bay City slowed us down, but even still we were at the mouth of the river by 5:30, the time when the guards unlocked the barracks at the *Saquaquom Iron* compound. The FBP inspectors came aboard and made a routine check through the cabins. In the cargo hold, one inspector stuck his head down the stern side crawl space and shone his flash light around. He saw nothing to cause alarm. We were back under way and clear of the Saginaw River by 6:15.

The captain called for me to come up to the bridge about an half hour later. He told me that the men could spread out, but that they had to stay in the cargo hold. He sent down as many blankets and coats as he could scrounge. He asked me to come back to the bridge after getting the men below settled-in. They had a police band radio for me to monitor as long as it was in range. It was not until after 7:30 that the news was out on the police channels that the escape had occurred.

I asked the captain how we would disembark. His manifest had him headed toward *River Rouge* and, any deviation would immediately be suspect. The captain told me that once in the open waters of Lake Huron, we would skirt close to the Canadian boundary. At some point we would have serious engine trouble and would have to notify the U. S. Coast Guard that we were going to stop over in Sarnia, Ontario, for repairs.

We were past Caseville by 9:00. We were well out of police band range, but we had satellite feed. *CNN* was headlining a *Spectacular Escape* from a "maximum security installation in Michigan." The captain turned the helm over to his first mate and joined me in front of the television monitor. He was worried that the Coast Guard might stop vessels that had been in the area. We were still in U. S.

waters and still had a way to go before even being within
reach of the border.

    CNN reported that, "About 800 suspected terrorists
have escaped from a maximum security detention facility
operated by the Federal Bureau of Protection near Saginaw,
Michigan. These men overpowered guards with the help of
outside accomplices around 5:00 AM this morning. The
men were believed to be heading north towards Bay City.
All residents in Saginaw-Bay City area have been advised
to stay indoors, as FBP and local law enforcement units
conduct a building-by-building search. Experts suspect that
these terrorists may try to hold up in a church in Bay City,
probably St. Stanislaus Catholic Church. [*CNN* flashed a
file photo of the church on the South End of Bay City].
These men are expected to be well armed and dangerous. A
$10,000,000 reward has been issued for information leading
to the capture of these dangerous men."

    I looked at the captain and said, "They are looking
for us in Bay City. They have no idea where we are." The
captain smiled and went back to the helm. We had been
pushing the *Mississaugee* at full steam, and he ordered a cut
in power back to three-quarter speed. I excused myself and
went down below to pass on the news to the men.

    We passed Port Austin and the captain began to
turn as his manifest required, which would take us due east
for about sixty miles. The captain ordered the engines back
up to full steam for about twenty miles, then back down to
one quarter speed. Then we steamed for about an hour,
taking us close to Canadian waters. At that point he picked
up speed again for about fifteen minutes, then back down to
one quarter speed. As planned, the U. S. Coast Guard
radioed him, wanting to know if the *Mississaugee* was in
trouble. The captain replied that the ship was having some
engine difficulties, but was still operating on two engines.
He told them that we should be able to make Sarnia without

any help, and he had called ahead to his home office, which would have a repair crew waiting there. In typically friendly Coast Guard fashion they offered to provide an escort. The captain assured them that one was not necessary.

When I went down below, it was mid-afternoon. Most of the men were resting as best they could. My presence caught their attention, and I passed on the good news. I think they were all still too stunned to believe they were really free. It certainly would not sink in until they were on land again. The cargo hold was really just another prison to them. Jimmy was sound asleep, but Marc and Scott were awake. They came over to me. Scott said, "Joe, you need to get some rest. There is nothing you can do now until we hit land. Why don't you lay down for awhile?" I asked them if they had gotten any sleep. They said, they had, intermittently. That was more than I had. Scott offered to go above and keep an eye on *CNN*. He promised me he would let me know if there were any developments. Marc put his arm on my shoulder and told me he had made a comfortable spot in the ore heap. He led me over to the spot he had hollowed out and lined with a wool blanket. I curled up in Marc's little den and fell into a deep sleep.

Some hours later, Scott woke me up. He said it was almost dusk. He thought I would want to come out on deck before sunset. We had just passed Goderich. I went up to the bridge. The captain had retired and left his first mate in command. Scott said we had about three hours before reaching Sarnia. That would put us in around 10:00 PM.

I went back down below, hoping to catch a little more sleep. The crew was down below serving supper to the men in the hold. I was quite amazed at the spectacle. Thirty rather salty and mostly hetero crew members were sitting on the ore heap with eight hundred gay prison escapees. They were chatting away, trading stories about

November storms on Lake Superior and imprisonment at
Saquaquom Iron. I debated with myself which group had
the toughest of men; for the moment my loyalties were with
both sides.

I walked around and talked with as many of the
escapees as I could for the rest of the evening. In all that
had happened, I had not been able to meet any of the men
from the other three barracks. Some I knew casually or
socially, but no more of my close friends were there. I was
overwhelmed that there were so many gay men in the Tri-
city area I had never met.

I finally found Kyle Reddick. I had no picture or
mental image, but as soon as I heard someone say the name
"Kyle," I wheeled around and introduced myself. Kyle had
run into some difficulties with the commandant. He had
swum to the *Mississaugee*, but had a cracked rib and was
badly bruised. He had some buddies who had looked out
for him. I did not tell him yet about Randy or Randy's
parents. I figured I would wait until we were in a more
secure environment for that. I was glad I had eaten that
second stack of pancakes.

Chapter 8   Rough Trade

The *Mississaugee's* horn announced our arrival in
Sarnia a few minutes before ten o'clock. We passed under
the *Blue Water Bridge*, and I ran up to the ship's bridge.
The captain was back at his post. We sailed down the St.
Clair River to the harbor in Sarnia. The captain told me he
had not made any advance communications as to the true
nature of his stop over in Sarnia. He called to the Foreign
Ministry office in town and told them he had 800 refugees
seeking asylum. He suggested they put him in direct
contact with the Foreign Minister in Ottawa. The captain's
phone rang after no more than three minutes. It was Prime
Minister McConihe. They talked; then the captain handed
the phone over to me. The Prime Minister congratulated me
on the unexpected success of our mission. He assured me
that arrangements were being made at that moment to get
the men into decent lodging for the night. A special train
would take them to Toronto the next day. We were not to
worry about any political issues. Asylum was granted *carte
blanche*. I thanked him for all that he and Canada had done
for us.

We would have to wait aboard ship for a local
official from the Foreign Ministry to arrive with temporary
papers. While we waited the captain said, "I think you have
some people to get out of the cargo hold." While on the
phone with the Prime Minister, the captain had arranged for
the crew to get their instruments together. With a proper
Canadian band of trumpets, bag pipes, and trombones, the

133

crew of the *Mississaugee* played *Oh Canada.* Scott, Jimmy,
and Marc joined me on the deck. The eight hundred
Saquaquom Iron survivors began spilling out onto the deck
with us. By that time, the *paparazzi* had arrived, and
curious onlookers were filtering-in.

Once all the escapees were on deck, the captain
called out on his P/A system. He made a brief speech to the
men on deck, and to the crowds gathering around the ship. I
could see the microphone booms hoist up from the *CNN*,
NBC, and *BBC* vans. He said, "I want to be the first to
welcome you to Canada, my country and my home, of
which I am rather proud. This boat tonight is filled with
some 837 of the bravest men in the world. In that number
are the members of my crew. They knew they were putting
their lives and their careers in danger on this mission, but
they trusted my judgment and followed my orders without
once raising an objection. Thank you men, you are the best
crew a captain could have.

"There are also these 800 men who, just twenty-
four hours ago, were political prisoners, in jail without due-
process, and subject to arbitrary acts of torture. Your
perseverance humbles us all. My greatest admiration,
however, goes to these four men in black suits, the men who
had already escaped from tyranny, but had the courage to
risk their lives to save others. You are the true Americans,
the ones who fight for the freedom that this continent is
supposed to represent. I salute you."

At that, the captain ordered the Stars and Stripes to
be run up the flag halyard next to the Canadian flag, and the
band broke into the *Star Spangled Banner.* All of us on
deck stood at attention during our national anthem. Then,
the captain introduced me as the captain of our team and
handed me the microphone. At first I was stunned and
fumbled for words, but I took a deep breath and spoke, "I
noticed that all of us from the other side of the river stood at

attention and saluted during the U. S. national anthem. I guess we all know that we are now the ones fighting for the freedom that used to characterize the United States. And I want the world to know, that we will not rest until we can watch our flag raised with honor once again in the United States. These times are the holocaust of the United States. I grieve for my country. But like De Gaulle and the Free-French of World War II, we will continue our fight for freedom from foreign lands as long as necessary. We thank all of Canada for the generosity and open arms you have shown us, but we want to go home."

It was nearly midnight before the Canadian Foreign Ministry personnel arrived with our papers. We were exhausted. The Foreign Ministry had shuttles to take us to local hotels. They had commandeered every available room. Everyone had to share a room with another. The men who were injured and sick were taken to the hospital for treatment.

My team was the last off the boat. As we climbed down the gangway, the reporters were lined up to beg us for interviews. The *NBC* people caught my attention and asked me to do an interview for their morning news broadcast. I said, "I hate to tell you this, but it is already morning, so if you want me to do an interview, it has to be right now, because I won't be awake at seven AM." They agreed. I said, "One more thing. I'll only do the interview if Mike Lindemann does it here in person." They said, "No problem. He's here and ready." Scott looked at me as though I were crazy. Our shuttle was the last one waiting, and Scott, Marc, and Jimmy would have to wait for me to do this interview that I really didn't want to give."

I saw Mike Lindemann running up to the dock in front of the boat. The *NBC* crews had shooed all of the other networks away. I looked terrible. I was still in the skanky black night suit that I had been wearing for the

previous twenty-eight hours. My face was still smeared
with grease paint, and the stubble of my beard was starting
to poke through. My team started to walk away as the
cameras and lights were getting in position. Marc turned
and gave me a once over look with a smile, "And you
thought I was rough trade?" He spun around and walked
off.

By that time Mike Lindemann was standing there.
He asked, "What did that mean; what is rough trade?"

I replied, "If I explained that on camera, you
wouldn't be able to air this interview."

He put his hands up, and said, "Don't need to
know."

NBC's equipment was all in place, and the director
told Mike he was ready to roll. He looked at me and asked
if I was nervous. I told him I was too tired to be nervous.
The tape started to roll and Mike started speaking into the
camera, "I'm here in front of the *Mississaugee*, a Great
Lakes cargo vessel with the *Canadian Royal Shipping
Company*. This ship normally makes a run from Sault Ste.
Marie, Ontario, down Lake Huron to Saginaw, Michigan,
where it delivers a load of nickel ore to a General Motors
foundry. On its run this past Tuesday night, it picked up
cargo on its way back down the Saginaw River. It picked
up a load of 800 men who, it is claimed by this man,
[camera panned to me], Joe Kelly, were illegal prisoners in
a Federal Bureau of Protection detention camp. Ironically,
they were being held at an abandoned General Motors
foundry, down river from the plant where the *Mississaugee*
was delivering its ore. Now, Federal Bureau of Protection
personnel tell us these men were suspected terrorists and
were dangerous and had to be detained. Joe, what can you
tell us about these men, and why did you get involved?"

I replied, "These men were not terrorists. Their
only crime is in being homosexual. That is my crime too. I

was a local activist in the gay rights movement in the
United States for many years. When Speaker Crooks
started pandering to right wing extremists I saw what was
coming, and I made plans to get out of the country with my
family before the arrests began. These men who were
imprisoned at the old *Saquaquom Iron* plant were not able
to get out of the country before Crooks closed the borders.
They had done nothing wrong, they had broken no laws, but
they were identified by the Federal Bureau of Protection as
members of the gay community and, therefore, were
branded as terrorists."

Mike then asked, "Weren't you putting your life at
risk by coming back into the United States to rescue these
men?"

I answered, "Yes, I was, but when I heard about
these detention facilities, and I think they are all over the
country, I had to do something. My home was in Bay City,
so I knew the area well. I figured I would have the best
chance at success by going to a place of familiarity."

"What did you find when you got there?"

"Deplorable conditions. The men were filthy,
hungry, and subjected to torture and other horrors."

"Can you be more specific?"

"These men were forced to perform sexual acts with
the camp's commandant. When they refused, they were
subjected to beatings and forms of torture that I would not
like to describe on television."

Mike was speechless. I continued, "What's
happening in the United States is a holocaust targeted
against gay men. It has to stop. I know there are good-
hearted people in the United States who don't approve of
what their government is doing. They need to stand up and
make their voices heard. I know they exist, I met some of
them these past few days."

By that time Mike had gained his composure. "Do you mean you had some assistance in the United States?"

"I cannot comment on that."

"Fair enough. What about the Canadian government; have they been helpful?"

"I can't say enough about the Canadian people and their government. Without them I would have had no safe refuge and neither would these men we rescued."

"What is going to happen to the *Mississaugee*?"

"I can't imagine that it will be sailing in U. S. waters anytime soon. I don't know."

"Is there anything else you would like to tell people in America?"

"There is much I would like to tell, but I'm too tired." The cameras shut off, Mike thanked me for the interview, and I walked to the shuttle.

As soon as Scott and I were in our room, I called Harry. It was after 1:30 AM, but I knew he would want to know I was all right. He and Allen were in Tobermory; they had gone up to Sault Ste. Marie to pick up my car. They were on their way back and decided to stay aboard the *Polar Star II* for the night. I told Harry we were back and safe, but no details. I told him to be sure to watch *NBC* in the morning.

He called me around 10:00 AM; he wanted to let me sleep as long as possible. I asked how the news was. Harry told me that we were the headline. The picture of the boat with all the men standing on deck was on every front page. My scruffy face from the interview was all over the news channels. In Canada, we were heroes. There was no comment yet from the White House, but some kind of reaction was expected. Harry said my interview was kind of choppy, like it had been heavily edited, probably by government censors.

Harry asked if he and Allen should come to Sarnia to pick us up. I wasn't sure if we would be needed here with the others, so I told him I would call him later. He said he and Allen were about ready to leave and would head on out. It takes almost two hours to get out of the Bruce Peninsula, I would know if we needed them by then.

Scott and I went down for breakfast. I realized while we were getting dressed, that we were the only ones who had clothes. All the guys from the prison had nothing except their prison garb. The Foreign Ministry had thought about that and had a fresh change placed in their rooms. Jimmy and Marc came down while we ate. They sat down with us. I said, "So how are you two getting along; it seems like we kind of pushed you guys together?"

Jimmy blushed. I knew they had done it. He stammered and said, "Oh fine. Marc seems like a nice person. I think we could be friends."

At that point I was looking directly into Marc's eyes, and I could read the situation quite well. I said, "I assume it was consensual."

They both muttered, "Of, of course."

I looked at Marc and said, "OK, you guys, what you do is your own business, but, Marc, you need to know that Jimmy is a very important person to me. Just don't lead him to think one thing and mean another. OK?"

Marc nodded. Jimmy upbraided me for being so paternalistic. I told him that I felt a responsibility for his happiness and well being, and I had a right to be paternalistic. Marc interrupted the fray, "Jimmy was the one who initiated the whole thing the other night. But if you want to know the truth, I think he is really hot. I hope this leads to something more permanent." Marc reached over and put his hand on Jimmy's.

I said, "The other night. You mean at the Voeglin's?"

Marc answered, "Yeah. It was a small bed, we couldn't keep from touching each other; you know, one thing leads to another."

My posture stiffened, "Yeah, well, Scott and I had the same size bed. We managed just fine without "one thing leading to another.""

Jimmy rolled his eyes, "Ah c'm'on. You can't tell me you guys lay there all night and didn't do anything."

I was aghast. "Scott and I are best friends. That would be gross."

Scott looked at me with an offended glare, "Gross? Are you saying sex with me would be gross?"

I shook my head, "No Scott. That's not what I meant. You are a fine looking man, and I would love to have sex with you."

Scott smiled, "Really?"

I stammered, "No that's not what I meant either. Look Scott, we've been friends for, what, almost twenty years? I know that you are utterly devoted to Allen and you know how devoted I am to Harry. That's the end of it, OK?"

Scott nodded, "Yeah, I know."

I turned back towards Jimmy and Marc, "Thanks. Now please tell me you didn't do more than make out at the Voeglin's."

Jimmy replied, "Sorry Joe. We went the distance."

I sighed, "Were you safe?"

Jimmy answered, "Of course. I always carry the right props, just in case."

I parsed my lips, "On this mission, you thought you might get lucky. That's nice. I thought we were here to do a good deed for mankind. Not to find a good fuck. So what did you do with the debris?"

Marc spoke up, "Oh shit. I completely forgot about that. When I took off the condom, I threw it on the floor."

Jimmy said, "You mean you didn't put it in the trash or down the toilet or something?"

Marc said, "No dude, I completely forgot about it."

I thought about that day: Martha going in to our rooms in the morning to pick up our dirty clothes so she could wash them while we were still sleeping; then again in mid-day to strip our beds so she could wash, dry, and press the sheets. In her spotless house, she would notice a stray wad of gooey rubber on the floor. She would also pick up on the cum-stained sheets. Then I thought, "What a classy lady. She said not a word, did not let on like she had noticed anything out of the norm."

We were about done with our breakfast. A woman from the Foreign Ministry came in to talk with us. She said that a special train was being arranged to transport the escapees to Toronto. They would be housed in whatever hotels were available for the time being. The train would be at the station at three in the afternoon. She said that the Foreign Ministry would really like to have us on board the train when it pulled into Union Station in Toronto. I called Harry and told them to meet us there.

The "*Saquaquom Iron* Men," as they became known, had been coming in and out for breakfast while we were in the hotel restaurant. They were clean, shaven, and starting to look normal again. Matt Crossly came down after we had finished breakfast. I told him he looked great. He said, "I've been up for a while. I relished the luxury of a fresh shave, a hot shower, and a toothbrush. I had always taken such things for granted."

I asked, "Are you going to make any contacts with any of your assets outside the United States?"

"I've already been on the phone with my broker in Toronto. He will have a driver waiting for me when we get off the train. As it turns out, my finances are not as bleak as I thought. My lawyer, who had power of attorney, had transferred most of our assets out of the country as soon as he got word of the arrest. All I've really lost are a few homes, cars, and some bank accounts worth about $300,000.00. And Bob, there will never be another Bob. I can replace the houses and cars, and the money doesn't matter. I can't replace Bob. He was everything to me. What will I do without him? In prison it didn't matter, because I felt my life was over anyway. Now I can live again, but I can't. Not without Bob."

Marc was sitting next to Matt and put his arm on Matt's shoulder. Matt looked up at Marc and smiled through his tears, which had started flowing again, "You know Marc, Bob would have chopped your arm off right about now if he were here."

Marc said, "Yes, I know. In fact, I think I feel something sawing at my shoulder right now. I think Bob is here, and I think he is terribly proud of you for leading all those men out of the barracks to safety. You will always be his hero."

Matt said, "Thanks. I appreciate your thoughts. I'll be fine. It's just going to take some getting used to."

I said, "Matt, there is something more you can do. Most of those men have nothing. I don't know who else in that crowd had money out of the country, but I expect that most of them lost everything. Those of us who do have means need to help them out for awhile."

Matt said, "I've already thought that through. I know those men. There were a few of us who had money outside the country. We had decided long before you knocked on our window that we would find a way to take care of the rest. That is why I insisted upon your taking all of us at one time. For a few of us to have gone and left others behind, would have broken the brotherhood we had developed. If you don't mind, I wish to take the lead on this. I want to organize the relief for them."

I replied, "By all means, Matt. I will support you every way I can."

We decided to go for a walk around town. Our hotel was near the waterfront, so we walked in front of the Blue Water Bridge. Port Huron was on the other side. There was a hotel Harry and I had stayed in a few years before. The Federal Bureau of Protection patrolled up and down the waterfront. I thought if they spotted me, they might send a bullet on over. We walked on down to where the *Mississaugee* was moored. The captain stood on the dock talking with some people who looked like they could be his bosses. He spotted me and waived us over. "You clean up real nice now, don't you fella? Joe, I want you to meet the President of *Canadian Royal Shipping Company*, Jason Fielding."

Fielding, with a slight brogue, said, "So you're the lad who has my boat stranded here." He grinned and shoved his hand at mine.

I replied, "I'm afraid so sir, but I thank you for helping us out."

Still grinning, Fielding said, "Not a problem. I want you to know that we are very proud of what you boys accomplished with my boat. It's going to cost us a bit, but we think it was a fair price to pay for helping out some people in trouble. Too bad those bastards on the other side of the river don't see it that way."

"What's going to happen to the *Mississaugee*? Are you going to get her on her way to *River Rouge*?"

Fielding laughed, "Your Coast Guard over there has threatened to sink her if she so much as ventures out of port."

"Oh no!" I exclaimed.

Looking dead serious, Fielding said, "Oh yes. The Canadian Defense Ministry has a few gun-ships on their way, and if the Americans give us any trouble, they'll have to pay for it." My eyes must have looked like saucers. He went on, "Don't worry. We'll be fine. I'll be standing in the bridge, alongside the Prime Minister when the *Mississaugee* sets sail this evening. If they want an international incident, we'll make it a fine one. The Americans already know that the Prime Minister and President of *Canadian Royal Shipping Company* will be taking her for a pleasure cruise to Sault Ste. Marie."

I began to grow increasingly concerned about the course of events I had helped to set in motion. If that ship went down, the holocaust that was, so far, confined to the United States, could spread to the entire world. I wondered if my conscience would enable me to cope with that responsibility.

We walked on back to the hotel. A shuttle waited to take us to the train station. The train was the *Canadian National*'s finest. The engines and twenty passenger cars had been washed and detailed thoroughly. All cars were fitted out with first class accommodations. It had a lounge car in the back with an open bar. The statement was obvious: The United States had these men living in conditions not fit for a dog; Canada gave them first class.

The Foreign Ministry had strapped banners to the cars reading "Freedom Train." I surmised that the Foreign Ministry wanted this to be a media event. We neared London, and the camera crews were there, along with cheering crowds, waving Canadian flags and banners saying things like, "Welcome to Canada!" At Kitchener the crowds were even larger, and from the outskirts of Toronto to Union Station, the tracks were lined with well-wishers.

The men on the train were ecstatic. They could not believe that a day earlier they had been prisoners. I was too nervous to sit and relax on the train, though. I walked up and down through the cars, checking on everyone to make sure they were OK. I did stop in the lounge car for a Bloody Mary.

The train pulled into Union Station, and I spotted Harry and Allen on the platform with Prime Minister McConihe and his entourage. I was in the third car. I waved franticly, but Harry never spotted me. The Foreign Ministry people on board grabbed me and shuffled me to the front of the train before we came to a complete stop. They wanted Scott, Marc, Jimmy, and me to be first off the train to be greeted by the Prime Minister. The conductor opened the doors and I stepped out onto the platform first. The Prime Minister was the first to greet me. He gave me a firm handshake and a pat on the shoulder.

Harry ran up to me and we embraced, tears streaming down his cheeks, cameras and all. Streamers and confetti were flying all over us. *People* magazine put us on the cover that week. *Time* had my scruffy picture from the boat. The *Saquaquom Iron* Men and their liberators were international heroes. We also made the cover of *Le Monde* and *Bilt*.

A podium was set up for several of us to make speeches. The Prime Minister went first. His speech was more of the same rhetoric we had been hearing. The most important thing for us was Canada's unwavering support for putting a stop to the illegal detentions of homosexuals in America. He said that Canada was outraged by the atrocities taking place across the border. McConihe told us unequivocally that our welcome would never be worn-out, but that he understood most of us simply wanted to be free to go home. He pledged his support for working to help us achieve that end.

My speech came next. Again, my comments were more of a rehash of earlier statements, but I did make it clear that one rescue mission was only a start. I addressed the Canadian people and thanked them for their help and the

welcome we had received. Then I addressed the citizens of
the United States, "I know there are many good hearted
people in the U. S. I challenge all of you to speak out to
your government. Tell them you don't like the idea of
innocent citizens imprisoned for no lawful reason. Observe
what's going on at those abandoned factories and
warehouses in your community. Has there been a sudden
flurry of activity? Have you seen Defense and Federal
Bureau of Protection vehicles going in and out frequently?
Have you noticed a sudden influx of government
contractors, especially *Ballithorun*? If so, you probably
have a concentration camp in your community. Don't end
up like the Germans sixty-five years ago, who feigned
ignorance, but knew what went on in those camps. They
had to carry the guilt of inaction with them the rest of their
lives. It has become a crime in the United States to criticize
the government. If you don't fight now to take back your
first amendment rights, you will lose them for ever."

  I didn't know who was speaking next, but to my
surprise, Matt Crossly stepped up to the podium. He was
now the official spokesperson for the *Saquaquom Iron* Men.
He told his story of arrest and imprisonment and the stories
of a few others. He thanked me and the Canadian
government and then closed with, "A few months ago, we
were carefree and living one day to the next. We were blind
to the course of events and even the warnings of our friends,
like Joe Kelly. We thought that people like Joe were
alarmists and a little flaky even. I wish we had listened to
them; I wish I had listened to Joe." He looked at me, "Joe,
you got my attention. One thing that happened to us at
Saquaquom Iron, was that it toughened us. I dare someone
to call me a "Pink-boy" now. You now have an army of
tough, battle ready soldiers to carry on the work of
liberation." He looked back at the cameras, "Speaker
Crooks, we won't rest until you have been brought to

justice. You are a war criminal and you will be tried by
Americans in American courts."

The ceremony concluded and Harry took me back
to the *Perseus*. Though I had slept well in Sarnia, I was still
exhausted. We had a quiet romantic dinner in our room and
made love. Harry brought me a snifter of *Dalwhinnie* after
we were done. We talked about the mission. I told him
about Marc and Jimmie. Harry thought they would make a
great couple. I started to drift off to sleep and mumbled
something about all the men we still had to rescue.

The next morning Harry asked me about what I had
meant about more rescues. I told him again about how bad
things were in Saginaw. I could not continue trying to live
a normal life without doing something about it. Harry tried
to forbid me from leading any more missions, but I insisted.
He argued, "You were lucky this time. If you do this again,
you had better have a well trained team to support you, and
you had better know what the hell you are doing. You can't
afford to make ad-lib decisions about how many men to
rescue in the middle of a mission."

Harry was right. We had to be well trained and
prepared for all contingencies. I called my contact at the
Foreign Ministry the next day and told him what I wanted to
do. The next day I was in Ottawa for a meeting with Prime
Minister McConihe. He offered to send us through a three-
week intensive training course with their Special Forces.
We decided to organize three teams of about four hundred
men each. Most of the *Saquaquom Iron* men who were
physically able would join, as would many of the refugees
already in the country.

McConihe's only conditions were that our teams
were to be made up entirely of U.S. citizens, and operations
inside the United States were to be free of any direct
Canadian involvement. He insisted that these operations do
minimal damage to his government's relations with the

United States, which were already troubled. Any misstep
on our part could be construed as an act of war.

We organized our teams according to internal
logistics, operations, and external logistics. We were to
become a sophisticated group of rapid-strike guerrilla
warriors. Internal logistics would operate inside the United
States under cover, organize transportation, and maintain
contact with underground cells. Operations teams would be
the ones liberating the camps. External logistics would take
the hand-off from internal logistics and get the liberated
men to safety. Though I would lead an operations team, I
would also be in charge of overall operations. Harry would
be in charge of external logistics, and a man by the name of
Roger Anthony would lead internal logistics. Roger was
from Louisville, Kentucky. He had worked at the world
headquarters of *International Delivery Service* (*IDS*) there.
His former employers were secretly sympathetic to our
cause and were willing to help with evacuation. We were
ready to report to the Special Forces training facility within
two weeks.

I had one more task to complete there in Toronto
before I could leave for training. Kyle Reddick, though
ambulatory, was in need of a brief hospital stay for his ribs.
He was released to our care at the *Perseus* Suites. Harry
and I were still there. Many of the others had found
housing and moved on, but for some reason, partly because
of my activism, we had never found a more permanent
residence.

One Friday afternoon I drove out to where Martha
had told me Randy lived. It was his cousin's house. I drove
to a nearby shopping center and parked. I went in and out
of a few shops to see if anyone was watching for me; I
knew U. S. spies had followed me in the past, and I did not
want to take any chances on connecting Randy's parents
with me or our mission. When I turned onto the right street,

I even walked on past several houses to ensure that nobody was following. I did not see any cars, so I assumed I was safe. I walked back to the house and rang the doorbell.

Randy answered the door. He looked at me for a second, and said, "Oh My Gosh, you're that Joe guy!" I kind of smiled and nodded. He went on, "You're every gay man's wet-dream, come on in!"

I put up my hands and said, "Whoah, that's not why I'm here, and I'm a happily married man. Besides, I've already slept in your bed."

He looked at me as though I were crazy. "What? No, I think I would remember that."

"No, I mean back in Michigan. At your parents' house."

"Now I know you are crazy."

"No Randy. I stayed at your parents' house in Carrollton. You've obviously heard about the mission where we released all those prisoner's from the *Saquaquom Iron* plant? [He nodded] Didn't you ever think about how close all of that was to home? [He nodded again] And no doubt you've heard about those "mystery people" somewhere in the Saginaw area that acted as accomplices to our mission? [He continued nodding.] Your parents, Fred and Martha Voeglin, were the ones who helped us."

"That's impossible. My parents would never do anything like that."

"It happened. I slept in your bed, the one with the blue chenille bedspread? Your little league softball uniform still hangs in the closet? Your *Hot Wheels* collection is in a glass case your father made, complete with your replica hot pink '59 Cadillac in the center of the display? Honestly, if your father didn't know then that you were gay . . ."

"I can't believe it. My parents helped you? I always thought they were too conservative for that sort of thing. I was shocked the day they called to get me out of the country. I can't believe it."

"I still remember the breakfast your mother fixed us that morning. The pancakes on the griddle and the aroma of warming Michigan maple syrup in a sauce pan wafting through the house."

"That explains it."

"Explains what?"

"What you just said; not too many people would be able to identify Michigan maple syrup by its smell. She just sent me one of her "care packages." In it were two half gallon jugs of Michigan maple syrup. She attached a note . . . let me go get it, hold on a sec."

He disappeared for a minute, and came back with a jug of syrup and the note still taped to it. He read it, "I know this is more syrup than you will use in quite some time, but I am sure you will find a good home for the second jug. Just make sure it is someone who will appreciate Michigan Maple syrup."

We both grinned, and I said, "She sent that jug to me, didn't she?"

"Yeah. That's my Mom's way of sending a coded message. So I guess she asked you to look me up, huh?"

"Oh yes, but there is more to it than that. There was one of the *Saquaquom Iron* Men that she wanted me to make sure you knew about."

"Who?"

"Kyle Reddick."

Randy was silent for a moment and grabbed his head, "I didn't know what had happened to Kyle. I was afraid he was dead. Is he here, is he waiting outside?" Randy started for the door.

I said, "No Randy. He is not outside; sit down. He is back at the *Perseus Suites* where Harry and I are living for the time being. Kyle is hurt. He's not doing so well."

"What happened to him?"

I explained, "He was beaten at the prison. He had some cracked ribs. When we escaped, he thought he was well enough to swim to the boat on his own, but that and the journey really wore him out. He was in the hospital for a few days in Toronto. He seems to be improving somewhat, but I think he would do a lot better, if a friendly face were there to cheer him on."

Randy said anxiously, "Let's go. Let's go right now. I have to see Kyle. I have hated myself for leaving without him. There was no time. My parents were rushing me, but if they hadn't, I would have been in that prison with him. C'mon, let's go."

I put my hands on his shoulder, "Hold on. We can't go together. I can't take a chance on you being seen in public with me. There are U. S. spies all over the place. I had to take extreme care in getting here. That's why I waited so long. I wanted to come the first day after I got back. If the U. S. government ever connected the two of us, they might figure out who helped us in Michigan. We cannot risk, under any circumstances, exposing your parents."

"I can't believe my Mom would have been concerned about Kyle."

"Your parents are part of an underground PFLAG network of families with gay sons either in prison or out of the country. They are part of a very quiet resistance."

"I'd give anything if I could have been there with you. I miss them so much."

"If it means anything, let me tell you what your parents did for us." I went on to tell the whole story of how his father picked us up at Tobico Marsh and put us up for the night. I also told him the whole story about Marc and Jimmy's dalliance.

He couldn't believe it, "I wish I could have been there to see the look on her face when she realized she had picked up a freshly used rubber. I would think the entire neighborhood would have heard the screech."

I told him to wait about four hours, then to go into town. I told him to walk into the hotel and go to the elevators. Any spies watching wouldn't take note of anyone acting like they knew their way around. I told him to call me when he got to Kyle's room. I also asked him to call his neighbors in back and let them know a strange man would be climbing over their fence and walking out in front of their house. I didn't want to go back the same way I came.

It was evening when Randy called me from Kyle's room. Randy said that Kyle had already made a marked improvement. I asked him to stop by to meet Harry on his way out. He said he would, but that it would likely be morning. I smiled and hung up. The next day Harry and I left for training.

Chapter 9   Where Have All the Flowers Gone?

Training made us a tough, battle ready, precision strike force. We were motivated. Eleven hundred and fifty-seven men joined. We accepted all of the *Saquaquom Iron* men who were healthy and physically capable of meeting the demanding requirements of training. That netted us six hundred men. The remainder came from refugees, many from Michigan, but a healthy representation from other states as well.

Aside from the physical testing of Special Operations training, we learned much more about stealth and the quiet techniques of intrusion. I learned that we had made over a dozen mistakes in the *Saquaquom Iron* rescue that could have lost the mission. We were lucky on that one; they weren't expecting us. We would never have that luxury again. All future missions had to be expertly planned and executed.

Creativity in planning the missions became a growing necessity. The Great Lakes were heavily patrolled after the *Mississaugee* incident. The days of freely crossing Lake Huron were over. To get back into the United States we had to employ elaborate disguises. I did my first drag on one of these missions. Matt DuPont worked on the external logistics team and helped me with my outfit. My image as a hyper-masculine tough guy with a scruffy beard had made drag a perfect ruse for getting in and out of the United States. The Canadian intelligence service assisted us in obtaining fake passports. As long as we were not recognized, we were able to cross the borders at will.

I dressed, however, as an older businessman on my second mission. Neatly shaven, drawn wrinkles, grey hair, and a three piece suit gave me the disguise I needed to cross the border. Marc, Jimmy, and Scott all came separately. We crossed at Detroit, supposedly one of the most secure crossings into the United States. My paperwork seemed in order to the U. S. Customs guard, and I remained my car.

I met my team on Woodward Avenue. The *Detroit Institute of Art* had always been one of my favorite place's to visit; I arrived early and enjoyed looking at the artwork. A French Impressionist exhibit was on display; it was particularly nice. Jimmy and Marc arrived together and met me in front of the Diego Rivera mural at the entrance as planned. Scott showed up a few minutes later. Winter was taking hold and it was brisk outside. We walked out of the front of the building facing Woodward Avenue. I looked at the Detroit Public Library across the street. I pointed to it and said, "I've spent many hours conducting research over there. Jimmy asked, "What is that?" I said, "It is the library, but inside is the *Burton Historical Archive*. That is the repository that houses the personal papers of many of Michigan's founding fathers. Lewis Cass, William Woodbridge, Stevens T. Mason; all of their papers are there. They looked bewildered. Jimmy said, "Who the heck are those guys?"

I rolled my eyes and said, "Stevens Mason was Michigan's last territorial and first elected state governor. He is the one who nearly went to war with Ohio over the city of Toledo. William Woodbridge was Michigan's next governor and presided over much of Michigan's early growth. Lewis Cass, probably Michigan's most important historical figure, was a governor, Secretary of War, Senator, and a presidential candidate. As Secretary of War, he negotiated the treaties with the Potawatomies, Chippewas, and Ottawas that ceded most of their lands in Michigan to the United States. Without those cessions, Michigan could never have grown much past Detroit." Scott thanked me for the history lesson.

Detroit had many closed factories, and we knew that there were several that had been taken over by The

Federal Bureau of Protection. At least two of them were being used as detention camps. We had no idea where they were, and our first duty was to find them. Roger's internal logistics team was already in place to sweep the detainees out of the country. Scott grew up in Detroit, so he knew the city well. He knew almost every factory site in town.

He had a hunch that an old *Chrysler* plant off Jefferson Avenue might be a site for one of the camps. It had been a *Dodge* assembly plant. *Chrysler* had closed it in the 1970s when they were near bankruptcy. It had sat there rotting for the last thirty-some years. This was a section of Detroit that was so neglected in the 1990s that street pavement had nearly turned to gravel. In past years I had busted a tie rod on a pothole on the street in front of the plant. When I turned into the area with my team I was shocked to see that the streets were all repaved – definitely the mark of FBP. We drove by and noticed teams of men in orange jumpsuits working as road crew gangs. We had found one of our targets.

We made a brief survey of the area and moved on to find our next target. We drove by every factory between Royal Oak and Dearborn. We found two more that appeared to be FBP working posts, but no camps. I knew there was one more in town, but we seemed not to be finding it. I suggested we go back by *River Rouge* one more time. Something I had noticed had been gnawing at me. Scott said, "*River Rouge* is still an operating *Ford* facility. There can't be anything there." I insisted, so we drove back to it. As we drove by, all the signs said *Ford Motor Company*, and there was no evidence of The Federal Bureau of Protection. The other guys said we should move on and look elsewhere.

We started to leave then Scott noticed something, "There. That cluster of buildings on the right; that was closed and boarded up two years ago. I can't believe that with the auto industry's sales as bad as they are, they would reopen a facility that had been closed for nearly thirty years." Then it hit what had been bugging me. The railroad cars sitting in the yard were livestock cars. A foundry would certainly have no livestock coming in and out of it.

Scott explained to me that the buildings had originally been a steel foundry for *Ford*, but *Ford* closed it in the 1960s. *Genereaux and Sons Machine Works* bought the buildings, refitted them, and reopened the property in the 1970s. That lasted until the company went bankrupt in 1983. After that the buildings were left to ruin.

We stopped at a *Denny's* for lunch across the street and watched for a while. We saw a train of nothing but livestock cars go out. It was empty. I was growing seriously concerned. We left and checked into the *Hotel Ponchartrain* downtown; we had to keep up our businessman image. Marc and Jimmy went to the airport to rent another car. Around midnight we drove back to the *Denny's*. It was a perfect spot for us to watch what was going on at the *Genereaux* plant. Around 12:45 we saw a train come in. Again it was made up entirely of livestock cars, but this one was not empty. I could not tell what was inside, but I could see that it was loaded down. The train pulled into an unloading bay inside a warehouse-like building.

The next night Jimmy, Marc, and Scott went to meet Roger's team to discuss evacuation plans. I should have gone with them, but I had to see what was going on at the *Genereaux* plant. Something wasn't right. I took a laptop with me. *Denny's* did not care if a person sat at a table for hours in the middle of the night, so I pretended to be working and drank way too much coffee. Another livestock train came in about the same time. The last car had a slight chink in the rear siding. I saw a human hand waving out of it. I nearly spewed my coffee. The trains came in full, they left empty, a human hand waved through the car; I concluded that the *Genereaux* plant was an extermination facility. I was unprepared for that realization. I knew Crooks had gone too far, but this was incomprehensible.

I packed up my computer and paid my bill. I went
to Scott's room where everyone was meeting. I knocked on
the door, and Scott let me in. I was visibly shaken. I told
them what I had seen. The others were silent as I described
the hand waving through the siding of the train car.

I said, "This changes everything. We have to
evacuate these camps and permanently close down the
Genereaux extermination facility. Every day we wait, who
knows how many more of our people will die. We have to
act now."

The old *Chrysler* plant would be easy enough to
spring. It was not much more secure than the *Saquaquom
Iron* plant had been. We made contact with the prisoners
there the next night. The conditions were just as bad. The
captives were grateful to see us and promised to be ready to
go two nights later. The problem was that we had no idea if
or how to get into the *Genereaux* plant.

The next morning, we drove to the main rail yard in
Detroit. We dressed as robbers with stocking masks and
overpowered the yard manager. We acted like we were
going to steal some equipment. Jimmy blindfolded and
gagged the manager and put him in a closet so he could not
know what we were doing. Marc and Scott held a security
guard as hostage while we worked. I searched the computer
logs for the trains coming in and out of the *Genereaux* plant.
After several tries I found them. The trains were manifested
as livestock trains. They had come from Toledo,
Indianapolis, Cincinnati, Dayton, and Grand Rapids. I also
found the manifests for the trains scheduled to come into the
Genereaux plant. There was one scheduled for the next
evening to come from Pontiac. It was supposed to stop in
north Detroit to pick up more "livestock." That meant the
Chrysler plant. We could not wait another night.

The yard manager did not seem like the sort of
person who would willingly be a part of genocide. I went to
the closet and un-gagged him. I explained to him, "Look,
I'm not here to steal anything or hurt anyone. I came to see

what was in your computer logs for in and out bound trains."

He exclaimed, "Oh my god, you're a terrorist."

I replied, "No, I'm trying to stop terrorism. Listen to me, what do you know about those livestock trains that keep going into the *Genereaux* plant in Dearborn?"

The yard manager answered, "I don't know what you are talking about."

I lifted up his blindfold enough so he could see the print out I had made of the logs. He thought I was going to kill him now that he had seen my face. I said, "I'm not going to kill you. Look at these logs, don't you see anything odd here? And look at the schedule for tomorrow night. What "livestock" is the Pontiac train going to pick up in north Detroit? Does that make sense to you?"

He answered, "No." He looked perplexed. "Is this something illegal going on? I've never paid attention to the cargo in these manifests. What is this?"

I explained to him, "The cargo is human livestock. They are taking them to be slaughtered."

He turned pale. "You, I recognize you. You are that Joe guy with the Canadian ship and all. How'd you get back into the country?"

I answered, "It's a long story. Can you help us? We have to stop the killing, we need your help."

He replied, "What can I do? I just shuffle trains in and out of here, I don't have any control over what they carry or what they do with their cargo."

I asked, "How about the engineers on these trains, do you know them? Maybe you could get to them or something."

He said, "Those trains are weird. They have their own crews. I think they must work for the Federal Bureau of Protection or something like that."

I nodded, "Yeah, I think they must. Didn't that seem odd, why wouldn't you be concerned about these trains?"

He replied, "In Crooks's America, you don't ask too many questions. It's best to be ignorant. Now I know, and I have to act." He went on to say that he could arrange for a diversion on the Pontiac train. The train had to come through his yard after picking up the prisoners from the *Chrysler* plant. He would order a random inspection of the train; the locomotive would not pass. He would then be required to replace it with another. I put the blindfold and gag back on him and stole some radio equipment to make it look like a real robbery.

In the meantime, Roger's team had gotten a closer look at the extermination facility. There were no prisoners there. Apparently, the prisoners who came in each night were dead and destroyed by the next day. The smoke coming out of the foundry's stacks was not from smelting steel.

The plant had to be destroyed. The Yard manager met us at the *Ponchartrain* that evening before we started our rounds. We told him we needed to load the replacement train with explosives.

The train from Pontiac arrived at the *Chrysler* plant around 10:00 PM. Roger had a member of his team watching the facility who then relayed the information to me. I was back in the rail yard with the yard manager. He had another train in waiting for us that was identical in cars to the one arriving from Pontiac. The "death train," as we called it, arrived in the rail yard a little before eleven. The yard manager had arranged to have a switchman call for a sudden maintenance check. He claimed that the engine appeared to have a leaky wheel bearing.

The engineer and two of his thugs jumped down from the engine and yelled at the switchman, calling him an idiot. The switchman had squirted some oil on one of the wheels. He pointed to it and yelled back at the engineer, telling him that the dripping oil was a tell tale sign of a leaky bearing. They argued a bit, and the yard manager ran down to jump into the fray. He stopped the argument by ordering the engine to the maintenance shop for inspection.

The engineer wheeled around and moaned that the Detroit rail yard was operated by a bunch of idiots.

The manager told him he would provide a replacement locomotive and they would be on their way in no time. He told the engineer to gather his crew and go into the yard building while his switching engineers made the trade. They had to keep the death train's crew occupied for about half an hour while they switched the explosive laden train with the train of human cargo. Each car was packed with enough explosives to destroy a building. The cargo doors were wired so that the triggers would snap upon opening.

As soon as the explosion train was out of the yard, we hooked up another locomotive to the train with the prisoners and headed west towards the airport. We stopped the train at an abandoned steel yard across from the Detroit airport. We had five cars loaded with about twelve hundred men, all in miserable condition and heavily drugged to keep them quiet. It would take three of *IDS*'s jumbo cargo planes to get them out.

Roger had four shuttle buses commandeered to get the prisoners from the rail yard to the airport. It would take eight trips to get everyone boarded. I was a nervous wreck the whole time. I knew that the other train had already arrived at the *Genereaux* plant and was about to light up the sky. The Federal Bureau of Protection could seal off the whole city. After the third trip, the first plane was loaded and took off without incident.

I kept watching the eastern sky. We were close enough to Dearborn and I expected to see a fireball any time. I saw nothing. Then I started worrying that they had somehow found the explosives and disarmed them. Then they would be looking for us.

The shuttles came back for the fourth load. Still no fireball, I gritted my teeth. Then, after they left, I saw a faint red glow on the eastern horizon. In the meantime, we had launched the second plane and were loading the last one.

Scott, Marc, Jimmy, and I were on the last shuttle. The Detroit men were in much worse condition than the *Saquaquom Iron* men had been because they had been marked for extermination. We could not have expected them to do more than walk from a train car to a shuttle and then to the planes. We climbed aboard the plane and began to taxi out to the runway. Roger had arranged for the customs officials at Detroit to have been bribed not to inspect the planes before takeoff. They were under the impression that the planes carried something illegal along the lines of marijuana.

We started to taxi out to the runway, and the plane stopped suddenly. The captain came on the loudspeaker and told us that he had been ordered to stop. He said, "This may be routine, so I don't think there is any call for concern yet."

Roger was on the plane, and I upbraided him, "Couldn't you have gotten more shuttles? We needed to be out of here an hour ago." He told me it was the best he could do and besides the planes needed to have their take-offs spaced out a bit so as to avoid suspicion. I didn't say anything more.

I was certain we would be caught. What a prize that would be for The Federal Bureau of Protection. Why, J. Paul Peterson might even appear in a press conference with my head. I was exhausted. I hadn't slept in three nights and just laid back to close my eyes while we waited to be boarded.

Scott woke me up and said that we were in Canadian air space. I had missed our take off. He explained to me how close we had come to exposure. The bribed customs official had not turned in the falsified inspection report as was required, and his supervisor was going to conduct an inspection himself. The captain insisted to the supervisor that we had already been inspected and were cleared for departure. He told him to call the inspector and ask for the paperwork. The captain frantically told the supervisor that he had perishable cargo and a tight

time schedule. Finally the supervisor relented and cleared
us for take off. That was too close. I told Roger that we
needed to get some kind of infrastructure in place to do a
better job on transportation.

Back in Toronto I met with Foreign Minister
Beckwith to debrief about our mission. The Canadian
government was outraged at learning of the extermination
facility. Beckwith asked me to sit in on a meeting with
several ambassadors from Europe, including Great Britain,
France, Germany, Sweden, and The Netherlands. At first
they were in disbelief. My evidence was sound and my
argument convincing. The Dutch ambassador agreed to
take this information to the war crimes tribunal at The
Hague. The other Europeans offered support in anyway
they could. I thanked them for their sense of justice.

The propaganda from Washington was as expected.
The White House issued statements condemning the
"terrorist attacks in Detroit that dealt a severe economic
blow to Detroit and the state of Michigan." It sounded like
they had no clue as to what had happened in Dearborn. The
rail yard manager had given the death train crew back their
original engine. He told them that the wheel bearing
checked out OK. They crawled back into their locomotive
unaware that the trains had been switched. The yard
manager had then altered the logs to make it appear that the
train had passed through without incident. When the FBP
forensic teams inspected the *Genereaux* plant explosion site,
they could come up with no explanation. It appeared as
though the train had gone from Pontiac to Dearborn without
interruption. As far as they were concerned, the prisoners
had all been killed and their bodies vaporized in the
explosion.

By the time we arrived back in Toronto, the other
two teams had left for missions elsewhere. In between
missions, we always had a two week rest and regroup
period. Harry was busy with his end of operations once
liberated men were inside Canada. He managed getting
temporary identification and visa processing with the

Foreign Ministry. After the Detroit mission, I used my
down time to hunt for a house. I found a stone Cape Cod
about six miles north of downtown. It had plenty of room, a
nice sized library, and private office. It would be perfect for
me to set up my office.

Our elation at establishing a new sense of normalcy
was brief. We both had much work to do if we were to
liberate all the incarcerated gay men inside the United
States. Nevertheless, when I came home from missions, the
most important thing for me was having a day or two with
Harry. While I was away, it was the thought of my family
that gave me the strength to endure the most difficult of
circumstances.

Our teams operated all over the United States.
Their priorities were first to find and destroy the death
camps, then to liberate any prisoners they could. The
missions continued for several more months. The Federal
Bureau of Protection began tightening its forces around the
remaining camps. We lost a strike team in March and knew
we had little time left.

My last mission was in Cincinnati. I had heard
about a particularly heinous death camp operating there. A
man by the name of Mike Kniffen had escaped from it and
found his way to Toronto. He had heard about our Saginaw
mission and clandestinely boarded a freighter at Cleveland
bound for Toronto. Once in port he scurried out of the
cargo hold demanding asylum.

Mike asked Canadian immigration officials if he
could meet "that hunky guy who rescued the *Saquaquom
Iron* men." I met him at the Foreign Ministry office
downtown, and he told me his story. Mike had worked for
an airline at Cincinnati's northern Kentucky airport. He
was a dashing fellow, about 5'8" with brown hair and a
broad chin. He had meaty arms and shoulders resulting
from a softball addiction. Mike had also been a party boy,
following the gay rodeo circuit and all the circuit parties
around the country. He showed up at work the day the
arrests began in Cincinnati the previous August and was

told that his security clearance had been suspended. He was
to go home until further notice. He was bewildered and
drove back to his apartment on Madison Street. When he
pulled in the driveway, FBP personnel were waiting to
arrest him.

The Federal Bureau of Protection had set up a
makeshift camp in an old organ factory. The treatment
there was particularly brutal. He had seen men taken in for
"interrogation" who returned with hands and feet missing.
There was no information The Federal Bureau of Protection
was trying to obtain; this was a torture chamber.
Apparently their goal was to see how much pain a person
could endure before loosing consciousness. He also had
noticed that after the men had been mutilated that they
disappeared altogether after a few days. He had also
noticed the livestock cars coming in and out of the
compound and surmised that there was an extermination
facility nearby.

He decided not to wait his turn. Mike found the
flaws in the security perimeter and crawled out from
underneath a fence the same night we arrived in Sarnia
aboard the *Mississaugee*. He had grown up in Cincinnati
and knew the town well, so he knew how to get around
without being noticed. He made his way back to his
apartment building to discover new residents in his
apartment. Mike had, however, kept a stash of money
hidden behind a loose brick on his patio. He snuck up there
while the residents were sleeping, carefully removing the
loose brick from the mortar. His cash was intact.

Mike hopped a city bus and went to the house of his
best friend, Lucy. She was, according to Mike, his "fag
hag." Lucy had been worried sick about him. She asked
him to stay at her place for awhile. Mike knew that the FBP
would be looking for him and refused, knowing that they
would likely look for him there. He asked her for a shower
and the spare set of clothes he kept there. He told her he
had to get out of the country and needed her help. It was

morning and she said she had to go into the office for about an hour, then could come back and take him wherever.

Mike showered and dressed. He turned on the morning news to see the headline story of the "escape of the *Saquaquom Iron* men." He watched my interview with Mike Lindemann. Lucy came back at the end of the interview and he said, "I have to go to Toronto." She told him they would be looking for him and watching her. There would be no way of getting him across the border or even near a port or border crossing. She had friends who lived on a farm near Akron. He could hide out there for a few weeks then make the attempt.

Lucy's friends, John and Sally, were aging flower children. They owned an organic farm that had recently become quite profitable. They welcomed Mike into their home and promised to do everything possible to help him out. They owned their own delivery trucks and put him to work driving and unloading produce. This was perfect because they had a route that included parts of Cleveland. He could learn his way around the city without arousing suspicion.

Mike watched the ports for five months, waiting for the ice to break in the spring to open the shipping season again. He learned what ships were coming in and going to Toronto. After hearing the story of how we hid 800 men on a freighter, he figured one man could easily hide. Security around the ports was tight, but he watched the people and figured out how to get on board. The ice broke in early March and ships started their runs early. Wearing only a wet suit on the night of his escape he rowed a black dinghy out in the frigid water of Lake Erie to a boat that had passed the mouth of the Cuyahoga River.

The ship had cleared final inspection and was powering up. He had enough time to dive in the water and grab the anchor line. He hung onto it at the water line until the boat was well out of sight. He clambered up to the deck and found his way to a cargo hold. There was only one crewman on deck and Mike evaded detection. He climbed down into the gravel below and waited. He thought about jumping off at the Welland Canal, but was determined to wait for Toronto.

I asked Mike if he had any idea where the death camp was in Cincinnati. He told me there was only one place it could be, and that was in the old slaughterhouse district. There were still plenty of abandoned meat processing plants there.

I asked him to join us on the mission. I told him how dangerous it would be. The Federal Bureau of Protection was passed its apprenticeship and was starting to anticipate our moves. Mike was, however, the only person we had who knew Cincinnati at all and was invaluable. He was happy to join us.

With the usual forged IDs and disguises, we had no trouble getting back into the country. We flew this time and entered at Nashville, Tennessee. There we rented cars and drove to Cincinnati, passing through Louisville, Kentucky first.

Roger was already in Louisville. He could not use *IDS* planes this time for the escape, but could use *IDS* trucks for ground transport through town. There he would make other arrangements for us.

Mike drove Scott and me around Cincinnati to assess the situation first. We drove by the camp where Mike had been interred. Then we went down to the waterfront to see the packing houses. There at the east end of the row on the Ohio River were the gates closed off by FBP guards. A livestock train was coming in. As at *River Rouge*, the train pulled into a covered area for unloading. Then the empty train drove on. The stacks at the plant were bellowing clouds of grim smoke.

Mike became hysterical. I told him we would save as many as possible. He sobbed wondering how many of his friends were fueling the smoke. I told him he could not afford to think about that sort of thing, that we had to be focused on saving the lives that we could.

The main camp was huge. Mike told us that it housed somewhere between two and three thousand men. The trains moved an estimated three hundred men in each load, and the trains ran twice a week. It would take us weeks to empty the camp if that were the case. I had been thinking about something else. Mike had left the facility more than five months earlier. Assuming that the FBP had been able to arrest another ten or twelve thousand men in that time, there could not be more than a thousand left. I did not tell Mike, but we scaled down our logistics.

Each of the camps operated somewhat independently of each other. They received orders from Washington, but rarely interacted with other camps. I hatched an elaborate scheme for taking control of the death camp.

It was operated by no more than twenty guards and a commandant. We went in with a well armed team of our best men. They were to take the camp. They would don FBP uniforms, and the death train crews would suspect nothing. We would receive our nightly shipment of "cargo" and send out the empty trains as usual. In essence, they would bring the prisoners to us.

Our attack unit completed the takeover without incident and dipped the American flag momentarily, our signal to enter the camp. We were unprepared for the gruesome scene we would find. It was early evening and the FBP contingency had almost finished their work from the previous night. Only a few had been on guard and the others were asleep. The crematorium was empty, but blood and body parts littered the floor. We held a brief memorial service and, after photographing the evidence, destroyed the remains.

The train signaled its approach and, as expected, we received our shipment. After the train unloaded and had departed from the facility, I went out to greet the men and told them who I was. They were in disbelief at first. I asked someone to tell me about the status of the main camp. Josh Reynolds saw Mike standing next to me and recognized him. Josh and Mike had traveled the party circuit together and knew each other well. Josh stepped forward and said he could help. He told us there were only 400 men left. He said they had run thousands of men through the camp since Mike had left, but they were all gone. He said the torturing had stopped about a month earlier. That was when they stepped up the movements from the main camp to the death camp. The trains were departing nightly.

We only had two more nights of work to perform. We held the men there at the death camp. It was tight quarters, but for two nights, we could manage. I sent Jimmy and Marc to Louisville to tell Roger to advance the escape date. No doubt, FBP personnel would arrive after the second night to close things down. Planes were out of the question. Although the airport was across the river, getting six hundred men to it at one time was impossible to do without detection.

Roger had arranged for a barge to pick us up at the packing house. From there we would ride down the Ohio River to the Mississippi. At New Orleans we were to move to an ocean going vessel that would take us eventually to Canada. It was no longer possible to get back across the Canadian border, so this was our only possible escape route. When the barge passed through the locks at Louisville, Kentucky, The Federal Bureau of Protection might perform a spot inspection. Roger had it arranged for us to disembark on the east side of town and be ferried to the other side of Louisville in *IDS* trucks. We were to re-board the barge down river passed the locks and the rapids.

We boarded without incident and made our way down river. About two hours later we were at the rendezvous point on River Road, adjacent to a city park. Roger was waiting for us with three *IDS* semi trailers. Scott and I sat up front with the driver of the last truck. We were east of downtown and could barely see the Louisville skyline.

As mid-sized American cities go, Louisville was one of the most striking. Its skyline was dominated by the *Aegon Tower*, which featured a glass dome. At night the dome was lit and could be seen for miles. One of my most important clients, a national liquor distributor, had been based in Louisville. They had signed a contract with the Russian government to import Russian vodka into the United States and sell American made liquors in Russia. They engaged me to advise their marketing department to develop a strategy for selling Kentucky whiskey in Russia.

On my first visit to Louisville I wondered whether it was a sleepy southern town or a bustling mid-western city. Perched at the northern end of Kentucky on the Ohio River, Louisville seemed to be both. Architecturally and culturally it had all the charm of a southern town, but had traffic, entertainment districts, and high quality restaurants that made Chicagoans feel right at home.

Like New Orleans or Charleston it was a fun place to be anytime, but the high point of the year was, without question, *Derby*. The *Kentucky Derby* was an event that put Louisville in the class of cities like New Orleans at Mardis Gras, or San Francisco's Castro District at Halloween. Louisville planned for *Derby* all year long and the events, parties, and festivals leading up to the two-minute horse race lasted for weeks. Women and drag queens spent more money and effort on hats and outfits than most brides spent on their wedding gowns and trousseaus.

No doubt the *Kentucky Derby* was steeped in Southern and English tradition, but it was just as much an excuse to party for the gay community as anyone else. *The Connection*, Louisville's mega-gay complex had a variance from the city to close down the street in front of the building so it could expand bar service and operations. Even that was not enough and the party simply spilled out onto surrounding streets, open container laws evaporating wherever people wandered. By closing time at four in the morning, gay Louisville would be partied-out, at least for the next week.

The *IDS* driver dropped us out in a quiet part of the riparian industrial district near Bell's Lane. The barge came by about an half hour later and we quietly boarded without incident. The rest of the trip was uneventful.

The barge dropped us off near an abandoned warehouse across the river from New Orleans. We could stay in the warehouse until our next ship pulled up alongside. We were fitted with rubber dinghies that we could inflate at the proper time. Our connecting ship was to pull up alongside at night and we were to row to it and be taken aboard. Roger had used this same facility and the dinghies on several rescues from the South.

In fact, there was a rescue from Oklahoma that was going out with us. Our original estimate was to have a total contingent of about twelve hundred. Because our numbers were so reduced from Cincinnati, Roger decided to put a six hundred-man rescue from Oklahoma City with us. I knew a lot of the people in that group. Among them was a young man by the name of Cameron Taylor. Cam was about eight years younger than me, blond, blue-eyed, and Brad Pitt-gorgeous.

In my college days before I met Harry I had a summer fling with Cam. It was one of those wonderful summer romances that make for the best novels. I had earned my journeyman's license and was nearing my twenty-eighth birthday. Cam apprenticed in the electrical shop where I worked. He was not out yet, but knew I was – as did everyone in the shop. One spring morning I had a rather nasty work order. It involved crawling under a house to run a new circuit for a kitchen. The dirt was damp and muddy in the crawl space. I told our dispatcher, Richard, that I needed an apprentice to do the crawling. I told him I would prefer to ask for volunteers rather than assign someone.

Cam volunteered. While driving to the job site, he said, "You're gay aren't you?"

Thinking, "Great a gorgeous redneck," I said, "Yeah. Is there a problem?"

He replied, "No, no problem, but I just, 'er, kind of wanted to talk to you about something."

"OK." I nodded.

He went on, "I think I might be gay too."

I asked him why he "thought" he might be gay. He told me about his desires for men and his lack of desire for women. I told him I thought that sounded pretty gay to me too.

We became instant friends, and I introduced him to a lot people in the community. I had an incredible crush on him, but thought that I was too old to be of interest to a young stud like that. I started noticing that he was assigned to me more frequently than not when I had need of an apprentice. I asked Richard what was going on, and he told me that Cam had bribed him to make sure he was assigned to me as much as possible. I wondered if he needed the security or if something else was going on.

In May we had another job that required crawling under a house. I was up in the house and Cam was underneath trying to drill a hole through the bottom plate to feed a circuit. He told me over the radio that he needed some help, that he was not sure where to drill. I tried to tap on the floor and offer some assistance that way, but he was still not sure where to drill. A little frustrated and angry I told him I would crawl under there and see if I could help.

I crawled up alongside him and said, "OK, what's the problem?" He shined his flashlight in my eyes and said, "Nothing." I was about to launch into a tirade when he planted a kiss on my lips. I was taken aback, but I liked it. I said, "Is this what you brought me down here for?" He said it was. That was the beginning of romance.

For the next three months we were inseparable. He virtually moved into my apartment. I had a vacation coming up in July, and I asked him if he could take off that same week. I had planned to go backpacking in the Rockies. Cam had never done anything like that, but thought it would be great fun. We took off driving through the plains of western Oklahoma, through the panhandle and into Colorado. By nightfall we were in the Rockies and found a quiet spot to set up camp. We spent the week climbing mountainsides, hiking through dense forests, and making love.

In another four weeks he was to leave for graduate school in another state. We had agreed that our summer fling would end in August. As September neared, though, I could not help how much I had fallen in love with him.

The week before Cameron's departure he spent back at his apartment packing and boxing what he needed to send either to storage or to school. He would depart on a Sunday in the middle of August and spent that last weekend with me. I told him how much I loved him and begged him to let us continue some kind of relationship. He refused, convinced that a long distance relationship was impossible. I behaved terribly, and finally, late Saturday night, rather than prolong the agony, he left. We never spoke again, though I had heard from some mutual friends that he had moved back to Oklahoma after I moved to Michigan.

I would not have recognized him in that warehouse in New Orleans. My team and our rescue party were already there. I was talking with Roger about where these people in Oklahoma had originated when they arrived. They unloaded, looking like the usual waifs we rescued everywhere we went. I saw someone with long blond hair and a filthy tangled beard staring at me. I thought he might be a crazy. Then he made his way over. We scarcely had more light than the moon provided through the gaps in the roof, but I could see his eyes. They looked familiar. I expected it to be someone I knew, but when he spoke my name, I was stunned.

I grabbed hold of him and hugged him. I said, "Cam! Thank God you're alive!"

Scott saw what was going on and came over to investigate. I introduced them and told Scott that Cam had, at one time, been the love of my life. I told Cam about Harry. Cam said he had heard I had gotten married. I told him he would get to meet Harry in Toronto.

We had to wait quite a while for our boat. Cam and I sat in the doorway looking across at the city lights of New Orleans. I told him about the times Harry and I had spent there. Cam had never been to New Orleans and wished he could go across to see what it was all about. I told him as much as I could remember about the city. The thing I remembered most was the food. When people talk about the "flavor" of New Orleans, they really mean the food. It is unique and distinctive and it cannot be reproduced anywhere else. Sure, I bought all kinds of Cajun and Creole spices and followed the recipes, but nothing tasted exactly the same. I've been to "New Orleans" style restaurants all over the east coast, but outside Louisiana, it just isn't quite right. The best meal I had there was in the French Quarter. I don't remember the name of the place. In New Orleans a person simply wanders the street until finding himself in a restaurant. Harry and I found one on Chartres, near Jackson Square. I had Cajun crab-stuffed gulf shrimp seasoned perfectly. Even years later, I could still imagine the taste of that delightful meal.

The *Vergulde Dreack*, a Dutch merchant ship, slowed as it approached the dock. That was our signal to launch the dinghies. It only took five trips to get everyone on board. Cam stayed with my team. The ship had passed its last inspection and was ready to sail into the Gulf of Mexico. From there we would go to the Bahamas where we would transfer to a passenger ship bound for Montreal.

It took almost two days to reach the Bahamas. Though we had to ride down below in the cargo hold, the Dutch had fitted out cleverly disguised sleeping quarters for us. Scott and I shared a bunk; I took the upper. I awoke in the middle of the night and looked over to the upper across the aisle from me. Cam lay there staring at me with a grin on his face. As though it had been the day before, I remembered awakening to the same vision so many years before.

I closed my eyes thinking that without his face in front of me I could regain control of my faculties. After a

few minutes I felt the bunk shaking. I opened my eyes and
Cameron was crawling into my bed. I whispered, "What
are you doing? I can't do this. I am in a relationship!"

He kissed my forehead and whispered, "Don't
worry, I'm not going to molest you, but I just wanted to be
next you one more time."

He pressed his lips against mine, and I melted. For
a moment I was in Oklahoma City on a hot summer day.
Holding Cameron in my arms seemed so natural, so normal.
Our rock-hard cocks rubbed together with our briefs as the
only barrier, and I felt myself losing control. In a moment
of passion we rolled around and I ended up on top of him. I
felt his legs begin to wrap around my waist, and I knew I
was in trouble.

Suddenly I felt a thump from underneath. Scott
loudly whispered, "Joe! Settle down. I can't sleep with all
the commotion."

I pulled off Cameron and whispered back to Scott,
"Sorry, I was kind of restless."

I wrapped my arms around Cameron and we lay
motionless until Scott started to snore. Cameron whispered,
"I could give you a blow job instead?"

I whispered back, "No. You are going to lie here
quietly until we are sure Scott is sound asleep. Then you
are going back to your own bunk."

I woke up a few hours later and my arms were still
wrapped around Cameron. I reached down and felt my
crotch; it was still dry, and my dick was safely inside my
briefs. I gently roused Cameron and made him go to his
own bunk.

The next morning we were eating at a makeshift
mess table, and Scott said, "I'm exhausted. I didn't sleep a
wink last night."

I was mortified and said, ". . . but I heard you
snoring several times."

Scott smiled and said, "I had hoped you would
think I was asleep. Otherwise you would never have gotten
rid of Cameron."

I said, "You shit. Why didn't you intervene?"

Scott replied, "I did and just at the right moment, too. What are you going to do now?"

I retorted, "What do you mean, what am I going to do?"

Scott elaborated, "What are you going to do about this Cameron character? Is he going to end up with us in Toronto and a continual distraction for you? How is Harry going to deal with this?"

I scowled, "Cameron caught me off guard last night. He's already broken my heart once, and he is not going to have that opportunity again. I have no idea whether he is going to Toronto, Montreal, or some other city, but regardless, he is not going to become a distraction. You know how I feel about Harry. I am not doing that sort of thing."

Scott parsed his lips, "You came awfully close last night."

I said, "Look. Whether you had thumped on the bunk or not, I think I would have had my wits enough to know when to stop."

Scott asked, "So you were in complete control?"

I shook my head, "No."

Scott said, "Then you need to stay away from this Cameron. He is nothing but trouble."

I got up from the mess table and went topside. I rang for the captain, and he invited me up to the bridge for an update. We were on schedule.

I went down to my bunk and Cameron was in his bunk. I told him we would be in port in about six hours. I talked nervously about Harry in hopes Cameron would get the message.

After a few minutes of my prattling, Cameron said, "Joe, I am sorry about last night. It was a weak moment for both of us. I've spent so much of the last year in shear terror. Suddenly there you were in the moonlight at New Orleans. I remembered how you had helped me out of the closet years ago, and then you were there to rescue me. I

was madly in love with you all over again. Yes, I am
jealous of Harry. I wish I could push him aside, but I love
you too much to interfere with your happiness. It won't
happen again. Please accept my apology."

When Cameron was done, I realized that Scott was
standing next to our bunk. He said to Cameron, "Joe Kelly
is responsible for rescuing thousands of men, who are safely
in Canada right now. I hope you meant what you just said,
because I won't sit quietly by and let you or anyone else
tarnish his armor."

The Bahamas had become a weigh station in our
Underground Railroad network. The northern borders of
the United States were sealed and impermeable, but one
could always slip out through the southern waterways.
Besides, the Canadian government wanted to take a much
lower profile in all of this. The tone from the United States
was increasingly hostile towards Canada, and the Prime
Minister thought it best not to agitate Speaker Crooks any
more than necessary. We were no longer issuing press
releases or participating in television interviews. We had
made our point, and we had saved many gay men inside the
United States.

The *Vergulde Dreack* moored at harbor after ten
o'clock, in the Bahamas. We disembarked under cover of
night and took shuttles quietly to hotels that the Bahamian
government had reserved for us. I noticed a small group
waiting for us on the dock. Harry was among them. I was
elated, but surprised. He was supposed to be in Toronto.

This time, instead of waiting for all the liberated
prisoners to disembark first, I ran down the gang plank and
into Harry's arms. It had been almost two months since I
had seen him. I asked him why he was there, and he said
that some things had changed during my absence. We
would be going back to Toronto, but all the newly liberated
men were headed for Europe. He was there to manage their
processing.

Harry's job was to get the men ready for integration
into a new society. They would undergo a routine medical

exam, be given a new set of clothes, a passport for their destination country, and tickets to board a cruise liner bound for wherever they were going.

We were to stay on Grand Bahama Island for two days until our ship arrived. Harry explained to me that it had grown too dangerous to continue bringing escapees into Canada. Countries in Europe and the Americas had offered to receive the men instead. I could not believe things had gone so awry in my absence. Harry's responsibilities in managing the receiving end of escapees had grown as a result of other countries' involvement. He had to learn over a dozen passport systems, along with gaining conversational fluency in two new languages. The unfortunate thing about both of us being in the Bahamas at the same time was that my work was done, but Harry's was just beginning. He had almost two thousand men to process.

Cam stayed at a nearby hotel with the other Oklahoma escapees. Scott and I walked over to Cam's hotel the next day while Harry was at work, Scott grumbling the whole way. I was pleased to find out that the Oklahoma boys were to board the *Queen Mary II* bound for Southampton. I told him they deserved it. They were to leave the next day.

I walked Cameron to the *QMII* the next morning. I hugged him. He smiled and said, "Well Joe, at least you're not so broke up about my leaving this time."

I told him to let me know somehow where he was and if he had to leave England. Otherwise, I would find a way to keep in touch. Scott walked with me back to the hotel. We had lunch and wondered how Allen was holding out in Toronto with the rest of us in the Bahamas. We had two more days before our departure; Scott and I spent our days on the beach. Harry had to work through the last day. I offered to help, but he told me I would have no idea what to do, and he had no time to train me.

We boarded the *Paradise*. It was a nice ship, but nothing like the *QMII*. The *Paradise* stopped in Bermuda for a few days. We rented bikes and rode around the island together. Bermuda was much quieter than the Bahamas, and Harry and I found ourselves using the time to have a bit of a second honeymoon. We visited some of the old forts and went scuba diving in the coral reefs. In the sunlight shining through the water I could see Harry's face in a distance while he gazed at a large clam. The clam was a fluorescent blue with bright green stripes. Harry beamed at the beauty of his find. That was why I was fighting.

Chapter 10   Stormy Weather

We were back in Canada a week later. I was unprepared for what greeted my return. We had to cease all operations. During my two month absence one mission in Harrisburg came close to total failure, and in Sacramento six men, including the commander, Ben Goodwin, had been killed. The Federal Bureau of Protection had learned to anticipate our actions, and security at every detainee camp was catching up with our tactics.

Along with the operational issues, the U. S. government took a more hostile approach towards the Canadian government. I understood why Cameron's group was sent to England. Canada needed to be less obvious in these operations. Trade across the border had come to a virtual halt and both sides had gunboats patrolling their respective borders on the Great Lakes. It was like 1812.

I tried to figure out a way to reverse the situation and get our operations up and running again. The Canadian government offered additional tactical training for our strike teams. The Canadians also worked with other countries to provide equipment and weapons; they did not want anything traced back to Canada. Even still, two months passed, and we had no hope of resuming operations anytime soon.

Early one morning in late summer I received a call from the Foreign Ministry. A man from the Toronto office, Oscar Wilke, called and wanted me to meet him at the airport right away. They had someone in custody who claimed to know me. Mounted Police had picked him up near the Canadian/U. S. border in the west. The Foreign

179

Ministry thought he was a spy. I dressed, kissed Harry and left for the airport. Oscar met me there with two Mounted Policemen. He said the plane was coming in from Vancouver and would arrive shortly.

Wilke would tell me nothing about whom I was to meet. I thought it all rather strange. We walked to the government terminal. The waiting area was in a glass building on the ground. It was another forty-five minutes before the mystery plane arrived.

Finally a small Mounted Police jet pulled up and parked on the tarmac. The door opened and the stairs set down. A group of men descended the stairs. One was in a suit, two were Mounted Police, and the third was wearing jeans and a t-shirt. Wilke said nothing. I stood up and looked at them as they turned towards the building. I could not believe what I was seeing and exclaimed, "Stormy!"

Wilke looked at me and said, "What was that?"

I said, "Stormy! Bob Fenton. Where did you find him?"

Wilke inquired, "Are you sure? How long has it been since you've seen him?"

"Of course I'm sure. Let's see, it's been about twenty-two years. Damn, he still looks good."

"If it's been that long, how can you be so sure it's him? Memories can be tricky after a while."

Then it dawned on me what this was all about. They needed me to be certain. I said, "Look. I had an affair with this man and he was my best friend. I know who that is. It's Stormy, Bob Fenton."

Wilke thanked me.

I asked, "How did you get him out of the United States? I thought the borders were pretty much sealed right now. Why is he coming from Vancouver? Why did you think he was a spy?"

Wilke went on, "That's why we needed your confirmation. We found him naked and wandering around the mountains in British Columbia just across the border. He claimed he had just escaped from a detention camp and had made his way through the mountains. His story was rather strange. We thought either he was a lunatic or a spy. After intense interviews, he seemed lucid enough, so we concluded he was a spy. We were either going to repatriate him or put him in prison. He spoke of you and gave details about you that we thought too personal. So we needed to know."

By that time Stormy walked through the door and I rushed up to him and we embraced. I said, "My God Stormy, you look great. You've hardly aged in twenty years."

He replied, "You have no idea how good you look right now. If you hadn't recognized me . . ."

"Of course I'd recognize you anywhere. Why the first site of that bushy mustache that used to tickle my balls, . . ." The MPs cleared their throats. I looked over at them, "Sorry." "So Stormy, how did you get out of the country? No one can get across those borders."

"It's a long story. I'll tell you all about it once we're out of here."

Wilke interrupted us with some official business. He gave Stormy some temporary papers and released him to my custody until he could be processed properly. I told them I would put him up for awhile.

We walked out of the airport and to the parking garage. I hit the remote to deactivate the alarm and unlock the doors, and Stormy remarked, "Woooo, a Beemer *M*6. Man I've wanted a six series for a long time. If I'd known you had one, I'd have been on your doorstep a long time ago."

"Yeah well, I don't take in gold diggers, and you would have had someone to fight with about that."

"I figured you were married by now. How long?"

"Nineteen years."

"Wow, you didn't waste much time. What's he like; is he a hottie, no doubt?"

"I certainly think so. You probably will too, but keep your hands off of both of us. He tends to be kind of the jealous type."

"I bet he'll be thrilled to have your ex-fuck buddy staying for a few days."

"Yeah, well, I'll deal with that when we get home. It might be a good idea for you to give me some time with him right after we get home. Hey, are you hungry?"

"Yeah, I ate on the plane this morning, but it wasn't much. I don't have any money though."

"My treat."

I called Harry and told him I would be late and that I was bringing a guest home to spend a few days. He asked me who it was, and I said it was a surprise. I knew he would hit the roof, so I figured I would wait until I was there in person to receive the full horror of it.

I took Stormy to a quiet sandwich shop on the way home. I said, "I think I told you about meeting Harry. It was when I was finishing school, and we moved to Michigan right away. With getting settled in and starting a new relationship and a new job, it was too difficult to do much else. I always hated the fact that you and I lost touch. I figured you probably hated me by now. So what's been happening in your life? Last I knew you were still in Phoenix. What happened since then, how did you get out of the country, and why did you know to use my name?"

He began, "I left Phoenix soon after you moved to Michigan. You probably couldn't have tracked me down even if you had tried. I decided to get into computers and took some programming courses. That was when it was easy to get a job in the Valley, so I moved to San Jose. I did well like most people there and got sucked into the trap of thinking we were creating a new world order where peace and justice would rule. I made and spent too much money, but had a hell of a good time.

"San Francisco is only an hour away, so on Fridays, I often took off for the city. I had some buddies in San Jose and we went in together and rented a hotel suite downtown. We would go into the Castro or over to the Eagle and pick up a bunch of horny guys and have a weekend-long orgy.

"I met a guy, his name was Randy. He was an ex-priest. He had moved to the Bay from somewhere in the Deep South. He and I dated for a while, but it ended up more like what you and I used to do; we were good friends and we liked to screw. There was nothing more to it. I never really settled down. I guess I'm not the type, or I haven't found the right guy yet. Or, maybe, I let the right guy go a long time ago."

There was nothing I could say. He continued, "Towards the end of the nineties, I woke up from my decadence and realized what was happening to my way of life. I knew it was unsustainable and I could see that the economy was about to take a nosedive. I scaled down my lifestyle and started saving, and I started looking for a new job. The lay-offs were already starting at other companies and I didn't want to be next.

"In 1999, I found a new job with a small IT firm in Seattle. I sold everything and moved only what I could carry in a suitcase. After I got there, I thought about all the things you and I used to do together. I missed the hiking and backpacking, going for long runs in the country, and camping out in the wilderness.

"Whenever I could get a long weekend, I took off for Idaho or Montana. Sometimes I took a friend,

sometimes I went alone. I always thought about you.
Sometimes I climbed to the top of a mountain and shouted
as loud as I could, "Joe, I'm here; c'mon up." I would sit
and wait for up to an hour, fantasizing that you would soon
climb up the other side, and we would make love on the
mountain top.

"I dated someone for awhile. His name was Carl.
He was about half my age. He enjoyed the outdoors stuff,
and I deluded myself into thinking it could work, but
children do grow up and need to leave daddy behind.

"It was about that time that I began to realize how
much I missed you. I had the best thing in the world, and I
couldn't see it. Joe, I'm not telling you this to make you
feel bad, and I am glad you have Harry. I would never
dream of coming between you two, but I love you and I
always will. I love you for what you gave to me, and I hope
I can find someone like you again."

I put my hand on his, "Stormy, I will always love
you too, for all those same reasons. We weren't ready yet,
neither one of us was. If we had tried to force something,
we probably would have ended up hating each other. We
needed time and space from the fucked up religious
mentality we had lived with for so long."

He continued, "I suppose, but I wish we had stayed
closer. I spent so much time, especially in the summer, in
those mountains between Washington and Montana that I
learned them like second nature. That is the only reason I
am here now."

I asked, "How so?"

"I didn't leave the country before Crooks closed the
borders. I kept thinking that things would calm down and
some sense of reason would prevail."

I was stunned, "Geez, if I had been able to talk with
you then, I would have screamed at you until you left the

country. I hounded all my friends to leave. Many of them did, even though they thought I was a nut case."

He continued with his story, "I'm not the historian you are, and I couldn't see it coming. After the borders reopened with exit monitoring, and things started getting so crazy, I decided to try to leave. I took my laptop, and dressed in a business suit. I bought a ticket for Calgary. I thought if I looked like a business traveler, they would leave me alone. I didn't realize I was in all of their databases. I was arrested at the airport and taken immediately to a work camp in Spokane.

"From what I've heard about the other work camps, ours wasn't so bad. We really were there to work, menial though the tasks were, and they fed us palatable food. Most of us were from the Seattle area, though after awhile, some new guys started to arrive from other parts of the country, like Utah and Colorado. I thought about Rob and Dean and wondered if they might show up. I never saw them though.

"We were building things for the military. Part of our operations were stamping shell casings, and part for rifle assembly parts. I'm not sure about the rest, but there were a lot of things going on there. We were not abused, though we worked eighteen hour shifts – slave labor, of course.

"About a month ago, some important looking guys from The Federal Bureau of Protection toured the facility. They watched us working and punched some kind of information into their hand-held devices. A few days later they pulled about thirty of us out of work to interview us. I had no idea what they wanted, but it was nice to sit down for twenty minutes. They asked us some questions about our physical strength and health. I never tried to give those guys too much information, but I am in great shape and it shows. I told them I would be healthier with a hot shower every morning and a shorter work shift. They thought that was funny and laughed. Then the little FBP Nazi that was interviewing me told me that I would be moving to a new facility. He said it would seem like a country club compared to where we were then. We would not be required to work long hours, and we would have a gym, a pool, and well rounded meals.

"I knew there had to be a catch, but so far I hadn't seen it. Without sounding too interested, I thought it would be worth a try. I really hated where I was, and perhaps a change would give me an opportunity to escape.

"They loaded us on a bus. The windows were painted over so we couldn't see out, but I scratched a small enough hole so I could see. We were headed west into the mountains. I knew exactly where we were the whole way. Our final stop was a new camp that had been set up in the mountains as a training facility for the new FBP Elite Forces.

"During our orientation, they told us about you and how you were releasing terrorists like us from prison and endangering America. We were there to help with the training. Someone back in Washington got the bright idea that it would be best to train these "Elite Forces" with real live homosexuals. We were to be used for target practice. They brought in about 150 men altogether from all over the country. They were all in excellent physical condition and would give the trainees a most difficult challenge.

"They would take us one at a time and let us go out in the wild like in a fox hunt. The "fox," as we called him, would have a twelve hour head start. He would be provisioned with a backpack loaded with a watch, a compass, a knife, raingear, a shovel, a mess kit, matches, and all kinds of worthless things one wouldn't need if he were truly trying to save his life. I think the whole point was to load him down so that he would tire easily. The rule was if he could survive out there for seventy-two hours, he would be allowed to live and go back to the camp until his number came up again. The rest of us were to stay there and work-out, swim, and eat, so we could be in top condition to put up a good challenge.

"I had no intention of dying in the mountains or of coming back to the camp to go for another round. The first three guys out were killed within twenty-four hours. The next one made it through his third day. Everyone cheered when he came back. I was next.

"I never let on like I knew anything about where we were. In fact, we were at an old campsite I had used for a staging area for some mountain climbs. I knew exactly where we were, about ninety miles from the Canadian border.

"They loaded me down with the backpack and set me loose at 6:00AM. I took a southeasterly direction away from the camp. That led me up a hill right away over to a mountain stream I knew well. I stopped at the top of the hill to look back, I was only an hour into my journey. I looked at the camp below and thought about how those bastards had ruined a place that had represented peace and serenity for me. I only lingered a moment. I had no time to spare.

"I quickly ran down the hill to the stream. There was plenty of water. The trainees brought dogs with them, so I knew they would be tracking my scent. I hiked upstream. I criss-crossed the stream several times to confuse the dogs. Then I went off into the woods and stripped all my clothes off. I took my knife and sliced my finger to draw some blood. I rubbed it into my clothing and then took the bread out of the backpack and broke it into pieces, rubbing it into my clothing as best as I could. I put the remnants of the loaf back in the pack and tossed the other articles from it randomly in a clearing. I took the compass and the knife. That was all I really needed to elude my would-be assassins.

"I found a good log that would float and launched it in the stream. The current was strong, so all I needed was a good stick to guide my makeshift canoe. I was well past the trail I had taken down the hill after six hours from the start. I still had six hours to put some distance between them and me.

"I followed the stream to its northern most point, about ten miles closer to Canada. There I left the log to continue on its way, while I headed due north into the woods. I knew a motel that was nearby on the main highway. It was after midnight. The inn was full so I darted around the parking lot hoping not to be noticed. There was someone's cherry 1964 *Pontiac Bonneville* in the parking lot. I knew those cars were a breeze to steal, so I took my pocket knife, jimmied the lock and quietly rolled it away from the rooms. Once closer to the street, I stuck my knife in the ignition like a key and started her up. I could tell someone had taken good care of it. I didn't want to do any more damage than was necessary.

"I had seventy miles to go, hoping that the owner hadn't awakened and called the police. I drove to within ten miles of the border and turned onto a dirt road that went east parallel with the border. I drove to a mountain I had hiked many times. It straddled the U. S. Canadian Boundary. It was too rugged for The Federal Bureau of Protection to have installed electronic border monitors. It was the only place I knew for sure that I could cross without being detected.

"I then had about forty-eight hours to get across before all hell would break loose. I jimmied the lock to the trunk and, sure enough, there was an emergency blanket. This was as much an emergency as I could imagine. I took that and an emergency kit with some rope, flairs, and matches. I cut some pieces off the blanket to tie around my feet. I knew it would be cold on the mountain and there was always the potential for frostbite. I wrapped myself as best as possible and started climbing.

"It was slow climbing. The grade is steep, and even with proper gear and boots it is about a four hour climb. This time it took me ten hours. I sat at the peak exhausted. One more step and I was in Canada. I walked down the Canadian side a bit and decided to lie down to rest for a few minutes. I slept through the rest of the night.

"I gathered my stuff and ran down the mountain as fast as I could. In the meadow below there was a cluster of small farms. I was starving and thirsty. I ran to the first one and banged on the front door. A startled elderly woman screamed when she saw me. My blanket was tattered, and it was impossible to shield completely my manhood. I told her, "Please call the police." She slammed the door and did just that. It was several hours before the Mounties arrived. I sat on her front porch and asked her for some food.

"There was dead silence for about twenty minutes then she came to the door, "You step away from the porch for a moment. I am going to set something out the door for you. Don't you dare make a move for it until I close the door and you hear the bolt slam." I did exactly as she asked. She sat a plate out with three farm fresh eggs, over easy, four pancakes smothered in fresh butter and maple syrup, and two sausages.

"I sat down and devoured what seemed like a heaven-sent meal. I thanked her over and over again through the door. After about the third time, she answered back, "You're quite welcome. I don't know what kind of trouble you are in, but I can't stand to see a young man like you starve to death." I tried to explain to her that I really wasn't a bad person, but that I had escaped from the United States. She didn't say another word.

"The mounted police arrived before noon. I explained to them what had happened. They seemed dumfounded. They first tried to treat me like I was a lunatic, but then they realized I was quite sane. Then they started interrogating me. At that point I demanded asylum. I knew they had to respond and take me to Foreign Ministry officials.

"They gave me these clothes at the Foreign Ministry office in Vancouver. I was allowed to shower, shave, and eat supper. They didn't want to believe my story. I think it seemed too far fetched for them. Besides, they had no idea that a concentration camp was barely across the border. Because I knew you had been leading rescue missions to the United States, I asked for you. I told them you were my friend and could verify who I was. As soon as I mentioned the name of Joe Kelly, they ran out of the room. They came back about thirty minutes later and said that we would check out my story together. I smiled and told them that I thought that was a great idea.

"They put me up in a comfortable room for a few hours so I could get some rest, heavily guarded though. We had to leave at two in order to be here by ten o'clock. I slept more on the plane. So that's my story, Joe, what do you think?"

I pulled my eyeballs back into my head and said, "That's amazing Stormy. I am always shocked at the actions of Crooks and his pack of hoodlums. Each time I think I've heard the worst, another story comes along that makes their previous low point of depravity seem not so bad. Thank God you got out alive." I smiled a bit, "Providence. It is God's Providence that you were put in a camp where you knew how to get out and come here to tell the story. Do you think even Pastor Stan could draw any other conclusion than that?"

Stormy appreciated the irony of the situation. It was the fundamentalist Biblical teachings we heard back in Oklahoma City twenty some years earlier that instilled in us a strong sense of moral outrage at the wanton destruction of human life. Yet, it was those same people who took their narrow interpretations of Scripture to such an extreme that devalued the lives of gay men, making this holocaust possible.

Harry called to find out how much longer we would be. I told him we would be home in fifteen minutes. On the way home, I asked Stormy if he thought we were the only ones from our little Presbyterian church that were fighting against the Crooks regime. We speculated about Brad, the Hammonds, and Brian.

We walked in together and I introduced Stormy to Harry. I told him Stormy had escaped from a camp in northern Montana. I said, "You've heard me talk about Stormy. We were friends some years ago." Harry asked me to help him with something upstairs. I knew what was coming and told Stormy to make himself at home, help himself to the refrigerator, or anything else. Harry said, in a somewhat icy tone, "Yeah, help yourself to *anything* in the house."

Harry didn't like the idea of Stormy staying with us. I assured him that whatever I had with Stormy was long gone and I cared for him only as a friend. Harry kept trying to turn things around and wondered what we had been doing for the previous two hours. After an half hour, Harry relented, "You know that I trust you and know you wouldn't do anything that would destroy our marriage. I need to remind you from time to time of how I would react if you ever strayed." We hugged and went back downstairs.

Stormy had the look of a scared puppy dog on his face. Harry went up to him and said, "I understand you've had a rather frightening experience. I want you to know that we are here to help you in anyway we can." Stormy thanked him for his hospitality. I asked Harry how long it would be for dinner, and he said he had a roast in the oven and it would be several hours. I told him Stormy had no clothes and no money. He suggested we all go shopping together. We did, and Stormy acquired a modest, but nice wardrobe.

The next morning, Stormy awakened Harry and me with breakfast in bed. He had made a stack of pancakes and found Martha Voeglin's Michigan maple syrup. Stormy was wearing his boxers and a kitchen apron he had found in the drawer. It was one Harry and I had picked up in New Orleans. It had a crawfish on the front that read, "Shut up and Suck it!" Harry said, "Hmmm, the only thing you missed was the bud vase for our tray." Stormy said, "Damn, hang on." He disappeared for a few moments and returned with a bud vase with three fresh roses. He had forgotten to put them on the tray.

Harry noticed Stormy's attire and remarked to me that he did not blame me one bit for having had an affair with him. He said, "If he looks that good now, I can imagine twenty years ago." I told him I would dig out some pictures later.

Stormy came back into the room and asked, "After your food has had time to settle, how about if we all go out for a run together?" I told him Harry was not a runner, but I was still at it. I had a great path I followed for my six mile runs.

It was like old times. We were both shirtless and still catching attention as we ran through the neighborhoods. Stormy asked me what I thought would happen. He was aware that tensions between Canada and the United States were getting worse. He wondered if we could do anything about the two camps he had left. I told him I definitely wanted to shut down the death camp, but was not sure if it was even possible. I told him I would call the Foreign Minister to see if we could do anything. Stormy speculated that he was probably the only one who could have gotten out alive. Even those that survived a thirty-six hour ordeal would eventually be killed. I told him that it was the policy of the Crooks government to murder homosexuals. Even the ones in the worker camps would eventually be killed. None were safe across the border.

I told Stormy I needed to spend some time with Harry in the afternoon. I took him downtown so we could shop for ourselves awhile. I told Harry that I wanted to do one more mission. On that he blew a gasket, "You told me the last one was the end. This is never going to end is it?"

I told him it could only end when Crooks and his cronies were in jail. I told him I doubted if the Canadian government would allow us to do another run, but I had to try.

Harry cried a bit, "I get so worried when you are gone. The last time I heard nothing for two months. I thought something had happened to you."

I told him this one would be fast, in and out. We would not be going deep in the country, just across the border and back. He replied, "Why won't you let me go? You know I am perfectly capable of handling the physical requirements. I could outlast some of those twinks you've taken on other missions."

I said, "Harry, we go through this every time. I risk everything when I make these runs. The only thing that keeps me going is in knowing that you are home safe, and that no matter what happens to me, you will be alive and well. If you were there with me, I would be more focused on you than with the mission. That's when I'd screw up and get caught. I have to know that I can come home to you."

As usual, Harry gave in, but more reluctantly than normal. I thought, "Good. That puts even more pressure on me to succeed." I called the Foreign Ministry and asked for a meeting with Minister Beckwith. They said he was going to be in Ottawa for several days, and if it was important, that I should go to Ottawa. I packed up Harry and Stormy and we took off for the national capital. I scheduled a meeting with Beckwith the next morning at 10:00 AM. Harry took Stormy sight seeing, but I told them to keep a cell phone handy and not to go too far in case I needed to call Stormy into a meeting.

Beckwith was completely unreceptive to the idea of another mission. He said, "As it is, the United States is looking for an excuse to declare war on Canada. Another mission, especially a cross border raid, would give them all the excuse they need. I cannot risk the fate of Canada to save a few hundred lives. I explained to him about the "fox hunts." He thought Stormy might have embellished the story a bit. I suggested getting a spy in there to investigate the matter. He agreed. I called Harry and told him to bring Stormy to the Foreign Ministry building right away.

We next met with Nelson Green, head of covert operations for the Foreign Ministry. Green had all the necessary maps handy. Stormy gave precise coordinates so they could locate the camp and the best way to get within observation range without being detected. After we were done there I went back to pester Minister Beckwith again. He pleaded with me to drop it. He knew Prime Minister McConihe would likely order the mission to go forward. Beckwith was convinced that this would be the mission that would start a war. I argued from the standpoint of the human rights case being developed at The Hague. I told him if we could get good photographs of the camp's operations and some concrete evidence of the horrors perpetrated there, it would strengthen the case. He told me I should have been a lawyer, that my skill at argument was immutable. He said, "Alright, let's get the reconnaissance done, and then we'll get the mission under way." I thanked him and bid my adieu.

Stormy was pleased. Harry still wanted to go along. He said he would be a lot more supportive if he could participate in some manner. As Harry and I normally do when at impasse, we compromised. We would have little Canadian support, and this mission would require a large number of operatives. I told Harry to lead the support team on the Canadian side of the border. He was alright with that. At least he would see me as soon as I came back and would be close if something happened.

I called Pete McHenry as soon as we got back home; he was my second in command of strike teams. I told him I might have a mission in the next few days for about three hundred of the best men we had. He replied, "I'll pull the best of the *Saquaquom Iron* Men together. You sure you don't need a few more?" I said I might.

The next few days were spent putting teams together. Pete brought the men we would need to a government training base for Special Operations. Stormy handed out maps marked with the routes we would follow. Roger was already in contact with *IDS* to pick up some trucks in Spokane. He also had the trucks on the Canadian side of the border ready to handoff to Harry's team.

Our goal was to do the strike without making the Canadian government suspect. All of our equipment was supplied by the Russian Army, a little something I was able to bring to the mission. By day three we were as ready as we could be until we heard back from Agent Green.

Harry, Stormy, and I were eating dinner around seven when Agent Green called. He told us to get our things together and head to the airport. When we got to Vancouver, Green met us with the spies who had done the observation. They confirmed everything Stormy had told them, but had one surprise for us. They had arrived in time to watch a "fox" set loose with his provisions. The victim wandered around the outside of the camp for about an hour trying to figure which way to go, he finally started heading up the mountain where they were stationed. They watched the whole spectacle. After eight hours, instead of the required twelve, twenty trainees came out with their dogs. They headed straight up the mountain where the fox was headed.

The spies could not stand to watch someone gunned down in cold blood, so they decided to perform a rescue. They ran down and grabbed the boy; he was scarcely twenty-one. At first he thought he had been captured by the trainees and started to scream. They pointed to the maple leaf on their uniforms. They stripped him down, shredded his clothes, sliced his finger to smear blood on the clothes, and whisked him on out of site. They left a miniature radio transmitter in a nearby tree.

They listened as first the bear came and devoured the bread and further shredded the clothing. Then, about an hour and a half later, the death squad arrived. They examined what was left of the clothing and backpack and radioed into the camp. They told their commander that the Grizzly must have beat them to it again. The Canadians whisked the kid back to Canada.

When the kid, his name was Cole Hardy, saw Stormy he rushed up to him and said, "Stormy, we thought you were dead. They told us you had ventured too far away from camp and had been killed by a bear. I guess you made them think that, huh?"

Cole wanted to go back with us to liberate the rest of the camp, but I firmly said no. He was disappointed, but I figured he had the rest of his life to get over it. I whispered to Stormy, that I thought Cole was sweet on him. Stormy blushed a bit and thought that was silly.

With the logistics we had in place, our plan was to get in and back out in less than seven hours. Harry took us in *IDS* trucks to "grandma's house," the name we gave to the elderly woman who had fed Stormy. She was thrilled to help us out when she found out what we were doing. From there, we would hike across "Stormy's pass." The spies had told us the *Pontiac* was still there, so part of our mission was to drive it somewhere else to draw suspicion away from the mountain. *IDS* trucks on the U. S. side were to take us to the outskirts of the camp. The drivers had falsified manifests, which would take us into the camp around 9:00 at night. The trucks would be a Trojan horse.

Everything went as planned. Stormy drove the *Pontiac* back to the hotel where he had stolen it and left $1,000 cash for damages and use, but no note. The *IDS* trucks entered the camp without issue. Once inside, the third driver tapped his horn, as had been planned, and simultaneously, we burst out of the back and side doors, guns blazing. We captured the gate guards, bound them and put them in the first truck. Immediately we cut all power and communications lines. Then we marched on the barracks where the trainees were sleeping. We got off a few shots and stormed the barracks. After that, all that was left was the commandant's quarters. We likewise bound him and put him in the first truck. We liberated the prisoners and escorted them to the second truck. We took the necessary photographs, some incriminating training manuals and logs, and set charges to destroy the camp on a timer about three hours later.

The trucks pulled out of the camp and drove straight to the Mountain. We marched both our new prisoners and the freed prisoners up and over "Stormy's Pass." The former death squads were to be sent directly to Amsterdam where they would be arraigned in The World Court on charges of genocide. They would, however, be offered leniency for cooperating with investigators. Except for Cole, who stayed with us, the freed men went to Stockholm where they would have temporary homes. This would help to absolve the Canadian government of some suspicion.

Harry's team was waiting at "Grandma's" house. As I would have expected, he had charmed her to the point of giving him a kiss on the cheek when he had to leave. Stormy said, "All she gave me was food and some harsh words." I told Stormy he lacked Harry's charm, it was pure and simple.

Harry's team had two objectives, one was to get all of us out of there post haste. The other was to go back up the mountain and make sure that no debris led anyone to Canada. Harry had to cross back over the mountain for about twenty minutes to make sure the site was clean. I fretted the entire time.

By the next morning, we were back in Toronto. I turned on the morning news to see the headlines about the FBP training facility that had been bombed. The news report described it as a place where Elite Forces received rigorous training. The report mentioned nothing about the "fox hunts." They went on to say that powerful explosives had leveled the facility, and everyone inside was presumed dead. Word was from the Whitehouse that because this facility was so close to the Canadian border, it was likely that the Canadian government was involved. The Canadian government denied any involvement at all.

The next day, the headline was news from The Hague. The World Court announced that it had 158 prisoners from the United States, who were being charged with acts of genocide. This was the first public acknowledgement that there was an investigation under way. The court officials explained that this "arrest" was part of an on-going investigation and that further indictments would likely follow. That evening, *CNN* had obtained an interview with the former commandant. He denied any acts of genocide and described the act of war perpetrated by some foreign government, probably that of the Netherlands, but he could not be sure. He told how men with American accents dressed in Russian uniforms invaded the camp and arrested them. He made no mention of their prisoners or of the camp's real function. He told how we had come into the camp in what appeared to be *IDS* trucks, captured them, and blindfolded them. They rode in the trucks for a ways and were forced to climb over a mountain then were loaded back into the same trucks and taken to a nearby airport. The next thing they saw was Amsterdam.

Speaker Crooks was furious. He held a press conference that afternoon and demanded the return of his "good Amer'kin soldiers," the dropping of those trumped up charges, and accountability from whatever government was responsible. He declared that an incursion like that was an act of war, and he did not care if it was the government of the Netherlands, they would pay as soon as he knew for sure.

Chapter 11   Dinner at Eight

I kept in close contact with Prime Minister McConihe and other members of his government. The Canadian government's role in clandestine operations was too obvious. Crooks's investigators concluded that Canada had some kind of pivotal role in all the liberations. For that reason McConihe wanted to make it obvious that other governments were involved too. He told me that the Russian uniforms were a nice touch. Some of the men liberated from the Montana camp went to Great Britain, others to Sweden, the Netherlands, Germany, South Africa, and New Zealand. What Canadian officials did not yet tell me was that it was also becoming obvious that they would have a difficult time keeping us safe inside Canada.

Getting other nations involved did little to defuse the crisis that was building in North America. It only broadened the scope. Although we finally ceased operations inside the United States, Speaker Crooks and his cronies continued pressing Canada for the return of the "fugitives" it was harboring. Canada admitted nothing, but kept pressing its concerns for the "humane" treatment of prisoners and detainees and for due process of the accused. Nothing yet was said publicly on either side about the death camps.

The World Court aggressively pursued its case against the Crooks regime. The camp guards we had turned over to them were starting to talk. Investigators needed

depositions and asked us to fly to Amsterdam to give
testimony. Harry, Cole, Stormy, and I booked our flights
and flew to Amsterdam. It seemed weird flying with our
true identities again. I wondered what would happen if the
plane had trouble and we were diverted to New York or
some other airport in the U. S.

Cole had moved in with us. He was a charming
young man, and we had two spare bedrooms. He was
enamored with Stormy. That was great. It deprived Harry
of any lingering suspicions, and Stormy needed the
attention. I had a talk with Cole when I realized the crush
he had on Stormy, "You know I had a crush on him before
you were born. I've known him for a long time and I don't
want to see him hurt. You have to promise that you will
always be honest with him, and if you feel you are growing
away from him, you will tell him." He promised that he
would be good to Stormy. My comment about the age
difference seemed to fly right over, though. It was about
that time that they started sharing a bedroom.

Cole had never been to Amsterdam. It was October
and perfect weather to show off a delightful town. Harry
and I had gone about ten years earlier, and Stormy had been
there a little more recently. We were all surprised with how
huge the gay community had grown. Many refugees from
the United States had gone there first. In our first night out,
we ran into people I knew from Bay City and from
Oklahoma City.

The ones from Oklahoma City were Rob and Dean.
We were walking down Kerkstraat on our way to the *Argos*
and they saw us coming from the other direction. I
happened to be walking with Stormy at the moment. Harry
was behind us with Cole, giving him some work-out tips.
Rob and Dean screeched, "It's Joe and Stormy!" At first I
did not recognize them, but as they came closer, I knew

who they were. They obviously had not continued their racquetball routine.

Dean remarked that it was a strange reunion. He wondered how Stormy and I had gotten back together. Rob said, "We've been watching you on the news. I thought you were with someone else?"

Harry stepped up, "He is."

I apologized and introduced everyone. Stormy explained how he had found me in Toronto. Rob smiled and said to Harry, "If you knew how those two carried on back in Oklahoma, you'd be a little jealous about their friendship."

I interrupted, "Harry does know." Then changing the subject abruptly, I continued, "So what are you guys doing here?"

Dean replied, "We live here now. We left the day of the Atlanta riots. We had been worried about what was happening. When I picked up our Sunday paper that day and looked at the headline, I told Rob we needed to go. He agreed. I went online and booked us a flight for that evening to Amsterdam. We packed, called our friends to say goodbye and to urge them to leave as well, and we left. We had Dutch bank accounts already, so after we arrived I had all our assets transferred. The only thing we lost was the house."

Rob asked Stormy, "Why didn't you get out?"

Stormy replied, "Just dumb I guess. I waited too long."

Rob apologized for his lack of tact and asked us why we were there. I could not divulge much, but I said that we were there to give some depositions in a pending criminal suit. I think they could figure out the rest.

They joined us in the bar for a drink. We reminisced about the night that Rob's world fell apart. I asked if he knew what had happened to Charlotte. Rob scowled and said, "That bitch. After she took everything I had, she went back to the church and got even more involved. Then she joined the Family Research Council."

I interrupted, "That's the most rabidly anti-gay fundamentalist lobbying organization in the country. They are the ones who wrote the Crooks agenda on extermination of gay men."

Rob continued, "I know. I wish I had let her slit her wrists that night. I heard from my sister in Washington that Charlotte lives in Georgetown and is a leading advisor to the Speaker's Committee on Reeducation. That is the group that is experimenting with ways to turn gay men straight."

I said, "I've heard about them. They are doing everything from electric shock to brain surgery. Those people are the Dr. Mengeles of our holocaust. I can't believe precious little Charlotte is involved in something like that. You know, she could go to jail."

Rob asked, "Do you ever think that will really happen? They seem so entrenched in power, and they have the U. S. military behind them."

I said, "In 1944 the Nazis were pretty well entrenched in Europe, but a year later most of them were on trial."

Dean said, "You know something, Joe, don't you?"

I replied, "Maybe, but here's what I know for sure. Regimes like Crooks's don't last. They are corrupt to the core. If war and pestilence don't destroy them, they will rot from within. Mark my words, within two years, Crooks and his cronies will be finished and on their way to jail."

Dean said, "You're pretty sure of yourself."

I replied, "Yes I am. It is what must happen, and I will do everything in my power to bring it about."

We finished our drinks and left the bar. Before leaving, we exchanged contact information. Rob and Dean

insisted we stay with them next time we came to
Amsterdam. I assured them we would.

Harry remarked after we left their company, "I
can't believe those two guys were ever married."

Stormy said, "I don't remember them being quite so
nelly. I think they've fagged out a bit."

I said, "Somehow I can picture Dean in a dress and
wig and on stage; I never had that mental image about him
before now."

We walked down the canals and watched some
ships coming into the harbor. I pointed to a merchant vessel
and told Harry it looked like the sister ship of the *Vergulde
Dreack*. Harry asked, "Do you really think those days are
over now?"

I said, "I hope so."

The next morning we hopped a train for The Hague.
I sat next to a window. We were in a four person face-to-
face seating arrangement. Harry, Cole, and Stormy carried
on a conversation about how impressed they were with The
Netherlands. I looked out the window at the picturesque
countryside with the windmills and thatched-roof farm
houses and thought about the train I was riding. Its route
had carried a host of high profile figures over the past
hundred-plus years. The one I was thinking about was
Count Muraviev in May of 1899.

Muraviev was the Russian Foreign Minister. He
was going to The Hague to try to prevent world war. The
results of my trip would likely start one. He was leading the
Russian delegation to the First International Peace
Conference at The Hague. The conference convened on 18
May 1899, the Tsar's birthday.

It was appropriate to honor the Tsar by convening
the peace conference on his birthday, as he was responsible
for the conference taking place. Nicholas II had inherited a
Russia that was struggling to modernize and catch up to the

other industrial powers of Europe and North America. The
biggest threat to his industrial agenda was the continual
threat of catastrophic war.

Europe in 1899 had not experienced a major war for
more than twenty years, and there were those *Fin de Siecle*
optimists who thought the year 1900 would usher in a new
era of peace and prosperity for the entire world. They
thought the wars of the Crimean and Napoleonic eras were
an obsolete concept. These optimists believed that
European countries were too inter-dependant and too
sophisticated to resort to war.

There were others who were more realistic and
grew increasingly concerned about the massive buildup of
armaments in Europe. Among them was a Russian
industrialist by the name of Ivan Bliokh. Bliokh was
somewhat of a Russian Andrew Carnegie. He was born a
poor Jew in Polish Russia. He started as an itinerant
peddler, and through hard work and discipline he made
enough money to study economics at the University of
Berlin. He built an industrial empire in railroads and
eventually served on the Tsar's Privy Council, Imperial
Russia's equivalent of the President's Cabinet.

In the 1890s Bliokh studied the arms industry in
Europe and concluded that Europe was headed for a
cataclysmic war. Bliokh published his findings in a six
volume work entitled, *The Future of War in Its Technical,
Economic, and Political Relations*. He drew attention to the
fact that when one country equipped its armies with bigger
and better guns that its rivals were compelled to keep pace.
Additionally, the application of technology to armaments
quickly made guns that had never been used obsolete. He
pointed out that European governments were bankrupting
themselves on weapons that were destined for scrap. Bliokh
expressed his gravest concerns for the destabilizing effect of
the weapons race. Rivals resented each others' buildups

and grew increasingly mistrustful of their neighbors' intentions.

He accurately predicted what would happen should European powers ever go to war with each other. The rival powers were so evenly matched that war would result in trench warfare and stalemate. War would drag on for years and consume whole generations of fighting men. Populations would grow weary with the depravations caused by long-term warfare and likely rise up against their governments. The entire European order would be destabilized and radical regimes would replace stable governments. Peace would result only for a time to allow countries to rebuild their arsenals, then, with the help of technology, greater and even more destructive warfare would resume, using weapons of unspeakable destructive power.

What Bliokh described in the 1890s was the first half of the twentieth century. One could almost read his predictions as some kind of psychic prophecy, but his all too accurate analysis was not based on the supernatural or paranormal; it was based on scholarly evaluation of available information. Anyone with ears to hear could have understood his message. Too many refused.

The most important person to have read Bliokh's book was the Tsar of all the Russia's, Emperor Nicholas II. Nicholas was so impressed with the book that he ordered it required reading for all officers in the Russian military. Albert Beveridge, a Progressive Senator from the United States, noted on his way through Siberia in 1902 that even officers in Russia's far eastern armies had well-worn copies of it with them.

The focus of Nicholas II's early reign was industrialization. He had been an integral player in Russia's economy since before his father, Alexander III, died. Nicholas had headed the committee that oversaw both construction of and economic development along the Trans-Siberian Railway. From the moment he became Tsar, he continued to be interested in Russia's economic development. Anything that might interfere with that agenda, including war, Nicholas viewed as a threat.

In the spring of 1898 his council of ministers informed him that Austria had ordered a complete re-supply of its army with the latest and greatest repeating rifles. Austria was locked in a defensive alliance with Germany against Russia. To remain at least on par with Austria, Russia would need to scrap its current supply of rifles and replace them with ones that could at least equal the Austrians. This was exactly what Ivan Bliokh had described. Rather than ordering the new guns, the emperor suggested calling a peace conference among all the great powers to discuss the possibility of drafting an arms limitation agreement.

At first he wanted to hold the peace conference in St. Petersburg, but other world leaders thought it hardly a neutral location. Most world governments were cynical about his proposal and had no intention of participating in an arms reduction conference. Peace movements in the United States, Great Britain, France, Austria-Hungary, and many of the minor world powers, such as the Netherlands, pressed upon their governments to participate in the conference. The government of the Netherlands offered The Hague as a neutral location to host the peace conference.

The Russian government was delighted to accept the Dutch offer. The Tsar expanded the list of invited countries to every government that had diplomatic relations with Russia. Each country's delegates came with their own agenda for peace proposals or with plans to derail any substantive agreements.

The concept of a world court to settle international disputes had been talked about for many years. All the major powers in attendance with proposals in hand included some kind of structure for a world court. That was the only issue with which most countries were in general agreement.

None of the other "great" powers, Great Britain, France, Germany, Austria-Hungary, and the United States, supported any proposals for arms limitations. Great Britain and the United States, however, had powerful pacifist electorates with which to contend. Those two powers brought proposals for arbitration agreements.

It was decided to incorporate the arbitration agreements into the structure of the World Court. The British and American delegates worked together to draft the language for the arbitration agreements. It really was a matter of reconciling language. Both countries' proposals were essentially the same.

The arbitration agreements stated that in the event of an international dispute of any kind that the nations at issue *could* use the good services of the World Court. Neither the United States, Great Britain, Germany, nor France were interested in any agreement that would require them to seek arbitration before resorting to war. That coupled with their complete unwillingness to discuss arms limitations, made World War I inevitable, and by default, World War II.

The Tsar had failed to achieve his primary objective, but did succeed in the establishment of the World Court, which was to be seated at The Hague. American and British pacifists were elated at the creation of the Court, thinking that wars would be a thing of the past and all disputes would be settled there. Among them was Andrew Carnegie, the great steel magnate in the United States. He provided funding to build a "Peace Palace" at The Hague to house the World Court.

In the first years several nations used the World
Court to settle disputes exactly as it had been intended. The
United States and Mexico used it; France and Germany
even used it; and smaller countries used it as well. In 1904,
however, the flawed nature of the arbitration clauses of the
agreements showed when Japan launched a surprise attack
on the Russians at Port Arthur in the Far East. In 1914,
when Europe was in crisis over the assassination of
Austria's archduke, Russia, Great Britain, France,
Switzerland, the Netherlands, and several other countries
lobbied and begged the German and Austrian governments
to use the World Court to settle their dispute with Serbia.
Germany and Austria opted for war instead.

Stormy, Cole, and I were going to take part in the
newer and expanded role of the World Court. After World
War II, its mandate was expanded to include certain human
rights violations, especially acts of genocide. I think
Nicholas II would have been happy about what we were
doing. Though he found himself embroiled in two
catastrophic wars, he was a man who preferred peace.
Though he has very wrongly been labeled an anti-Semite,
Russia was an anti-Semitic country long before he came to
power. Apart from an aggressive educational agenda he had
little control over his subjects' ignorance.

As for gays, if anything he was supportive. He
knew of two uncles, a nephew, and several other relatives
who were gay. He might not have approved of his brother's
morganatic marriage to a divorcee, but Nicholas never
criticized his male relatives for having male lovers. It was
the Bolsheviks who turned Russia homophobic. Lenin and
his cronies considered homosexuality a decadent
manifestation of the tsarist regime.

As far as I was concerned Crooks and Lenin were
of the same evil intolerance. Crooks was wrecking my
country as horribly as Lenin wrecked Russia. If Crooks

were allowed to finish his agenda, the United States in the twenty-first century would, like Russia in the twentieth century, be a place of a decaying standard of living, stagnant economy, and oppressive society.

The depositions we were about to give would be key evidence in the trials against Crooks and his regime. Once an indictment became public, Crooks would consider it an act of war. If he were to declare war on the Netherlands, or worse yet, the World Court, it would be viewed by the rest of the world like the Kaiser invading Belgium or Hitler invading Poland. Crooks would be looking at the nuclear arsenals of Russia, China, Great Britain, and France. I very well might be responsible for turning a human holocaust into a nuclear holocaust.

Our train pulled into the station and Wilhelm Ten Broeck was there to meet us. He was the attorney that would conduct the depositions. He asked all the usual niceties such as how our train ride was. We walked into Carnegie's Peace Palace and into the room where we would wait our turns. He took Stormy first, then Cole, and saved me, which would take the longest, until last.

While Stormy was in there, Cole asked me what to expect. I told him the attorney would not be friendly. He would badger Cole and try to find any holes in his story. Since he and Stormy would be telling essentially the same story on the Montana camp, he would be looking for two things: One would be if they had synchronized their stories beforehand, which would discredit their testimony; the other would be to try to find contradictions in their stories. Cole said that it seemed like no matter what, Ten Broeck would clobber them. I said, "No, he's not out to get you. He simply wants your testimonies to be credible in court. Tell the truth. That's all you have to do. Don't embellish, don't leave things out. Simply answer the questions completely and accurately."

Stormy came out, and Ten Broeck asked for Cole. I asked Stormy how it went. He said that he was able to tell the whole story about both Seattle and Montana. He said there was not much cross examination or whatever it was. I told him that Cole would get the tough questions on Montana.

Harry seemed distracted, so I suggested that he and Stormy go outside. I told them, "*The Little House In The Woods* is not far away. That is where the peace conference was held."

Harry asked, "Don't you want to go? I would think that you would want to lecture us or something."

I said, "No, I have to stay here. Besides, I've seen it a few times."

Harry replied, "You never told me you had been there. When was that?"

I said, "I came here first while I was doing some European research for my dissertation, but I've come here a few times since on some business trips. I don't necessarily tell you everywhere I go."

Harry scowled, "Hmmm. I wonder where else in this country you've been that I don't know about."

I shrugged my shoulders and threw my hands up. Harry and I were toying with each other. We knew that, but Stormy started inching away like he thought a bomb was about to explode. I said, "You guys go on. Enjoy the afternoon. I know this will take a few hours."

They walked outside. A little while later, Cole came out. I told him to call Harry on his cell phone and he could meet up with them. Ten Broeck motioned for me to come in to the deposition room.

My deposition was intense and did take more than two hours. He started right off with Stormy's testimony about the Spokane camp. He said, "You have filed some reports and evidence that makes these work camps sound horrible. The testimony I've heard today from someone who lived through one makes it sound not that bad. How do you reconcile this seeming contradiction?"

Whew, he wasted no time zeroing in on the tough stuff. I answered, "If you are talking about the one in Spokane, I've never seen it. All the "work camps" I've seen were places not fit for vermin. I don't know why, but it seems that this one camp in Spokane is the exception to the rule. I think when this is all over you will have testimony from plenty of people who lived through the other camps to corroborate my observations."

"So how many of these potential witnesses have you coached?"

This was going to be an unpleasant two hours. I answered, "I haven't coached anyone. They're the ones who have told me what they lived through."

"What about this Cole, did you coach him before his testimony? He indicated that you had?"

"I didn't coach him. He asked me what to expect, and I told him it would be exactly like this. The only advice I gave him was to tell the truth."

"Tell me about this camp in, what is it, S-a-g-i-n-a-w, Michigan?"

I caught a hold of myself. This guy was a damn good lawyer. He was doing exactly what he was supposed to do. He knew I hadn't coached Cole; that was just friendly lawyer badgering to firm up my credibility. I described the *Saquaquom Iron* camp, and how the men had been subjected to rape and torture, had been left to live in filth, and were without adequate food. It might well have been a death camp. In fact, about 20% of the men had been diagnosed with various diseases directly associated with their internment. Most of them had been raped by the camp's commandant. He went on to question me about the death camps. When I described the one in Cincinnati with the body parts laying on the floor of the crematoria, his face turned pale.

When he was done questioning me, he shook my hand and said that everyone had given excellent and useful depositions. Then he was ready to be friendly; that is the lawyer's way. He opened up a bit and told me that charges of genocide were being drawn up against Crooks and would be made public within the next few months. I was not to tell anyone.

I asked him about his face color during the Cincinnati answers. He said that his great aunt had survived Dachenau. It hit a little too close to home. He put his hand on my shoulder and said, "I can't tell you how much respect I have for the work you are doing. You will have saved the world from another bloodbath." I told him my fears that I might start one, but he dismissed it. He said, "God knows that you are doing His will; He will not let your work be in vain."

I walked on out and told Stormy about Ten Broeck's ending comment. Stormy shrugged a reply, "This is supposed to be a Calvinist country."

We finished a tour, the others never made it to *The Little House In The Woods*, and so I led a tour there before we caught our train back to Amsterdam. Somehow I missed their excitement at seeing the birthplace of the World Court.

Our flight back to Toronto left at noon the next day, so we had time for one more night on the town. I insisted we call Rob and Dean. They joined us for dinner and later took us to a stripper bar. I figured Harry would have a cow at that suggestion, but he had taken some hits of marijuana. He would go along with just about anything. As are most stripper bars, the clientele were mostly trolls. Somehow Rob and Dean seemed to fit right in. The rest of us seemed rather out of place. The only other people who looked like us were looking for a nighttime job. The strippers,

themselves, were a little homely. Dean kept hooting for me
to drop money on this one red headed number. I thought,
"Harry, Stormy, and Cole could jump up on the bar and get
rich tonight."

I excused myself to go to the bathroom. When I
came back Harry's shirt was off his shoulders and hanging
loose around his waist. A strange German had his hands all
over Harry's chest. I pushed the German aside and said,
"Keep your hands off my husband."

He said, "Verstehen Sie nicht."

I said, "*Sie verstehen mich*; Keep your hands off my
husband." Then I turned to Harry, "What were you doing?"

He smiled a broad grin and said leisurely, "I don't
know; it was hot in here. I needed to cool down."

I rubbed my head and turned to Stormy and Cole,
"Why didn't you guys do something?" Then I realized they
were googooing at each other and were oblivious to the
world around them. I told everyone I thought it was time
for us to go back to our hotel. I thanked Rob and Dean for
showing us such a great time.

Back in Toronto things were quiet for a few
months. I was actually able to go back to work and earn
some money, which I sorely needed to do. Supporting a
household of four was expensive. We were, for those few
months, the Cleavers. Cole was every bit the Beaver.

One night after we had all gone to bed, Harry, or
"June" as I called him then (he really hated it too), told me
about Cole's excitement for the day. He had gone out for a
run and when he came back he said a stranger had stopped
his car and asked if he wanted to go fly fishing. Cole said,
"I didn't know there were any good fishing spots around
here."

I rolled my eyes and said, "I don't think Cole was
out very long before he was arrested. I think I should go
have a good "Ward" talk with him." Harry said that he had

already done that, and, "thank-you very much," he was not June Cleaver and was perfectly capable of having his own "Ward" talk with Cole.

I left for St. Petersburg the next day. I had clients there to meet. A Canadian firm was negotiating a contract between an Argentine beef export company and a Russian import company. I was there to help with cultural reconciliation issues.

While there I visited some Russian friends in St. Petersburg. I had met them in Michigan. They had been students at a state school. Dmitry was a musician and was gay. I had met him at a Christmas party in Bay City. He was dating Jerome Madigan. Jerome was not one of my favorite people, but having a Russian to talk to made it worth while.

Jerome was an arrogant character who had little on the ball to be so arrogant. Jerome taught English at *Bay City State University*. He prided himself on correcting other people's English, even when he was wrong. Once I was having a conversation with Dmitry and I was saying something about, "If I were you, I would do . . ." when Jerome interrupted me.

He said, "You mean if I was;" I want Dmitry to learn proper English."

I looked at him as though he were crazy and said, "No, I mean what I said. That was a condition contrary to fact, which means I was speaking in subjunctive mood. "If I were" is a proper subjunctive mood statement."

Jerome and I got off to a bad start. Right after I had begun teaching at *Bay City State University* I had joined the Faculty Food Bank, an organization that distributed food to needy families throughout Bay County. Each year on Fat Tuesday the organization held its biggest fund raiser, a *Mardis Gras* themed celebration. The proceeds from this one night usually funded nearly the entire annual budget. I was on the steering committee that designed the marketing campaign for the fund raiser. Jerome was also on the committee.

He was dictatorial, surly, and at times downright nasty. Jerome had a Dr. Jekyll and Mr. Hyde personality. In public environments he was sweet, charming, and the very picture of enlightened friendliness. In private settings, he was a beast. The hypocrisy of his character, however, left me dumbfounded while working on that food bank committee.

Betty Stanton and I had been designing a poster that was going to be printed for display in grocery stores, drug stores, and other retail establishments. It featured a woman, nicely appointed in a knee length skirt with a simple string of pearls around her neck pushing a shopping cart. She had a serene smile. A thought bubble from her head read, "For the price of a new set of earrings I can feed a family for a week!" It was meant to be humorous. Jerome took one look at it and screamed, "That's misogynistic!"

The next day Betty and I decided to stop by his office to see what kind of poster he would find inoffensive. We opened the door to his office to witness him screaming at the top of his lungs at his secretary. Apparently her seven year old child was running a fever and she had to leave to pick him up from school. With his hands waving over his head, Jerome screamed, "This is exactly why I will never hire another single mother again. All you do is take off for your children. Who is going to answer the phone while you are gone? I swear, there is too much estrogen at this university anyway!"

He had no idea Betty and I were standing there. Betty pointed to him and exclaimed, "Now that's misogynistic." We turned and walked out of his office. We both resigned from the poster committee in protest.

Jerome and Dmitry did not last too long as a couple. It was, what I called, a needs based relationship. Jerome needed a trophy-husband; Dmitry needed a meal ticket. After Jerome caught Dmitry screwing Jerome's best friend, they broke up. Dmitry moved back to St. Petersburg where he found work teaching at the conservatory. He was much better off, and I made it a point to see him anytime I was in St. Petersburg.

He was doing well. He was a respected concert performer and played in all the major Russian cities. Dmitry said he had watched me in the news. I was a big hit with the Russian gay community and people were amazed that he knew me. He insisted I go out with him so he could introduce me to some of his friends.

It was great fun. I met some very nice Russians at *Грешники* (*Greshniky*), St. Petersburg's leading dance bar. Dmitry kept trying to hook me up with someone for the night. He pointed to different men, saying, "*Смотри, какой видный паренъ! Ты просто долҗен взятъ его с собой в твой номер.*" (Roughly: "Look at that hot piece of man-flesh. You should take him back to your room.") I kept saying I was not interested, but he took that to mean I was not interested in that individual. Finally after he could not find anyone to trot in front of me, he said, "Then you go home with me." I thanked him and said that I wanted to go back to my room alone. I think going home alone from a bar was a new concept to Dmitry.

The next day I took a flight for London where I changed planes and flew to Toronto. Harry picked me up at the airport and told me that Cole had gotten a job at the Diesel store downtown. Cole was perfect for a job like that. Stormy interviewed for an IT position at an insurance company, and Harry applied with a security company. Things started to seem normal again.

I suggested that to celebrate our return to "normalcy" we should host a dinner party. Harry groaned and argued that the china was packed away, and it would take too much time to prepare. I told him I knew exactly where the china was, and I insisted.

We threw fabulous dinner parties back in Bay City. Having been raised in a home where etiquette carried a southern flair, I always set a proper table, using the best china, freshly polished sterling silver, sparkling crystal stemware, and pressed Irish linens. Our china was *Ansonia*, an old *Noritake* pattern. The plates were white with a narrow painted band with six sets of pink roses. It was a clean and graceful pattern that had the right amount of flair without being too fussy. We had found a set of it at a flea market in Indiana. The original set was a complete service for twelve, with all three serving platters, a gravy boat, a covered casserole, and cream and sugar bowls. We purchased the entire set for $300, which was a steal. We added to the set and replaced a few pieces that were chipped, and in so doing more than tripled our investment. We ended up with service for sixteen.

Our silver pattern was *Colfax*, by *Gorham*. It was a classic 1920s pattern. It was free of frilly scroll work and had an understated, delicate border, somewhat Roman in design. We had service for twenty, plus serving and specialty pieces for almost any occasion.

Steuben Century was our stemware pattern. It was current and new. *Century* embodied the austere elegance of *Steuben* design. It had no gold or etching. It simply was perfectly made glassware, and it completed the setting for a table welcoming to guests.

Our dinner parties were all evening events. We followed that old European notion of preparing for a meal for a full day. Guests sat down at the table for their first course around eight, and finished dessert around midnight.

Often times, we would leave the table sometime around one in the morning.

Those events were among my happiest. Harry and I prepared the meal together, each responsible for certain courses. We always planned these dinners for a Saturday, so we would have all of Friday night and Saturday to prepare, and Sunday to clean up and put things back in order.

We prepared the guest list and mailed the invitations. Our dinner companions would be Matt DuPont, Matt Crossly, Jimmy and Marc, Scott and Allen, Randy and Kyle, and the four of us, twelve altogether. They began arriving at seven. We served cocktails and hors d'oeuvres until eight. The first course was a shrimp and oyster *Sabayon*, the soup was red pepper bisque, garnished with a swirl of *crème fraiche*. Harry prepared walnut and blue cheese dressing for a mixed green salad. We slow roasted beef tenderloin and served it with a cabernet reduction sauce. I baked fresh rolls to serve throughout the meal. Harry made *Crème Brule* for dessert.

The two Matts had never been terribly fond of each other, so I made sure they were not seated together. Though I rarely put place cards out, I did for this occasion. I always seat couples apart at a dinner party, and I try to intersperse the new or different with the familiar. With Harry and me at either end of the table, I sat Marc to my left. Next to him was Matt DuPont; on his left was Stormy; to Stormy's left was Scott, and Kyle was on Scott's left and Harry's right. Going down the other side of the table was Jimmy, Matt Crossly, Allen, Cole, and Randy on my right.

Matt DuPont and Scott grilled Stormy. They wanted all the details about my life in Oklahoma City. Stormy resisted as much as possible, but a peppery Shiraz loosened his tongue. I was wrapped up in listening to Marc telling Randy about fucking Jimmy in Randy's parents' house. I missed most of the conversations at the other parts of the table, but I did hear Stormy telling Matt and Scott about us having sex in the Oklahoma state capital building. After Stormy finished the story, Matt and Scott looked over at me and their eyes, in perfectly simultaneous choreography, looked up and down as if to say, "We had no idea you were the type."

I blushed and the evening went on. It was, for the moment, as though nothing had interrupted our lives. We gossiped about those who were not there and drank too much wine. As Harry served his renowned *Crème' Brule*, Matt DuPont tied knots in his napkin so he could make a fetching hat. He arranged it just so. Harry looked at him as if he were going to say something about ruining our finest linen, when Matt quietly, at first, began singing,

> I am what I am
> I am my own special creation
> So come take a look
> Give me the hook or the ovation
> It's my world that I want to take a little pride in,
> My world, and it's not a place I have to hide in.[3]

Then, the rest of us, one by one, joined in to finish the song,

> . . . Life's not worth a damn 'til you can say,
> "Hey world, I am what I am!"[4]

---

[3] Jerry Herman, "I Am What I Am," *La Cage Aux Folle* (Winona, MN: Leonard Publishing Corp., 1983).

[4] *Ibid.*

Chapter 12   Mechanicsburg John

Part of my purpose in throwing a dinner party was to remind myself and those around me why we were fighting. We were not simply fighting a government that was evil incarnate. All of the reunions I had experienced in the past year and one half with Stormy, Cameron, Matt Crossly, and Randy and Kyle had been great, but they were all reminders of the horrors occurring in the place that was my home. We were fighting for the right to have a normal life, all of the things we used to take for granted. I wanted desperately for life to be fun again.

Sunday Harry and I spent most of the day putting the house back in order. Stormy and Cole went to a movie and spent the day downtown. In the evening they went for "tea" at the *Woody's/Sailor's* complex. I went to the gym in the afternoon, and Harry and I watched some old movies in the evening. We watched *Lady Eve*, my favorite Barbara Stanwyck movie, and *The Train*, a post-World War II movie staring Burt Lancaster.

The next morning everyone else went to work, and I went into my office to work on my report. I was in the process of assembling all the treaties and trade agreements into a manageable form by entering the terms and conditions of them into a database that could be sorted later. My clients were, as always, pleased with my work.

I worked until three in the afternoon then decided to go to the gym for a long run on the track. It was a cold November day, but the gym was almost sultry. My mind slipped into a reflective state while my feet pounded the track.

I missed the *Polar Star II*. I had sold it in Tobermory a few weeks earlier. I knew I would never be able to sail the Great Lakes safely again, so there was no point in keeping her. In the sales contract I insisted that the purchaser re-christen the boat with a different name.

While I was running I closed my eyes and I could feel the *Polar Star II* running with the wind fast enough that the boat clipped the peaks of the waves. I could imagine the mainsail ballooned out on the starboard side and the headsail filled out on the port side. All I could hear was the fluttering of sails and the squawk of an occasional seagull.

I stopped at the corner market on the way home to pick up some things. The rest of the family was at the gym, so it was up to me to fix supper. I bought a couple of acorn squashes, some mustard greens, and a fresh young hen. I put the chicken in the roasting pan, while I cut and gutted the squash. The boys came in while I was setting the table. After Harry showered I told him to watch the greens so I could shower.

Stormy talked about the news that had been running on the monitors at the gym. He said that there was a story about some Canadian tourists being hassled at the border. They were coming back from New York and were crossing at Niagara Falls. It was a group of twenty-something men, and border guards thought they were gay Americans trying to flee. It seemed that the young men's passports were in complete order, but they were detained for three days. The men had not been allowed to make any phone calls and were refused counsel. Finally, their worried parents contacted the Foreign Ministry.

I commented that the men were probably about to be sent to a camp. Stormy said the Foreign Minister demanded an explanation and an apology. I replied that he would have fat luck getting either.

The next morning I was in my office reviewing documents, and the phone rang. It was Matt Crossly. He asked me to come downtown as soon as possible. He sounded worried, so I marked my place and left right away. I went to the refugee center he had established for helping escapees with no financial means. Matt pulled me into his office and shut the door.

He said, "Joe, we have a big problem. Do you remember the team that was operating in Harrisburg while you were on the Cincinnati run?"

I did remember them. That was Pete McHenry's team. They had a near disaster on their way out. Pete had arranged for the *IDS* trucks to pick them up outside the camp they were liberating in Mechanicsburg. The trucks came too close to the camp and alerted the guards who were sleeping. The sirens and search lights went off. The trucks were almost spotted and would have been, if it had not been for the quick thinking of one of the escapees, John Beale. John saw the search light coming towards the truck and ran away from it and screamed. The lights panned over towards him, while he crawled back to the truck. Pete grabbed him up and pulled him into the cab as the trucks took off in the opposite direction.

Pete introduced John to me as the man who saved the mission. I had wanted to do a media blitz with John as our poster boy, but he said he was too shy and refused. I always thought he was and odd duck. He never went out to any of the bars, he did not date, but once in awhile he showed up at the refugee center to do some volunteer work. He was handsome enough, built, and sported a blond flattop. He did not seem quite right, though.

Matt told me that John had disappeared. He was supposed to work two volunteer shifts and had not shown for either one. I said to Matt, "I know you didn't call me down here to tell me about a volunteer who stood you up, what's going on?"

He replied, "John was here last Thursday. I had a meeting with some potential donors, and I was in there for about two hours. John was working the front counter. When I came out of the meeting, it looked like he was walking out of my office. He had no reason to be in there. He smiled and said, "I have to go Matt, I have a dentist's appointment." I went on into my office and my computer screen was up. I have my computer set to go on password-protect after five minutes. Joe, I was in the meeting for two hours!"

"What do you think he was doing?" I asked.

Matt replied, "I don't know, but how did he get my password?"

I said, "That's a good question. Does anyone in the office know it or have access to it?"

Matt was firm, "Absolutely not, I keep my password strictly to myself. No one in the office has access to it. I checked my files. My database that connects all the refugees with the camps from which they were liberated, the team who liberated them, and when they arrived in Canada had been accessed while I was in that meeting."

I speculated, "Maybe he was trying to get a phone number for a friend from his camp or something."

Matt shook his head, "Joe, he has that. I keep everyone's current phone numbers and addresses updated and available on the public monitors for all the refugees. What John accessed was sensitive information, and in the wrong hands, it could cause some major problems."

I started thinking about that database and began to worry myself. If that information ever crossed the border, Crooks would be in the catbird seat. I suggested we go over to John's apartment and check up on him.

His landlady said he had not been around in several days. She thought he might have gone on holiday or something. I told her we were his friends and were worried about him and asked her for the key to check and make sure he was not hurt. She went up with us and opened the door. She was afraid of what we might find and waited in the hall.

The girly magazines on the sofa and the half eaten bags of chips littering the floor were our first clue that we, indeed, had a problem. Matt looked around his computer while he booted it up and noticed a CD that looked like one off the spool he kept in his office. Matt's database was burned to it, and the database was on John's computer. Matt searched the computer for any other incriminating evidence, finding an address book with some contact information for some local women, probably hookers, and his superiors with The Federal Bureau of Protection. He was a mole. After we harvested anything else that might be useful, I set his hard drive to format, and we took the CD. His landlady had gone back to her apartment; I told her, "He's not there, so don't worry. I think you were probably right about him going away on vacation for a few days. Now listen, when he comes back, don't tell him we were here. He would be furious with us for being so worried."

Matt and I talked about what was likely to happen next. He knew everything about our operations and our relationship with the Canadian government. This could start a war. I told Matt to take us on over to the Foreign Ministry office instead.

They put me on a secure line to Ottawa. The Foreign Minister told me they would conduct a little counter-espionage themselves. They bugged his phone, and set surveillance around his apartment building.

As it turned out John, or whatever his name was, had gone to Ottawa to the United States Embassy, presumably to hand over a copy of the disk. The Foreign

Ministry had tracked him boarding a return train to Toronto. They would also try to prevent any embassy personnel from leaving the country.

Harry had supper ready for us when I came home. I told the story about my day. Harry said, "Joe, I don't want you getting mixed up in that sort of thing. That is how people get killed." I told him it was too late, but that it probably would not drag out too long. I suggested that we start packing non-essential items.

The next morning I went down to the refugee center with Matt. I had called Pete and asked him to come down to the center as well. When he heard the story, he said, "It all makes sense now. I always wondered why we had averted disaster. The whole thing was a set-up." We waited in Matt's office.

The Foreign Ministry called; it was Oscar Wilke. He said that as soon as John had gotten back to his apartment, they had taped a phone call I should hear. He put the tape on for me. John was talking to someone on the other end of the line, "Someone's been here. They've taken the CD I forgot to bring with me, and trashed my computer. I'll have to try to get another copy."

The person on the other end said, "Make sure you don't fuck up again. I might start thinking you are siding with those fairies. Maybe one of them poked you and you liked it, heh heh heh."

At least The Federal Bureau of Protection did not have the entire database. It sounded like John had given them what names and places he could remember, but at least there was no documentation. Oscar seemed somewhat relieved with the contents of the phone call.

We sat there and talked for a while with Pete getting angrier with every sentence. Matt shushed us when he heard John's voice greeting everyone at the counter. John apologized for missing the previous two days, but said he had been ill. Pete walked out to greet John, and extended his hand, "Now Johnny my boy, tell these folks again how you saved our mission back there in Mechanicsburg."

John blushed and said, "Oh they've heard it a thousand times, how are you Pete; it's been awhile?"

Matt and I walked out and I said, "Yeah John, tell us exactly how you did it. I've always been curious about how you timed your scream just right to divert the search lights. Why, it almost seems like it was planned that way."

John said, "So it was you guys that fucked up my computer."

Matt shrugged and said, "I don't know what you are talking about John, but maybe we should continue our conversation in my office."

John replied, "No, I think maybe I should be going." He started to turn to run out the door, but I had arranged for Marc and Jimmy to be there that morning. They were standing behind him and each grabbed an arm.

Marc said, "I would like to hear that story explained in Matt's office."

As soon as we were all in the door, I asked Marc to conduct a search. John had two guns and a knife on him. Pete told Marc to do a strip search, with all of us watching. Pete waited until John was buck naked, and said, "So you're not really gay? How would you like to find out what it's like? You might enjoy it." Pete started to unfasten his belt buckle and John started to squirm.

Horrified, I said, "Pete! You can't do that."

Pete said, "I was just messing with him, you know me better than that. Besides, I wouldn't soil my dick inside this filthy vermin. He'll get plenty of that in prison."

The strip search revealed a Federal Bureau of Protection ID. His name really was John. He had a few more weapons and a micro-camera. Matt called Wilke to send Mounted Police over to arrest John.

The crisis had been resolved for the moment, but damage had been done. John would not reveal to interrogators what he had told his superiors. It was then up to Crooks to make the next move. We had to wait for them to realize that John was out of circulation. While we waited, the Foreign Ministry conducted a thorough investigation of John's activities from the moment he surfaced.

All the warning signs had been there for us to see. We never thought about the possibility of infiltration. John appeared in the internment camp about two weeks prior to Pete's mission. That should have been our first warning. In all of the rescues we were liberating communities of people. The camps were, in there own macabre way, like a night at any local disco. One did not necessarily know everyone, but everyone was a familiar face. There had been the occasional stranger in the crowd, but he always had the explanation of a traveler caught in the wrong place at the wrong time. John had claimed he was from Harrisburg, but nobody from Harrisburg knew him.

After the rescue, John never socialized or tried to make friends, except as was necessary at the refugee center. He was very private about his life, never letting anyone get close. When some of his co-workers at the center made advances towards him, his refusals bordered, at times, on the violent. The man was obviously not gay, yet everyone refused to believe it. It was his hero status from the rescue that gave him such immunity.

The female prostitutes knew John well. He had several favorites, Miranda, Connie, and Natasha. They told us that he spent at least five nights a week with one of them. Connie said he talked frequently about being in the middle of something big. He kept saying they should get out of Toronto, because it was going to get ugly there. Miranda said John had given her a sealed envelope that she was to

take to the United States Embassy, should he ever
disappear. He paid her a $1,000 in US currency to keep it
in a safe place. The Foreign Ministry gave her another
$1,000 to purchase it. The envelope contained a detailed
flowchart of our entire operations – with me in the top
square. He had also written a long narrative describing my
house, inside and out, and concluded that Harry, Stormy,
and Cole were a part of my "harem of degenerates." As far
as I had known, he had never been inside my house.

John's narrative also contained details about Matt
Crossly's house and personal life. He had all of Matt's
bank accounts all over the world listed with estimated
balances. We wondered if John was the only spy. Over the
next several days, Matt and I poured over the records of
everyone we had rescued trying to find anything that was
suspicious. There seemed to be no one else.

Stormy laughed when he heard about John's
conclusion about our relationship. He said playfully, "Well,
we could make an honest man out of him," and winked.
Harry flashed him a glare with daggers. I told them that we
had to sell the house and move. We had no idea what
information John had passed to his superiors. If there were
other spies in town, we could all be murdered in our sleep.
They thought I was being silly, but I insisted that we pack
up the house and put it back on the market. We moved back
to the *Perseus*. Stormy was concerned that he and Cole
could not afford the hotel. I told them not worry, that I
would take care of them. Stormy said, "You know Joe, I
managed just fine for twenty-some years without you taking
care of me, I'm not sure I can keep mooching off of you."

I replied, "Nonsense. You are not mooching. You
are still recovering from loosing everything you had. I
know that when the time is right you will be on your own
again. In the mean time, this is what friends do for friends.
We take care of each other." Harry knew that there was

another issue. He knew how devoted I was to Stormy. It
was not a sexual devotion, and Harry felt no longer
threatened by my relationship with Stormy. He knew that
my love for Stormy was that of a brother.

Harry had also grown to care for Stormy. He was
part of our family now. Gay rights activists had always
talked about alternative definitions of family. What we had
developed with Stormy and Cole was a new one of those
definitions. I suppose anyone observing us might have
concluded the same thing that John had concluded. Maybe
he even heard speculation about our relationship at the
refugee center. As far as I was concerned, the four of us
were lucky to have each other.

It did not take away from my other friendships
either. If Stormy and Cole were our nuclear family, Scott
and Allen were still our best friends. In a sense it was good
to be back at the *Perseus*. Living in the heart of the city
was attractive. Harry and I were back in the nightlife
circuit. Several nights a week we had supper at a fabulous
up-scale restaurant with Scott and Allen, another couple, or
several of our friends. We often met at a martini bar near
the hotel for cocktails and finished off the evening at a
show.

For the time being I set up my office at Matt's
Refugee Center. It was only a few blocks from the hotel, so
I walked to work. It was more convenient than working
from home. I often needed to use the downtown libraries of
both the city and university. Working out of the house, it
had been necessary to drive downtown to use those
facilities. Between traffic and parking, I could easily waste
half a day to look up information that took thirty minutes to
find.

We put all of our belongings in storage, except for
what we needed at the hotel, and placed the house on the
market. A middle aged couple, who had transferred to

Toronto from Hamilton, bought the house. A few days
before closing, someone firebombed it. The house was a
total loss.

Obviously there were other Crooks regime
operatives in Canada. They had to have known we were not
living there, so the bombing was a shot across the bow. The
Canadian government purposely ignored it and let the City
of Toronto treat it as though it were an inexplicable house
fire. To have done otherwise, would have been to
acknowledge the incendiary material to have been made in
the United States and the action an act either of terrorism or
war. The latter was what the United States was hoping to
provoke.

In the weeks after the firing of my house the
Foreign Ministry picked up a flurry of activity going on
between the United States Embassy in Ottawa and the State
Department in Washington. Some months earlier, Speaker
Crooks announced that operations in the Middle East had
achieved their objectives and he would be initiating a
phased pullout of all U. S. troops from the region. The
Middle East was a bigger mess than before the United
States had first set up bases in Saudi Arabia, so I was not
sure what objectives had been achieved.

I thought that in bringing the troops home, he might
be looking for a way to reduce government spending by
decommissioning some divisions. That was not the case.
As divisions came home, he began re-opening military
bases that had been closed for anywhere from three to
twenty years. The most notable bases that were reopened
were in North Dakota, Minnesota, Michigan, New York,
Pennsylvania, Montana, and Washington State. He opened
new bases in Vermont and Maine. Crooks was massing
troops along the Canadian border.

Still, things were quiet. Relations between Canada
and the United States remained at the lowest point they had

been since 1812. The foreign services in both nations had reduced their staffs to a minimum and closed most consulates. The borders were nearly sealed and cross border trade was non existent. Everyone knew military action was coming, but Torontonians went about their business as though the enemy were thousands of miles away, rather than the thirty miles it was across the lake to New York.

Speaker Crooks was still looking for a Canadian provocation. They obviously had whatever information John had given them, but he had given no evidence. Without that, officials of Crooks's administration could make allegations, but had nothing with which to declare a provocation.

The World Court, oblivious to rising tensions in North America, concluded its investigations in March and announced that it would be issuing public indictments in coming weeks. The investigations had expanded to abuse of power and abrogation of constitutional law, along with the original investigations of genocide, torture, and violations of basic human rights. The indictment named Crooks, every Cabinet member, and several key leaders in Congress. It asked the House of Representatives to elect a new Speaker, purge itself of criminal elements, restore President O'Hara to power, and abandon martial law. Should Congress fail to take necessary action, it called upon the Joint Chiefs of Staff to arrest Speaker Crooks, his associates, and the other named officials, and turn them over to the World Court for prosecution.

The next morning Crooks called a press conference in the Blue Room at the White House. He was there with the indicted members of his staff and Congress. Crooks gave one of his cocky speeches about the evils of the World Court, accused them of ignoring genocide in other countries (trying to deflect criticism elsewhere, as usual), stated

defiantly that he had nothing to be ashamed of, and, "make
no mistake," he would not surrender. Then, in his verbal
counter-attack, he called upon the European Union to
"disband this worthless sham of jurisprudence called the
World Court."

He went on to accuse Canadian Prime Minister
McConihe of "deviltry" in providing falsified evidence to
the World Court. Crooks then launched into his tirade, "I
hope McConihe comes clean with all the evil doing he has
been promoting. Not only has he sheltered known
American criminals and terrorists, he is now, upon the
testimony of a bunch of fag – er these criminals and
terrorists, leveling charges against me. Well I'll tell you
one thing Mr. Prime Minister, you are about to make me
mad, and I think terrorists in the Middle East can tell you
what happens when you make me mad. Well, [with that
cocky grin on his face] they would tell you if they were still
around to do so."

The first question came from Robert Hammill of the
Dallas Morning News, who asked, "Does your last
statement mean that you are about to declare war on
Canada?"

The Speaker replied, "Only Congress can declare
war, and anytime Congress thinks an appropriate response
to a provocation is war, then, as long as I am acting in the
role of president, I will lead our troops to victory."

Dorothy Asbury of the *Chicago Tribune* asked,
"What evidence do you have that the Canadian government
has been involved with terrorists?"

Crooks answered, "I can't discuss sensitive
information like that in public, but let me say that when our
forensic teams uncover explosive trace elements that were
manufactured exclusively for a particular government's
military, then we tend to suspect that government." I knew
that Crooks had to have pulled that one out of the air. Any

explosives any of our teams had used were either U. S. issue or Russian.

Mark Gatlin of *CBS News* posed his question, "I want to go back to the indictments issued by the World Court. There must have been some shred of truth to them; I cannot imagine that a respected body like the Hague Tribunal would have based such serious charges on faulty evidence. Can you think of anything that they might have misconstrued to warrant these charges?"

Crooks's face flushed red, "I don't think those idiot judges at The Hague are all that respected. I have nothing further to say; this press conference is over." With cries of "Mr. Speaker," Crooks and his entourage exited the room.

Prime Minister McConihe called a press conference of his own soon after. In it he denied that Canada had been involved in harboring terrorists and legitimate criminals, but that Canada would always be a safe haven for people oppressed by a government simply for being who they are. He went on to talk more freely about the indictments, clarifying that Canada had assisted in the gathering of evidence to be used in the trials. He went on to say that the World Court's call to the U. S. Congress and military was the right way to pursue justice. He said emphatically that the United States need fear no invasion of Canadian armies and that he hoped tensions on the borders could be eased. McConihe went on to say he hoped Crooks would be arrested in the United States, but if he were to travel outside the country, he would have no immunity as a head of state.

McConihe was not interested in starting a war; he was trying to put pressure on Crooks to resign. In the interest of keeping dialogue open, both embassies maintained missions in their respective capitals. Nevertheless, Crooks was intransigent and the situation continued to deteriorate.

Exchanges between Ottawa and Washington became increasingly feverish. Secretary of State Carmen Ranciford and Foreign Minister Beckwith became talk show favorites for exchanging barbs. Ranciford claimed that Canada had knowingly and willingly violated the sovereignty of the United States by conducting secret and clandestine operations of espionage within the territorial confines of the United States, and had broken its treaty obligations by refusing to extradite fugitives from justice. Beckwith typically retorted that Canada had never violated U. S. sovereignty and that it had never failed to extradite legitimate criminals, but that it would never send people, who would be arrested as political prisoners, to their certain death. He went on to accuse the United States of sending spies into Canada to commit acts of violence targeted at those same people.

Foreign Minister Beckwith gave an interview in mid-May on the cable news show, *Lottie Roy Live*, and expounded upon the reasons why Canada refused to extradite the escapees. Beckwith insisted that the men given refuge in Canada were not criminals, but were political prisoners. Lottie Roy proceeded to read off a list of the charges leveled against some, which included tax evasion, racketeering, conspiracy, and fraud. Beckwith replied, "Those kinds of charges are typically used by governments to convict people who are guilty of other crimes for which they lack adequate evidence or legal authority to convict. The burden of proof is so vague that most anyone could probably be brought up on those kinds of charges." Roy understood Beckwith's point.

Beckwith went on to talk about the plight of the refugees should they be forced to return to the United States. He emphasized that Canada had certain clear and inviolable standards for granting asylum and that it was not something granted easily or lightly. He went on to say that these men faced torture and death for no other reason than that they were homosexual. He went on to say that the Canadian government had obtained conclusive evidence that the United States, under orders from Speaker Crooks, was pursuing a policy of arrest, torture, and murder of its homosexual male citizens. He finished his statements by saying that some of the men granted asylum in Canada and other countries had been freed from Nazi-style death camps.

Harry and I watched that interview together and knew the waiting would end soon. I spent more time in Ottawa than in Toronto, consulting with the Prime Minister and the Foreign Minister. Secretary of State Carmen Ranciford scheduled a meeting in Ottawa with Prime Minister McConihe in early June. Their hope was to come to some kind of agreement on the matter so that relations could normalize. McConihe asked me to come to Ottawa for the meetings. He needed my input, but also required my acquiescence to any agreement that might result.

Ranciford was insistent that extradition had to take place. McConihe was equally adamant that extradition could not be considered. She offered assurances that the men would not be killed. He insisted that due process would be the first requirement and that Canadian observers would have to be permitted in the courtrooms and detention facilities. Ranciford could never agree to such terms and the first round of meetings ended with no progress.

I expressed my concern to McConihe for even discussing extradition. What if she had accepted those terms; going back on any terms while a criminal like Crooks was running the country would be unacceptable. It would have been like expecting Hitler to be nice to Jews.

McConihe explained that it was necessary to attempt to negotiate. He knew there was no chance of her acceptance, and his dialogue increased his credibility for the next round. The next morning they met again. There had been no state dinners, as would normally have occurred. Ranciford stayed in the U. S. Embassy that night, making no public appearances in town. The next morning McConihe raised the issue of the camps. He told Ranciford that his government insisted that Speaker Crooks issue a statement outlining his role in and knowledge of the camps that had operated in the United States in violation of international law and treaties. Ranciford, of course, refused to acknowledge even the existence of the camps. It appeared that no point existed in the continuance of these talks, and Ranciford prepared to leave. McConihe's last words to her were his confidence in the prevalence of justice.

The day after she returned to Washington, Crooks recalled his ambassador from Ottawa. The Canadian Prime Minister did likewise. McConihe called a press conference to discuss the worsening relations between the United States and Canada. He opened with a statement that read, "I am legally and morally bound to ensure that Canada does business with nations that are in full compliance with international law, any treaties to which they are signatories, their own laws and/or constitutions, and the basic laws of human decency. When it comes to my attention that a sovereign nation's government is in violation of not one, but all four of those criteria, I have no choice but to break all normal relations with that government. I have just signed a directive, with the advice and consent of the leaders of our Parliament, which ceases to recognize the legitimacy of the government of the United States of America. Until such a time that the American people or the U. S. Congress replaces the criminal and rogue regime of Michael Crooks, the people of Canada shall maintain no relations with the United States."

It appeared that war was imminent. I pledged to the Prime Minister that we would form a refugee army to fight alongside Canadians if necessary. He thanked me and hoped it would not be necessary.

The situation grew critical soon after the press conference. The United States issued an ultimatum to Canada. The ultimatum listed the highest profile "terrorists" and demanded their immediate extradition; I was on that list. The Canadians had forty-eight hours to comply, or the United States would send in its own teams to make the arrests.

Within two hours of the Prime Minister's receipt of the ultimatum, we had Foreign Ministry personnel knocking on our door. They showed us a copy of the ultimatum and told us to grab whatever we could; the Prime Minister would meet us privately in Montreal. They had a car waiting for us, and the four of us were whisked away without any chance of notice by spies. We boarded a government jet. Scott and Allen, Jimmy and Marc, and both Matts were with us. The Foreign Ministry people assured us that we were not being sent back to the United States. We were being sent out of the country for both our safety and to give the Canadian Government an excuse of plausible deniability. If we mysteriously disappeared, then Crooks would have no theoretical reason to go to war with Canada.

We arrived in Montreal late at night, around eleven, I think. Prime Minister McConihe was there waiting for us. He walked up to me and we embraced. He apologized for reneging on his promise to protect us. He said, "I wish I didn't have to send you on, but against the U. S. army, we cannot protect ourselves, let alone you. You are going to London for now, there the British government will help you find more permanent quarters. This may be the last act of my government. U. S. troops are mobilizing along the entire border."

I thanked him again for his hospitality, and I apologized for putting him and his country in such grave danger. We boarded our planes. There were more than four hundred of us on the ultimatum list.

I was despondent on the flight across the Atlantic. It was late at night, and I needed to sleep, but could not. I kept thinking about everything we had been doing. I was scared to death that I was the one responsible for starting a world war. Harry saw the look on my face. He knew I was on the edge of a breakdown. He put his arm around me and pulled my head against his shoulder.

I said I was tired of running, running for my life, running to save others, running to do everything I had ever accomplished, and even tired of running to stay in shape. All I wanted to do was to take him to a club and go dancing where we could forget about all the horrors going on around us.

Harry replied in his soothing tone, "Joe, you just keep on running and don't ever stop. Look at how many thousands of lives you have saved this year. There is not a soul on this planet with a bigger heart than yours. I know I bitch at you about going away and being so involved in things, but that's just me. I wouldn't live with a Joe Kelly who didn't care enough to act on his convictions." I fell asleep in his arms.

We landed at Mildenhall Royal Air Force Base, about eighty miles north of London in mid-afternoon. British Foreign Ministry personnel were there upon our arrival and escorted us to temporary quarters on base. They told us to get some rest and we would be meeting with the British Foreign Minister the next day. He told us to be sure to watch the news and showed us how to get to a *BBC* channel.

We were still within the forty-eight hour deadline, and events had progressed rapidly. The Canadian Prime

Minister had gone on National Television to announce the mobilization of all Canadian forces along the United States border. He told Canadian citizens to prepare themselves for the struggle of their lives. He also told them that they would not be fighting alone. He said that other governments were outraged by the demands of the U. S. ultimatum, and that he was building an international alliance to defend Canada in the event of an attack.

News pundits rehashed the meaning of the Prime Minister's statements for hours. Then, the *BBC* announced that programming was being interrupted by a statement of Her Majesty, Queen Elizabeth II. This was unheard of. Not the British Prime Minister addressing the nation, but the Queen addressing the realm. I guess it made sense. She is, after all, the sovereign of Canada. In her speech, she recalled how Canadians and other peoples in the British Empire had come to the defense of England in two world wars. She said that it was time for the British Commonwealth to band together once again to defend the realm. She announced that, at that very moment, the British Navy and the Royal Air Force were sending troops to Canada to assist in its national defense. Alongside troops from the British isles, were forces from South Africa, Rwanda, Australia, New Zealand, India, and Pakistan. She had personally spoken with the governing councils of the European Union and NATO. Any act of aggression against Canada, would be viewed by these entities as warranting a military response. France, Great Britain, and India were placing their nuclear arsenals on high alert. She had even spoken with President Golitsyn in Moscow. For the time, he remained neutral, but made it clear that Russia would not welcome an expanded U. S. presence in North America.

The gauntlet was thrown and what happened at the expiration of the ultimatum's time limit, could very well determine the future of humanity. I wanted to call the

Prime Ministers of both Canada and Great Britain and volunteer to return to the U. S. if it would prevent a global war. It was too late for such maneuverings.

The time limit passed with no action. The British ambassador in Washington had informed Secretary Ranciford that all of the men on the list were safely in Britain. If Crooks wanted us, he would have to send his armies to England.

Several more days passed, and all was quiet. U. S. troops were still amassed along the Canadian border, and coalition troops were taking their places on the other side. The crisis seemed to have passed. A few days later reconnaissance revealed that U. S. troops were backing away from the Canadian border. Quiet tension remained with no word from the United States for several weeks. The world seemed to hold its breath.

Chapter 13   Hvidore

Though we were grateful for British hospitality, three weeks of barracks life was enough. Crooks appeared to be backing away from war, and we began to ponder refugee life in Europe. We were free to consider settling in any of several host countries.

I contacted Cameron, and he was excited at the prospect of us finding a place in London. He took us to London on an excursion to look for a place to live. Cam had cleaned up and looked more like I had remembered him. He showed us his flat and talked about how crowded London was. I told him it seemed just like any other big city I had seen. We found a few possibilities, but nothing definite. We went back to the barracks without any strong convictions towards any of the places we had seen. We were refugees, and it felt like anyplace we might try to settle would be temporary.

The next day a British Foreign Ministry official, Bruce Haslingden, arrived. He asked for me and told me that a new situation had developed that might offer an end to present circumstances. He asked me to leave immediately for a meeting in Spain, I would be debriefed *en route*.

Haslingden and I boarded the plane, and he introduced me to British Foreign Minister Lord Ramsey. Lord Ramsey told me what had transpired. Several top leaders of the United States military were prepared to discuss terms for the arrest of Crooks. He said that two Air

Force generals, the Chief of Naval operations, The Chief of
Staff of the Army, and one Marine general had suddenly
appeared in Madrid at the British embassy. They were in
Spain, ostensibly for meetings with Spanish military
leaders. Their staffs had conducted their own investigations
and had confirmed many of the allegations contained in The
Hague indictments.

They wanted to interview me to confirm some of
what they found and to make the other allegations credible.
I told them we should have brought Scott and Stormy; they
could have further lent credibility to my stories. Ramsey
understood that, but the American brass did not wish to
meet with anyone else. They insisted that I come without
any other accomplices.

The flight from London to Madrid was a little over
two hours. Ramsey spent most of his time conferring with
other colleagues. Haslingden sat with me after Ramsey was
done debriefing. He apologized for the accommodations we
had been given; they had not much warning and had to
come up with something rather quickly. I assured him the
accommodations were fine, much better than we would
have had in the States, and that we were grateful to be safe
and alive. He told me that his countrymen had been baffled
by the course the United States had chosen. He said that it
was such a shame that their closest ally had to have taken
such a wrong turn. I replied that unfettered democracy was
always in danger of running amok. I said that if Britain,
Canada, Australia, or any others of the British
Commonwealth ever went too far out of line, that the Queen
or King could always appeal for sanity.

I asked Haslingden if he thought war could be
averted. He replied that it depended on how one defined
war. Crooks had already declared war on a segment of his
own country. Now it was a matter of him deciding if he
should sue for peace or expand the war outside the

boundaries of the United States. Haslingden assured me
that whatever action Crooks chose, the world was prepared.
Haslingden went on to say that the defection of about a third
of Crooks's military certainly improved the prospects for
international peace.

We landed to a sunny summer afternoon at *Madrid
Barajas Airport*. Spanish security personnel escorted us to
a private area of the terminal. Waiting inside there was
Spanish Foreign Minister Hernan de Alvarez y Sotelo and
Canadian Foreign Minster Beckwith. Beckwith greeted me
warmly, "I knew we hadn't seen the last of you. Is the
mother country was treating you well?

I replied, "The barracks are no *Perseus*, but they
will do for now."

Alvarez greeted us all in the name of the King of
Spain and told us that his majesty wished for us to pursue
the course of peace with all haste.

We drove in sealed motorcade to the *Palacio Real
de Madrid*. Journalists speculated about the secret
emissaries arriving at the King's official residence, but
security had been sufficient to have kept all participants'
identities secret. Alvarez led us into a long room with
ornate press-plaster ceilings. The only furnishings in the
room were the twenty-foot long mahogany table and the
eighteen red-leather padded armchairs pulled up to it.
Alvarez positioned himself at the head of the table, with me
to his immediate right. Beckwith was next to me, followed
by Ramsey, and Haslingden. After we were seated, four
American generals and one admiral entered the room. Chief
of Naval Operations Admiral Hewitt was the most senior
member of the group and sat to Alvarez's left. He was
followed by Army Chief of Staff General McIntosh, Marine
General Dwyer, and Air Force Generals Stevens and Meeks.

Alvarez opened the proceedings by introducing
both sides to each other as far as was necessary. McIntosh,

a tall dark-skinned man with a severe butch cut shook my
hand across the table and said, "I understand you are an
Oklahoma boy." Not sure where that was going, I nodded
cautiously. He continued, "I'm from Checotah."

I smiled and said, "My mother is from Eufaula.
I've driven through Checotah many times. I know that
country well. I suppose with a name like McIntosh, you
must be Muscogee Creek."

"Well, of course. What was your mother's maiden
name?"

"Foley."

"They were white farmers down on the Canadian
River before the lake went in, weren't they?"

"Yeah. My granddad had a pretty good homestead
down there. You know, my aunt married a McIntosh. John
Henry was his name. He passed away a few years ago."

"I know exactly who he was. He was a decorated
World War II veteran in the Air Force." McIntosh looked
over at Air Force Generals Stevens and Meeks and said,
"John Henry could have flown circles around you fellows.
That's the kind of family this boy comes from; no wonder
The Federal Bureau of Protection couldn't catch him."

That was a good ice-breaker. Everyone except the
stoic Admiral Hewitt was laughing as they sat down. I
chuckled cautiously as well. Hewitt was nearing retirement
and had a flowing mane of grey hair. He spoke precisely
and used few adverbs. As the most senior member of the
group, he was in charge and directed their side of the
discussions and questioning. He neither cracked a smile nor
winced. He must have won every game of poker he had
ever played, which were probably few. Hewitt's scratchy
voice quieted the room, "Now that family reunions have
been concluded, I would like us to proceed with our
itinerary. Mr. Kelly, I hope you know that we have placed

our careers and our lives in jeopardy, I want you to listen to
our questions and answer them with direct candor."

I responded with, "Admiral and Generals, I fully
appreciate the gravity of the circumstances in which we all
find ourselves. Your actions in coming here are among the
bravest I could have imagined. General McIntosh, my
uncle, John Henry McIntosh, only gave me one piece of
advice. It was to have the "courage of my convictions." It
would have been easier, once I was safely in Canada, to
have resumed my life and never given another thought to
anyone inside the United States, but my uncle's voice
echoed in my head. I could not sit idly knowing that
innocent people were being tortured and murdered. My
actions were not aimed at you or the proud military
traditions of protecting the freedom you represent. I was
reacting to the agenda of a criminal regime. I do not want
any more killing, I want to do everything in my power to
prevent global war. Ask me any questions; discuss with me
anything you wish."

Admiral Hewitt asked me, "If it would stop a war,
would you come back to Washington with us?"

I stared at his steely eyes and replied, "If it would
stop the killing and torture, and prevent war, I would
without hesitation."

He said, "You know that you would be put on a
show trial and executed?" I nodded and he continued, "But
the only thing your return right now would accomplish
would be your own execution. If the return of the rule of
law is to be reborn in the United States, we must find
another alternative. General McIntosh, will you explain to
our friends on the other side of the table what we have
learned in the past few months?"

McIntosh started to speak, "When Joe here made
his debut on the national television it got our attention.
Keep in mind, we, as military personnel, were forbidden

from entering certain FBP facilities. We didn't even know where most of them were. I started hearing stories coming up through the ranks that some of the newer inductees were talking about the Federal Bureau of Protection buying up old abandoned factories and the like and turning them into some top secret operation. Those stories kept haunting me. I had seen your interview and, at the time, thought, "How absurd, we don't do things like that in America." I thought you either were nuts or a subversive fag. Well, those stories kept coming from Cincinnati, Pittsburgh, Detroit, Denver, Spokane, Albuquerque, Los Angeles, Sacramento, Tulsa, Kansas City . . . they came from every part of the country. At first I thought you boys were real good at spreading propaganda. After a bit, I began to think that you were better at it than the Speaker of the House.

"Finally, I got a call from General Ritchie at Camp Shelby. He asked me if I could come down to Mississippi. He said it was a matter of the utmost importance. I told him it had better be important for me to throw a kink in my schedule like that. I flew on down to Hattiesburg. It was in the middle of August and not a pleasant place to be. The commandant met me at the airfield and we went straight back to his office. On the way it was nothing but pleasantries and talking about the weather.

"Ritchie told me that he had heard more than his fair share of stories about these so-called concentration camps. It had gotten to the point on base where most of the soldiers took it as a matter of fact. One weekend a carload of soldiers on pass headed in to Pensacola. They had heard about one of the camps there. They drove around all hours of the night looking for it, until they stumbled onto it around dawn. The boys saw the FBP signs warning people not to linger. They were under strict orders, whether on leave or on duty to stay away from anything that said FBP. They snuck off into some bushes and watched for awhile.

Pretty soon a train came with a bunch of cattle cars attached. It stopped inside the compound and the cars emptied their load of human cargo. Some of the men looked like they had been beaten, others were filthy and despondent.

"They stayed there and watched until all the prisoners were inside the building. They tried to get back to their car quietly, and, guess what, one of them made a noise. They were detained by FBP officers at an office in town. They were questioned for two days. By that time they were AWOL from their base, and their sergeant started calling the hospitals and police departments. Finally, General Ritchie received a call from someone in Washington that said his men had been detained in Pensacola.

"He sent a detachment to bring them back to base. Ritchie said he chewed them out royally for hanging around a Federal Bureau of Protection compound. One of them broke down and started crying. He said, "All those stories are true. Those are death camps." The rest of the soldiers starting spilling their guts about what they had seen. Ritchie asked them if they had let on to any FBP personnel about what they had seen. They said they were careful not to. In all their interrogations they had consistently said they had only been there for a few minutes and were going to pass out after drinking too much. That was good. They probably never would have made it back to base if they had told the truth about what they had seen.

"Ritchie had sent a more professional team down there after that, who confirmed the soldiers' stories. That was when he called me. I couldn't believe it. What in the Hell were those FBP people doing? They were going to spoil everything we had fought for in the Army. I asked him to let me meet those soldiers.

"I sat them down and I said, "You had better listen up, because you will never hear anything like this from me again. I am proud of you boys for failing to follow orders in this, and only this situation. You may well have saved your country from destruction. There is something we teach you about orders. You are to follow them without question or hesitation. There comes a time in some countries though, when orders should be disobeyed. When a commander gives you an order that is in violation of the basic laws of humanity, you must not follow those orders. I don't care if it is a platoon commander or the Commander-in-Chief, if you are given an order that you know in your heart is morally wrong, you disobey. You might not think much of gays, fags, fairies, or whatever you call them, but they are human. They deserve the same right to life, liberty, and the pursuit of happiness as you and me. That is what we fight for; that is why we are soldiers. I am telling you here and now, that I will fight for their freedom as much as I will for your hometown. Are you with me?" They said they were. After the soldiers left, I told Ritchie that we had some work to do. I told him that we were about to face the most difficult struggle we could ever imagine. I didn't need to tell him we were about to turn against the government; he knew what I meant. He assured me that Camp Shelby would follow my lead. He also assured me that I could count on most Army commanders. I saluted and told him I would expect nothing less.

    "At my next meeting with the Joint Chiefs, I decided to probe the other chiefs and see if and what they knew. During breaks I asked in a joking tone if others had heard some of those crazy rumors about concentration camps. Several laughed and said they had. We started our meetings again, and General Green of the Air Force, who is the Chairman of the Joint Chiefs, said, "I don't know why we have to waste time talking about silly rumors, I don't want to hear any more of this "camp" talk. It ends right here, and you need to pass that on to your subordinates.

This order is straight from the acting President." I knew then what I was facing.

"Admiral Hewitt came up to me after the meeting and said, "Mildred and I would like for you and Carolyn to join us for supper tonight." I told him we would be delighted. We met at their house for cocktails at seven sharp. Carolyn went off to the kitchen to help Mildred with the hors d'oeuvres. The admiral asked me what I thought about the camp stories. I needed to be a little cagey, so I said, "Well, it seems funny to me that these stories keep popping up all over the place. I can't believe everyone is making them up, how 'bout you?" He told me that he more than believed them. He had some pretty reliable sources. At that I opened up and told him about Pensacola. He said he knew about that one.

"We agreed to conduct an internal investigation within our own commands. We would share our results and collaborate as much as possible. The Marines and Air Force didn't seem open on the subject yet, but maybe after we had the evidence, they would come along. We went back to Pensacola with the hope of sending in some undercover agents to see what was going on. Unfortunately they arrived two days after one of your teams liberated it. That seemed to happen almost everywhere we went, Pittsburgh, Rochester, Los Angeles. We finally got into Madison a few weeks before your boys arrived."

I said, "I led the team that liberated that camp. Were your people inside there at the time? That was back in the spring of last year I think."

McIntosh said, "No, our people were just in there for a few days. They were horrified at what they saw. They saw guys being taken out and beaten for no reason. Living conditions were worse than would be considered humane for a dog. Is that how all the camps were run?"

I said, "No, Madison was just a work camp. It wasn't as bad as many of the others. The death camps and the holding camps are where conditions are really bad. At least a guy has a reasonably good chance for survival in a work camp. Did your investigators go into any others?"

McIntosh answered, "Yeah, but they were all about the same. We sent reconnaissance into four other camps. Actually we sent one last batch to a camp, but they didn't come back. We figured they must have been found out. By then we had enough information, so we stopped the investigations."

I asked, "Where was this lost team sent?"

"Cincinnati."

I rolled my eyes, "How did your teams go in, were they disguised as inmates, guards, or support staff?"

He replied, "We tried going in as support staff, but realized we couldn't get a good survey of what was going on. Most of them went in as prisoners. That's what the team in Cincinnati was."

I said, "Cincinnati was a death camp. If your men went in as prisoners, they were probably executed and their remains destroyed."

McIntosh looked like he was about to explode. "How do you know?"

"I liberated the last load of prisoners. They were shipping them to a destruction facility on the river. Your men would have had no idea what was coming. They never had a chance."

Admiral Hewitt took over the questioning at that point, "That is precisely the kind information we were seeking. We received a copy of the World Court's indictment, and were baffled at the charges about the death camps. What can you tell us about their operations, and what evidence do you have?"

For a moment I wondered if this might be a fishing expedition sent by the administration to find out just what we had. I knew, though, that telling them what I had seen would not compromise my integrity as a witness, besides I had already given my deposition. I described in detail what I had seen and told them about the evidence we had collected, though I did not give a lot of detail about the evidence. The admiral and generals were most horrified when I told them about Montana.

A furious General McIntosh commented to Admiral Hewitt, "This is the sort of thing I was afraid of when the Federal Bureau of Protection started building its own military forces and took control of certain functions from the armed forces. We now have two military structures in the United States, one under Joint Chiefs command and the other under no accountable command, except that of Speaker Crooks. In a sense they are his own private army. Should we decide to oppose him, he will have a formidable defensive structure that we will have to break down. That assumes, of course that the Joint Chiefs are united. If it is only the Army and the Navy with a few battalions of Marines and a few planes, I am not sure we can prevail. Congress should never have authorized the creation of a military structure outside the command of the Joint Chiefs. I opposed it then, and I was right."

Dwyer assured us there would be more than just a few battalions of marines. He insisted there were two complete companies that would join. Stevens and Meeks, however, agreed that the Air Force would be the toughest of the armed services to bring along. If their chief of staff failed to support the opposition, we would not be able to count on much air support. Without air superiority at the outset, a quick ouster of Crooks would be impossible. They could fly him all over the country and there would be little the other armed services could do about it.

Stevens and Meeks also tossed out the possibility that if stalemate dragged out too long, civil war would wreck the country. Crooks could toss what was left of the Constitution aside and declare himself dictator for life. Meeks began to argue that as bad as Crooks was, maybe they should only try to ride out the remainder of President O'Hara's term when a new president could be elected.

The generals came back around and agreed that their goal was to eliminate Crooks and restore President O'Hara to the head of government. Part of the problem with that, however, was that no one knew where the President was. Shortly after the coup, Crooks had moved the President and his family from Belgium to a black site. None of the Joint Chiefs had been privy to the exact location. The generals were worried that the President might be executed the moment a counter-coup started.

They understood, however, that they had reached a point of no return. When they went back to the United States it would be to shore up their support structures and win as many converts from the other side before the other side could figure out a mutiny was in process. I offered my forces to the struggle. McIntosh thanked me, "You and your boys have done a great service to your country already. As far as I am concerned you all are national heroes. We have plenty of troops to succeed, and we need all of your men alive to tell their stories at trial when all of this is over. You need to understand that it may take several years before you can come home."

I pleaded with them to let us take part, "If people see us fighting along side regular military, they will start to accept us. They will understand that what we have been fighting for is freedom for the entire nation, not just ourselves." Hewitt told me that the decision was made and I needed to respect it. I continued, "All I want is to be able to pull up in my driveway and walk into my home without fear of anyone or anything. Why can I not be a part of making that happen? It is my home for which I am fighting."

McIntosh said, "I know where your home is, and you will return when it is safe. Until then, I don't want to catch you inside the country again. If I do, I will arrest you for your own safety, is that clear?"

I could not stand the thought of no longer being at the center of the action, but I agreed. They did, however, ask me for tactical assistance, which I gladly provided. I was reluctant at first to give names of contacts inside the United States, but we worked out a system where I and my men would make the initial contact through third parties. A cell system was already in place to protect the resistance we had built. That resistance would help to counter-balance any advantage the Air Force might give to Crooks. A good many of our resistance fighters were air traffic controllers.

Our meetings continued for two more days. I gave them every piece of logistical information I could remember. We set up a secure communications network, so that we could continue to funnel information to our military forces. Hewitt and McIntosh promised to continue sending prisoners from liberated camps to us in Europe.

The Admiral and the Generals had to depart before they missed their scheduled return from their supposed meetings with the Spanish military. I spent the next day with Canadian Foreign Minister Beckwith. He apologized for not being able to invite us back to Canada. He said that even though the threat of invasion had passed, with the difficulties about to start inside the United States, they would still not be able to guarantee our safety. I thanked him for all that he and McConihe had done, and told him that we certainly respected their decisions.

Harry was at the airport awaiting my return. Stormy and Cole were there as well. I told them all about

the defections to our side and they were elated. They
wondered when we could all go home. I told them it would
be quite a while. We might not be able to go home for
several years, if ever.

We chose Zurich for the command structure to
communicate with the Joint Chiefs. Matt Crossly had
moved into his chalet there. We figured that would be a
great place to direct our activities.

Most of the men we had freed, who had been in
Canada, had gone to southern France, Switzerland, Southern
Germany, or the Netherlands. A few groups had gone to
Scandinavia, and some stayed in the British Isles. Most of
the Bay City crew had gone to France. I thought we should
move there as well, though I was no great fan of French
culture. Harry and Stormy both, however, had received
excellent job offers in Denmark. With the rail and air
transportation system in Europe, it did not matter where we
lived as long as we were on the continent.

I went on to Zurich for two weeks to set up our
command center. Harry called me from Copenhagen to tell
me he had found a wonderful home for us. I told him to go
ahead and buy it, but he insisted I come to Copenhagen. I
trusted his judgment and knew he would find the perfect
thing for our lifestyle, but he insisted. He picked me up at
the airport and drove me north along the coast. I kept
asking where we were headed, but he wanted to surprise
me. We continued on and Harry told me I had to close my
eyes. Stormy was in the back seat and he reached around to
put a blindfold on me. We drove for another fifteen minutes
before we stopped.

Harry removed the blindfold. I knew instantly
where we were, it was Hvidore, near the villa that had been
the 1920s home of Marie Feodorovna, the Russian Dowager
Empress. She was born Danish Princess Dagmar, and had
married Alexander III, moved to St. Petersburg, and was the

mother of the last reigning Tsar, Nicholas II. After her
escape from Russia during the revolution, she moved into
her home there. It seemed appropriate for us to live near
her last home. She was a refugee from Russia, and we were
refugees from America.

I finished my work in Zurich and went home to
Hvidore. Most of our furniture was new; Harry had gone on
a much needed shopping spree in Copenhagen. The
remainder of our personal belongings had just arrived from
Britain. At one point I marveled at how the ever-so-delicate
Steuben glassware had survived a midnight boat ride to
Tobermory, and shipment to Copenhagen. Nothing was
broken, chipped, or missing.

While I had been working in Zurich, the battle
began in earnest in the United States. Hewitt and McIntosh
timed their challenge perfectly. Upon returning home, they
secured their base of support. A few more corps defected
from the Air Force, but most of the Marines and Air Force
remained loyal to Crooks. Crooks knew there had been
some rumblings of discontent in the armed forces after
having had to back down on his invasion of Canada, but he
had no idea that disaffection reached to the highest levels.

At a meeting of the Joint Chiefs in which Crooks
presided, McIntosh and Hewitt made their moves. Crooks
entered the room and the two generals remained seated,
refusing to stand at attention or salute. Crooks angrily
ordered them to apologize or risk losing their positions.
They refused. Crooks threatened to have them arrested,
and, at that point, armed guards entered the room to
guarantee the safety of Hewitt and McIntosh. Hewitt
replied with indignation, "Mr. Speaker, it is time for you to
resign and allow the duly-elected President of the United
States to return to office. You can save the republic and
avoid bloodshed, but neither General McIntosh, nor I will
permit you to remain in power."

General Green, Commandant of the Marines,
buzzed his security teams and ordered them to intervene.
They were under the direct command of General Dwyer and
refused to obey. Their colonel entered the room, siding
with Hewitt and McIntosh. By that time, Secret Service and
FBP forces loyal to Crooks entered the room, all with guns
drawn.

Hewitt spoke up, "Mr. Speaker, I'll ask you again to
resign. Barring that, however, the rest of us appear to be at
a standoff. Once the first bullet flies, every man in this
room will be killed. I suggest that if you fail to resign, we
declare a truce until we all exit the room safely and have
returned to our bases."

Crooks asked, "What if I do resign; then will you
simply let me walk out of here?"

Hewitt replied, "No, upon your resignation, we will
arrest you and all of the others named in the World Court
indictment. Congress will then be free to elect a new
Speaker, who will act as president until the real president
can be returned to serve out the remainder of his term in
accordance with the Constitution." At that, the Joint Chiefs
agreed to retire under flag of truce for twenty-four hours,
while the Speaker weighed his options.

Crooks had no intention of resigning. He went
straight to Andrews Air Force Base to entrench. Hewitt,
McIntosh, and the generals supporting them retired to their
strongest points of operations. Admiral Hewitt set up base
in San Diego. A big concern in the beginning had been the
national defensive structure's base in Central Colorado. It
was under Air Force administration, but it controlled
delivery of Presidential orders to all nuclear missiles. In the
first hour of the truce, General Meeks, in joint operations
with General Dwyer, had seized control of the facility.
McIntosh moved his central operations to the base, which

had communications capability with every base, in the country.

With that capability, McIntosh effectively became the supreme authority in liberated America, though he made it clear that he served at the pleasure of the rightful President. Hewitt's navy quickly secured all major ports, and Crooks had to move inland. Crooks was far from finished. He still had popular support in the southern and central parts of the country. The coastal states in the north and west quickly ousted the remnants of the Crooks regime and declared loyalty to McIntosh, who with his southern brand of Native American charm easily won support amongst many who might have tended to support the Crooks regime.

In the first months of the struggle both sides focused their energies on securing the territories where they could entrench. The battleground areas that emerged were in the southern coastal cities and the northern states in the plains and Rockies. In the northern tier of states McIntosh controlled Idaho, Montana, Wyoming, and the northern part of North Dakota. To keep the northern states connected to the west, it was critical to keep those states in tact, especially the right of way of the *Great Northern Railway*. If the Crooks Army could seize even a small chunk of that link, communications and shipping capabilities between New York and the west coast would be effectively severed.

The southern coastal cities, especially the Washington/Baltimore area would be the next major battle area. What was left of Crooks's government set up shop at Andrews Air Force Base. They considered Washington no longer a safe place. Baltimore was occupied by the Navy, and a large squadron of the Atlantic fleet controlled the waters of the Chesapeake. If Crooks could take Baltimore, he would not only have a seaport, he could re-occupy Washington, which would go a long way towards relegitimizing his government. At the moment Washington was a free city, with neither side in occupation.

The first real fighting was the battle of Andrews Air Base. An army under McIntosh's command was entrenched at Fort Meade. They had discovered that Crooks was moving Marine and Federal Bureau of Protection forces into Andrews for their attempted attack on Baltimore. With a well coordinated effort on the part of Navy air patrols, ship to surface missiles, and an infantry attack, Crooks was forced to abandon Andrews. His army pushed inland as far back as Wheeling, West Virginia. With the capital area secured, McIntosh flew into National Airport on an army transport. With a cheering crowd of Washingtonians, he ordered the lights to be turned back on around all the national monuments."

From the capitol steps McIntosh held a news conference that broadcast throughout the territory he controlled and some of Crooks's territory. In his address, he said he had no interest in establishing a military dictatorship, but his only motivation was for the return of legitimate, democratically elected civilian government and the complete restoration of the Constitution. He outlined Crooks's crimes, apologizing to the American people for having to take such drastic actions. He said that Congress would be welcome to return to the Capitol building and resume its work, but that Congress must first purge itself of any criminal elements, namely those members who were Crooks's accomplices. Once a new Speaker of the House had been elected by Congress, he offered to turn all aspects of government, including the military over to the new Speaker, who would then return power to the President as soon as the President could be found and brought back to the country.

Within a few hours, McIntosh had heard from Congressional leaders in the states he controlled, and with his assurances that Washington was safe, they agreed to return to the capital, officially purge their own errant members, and select a new Speaker. Congressional leaders pledged to select a new Speaker committed to the restoration of constitutional government. At that point, the new Speaker could legitimately take control of civilian government where it existed.

Regardless what Congress did, Crooks was far from finished. He launched a counter attack in North Dakota, hoping to cut the northern lifeline. At the same time, he launched a massive attack in Colorado to oust McIntosh from the central command post. McIntosh's armies guarded both and were ready for anything Crooks's marines could attempt. They held out famously in both locations.

McIntosh's first priorities after fending off the northern attack were to expand control along the plains, so as to strengthen his connection between Montana and Minnesota. He also moved the eastern armies into stronger positions around the capital to secure the rest of Maryland and much of Virginia. Virginia was a challenge as much of its population was hostile. Nevertheless, three House members and one Senator from Virginia returned to Washington. Richmond was free, and the governor, though one who had supported Crooks's regime, declared his support for McIntosh and O'Hara. The rest of Virginia reluctantly followed.

Congress reconvened with the Virginia delegation and about half the delegations from states still under Crooks's control. Congress had a legitimate quorum and went to work restoring constitutional government. Several other governors followed the lead of Virginia's and, though occupied by Crooks's armies, declared their support for Constitutional restoration.

The new Speaker of the House, Richard Schumacher from New York, gave a press conference from the East Room of the White House. As the Speaker succeeding to the acting presidency, he said that the Constitution was functioning as it should and that the United States system of government would prove to the world that even when subjected to utterly corrupt officials, it could survive and freedom would once again be the law of the land. He again pledged to hand over civilian authority to President O'Hara as soon as he could be located and retrieved.

Admiral Hewitt and Generals McIntosh, Meeks, and Dwyer were at his side. Schumacher said that in the interest of restoring a sound defensive structure, he had ordered the restoration of the Joint Chiefs, with General McIntosh as its head, who would report to him in the interim. He strongly encouraged military commanders then fighting the new legitimate government to declare their loyalty to the new heads of their respective branches of the military. He promised no recriminations once they had sworn loyalty to the new government.

Some generals did abandon Crooks. It appeared that the Crooks regime would be finished soon enough, but McIntosh and Schumacher favored a strategic policy that spared U. S. cities the destructive forces of total war. Their targets were purely military. Population centers would be brought back under national control only when it was safe to do so. Though less destructive, such a policy threatened to take years to restore peace again in the United States.

After losing the east coast Crooks set up a temporary capital in Dallas, Texas. He was relatively safe there, knowing that Texas would be the last place to fall to the new government's Army. It was also his hometown. Crooks's army tried several counter attacks, but having lost much of its resources and manpower, the best it could hope for was stalemate for a long enough time that both sides would welcome a compromised peace.

Chapter 14   Greenleaf

I appreciated the beauty of the Baltic Sea, even in the grip of winter. I began to long for a sailboat and looked for a craft suitable for sailing on the Baltic. I found an old yacht that had at one time been owned by a member of the Danish royal family. It was a 56' Ketch. It was in terrible condition, but was a stunning boat. It was a fitting successor to the *Polar Star II*, though it would take at least a year to get it seaworthy and fitted out properly.

I took some time off to get the yacht into a shipyard where it could be dry-docked. In Copenhagen I had no trouble finding shipwrights qualified to begin the restoration. I had always done my own restorative work, but a boat as large as this one required skills, facilities, and tools that I did not possess. Still I insisted that the shipwright allow me to do at least some of the chores, mostly in the tear-down phase.

About two weeks into the project, Harry came into where I was working. He asked me why I had not answered my cell. I told him I had it off, wanting to work without distraction. Harry said that General McIntosh had called the house for me and wanted me to call him right away. I dropped what I was doing and rode back home with Harry.

I called for McIntosh on the way. His secretary returned my call after we were home and transferred me to McIntosh. His first words to me were, "Your country needs you."

I replied, "What can I do?"

He said, "I apologize for breaking a promise. I didn't want you back in the country until this mess is over, but I have a job that needs to be done, and you are the best man for it. We are still encountering detention camps. I need you to pull some of your men together to help us clean them out for good. I can get you on a civilian flight out of Copenhagen to *Heathrow* in three hours, is that enough time?"

I said, "I have to shower and pack, but I think I can make that. I don't know what you want us to do, but I already know who I will want on my team."

McIntosh replied, "Right now I only want you to come. We will get your team on their way probably tomorrow. I'll have my boys in London at the airport to meet you. We've got a plane commandeered to bring you to Washington. You'll be flying into *National*. Just bring enough clothing for a couple of days, and tell Harry to be prepared to leave soon. He can come on to Washington with the others in a day or two." I told McIntosh I would see him later that evening and hung up the phone.

Harry was already red-faced with fury. I explained to him that it had something to do with the camps. It helped ease his anger when I told him he was coming to America a few days after me. I told him to get Stormy, Cole, and the others ready to go as well. I would probably need them. I jumped in the shower while Harry pressed a shirt and got my clothes ready. We arrived at the airport with about fifteen minutes to spare.

Two men in U. S. Army uniforms were at the gate for me when I landed at *Heathrow*. Sergeants Miller and Peabody introduced themselves and told me our flight was ready to leave at that moment. They were the very portrait of military stoicism. They never smiled, and every answer was "Yes Sir," or "No Sir." I tried, without success, to open them up a bit. I asked if they knew anything about why I was going to Washington or what I was expected to do. They were merely escorts and knew nothing. Miller suggested I get some rest, as I would probably have a long night with the General when I got to Washington.

We had one flight attendant on board. I asked him if, since we were the only ones on the plane, I could get comfortable. He smiled and said, "You can get as comfortable as you want." I took off my coat, trousers, and shirt, leaving only my t-shirt and shorts on. He brought me a blanket. I asked to be awakened about an hour before our initial descent so I could freshen up and dress.

Peabody woke me up at the appointed time. He had a cup of coffee for me. I thanked him and asked him to sit for a few minutes while I sipped my coffee. I said, "You have to know something, besides the fact that I am going to meet with General McIntosh."

He dropped his guard a bit and cracked a short smile, "All I know sir, is that you are a very famous person. Anywhere you go something spectacular is bound to happen." I went into the restroom to splash my face and put on some fresh deodorant. I was dressed and ready when the flight attendant announced our preparation for landing.

It was about eight at night and Washington was lit like always. It had been almost four years since I had been to Washington. From the air everything looked normal as we circled around for the initial approach, the Capitol was ablaze in amber lighting, and the Washington Monument and Lincoln and Jefferson Memorials were lit around their perimeters. I thought about how those monuments again stood for something worthwhile.

We landed at the old *Northwest* terminal at Washington *National Airport*. The Army had taken use of the terminal for transports like mine. Miller and Peabody escorted me down the jet way. I spotted General McIntosh there waiting for me with a big grin on his face. I remembered the white terrazzo floors well. I started to walk on ahead and Peabody said, "Sir." I stopped and looked back at him. He smiled broadly and said, "God Speed, sir." He and Miller saluted and walked away.

McIntosh shook my hand and asked me about my flights. We walked down to his limo that was waiting at the old taxi curb in front of the terminal and drove straight to the Pentagon. He wasted no time in telling me why I was there, "I told you that we are still encountering camps when we liberate areas. At first they were pretty much just work camps. Conditions were deplorable, but the men were at least alive. That situation has now changed. We have started seeing more death camps, and it appears that Crooks is now converting work camps into death camps. He knows he is losing the war and wants all the gay men in his territory destroyed before we arrive. I think he knows he will, at the very least, go to jail and very possibly be executed for treason and genocide. The man is a dangerous animal now, and we have to accelerate our timeline for total victory.

"I would have preferred to do this with Army personnel, but I need you and your men. Quite frankly, I don't have the manpower to go after these camps as quickly as I want. Your men have more experience with these camps than anyone else. We have also had some issues with liberated prisoners thinking we were there to kill them. They just see us as another arm of the government. I think you and your men could diffuse those fears right away and avoid the risk of blowing the whole mission at the outset. I need you to get your boys together and go behind enemy lines to liberate as many camps as possible. I don't want those death camps operating any longer than possible. That is your mission; are you up to it?"

I replied, "I am up for anything to save lives and liberate camps. You know, we had to stop operations because Crooks and the Federal Bureau of Protection had learned too much about us and were beginning to anticipate our moves. Security around those camps will be tight. I am not sure we can get in."

McIntosh assured me, "Back then you boys were doing it pretty much on your own. It amazed me at how successful you were with only peripheral help from the Canadians. Now you are going to have the support of the most sophisticated military intelligence structure in the world. We can get you in and out. I need you to get to the camps and liberate them."

I reminded him of the "John" incident at Harrisburg. I was concerned that we could be bringing spies back with us. McIntosh said, "I share that concern, and for that reason, as well as the safety of the liberated prisoners, they will be going directly out of the country until this thing is over. The Canadian government has agreed to start taking them again, but this time they will be screened and monitored. We have ways to identify spies."

We were at the Pentagon and went in to McIntosh's office. Some Congressional leaders came in along with General Andrews, who was the Army General in charge of Intelligence and Clandestine Activities. McIntosh told me I would be directly responsible to him, but that Andrews would help to coordinate my activities. I said, "Responsible? How so?"

McIntosh explained, "This will be an Army operation. You and your men will, for the duration of your missions, be inducted into the Army."

I smiled, "But we are all openly gay. I thought that was illegal again."

McIntosh said, "A lot of things have changed here in Washington in the past months. Our current Congress repealed all of the Crooks era laws criminalizing homosexuality. A new law once again permits gay men and women to serve their country with honor and forbids discrimination against anyone on the basis of sexuality."

I said, "I have never been in the military. I am not sure I would know how to function."

He replied, "You'll be fine. Yours will be a special unit entirely under your command and directly responsible to me. You will hold the rank of Colonel. You will have total liberty to determine how your command is structured. What I would like to see is for you to operate just as you did before. Structure your unit so your men can go to work right away. I would like all three of your teams in operation. One team will be based in California and will operate in the Great Basin and southwestern states. Another team will be based in Des Moines and will service the Plains and Mountain states. Another team, yours, I presume, will be based here in Washington and will take care of the Deep South."

I told him, "We need more than just the operation teams. What made it work before was having the logistics teams both inside and outside the country. Here is the structure I want. We'll send Matt Crossly back to Toronto to coordinate refugee services and screen for saboteurs and spies. I want Roger working with your logistics personnel inside enemy lines and Harry in charge of Logistics on our side of the lines. Pete will operate the Plains group and Dan Shotwell will operate the West Coast group. We will get into situations where we will need Army support. My commanders will need direct contact with a member of General Andrews's division. I will want them standing by to help us with any difficult situations. Do you know where any of the camps are? Locating them is always the most time consuming part."

General Andrews answered, "I've got my teams working on that right now. We know where some are. I do know that they have reestablished some of the ones you took out. Cincinnati's organ warehouse is back in operation. I want you to make that one a priority. We are preparing to launch an offensive along the Ohio River between Cincinnati and Owensboro. We are anxious to reopen navigation on the Ohio. St. Louis is already back under federal control, so we are ready to open the Mississippi right now. The only thing holding us back is the Ohio. I am afraid that as soon as we launch the offensive, the enemy will mass execute any prisoners in the area."

I asked for a phone so I could call my lieutenants. McIntosh said he would have transport planes in Copenhagen, Amsterdam and Zurich by morning. I called Harry; it was about six in the morning in Denmark. I told him to have everyone there ready to go by noon. I told him I would meet him at the airport when they arrived. I called Pete, Scott, Roger, and Matt next. I told them to get their teams together and be at their respective airports by noon as well. I told them they would be coming on ahead of the men. The rest would leave in the next several days. They all wanted to know what was happening, but I told them they would be briefed in Washington.

They set me up an operational headquarters at the Pentagon, but my base would be at Manassas, Virginia. It was about two in the afternoon when Harry's plane arrived. He and Stormy stopped dead cold when they saw me in a colonel's uniform. I saluted as they approached. Harry said, "Can't you get arrested for dressing like that?"

I said, "It's not illegal when you *are* an army colonel."

I took Harry, Stormy, and Cole back to the Pentagon. Stormy commented as we passed the security checkpoint, "Into the lair of the beast we go."

I told him, "You might want to tone that kind of language down when we get inside. They are our allies now."

Stormy said, "It's too much to comprehend. If you had told me two months ago that today I would be walking, unchained, through the halls of the Pentagon, I would not have believed it."

It would take several weeks to get all the men together and get all three teams operational. That was more time than we had for Cincinnati. I asked Stormy and Pete to stay with us at Manassas so that with whatever team we could piece together we could proceed. We had to be operational within a few days. Harry and Roger went to work coordinating logistical support. Harry would have army transport trucks and planes to get the men away from the checkpoint and into Canada. A hospital plane would be standing by for any men who needed medical attention. The goal was to have everyone airborne within one hour after crossing back into friendly territory.

Roger had a few new challenges. After the "John" incident *IDS*'s cover was blown and they were under tight scrutiny by the Crooks regime. In fact, Federal Bureau of Protection forces had set up a command post at the *IDS* brain center in Louisville, Kentucky. Any misstep by *IDS* personnel and Federal Bureau of Protection was under orders to destroy the Louisville facility. For internal transport, Roger had to rely on a patchwork system of moving and trucking companies. In Cincinnati he would use a local moving company.

Most of Ohio was secure, but the southern third of the state from south of Columbus to the Ohio River was still under control of the Crooks regime. The same was true for Indiana to about Evansville. Friendly forces controlled western Kentucky from Owensboro west to the Mississippi River. The new federal government controlled the

Mississippi River as far south as St. Louis, Missouri.
McIntosh wanted to control the major river systems, a
strategy dictated by geography. If he could secure the
Mississippi and Ohio Rivers, Crooks's realm would be
divided. With his capital in Dallas, the Deep South might
be regained without prolonged and destructive military
operations.

     We made our reconnaissance mission within a few
days. There we met up with some army intelligence men
who gave us the lay of the facility. They told us Crooks
knew he could not keep territory in Ohio and Indiana and
was planning to abandon south of the Ohio as soon as the
offensive started. They were planning to entrench on the
other side of the river.

     I told them I needed to get into the facility to scope
it out. They told me that would be difficult. Security was
too tight and FBP personnel would spot me instantly. With
the right disguise, however, I might get in unnoticed. The
Army Intelligence men wanted to go with me, but I told
them they would be too obvious. I suggested that Don
Sweetwater, their commander, go with me.

     Don told me he was gay and was one of the first
Army men to have come out after the new law passed
permitting gays and lesbians to serve. I asked him how the
other men had taken it when he came out. He said that most
of them had been great, but there were a few who were
unsure about sleeping in the same bunker with a fag.

     Roger had contacts at the switching yard in
Cincinnati where the trains came through carrying
prisoners. Don and I boarded a train while it was being held
in the yard. We were in the third car from the rear. The
men there were surprised to see strangers boarding at that
point. We asked them where they had originated. They had
come from West Virginia and eastern Kentucky. As

Crooks's forces retreated, they swept through the towns and cities and rounded up any homosexuals they could find.

We told them we were with the United States Army and were there to liberate them. They asked us where we were; they had been traveling for more than a day and were disoriented. I told them we were headed to a death camp in Cincinnati, but that we would liberate them before anything could happen.

The camp was in worse condition than when we were there the first time. It was crowded, with about twelve hundred prisoners. The old organ factory was still a holding area. An execution camp was set up nearby. We could see the smoke stacks from where we were. Security was much tighter, but it did not take Don and me long to figure out an escape route. Old buildings are terrible for security and a breeze for getting into and out of without notice. There was an old loading dock that was boarded up and sealed off from the camp. No guards were stationed there. We figured out a way to remove and replace the boards easily without it looking like anyone had tampered with them.

The next night we were back with the rest of our team. While we had been at the main camp, Stormy, Marc, and Scott had gone to the death camp. It was an old foundry on the outskirts of town. There was only one rickety railroad track leading into it. They determined that they could easily sabotage the tracks making it look like track failure. All they had to do was, by hand, loosen some of the clamp plates from the ties. When a train came by, the tracks would spread out and derail the engine. That night they watched from the bushes while the train made its run to the death camp. The engine tipped over as the tracks spread out underneath it. It would take at least two days to get the tracks back in service. That would be enough time to liberate the main camp.

The Army intelligence squadron was to create a diversion outside the front of the camp. That would enable us to go in the back way, and open up the loading dock. We had moving trucks ready to roll in, back up to the dock, and load up the prisoners. It would take ten trucks to get everyone out. The dock had five bays, so we could do it in two shifts. The men from our train car were supposed to have networked through the facility and have everyone ready.

We got to the woods outside the compound and waited for the diversion. Something held up Don's team; they were almost an hour late. I was almost ready to take a crew and go around front to start our own diversion when the rockets started firing. The search lights went on and, as planned, the FBP guards went out the front gates, leaving a skeleton crew to guard the prisoners. We easily took them out, but the camp commandant must have called for backup when the diversions started. Within fifteen minutes another two hundred FBP troops were on the scene battling with Don's squadron.

I was afraid they were about to be lost. The trucks loaded the first shift and pulled out for the second shift. I asked the trucks to load the first four as heavily as possible to see if they could get the rest of the prisoners in them. They did, and that left the fifth truck to stay behind to wait for us. I sent it to a safe rendezvous point a quarter mile down the road. The other four went on for their trip to the stretch of I-70, where the transport planes would land to pick up the prisoners. I took my team out into the woods to create a secondary diversion, hoping to take some of the heat off of Don's team. We launched rockets directly inside the compound, destroying the main building. It did the trick. The fighting stopped on the front end of the compound as the FBP troops wheeled around to come after us.

We disappeared into the woods and moved around to hook up with Don. His men were battered, but no one was lost. I told Don to bring his men with us to meet the fifth truck. The truck could not go anywhere near the site where the escaped prisoners had taken off. That area was crawling with FBP squads. Instead, the truck took us across the Ohio River into Kentucky. Don had a place in the mountains where a helicopter could pick us up.

I had not noticed until we were at the site that Stormy was bleeding. I pulled his shirt back to see that a bullet had grazed his shoulder. At first I thought it was worse than it really was. It looked like he had lost a lot of blood, but he was alert. He said had felt some discomfort there, but thought it was just a blister from carrying his gear.

We only had to wait an half hour before the helicopter flew in to rescue us. We climbed aboard, I had to help Stormy; his shoulder was getting particularly sore by then. The medic opened Stormy's shirt and remarked that if Stormy had been standing two inches back from where he had been, the bullet would have been at an angle to pierce his heart. I held his other hand while the medic cleaned and stitched the wound. After the medic was done, Stormy gripped my hand tighter and pulled me closer to him. He said, "Thanks Joe, but stop worrying about me. After all these years, I am not going to leave you now." I told him to rest; I thought he must have lost too much blood. I bent down and kissed his forehead.

We landed in Pittsburgh. An ambulance took Stormy to a hospital for follow-up treatment. Scott walked with me to the plane that would take the rest of us back to Manassas. He said, "I can tell how upset you are, you still care for him, don't you."

I replied, "Yeah, I do, but it's not just Stormy. If anything ever happened to you, Allen, Marc, Jimmy,

Stormy, Cole, or especially Harry, I would be devastated. It would feel like having my heart ripped-out."

Scott put his arm on my shoulder, "That's why we all are fortunate to have a friend named Joe Kelly."

I went to Washington the next day to report to General McIntosh about our mission. He thanked me for staying behind to help Don's team. He went on to tell me that after we left, guided missiles had destroyed both that camp and the death camp nearby. He said that they would be ready to move on Cincinnati as soon as Don's team went back in and cleared the explosives from the bridges. Crooks's army had planned to blow up all the bridges across the Ohio after they evacuated the city.

I asked McIntosh when Don would have his team back there. He said they needed a rest and would be able to do it in three days. I told him I could do it that night. He said that was out of the question. My mission was to liberate camps. I told him that Don had used his men and resources to help me. The least I could do would be to return the favor. I reminded the General that I had conducted three undercover missions in Cincinnati. I also told him that Mike Kniffen and some of his friends from Cincinnati were back from Europe and were at Manassas. They would be thrilled to help liberate their hometown.

McIntosh said he would like to start the offensive now rather than having to wait a few more days while Crooks's army brought up more reserves. He called for ordnance engineers to give us a crash course in disarming set-charges and told me to proceed. I called Scott back at the base and told him to get the men ready, we would leave immediately.

Apparently the bridges were already set with charges, so that when Crooks's forces had to make their escape, they would ignite the triggers. Our job was to get in there and disconnect the triggers and disable the explosives

without it looking like they were disabled. Two helicopters
flew us to Don's pad in the mountains. Roger was waiting
for us with a couple of vans. He greeted me and said, "Man
it's good to be back in action. I couldn't stand being over
there in Europe doing nothing while all this was going on."
I told him I felt the same way, but that I would be glad
when we could go home.

Mike Kniffen's team took us to the bridges. They
knew how to get to the abutments without being noticed.
We did it from the Cincinnati side. The triggers were on the
Kentucky side so that they could be ignited after the last
Crooks vehicles had crossed the river. Security was all on
that side. By scaling the bridges on the Ohio side, then
crossing the river in the steel and concrete frameworks, we
could complete our mission without disturbing security at
all.

It took us a little more than two hours to finish. We
cut the trigger wires at the first junction as we had been
trained, spliced in a piece of nylon cord, which would act as
an insulator instead of a conductor, and taped it up to look
like it had before we tampered with it. If anyone inspected
the bridges, they would not detect a thing. We were done
and on our way back home in six hours.

In the next week Dan moved to San Bernardino,
California, and set up operations there. He had targets in
Phoenix, Reno, and Salt Lake City that were first priorities.
After that his group had to liberate two remote camps in the
desert of New Mexico and one in Albuquerque.

Pete set up shop in Des Moines, Iowa. He had
missions in Topeka, Wichita, and Oklahoma City. After
that he had one camp to take out in Springfield, Missouri.

My missions were frightening enough. The
southern camps were in parts of the south that would have
frightened Scarlet O'Hara. They were in places like
Greenwood, Mississippi, Albany, Georgia, Chattanooga,

Tennessee, and Tuscaloosa, Alabama. These were the
places where local custom welcomed white supremacy, as
long as it was distinctly heterosexual and protestant. These
were the places where landlords could be heard to say
unabashedly, "No Kikes, Fags, or Niggers."

In the South, we had to worry more about the local
population than the FBP guards at the gates of the camps.
Although I had grown up in a pseudo-southern state, I was
never a fan of the repressive elements of southern culture.
As much as I disliked the South, I was the best one to lead
the incursions there. I knew how southerners think, and I
knew how to talk like them. I could put on a phony
"Southern hospitality" smile like the rest of them.

Greenwood, Mississippi, was the most daring of our
raids. It was summertime and hellishly hot. There, just like
everything in that part of the country, everything had to be
done backwards. Instead of doing our raids at night, we had
to do it in the middle of the afternoon.

I took Harry on this mission, because he knew the
area and could talk southern. We drove into town in a 1976
Eldorado convertible. It was candy apple red with white
leather interior. We wore white linen suits with panama
hats. It looked like we could have been filming *Cat on a
Hot Tin Roof.* Harry and I drove into downtown and
stopped some people shopping. I asked, "Whea can we find
the Florewood River Plantation?" I told them that we were
some investors from Texas. We were interested in buying
the property for development as a resort.

A pretty young woman with white gloves and
perfectly sprayed hair replied, "Why that place is gov'ment
prop'ty. I don't thank it's fo sayel."

Harry replied, "We know that, but when the wah is
ovah, it weall be fo sayel."

I said, "Pahdon me Miss; Pahdon my manners!
Allow me to introduce myseph. I am Beauregard Austin

Kingston and this here's is my pahtnah William Jonathon
Smythe-Wilkerson. You can call me Beau and him Billy
Jon." Harry bowed and extended his hand.

She smiled and replied, "I am Junia Edwina
Teague. Ya'll may call me Miss Teague. Mah Daddy owns
the plantation jest dowan the road from Florewood. Ouah
family has lived theah fo' nine generations. The gov'ment
man who runs Florewood is Jimmy Bob Tarleton. He used
to be the ovahseah at Daddy's plantation, but Daddy said it
was the Lord's will to let him move on into gov'ment work.
Jimmy Bob has hired some of the sharecroppahs from our
prop'ty. Daddy still says it's the Lord's work. Wheah are
ya'll stay'n?"

I told her we didn't have accommodations yet and
that we were going to drive on to Jackson for the night. She
said, "Nonsense. It is too late in the day to be drivin' all
that way. If'n ya'll will wait just a bit, I have to pick Mama
up from the beauty shop. Aftah that, ya'll are moah than
welcome to stay at Greenleaf, ouah family home." I asked
if I could buy her a "Cocola" while we waited for "Mrs.
Teague."

Mrs. Teague was a proper and genteel southern
lady. She was in her fifties and wore the latest haute
couture from Paris. Her hair was a work of art and would
probably keep its style for several days. She was charming
and smiled sweetly, but kept an air of reserve until she got
to know a person better.

On the way to Greenleaf Harry remarked, "Do you
remember what Stormy said at the Pentagon about going
into the lair of the Beast?"

I said that "Daddy" was probably the son of the
Beast. Greenleaf was everything one would expect from
white Southern wealth. The quarter mile long drive was
lined with Live Oaks, all dripping with Spanish Moss. The
façade of the house was a stereotypical antebellum

plantation house with a pillared front and a veranda across
the length of the top floor. The house was about five
thousand square feet. The inside was tastefully decorated in
traditional fashion. The house had been updated and,
thankfully, was air conditioned. Mrs. Teague introduced us
to Bessie, the African-American maid who ran the house.
Bessie was a round woman with large breasts. She wore
homespun and fit the role of a southern mammy. She told
us if there was any problem with our rooms or
accommodations, to let her know personally.

Mrs. Teague excused herself and told us supper
would be served at 7:30 sharp. She asked us if we had an
appropriate jacket for the table. We told her we did. Junia
showed us to our rooms. They were in the same end of the
house, and were separated by a sitting room that was
directly accessible by private doors from each room. That
was great. We could get to each other without disturbing
anyone else.

From the veranda all we could see were fields of
cotton. I asked Junia where Florewood was from there.
The front of Greenleaf mansion faced east; Junia pointed
northeast from the veranda. She said it was about six miles.
It was around five and Junia excused herself so she could
rest and freshen up for dinner. Harry and I went into the
sitting area where it was cool. Even in the shade it was
ninety-five degrees outside.

We talked logistics for a few minutes. I told Harry
that the best advantage of the camp's location was that it
was a few miles from the *Illinois Central*'s mainline. We
could get a couple of boxcars attached to a freight train and
load the prisoners there for a short trip.

"Daddy" came in and knocked on the sitting room
door. He welcomed us to Greenleaf and told us we were
welcome to stay as long as we liked. "Daddy" fit the part of
a fat-cat southern businessman-plantation owner. He owned

the bank and half the businesses in Greenwood and several in Jackson. He would not be an easy sell. I told him that we were hoping to conclude our business the next day and would be on our way then. He said, "Nonsense, Ya'll can't git anywhere near that compound. I'll get Jimmy Bob over heah tomorrow night fo' suppah and ya'll can talk." "Daddy" excused himself so he could freshen up and change. I told Harry we should do the same.

"Daddy" had invited us down to the drawing room for a cocktail at 6:45. When he asked what "my poison" would be, I thought I should order something manly like a *Dewar's* on the rocks. As hot as it was I would have preferred an icy martini, but I was afraid that would appear too northern. Harry followed my lead and asked Mr. Teague if he had a good Kentucky sour mash. Cocktails in hand he proceeded to check us out.

Teague asked us what our plans were with the old plantation. I told him we wanted to restore the mansion house as the main structure and build private cottages around the perimeter of the old gardens. That would be where people would stay. The new structures would be in the same architectural style as the main house. The gardens would be restored, but a swimming pool and tennis courts would be added. Shuttles would carry guests to a dock on the Mississippi River so they could board gambling boats.

Teague said he was not crazy about the idea of commercializing the property. He liked things nice and quiet the way they were. I assured him this would be a small scale operation. It would be priced and designed to attract only the wealthiest elements of society. The patrons there would be the kind of people his wife would invite to a dinner party. On that note he said, "We best drink up boys, Mrs. Teague isn't fond of people settin' down late to her table."

We continued our conversation at the table. Teague asked us how we knew the property would be for sale soon. I told him, "Our venture is purely speculative. This war cannot last much longer, and when Speaker Crooks has restored order, he'll need to be selling off some of these recent acquisitions to pay down the deficit. That's why we want to go over and meet whoever's in charge of that facility tomorrow. We want to let him know we are ready to pay top dollar for it as soon as it is available, and you would be good to get on our side on this. If another developer gets a hold of it, they'll likely turn it into a circus. We want to preserve the dignity of the property, while making it commercially viable."

Teague was on our side. Junia asked, "How are you so confident that Crooks will win? It seems to me things are awfully a mess right now."

Teague joined in on her question, "Yeah, you boys are from Texas; what's the mood in Dallas? Are we in as much trouble as people around here think?"

I replied, "Heavens no. Crooks is as confident as ever. Why, he's still got the Marines and Air Force on his side. I've even heard rumor that about half the Army generals are going to switch back to our side. These setbacks you've seen are part of the art of war. Pretty soon, we'll launch an offensive that will have the other side reeling."

Mrs. Teague commented, "Those damnable generals. How dare they rebel against the finest leader we have ever had!"

Mr. Teague spoke up, "Now Mother; you don't need to get yourself all worked up. That ring leader is a good fer nothin' Injun. They're the ones our ancestors booted out of Alabama and Mississippi. I knew somethin' like this would happen when the Army started promoting coloreds, spics, and injuns to responsible positions. Those people cannot be trusted. I don't know what's gotten into this country, thinking we have to kowtow to every mongrel race on the planet. And do you know what started this whole thing? That damned general was worried that the government was mistreating a bunch of perverts. Perverts!"

I could barely finish my dinner. Harry looked like he was about to explode, but neither of us said a word. I kept thinking to myself, "Lair of the Beast." Mrs. Teague, with her voice of Southern gentility regaining control said, "I apologize for my and my husband's outburst! Why you boys look like you are as angry as he is, but you haven't lost your manners and have kept quiet. Your mothers raised you right."

I put on my sweet Southern genteel face as sincere looking as theirs and said, "Well, I think we all share certain sentiments at this table, but let's talk about something more pleasant."

Mrs. Teague said, "Yes, of course. Now tell me Beau, do you have a family?"

I wasn't about to say, "No we are two single guys in our forties, traveling together." I answered, "Why yes. I've got a little woman back in Dallas right now with my youngest daughter. My wife's name is Melissa Sue. She's probably at *Neiman*'s right now spending all my hard earned cash. By the time she's done there today I won't be able to afford that plantation up the road anyway." Everyone laughed.

Junia asked, "Do you have any other children?"

I replied, "I was waitin' for you to ask. I have a handsome young boy just about your age at Baylor studying to be a doctor right now. Would you like to see his picture?" I pulled out my wallet and took a picture of Jimmy sitting on the bow of the *Polar Star II*, shirtless of course. I handed it to Mr. Teague first for his approval.

He said, "I'm not sure I want to pass this on to Miss Junia, she might swoon." He passed it over to her anyway and continued, "Now I assume Beauregard, that if'n you're passin' this fine lookin' photo of a young man around he is not spoken for?"

I replied, "He is available."

Junia batted her eyes, "Oooh, he's handsome. Do you think he would even pay any 'ttention to an old spinstah like me? He must have evah purty girl on campus chasin' after him."

I said, "Well, Miss Teague, I can assure you that Jimmy Beau would have no interest in any girl that chased after him. Besides, the girls at *Baylor* are no purtier than you. I am sure he would be smitten the moment he laid eyes upon your delicate face."

Junia blushed and handed the photograph to her mother. Mrs. Teague commented, "I see he is sitting on a boat of some sort, is that a family boat?"

I said, "No that's Jimmy Beau's. That boy loves the water and pestered me and pestered me to buy him a boat. Now mind you, I don't spoil my kids with all kinds of expensive toys, but I figured a sailboat would build character and responsibility. He loves that boat. Whenever he has any spare time, he's down there cleaning or polishing something. I figure it's about time to pour some of that attention into starting a family. I'm about ready for some grandkids."

Mrs. Teague chuckled, "Oh, Mr. Kingston, you are fah too young to be thinkin' about grandchildren." Everyone laughed. Bessie was starting to serve dessert and asked if we wanted coffee.

Daddy Teague said, "I s'pos'n you boys will want to drive by the old plantation tomorrow. Now you know you can't get within a mile of that place. You can see the Mansion on the hill from the road, but that's about it.

Whatever's goin' on there is top secret gov'm'nt stuff. I
cain't even git in that place, and Jimmy Bob, the
commander, let's see, he calls himself "commandant,"
whatever that's s'pposed to mean. Anahway, he used to be
my overseah befoh he got this job. He won't tell me a darn
thang. Can you 'magine that, he used to work for me and
now treats me like I'm almost a terr'ist. "

I said, "That's government work. I am sure it has
something to do with the right side winning this war, so it's
best just to let him keep his secrets."

Daddy Teague said, "I s'pose so. Well, if'n ya'll
would like to meet him and talk shop, we could invite him
for supper tomorrow night."

I said, "I wouldn't want to put ya'll out two nights
in a row. I wouldn't hear of it."

Mrs. Teague said, "Really, we have Jimmy Bob
over about once a month anyway, and we are overdue. It is
no trouble at all. I insist."

Daddy Teague said, "I imagine you boys will have
some runnin' around to do tomorrow and will want to drive
around the area to get ideas, but if you will plan to be back
here around three tomorrow afternoon, I'll have Jimmy Bob
here and you fellas can talk business in my study.

I said, "Actually we do have some business in town
first thing in the morning, but we can easily be back here by
then. I can't thank y'all enough for your hospitality."

We retired from the table and went into the parlor
for a sherry. I proposed a toast to new friends and new
opportunities. The new friends would be the men we
liberated and the new opportunity was the one Daddy
Teague had just given us. Harry and I went upstairs and sat
in the ante-chamber for a few minutes. He whispered to
me, "Are you thinking we might do our job tomorrow?" I
told him that with the commandant tied up here for at least
six hours, we could get the camp cleaned out in broad

daylight. He asked how "we" were going to do it. I told him the team was in place and Scott and Marc could lead it just fine. We could keep Jimmy Bob tied up here while they did the rest.

We gave each other a peck and went into our respective rooms. I slept like a baby until around three in the morning. I stepped out on the veranda. It was a gorgeous evening. The stars were shining brightly, but everything else was pitch black, except for the halo of amber lights glowing up from where the Florewood camp was. A day job would be much easier to pull anyway.

I slept a few more hours then woke up around five o'clock as usual. I went down to the kitchen to see if I could find some coffee. Bessie was already in the kitchen and had just finished brewing a pot. She invited me to have a cup with her. She said, "Nobody else is up and won't be for another hour or so. I've got some questions for you Mr. Kingston."

I said, "Sure Bessie, anything you ask."

She cut right to the point, "I know who you really are. I recahnized you the minute you walked in this doah. What are you fixin' to pull? You better not be plannin' to hurt anyone in this house or damage any of the property heah. They might be bigots and fools, but they have taken care of me and my family for years. I was there with Mrs. Teague helpin' her to deliver Miss Junia Edwina. I've helped to raise that little girl. I've tried my best to expose her to some different values, and when she is mistress of this plantation, she'll make some changes. Please mister, give her a chance."

I said, "Bessie, I have no intention of harming these people in any way, shape, or form. You're right. They are bigots, but they have been kind to us, and I can see that behind that damnable white southern façade are some decent people. All I want to do is to stop the killing up the road. Are you going to turn me in for that?"

Bessie replied, "If'n I was goin' to turn you in, it would have been in the first half hour after your arrival last night. I know what's goin' on up the road, and it's down right disgraceful. In a country like this, it makes no sense. Why this is worse than the lynchings they used to do around here with my people. What can I do to help?"

I said, "I think my teams can handle it, but thanks for your offer. The one thing you can do is to make sure no phone calls get to Jimmy Bob this afternoon."

She said, "I can handle that, but how you gettin' your people into the camp in the first place?"

I said, "We are going to ride around the area today and figure it out."

She said, "My brothah Roscoe can get ya'll right in by way of the secret entrance."

My eyes bugged out with interest. She told me that back in the Civil War the slaves at all the plantations around there dug a series of tunnels in and out of the plantations. They figured when the Union Army came, they could use the tunnels to escape. She said the white people knew nothing about the tunnels and that they had been maintained for all these years. There was one that would get us right into the cellar of the old plantation house. That was where the commandant stayed, so with him away, the mansion would be virtually empty. Timing couldn't have been better. I told her we were meeting a colleague in town around eight. She said Roscoe would meet us there. I finished my coffee and started upstairs to wake Harry. Daddy Teague was coming down for coffee as I was putting my cup in the sink.

He asked if we were going to stick around for breakfast, "Bessie stirs up a fine mess of grits." I thanked him, but said we had a lot to accomplish in order to be back at Greenleaf by three. He said he understood.

Roger waited for us at the post office as planned. I told him we were going to do the job that afternoon. We walked outside after mailing our letters. Roscoe was standing at the *Eldorado* admiring it. He said, "Sho is a purtee car. I've wanted one of these since they was new." I asked him if he would like to go for a ride.

Roger and Roscoe piled in. Roscoe dropped his "Uncle Tom" act and told us all about the tunnels. He said he would be at the entrance sight to act as a guide.

We drove out to the site where Scott and Marc were waiting. Roscoe showed us where the tunnel went in to the compound. It was a few hundred yards from the tracks of the *Illinois Central*. A Shreveport to Memphis train was due to cross the area at five in the evening. Roscoe said he could have some cows and goats crossing the track at that time. The train would already be loaded with two empty cars. We could get the prisoners on board while the train stopped to clear the tracks. Roger would cut the cars loose about thirty miles down the road, where they would be picked up by transports that night.

Harry and I drove back to Greenleaf. It was almost three. Bessie brought us some mint juleps to enjoy while we talked. Daddy Teague's and Jimmy Bob's drinks had a shade more whiskey than Harry's and mine. Jimmy Bob had all the charm of a salamander and the intelligence of a three week old calf. I could easily picture him in his roles as both plantation overseer and camp commandant.

We chatted and charmed him as best we could, assuring him he would have a handsome cut of the deal if we were the successful purchasers. I asked him if he had any idea when the property would be available. He said he thought his mission would be done in about six months. He thought it could be made available then. He suggested we

set up an escrow account the next day with an appropriate
down payment so we could appear more serious to the
government. Harry said that was a splendid idea, and we
would run down to Mr. Teague's bank first thing in the
morning to set up the wire transfer.

Around six-thirty I said it looked like we were
pretty much as done as we could be with business. Daddy
Teague agreed and suggested we step out on the porch for a
cigar before we head to the dining room. Scott was to have
set the charges to blow the facility an hour after they had
left the camp. The FBP guards were supposed to be tied
and gagged and in a safe place; I had promised Bessie that
no one would be killed if at all possible. Daddy Teague lit
his cigar and took in a nice drag. Jimmy Bob lit his cigar
and did the same. Harry and I lit ours together and at that
moment we heard a concussion followed by a bright light to
the northeast.

Jimmy Bob pulled his cigar out of his mouth and
said, "I think that came from over by the plantation."

We stood there for the longest time trying to figure
out what it could be. Finally Daddy Teague said, "Jimmy
Bob, I think you and I ought to hop in my truck and run
ovah to Florewood and see if the place is still theah. You
boys excuse us just a minute. I'm sure we'll be back in time
for suppah."

As soon as they were down the driveway, Harry and
I ran upstairs, grabbed our bags and ran back down the
servants entrance. We hopped in the Eldorado and headed
the opposite direction. A helicopter was due to pick us up
about twenty miles south of there.

I met with General McIntosh the next day and told
him what Daddy Teague had said about "Injuns" running
the military. His reply was, "Yeah, well the best they could
come up with was Robert E. Lee, and look at what a loser

he was." I told him he should repeat that to Daddy Teague when the war was over.

The war was nearly over. While we were in Greenwood, the Army was securing Tennessee and most of Missouri. What was more important, though, was that the roads were now clear to head on towards Chattanooga and Birmingham. With the Ohio open, they could push there way on down the Mississippi and rejoin New Orleans with the rest of the country.

My teams stayed busy in the east, liberating camps just ahead of the battles. The camps grew grimmer and grimmer as Crooks's territory dwindled. Neat and orderly death camps gave way to mass graves of men who had been shot. No matter how feverish we worked to liberate the camps, it was never enough. There were still too many times when we arrived too late to save more than a handful of people.

The western states were easier for the Army to retake. Without the compact population centers of the east, states like Arizona, Nevada, and Utah could be swept in a matter of weeks. That gave Dan his own challenges. Things moved too fast. He often pleaded for help from Pete and me. He needed the ability to liberate several camps at a time.

The plains states were the slowest going for the army and their lowest priority. McIntosh's strategy was for securing the entire eastern states region and the Great Basin and Desert Southwest. He bargained that when Texas, Arkansas, Kansas, and Oklahoma were all that was left, the remainder of Crooks's power structure would abandon him.

McIntosh called me in September to come to Washington for a planning session. He was ready to run the Mississippi and split Crooks off from the rest of the South. He had gun boats that would come up from New Orleans and down from St. Louis. At the same time, he planned to cut a fifty mile wide swath through Mississippi along the river.

McIntosh planned to destroy almost every building in his path to ensure a strong foothold along the Mississippi River. I pulled him aside during a break and asked him about Greenleaf. He shook his head and apologized, but it was in the way. Besides, why would I care about protecting a bunch of racist and homophobic pigs? I told him, they, in there own way, had treated us well. More importantly, I owed a debt to Bessie and Roscoe. If Greenleaf fell, so would my honor. McIntosh told me I was starting to sound like the Teagues. He asked me if I thought the Teagues were colluding with the enemy. I told him they sided with the enemy, but I had seen no evidence of collusion. He relented and promised me it would be spared. He told me to get my unit ready, though because I was to be the one to knock on their door.

Memphis was already under federal control. Crooks's armies were retreating along the Mississippi, and our armies were quickly rushing to fill the void. McIntosh was serious when he said he wanted to cut a fifty mile swath along the river. They skirted towns and cities, but along the countryside they razed every structure along the way. He wanted no opportunity for snipers or rogue squadrons to hide out and menace their advance. We drove in convoy down I-55 and exited at Enid. Greenleaf was off US Highway 49E north of Greenwood. Engineers were already busy razing buildings in the area. I figured the Teagues must have been terrified.

Marc, Scott, and Jimmy were riding in my jeep, Marc was driving. I told him where to turn. We had two more jeeps of regular troops following us. We drove past the rows of Live Oak up to the mansion. Daddy Teague was waiting on the porch with a shotgun in hand. He yelled at us to "git on out. If'n ya'll are fixin' to destroy my home, yah gonna have to destroy me first." He cocked the gun, and my men started to pull their guns. I ordered them to put them back in their holsters.

I yelled out, "Mr. Teague, we mean no harm."

He yelled back, "Who is that? I rekonize your voice." I started to walk towards him with my hands in the air. He looked at me and said, "Beau, is that you?" I smiled and started to lower my arms. Then he got angrier, "Git your hands back up there. What are you, a goddamn carpet baggin' Yankee? What's the meaning of this? You come here to destroy the bed you slept in and the table you et at? You come here to rub it in my face that I'm a fool?"

I said, "No, Mr. Teague, we are not here to destroy your house or to cause you any harm whatsoever. I am here to tell you that Greenleaf is to be spared."

He started to lower his gun, and I lowered my arms somewhat. He asked, "Why, Mr. Kingston, well, I guess that really ain't your name, huh? Why are yah savin' mah house? You used me to destroy that gov'm'nt operation up the road, didn't you?"

I replied, "My name is Joe. I am with a Special Forces division of the United States Army. I apologize from the bottom of my heart for deceiving you and your family, but that facility was a camp used for executing innocent people. Before we liberated its prisoners and destroyed it, your former overseer, Jimmy Bob, had ordered the execution of more than a thousand men. You might think they were just "a bunch of perverts," but those men did nothing to deserve the brutal execution they faced there. I appreciate the hospitality you and your family showed me. Saving your home is my way of paying you and yours back. Your home was to have been destroyed, but I pleaded with General McIntosh on your behalf."

By that time Bessie and Mrs. Teague were on the front porch as well. Mr. Teague turned to them and said, "He says his name's not Beau; it's Joe something."

Bessie smiled and interjected, "I know that Mr. Teague. He's that fella from the Canadian boat. He's the one that's been runnin' all over the country freein' the homasekshals. He appears to be a man of his word, because I made him promise he wouldn't harm a blade of grass at Greenleaf."

Mr. Teague raised his gun back up, "You mean to tell me I've had a homasekshal under my roof, and you knew about all this Bessie? I am ashamed of you! You betrayed us."

Bessie said, "And I am ashamed of you, Mr. Teague. It's high time you left all those old fashioned ways of yours behind. Actually, you had two homasekshals under your roof, because when he said Billy John was his pahtnah, he didn't mean business pahtnah. They live togethah and they have sex togethah." Mrs. Teague clutched her throat and gasped. "An' you Mrs. Teague, quit actin' like you never heard the word sex before. In fact, maybe you ought to think about it more often. If'n you did, you might be awaah of what all those boys from school are doing with Miss Junia when they are s'posed to be studyin'. Now, this boy has gone to a lot of trouble just to fulfill a promise he made to me. Why, after you called him a pervert, he would have every right to let this place burn to the ground. Now y'all git ovah yourselves raht now!"

Mrs. Teague was in tears and ran inside the house. Mr. Teague said, "Now look what you've done Bessie, you made Mother cry. I guess you're right though. Now, Beau or Joe or whatever your name is, are you really going to let us alone?"

I said, "Yes sir, Mr. Teague. There are a couple of things, though that we will require. This area is a designated war zone, and, for the time being, you are under military law. The first thing we need you to do is to remove that Confederate Battle flag and that Crooks Union Jack or whatever you call it from your flag pole. The Stars and Stripes may stay." He told Bessie to have one of the yard hands tend to it right away. I continued, "Thank you. I must ask you and your family to stay in the house as much as possible and you cannot leave your property until the area is secure. We will station some guards here to protect Greenleaf. The general is afraid that snipers and renegade detachments may try to infiltrate. We cannot take any chances. If you have more than one fire arm, you need to keep them handy at all times. We will have about twenty men camping out on your grounds to protect it, but undesirable elements could still get through. I apologize for any inconvenience all this may cause, but we will do everything possible to keep you and your household comfortable and safe. Can we bring you any provisions?"

He replied, "We have a cellar stocked with provisions for six months. We have cows for milk and chickens for eggs. I think we can manage just fine. Would you and your men please come inside for refreshments? I think Bessie could bring us a pitcher of nice cool lemonade. Mother just made peach cobbler and I think there's enough to go around."

I told the regulars to start securing the perimeters, and I took Scott, Jimmy, and Marc inside. When Jimmy took off his helmet, Mrs. Teague said, "Why you are that handsome young man from the picture." He looked perplexed, and I told him the story. We told her how delicious her cobbler was and thanked them for their hospitality again. I gave them my direct line at the base and my cell phone. I said, "If you need anything at all, or if these men do not take care of you, call me."

Our operations in the east slowed down in the next weeks. We had cleaned out every camp we could find, and while the war in the east was coming to a rapid close, it appeared that Crooks lacked the resources to set up new camps. Within a month the entire length of the Mississippi was under federal control. The few remaining armed units in the Old South started negotiating for terms. I started transferring units from Manassas to Pete and Dan so they could finish their operations.

Texas was the only state still under Crooks's control by early November. He started making overtures to third party countries to explore the idea of having Texas recognized as an independent country. Speaker Schumacher warned them not to take such a step while Texas was still officially part of the United States.

Dan and Pete finished their work and closed their units down, leaving mine as the only operating unit. Pete asked for a discharge, but told us if we got into trouble to call him. There were no more camps as far as we knew. I began to wonder why we hadn't been decommissioned all together.

Finally, General McIntosh called me to the Pentagon. He asked me if I would like to go on one more mission. I was perplexed. I thought we had cleaned out all the camps, even in Texas. He said, "There aren't any more. This mission is for the gold. We're going to take Crooks. I would like you and your best men to help us do it. I think it would be a fitting end to this war for you to be the one to escort him to Washington in chains for all the press to see."

I replied, "I would be honored." He told us that the few generals Crooks had left had contacted the U. S. Embassy in Mexico City. McIntosh flew down there to meet with them and discuss terms of surrender. They also had handed over the location where the President was being held. It was at a site in Saudi Arabia. The generals would get off on treason charges, but would be forced to resign in disgrace and would still face a multitude of civil charges. In turn, they would hand over Crooks to a team they would let into Texas. General Andrews would arrive first to secure the route, then we were to arrive.

On this mission I took Harry, Stormy, Jimmy, Scott, and Marc. Crooks's Generals had convinced what was left of his Secret Service contingent that they were protecting the wrong person. Unbeknownst to Crooks, he was held hostage in his Highland Park home for about eighteen hours. We flew into Love Field on an army transport. We were dressed in our covert operations black uniforms that were meant for nighttime duty, although it was mid-afternoon when we arrived.

Stormy said, "Hey Joe, do you remember the last time we were in Dallas together?"

I just nodded. From the freeway I could see the tower of the *Sheraton-Dallas* and remembered our weekend there so many years ago.

We arrived at Crooks's mansion and the Secret Service guards waiting outside escorted us. Crooks was at his desk trying to make a phone call when I walked up to him. He recognized me immediately and ordered his Secret Service men to arrest me. They stood silent. I said, "Mr. Michael Crooks, you are under arrest under charges of treason against the United States of America, genocide, and other human rights violations, and violations to your oath to uphold the Constitution of the United States of America. You have the right to remain silent, you have the right to an attorney, . . ." While I finished his *Miranda* rights, Scott and Harry cuffed him at the ankles and wrists. We led him out of the house with reporters' cameras flashing the entire length of his graceful walkway.

I reported to the Pentagon the next day with Harry, Scott, Stormy, and Marc. McIntosh congratulated us on the success of our entire operations, for enlightening the country, and helping to restore a free and open democracy. He told us that President O'Hara was on-board Air Force One and would be back in Washington by evening. He asked me if there was anything the Army or the U. S. government could do for us. I answered, "I only wish we could go home in time for Christmas."

McIntosh said, "Then that is what you should do."

I said, "But, how? Our homes are all gone. The only place here we can call home is the base at Manassas."

McIntosh spread an ear to ear grin across his face, "While you boys were finishing up this war, Speaker Schumacher ordered the Justice Department to work on getting titles to your homes restored. We don't have all of them done yet, but the homes in Bay City are now titled to their rightful owners. Go home." He handed me a large envelope containing a fresh deed to our home and our honorable discharge papers.

It was early December. We took Stormy and Cole with us. They were not sure about going back to Washington State. Besides, they wanted to give Bay City a try. We flew out of National Airport, connected in Detroit, and then home. Our house was a mess. It had been occupied by people who worked for The Federal Bureau of Protection. There were crayon marks on the bedroom walls, the terrazzo floors needed polishing, and the whole house needed a good cleaning. We hired a professional cleaning company and some painters. While they got the house ready we went to Detroit for a week to look at furniture, dishes, clothes, silverware, and all sorts of other necessities. Everything we had kept and moved around for the last three years was still in Hvidore. There was no way we could have gotten all of that packed and moved by Christmas even if we wanted. Harry suggested we keep the place in Denmark anyway. I thought it a splendid idea.

While Stormy, Cole, Harry, and I worked on putting our home back together, Scott and Allen, Matt DuPont, Matt Crossly, and all the others did the same thing. It was as though we were all in a race to see who could have our homes ready for the first Christmas party. The painters were done on the fifteenth and the furniture started arriving the next day. We spent the next week unpacking and shopping for incidentals. On the twenty-first the house looked great, and I said at breakfast, "Let's go get a tree."

Michigan was a magical place at Christmas time; every home could be the subject of a Currier and Ives print. We had about two feet of fresh snow on the ground. All the spruces and yews in the front yard were covered with white powder. We drove out to a tree farm in Midland County. It took us an hour to pick out the perfect tree. Harry was the one to spot it. He knew the corner by the front window where the tree went, and he knew the right shape. It was a Blue Spruce, about nine feet tall and had plenty of open spaces for ornaments.

We got the tree home and strung the lights on it. I commented that I wished we had time to decorate the outside. Stormy and Cole went for a walk while Harry and I left for some last minute shopping. In the afternoon an *IDS* truck arrived and there was a knock on the door. The day before, I had called the caretaker at our house in Hvidore and asked her to overnight the two boxes that contained our best ornaments. Harry was surprised to see them.

That night I roasted a duck in the oven and stuffed it with a cranberry-walnut dressing. While it was roasting Stormy asked us all to step out front for a few minutes. Harry, Cole, and I walked on out. Stormy lingered. I asked Cole, where Stormy could be. He just shrugged. All the homes on the street were decorated for Christmas except for our house. Then suddenly, the lights came on, and all the

yews and spruces in front of our house were ablaze with
light. Stormy and Cole had decorated the outdoors earlier
that afternoon while we had gone shopping. A fresh shod of
snow had fallen since, so all we could see were the lights
shining through the snow on the bows of the trees.

Some carolers were singing *Bring a Torch,
Jeanette, Isabella* several doors down. I took Harry's hand
and we started began to sway with the rhythm of the song.
As the carolers approached and saw what we were doing,
they began singing *Silent Night.* They walked towards us
until they were standing in front of us and for some time
after. It was about eight degrees. Neither Harry nor I had a
winter coat, but we danced while large snowflakes floated
down from the sky swirling and tossing in the air around us.
We were home for Christmas.

Aarquives Publishing Group, a division of *Aarquives Unlimited, LLC*, was created to assist aspiring writers to break into the publishing world. It is committed to concepts of:

> Full editorial control by the author
> Social justice for all
> Full equality for the GLBT community
> Respect for all sovereign peoples
> Peace

Aarquives Publishing Group is committed to publishing worthwhile works in both fiction and non-fiction. Our authors have full creative license to let their knowledge, experiences, and imaginations weave stories of unlimited fascination. If you are interested in becoming an *Aarquives Publishing Group* author, or if you are a bookseller and would like to carry any of our publications, please contact us at:

authors@aarquives.com

 Do not send writing samples, drafts, or any other attachments unless specifically requested or authorized. Electronic mail messages containing any unauthorized attachments will be deleted, will not be read, and will not receive a reply.

Look for other titles scheduled for publication later this year, including:

The first volume of a trilogy entitled, ***Particularly Dangerous Work***, by G. Russell Overton will soon be in print. It is a piece of historical fiction about a Spanish diplomat pulled into the world of espionage during the early years of World War II. The second and third volumes will continue his journey through the remainder of the war and into the early years of the Cold War.

Rusted Steel is a story about a young man struggling with mental illness, drug addiction, homelessness, and an abusive father.

About the Author

G. Russell Overton is an historical researcher in Lansing, Michigan. He has produced and co-authored a number of works, both fiction and non-fiction. He authored a non-fiction essay published in 2006 and a short story published in 2007. He has planned two novels and a non-fiction work for publication in 2011-2012.

Overton studied for both a bachelor's and master's degree in history and minored in his bachelor's degree in English, with an emphasis on creative writing. His fields of study in history include pre-Revolutionary Russia and Indigenous Americans in the nineteenth and twentieth centuries. His fictional style, unbounded by the dictates of political and cultural agendas, is to create romantic adventure and thrilling action, while challenging his readers to ponder compelling arguments.

He is a member of the Historical Society of Michigan, the California Historical Society, Friends of the Bancroft Library, the Publishing Triangle, and Michigan Writers.